Advance Praise for

"Dark and gritty ... an exceptiona
of raw emotion, deep-seated fear, ;
and innocence. Deeply atmospher
porary mysteries/thrillers." — Pub...
Semifinalist

"In Emily, author Dorian Box has created a rarity—a teenage
protagonist that is at once sympathetic, vulnerable and large-
ly fearless. ... This sharp characterization within a fast-paced
work of suspense makes The Hiding Girl one of the year's most
exciting series openers." — BestThrillers.com (named a 2020
Best Thriller of the Year)

"The story that author Dorian Box has created for Emily Calby
is nothing short of thrilling, but it's THE HIDING GIRL's
masterful interplay of character, setting, and theme, along
with its fast-pace and high emotional stakes that makes it a
real page-turner." — IndieReader (starred review, Official Seal of
Approval)

"[S]tunning, captivating, heartbreaking, but also heartwarming.
... [T]he characters were so alive, believable, with heart and
warmth, humor and love. ... This book is certainly on my 'best
ever books' list." — NetGalley

"[A] unique mix of hope, shattered innocence, pain, fear, and
vulnerability ... a great, suspenseful read." — Reader's Favorite

"This is a fantastic book that completely demolished my expec-
tations. ... This novel is fast-paced and action-packed but it has
a profound human element that sets it apart from other novels
in its genre." — BookishFirst

"Author Dorian Box keeps his audience on the edges of their
seats with the gripping first installment in his new Emily Calby
Series." — FeatheredQuill.com

Emily Calby Book 1

THE HIDING GIRL

DORIAN BOX

FRICTION
PRESS

THE HIDING GIRL

ISBN 978-1-7346399-0-2

*To the people in our lives who make us feel like
Emily, a scared child who will survive.*

Who in the world am I? Ah, that's the great puzzle.
—Lewis Carroll, *Alice's Adventures in Wonderland*

Before

TWO MEN. I noticed them when I was unloading groceries from the F-150, handing the heavy bags to my little sister and daydreaming about the end of the sixth grade. They got out of a blue pickup truck with a crooked camper-top, parked down the road in front of nothing. Dilfer County is Georgia farm country. The next house is a half-mile away.

They walked to the back of the truck and I went back to daydreaming. Only two weeks until summer softball camp, my first year in fastpitch.

"These are too heavy," Becky whined.

"It's good for you," I said, distracted. The two men were coming our way.

The driver was short and stocky, in a muscley way, with black hair and black clothes over pale skin. The passenger was a string bean with curly brown hair, wearing shorts and a t-shirt. He was carrying things, an orange sack and something with a handle.

They reached the long driveway just as a red-tailed hawk swooped low in the space between us, scanning for prey. I swore it looked right at me.

Mom came out of the house. I pointed. "Mom, look. Who are those two men?"

"I have no idea, Emily. Becky can't carry those big bags. Give her the light ones."

"They're on our property," I said.

"Yes, I can see."

"They're trespassing."

"I'm sure it's nothing to worry about. Maybe they're lost. Come on, girls, get to work."

Becky crept up beside me. Eyes wide, "Who are they?"

"They're no one," Mom said. "Emily, stop worrying your sister. You don't have be suspicious of everyone."

I do. *Take care of your mom and Becky.*

The stocky man grinned and waved.

"Emily, get those bags inside before everything melts," Mom said.

"But Mom—"

"No buts. Now."

I climbed the steps to the kitchen deck and held the screen door for Becky. The men stopped ten feet from Mom.

"Can I help you?" she said.

"Sorry to disturb you, ma'am," the stocky one said. "We ran out of gas and was wondering if you might be able to spare some."

She smiled an apology. "We don't have any gas. Someone else cuts our lawn."

"Actually, we were hoping you might let us siphon a little from your truck. Those F-150s hold a lot. Just need enough to fill this one-gallon can."

The tall man held up the can, a dented, rusty-red rectangle with yellow letters slashing down the front. *GASOLINE.* "Juss dis," he said in a strange accent, eyes twitching between me and Mom. He had tattoos, one on his arm looked like a zombie, and sores on his face.

Mom hesitated. "Well, I don't know. Are you men from around here?"

I let the screen door slam and stepped out on the deck, Becky attached to my hip.

"Why didn't you get gas at the Exxon station at the bottom of the hill?" I said. "You had to pass it to get here."

The stocky man chuckled. "That is a very observant girl

you've got there, ma'am. She is to be commended. Young lady, you are the spittin' image of your mother with that blonde hair of yours. Anybody ever tell you that?"

Only everyone. Mom smiled at me. I rolled my eyes. *Answer the question.*

"The fact of the matter is our gas gauge broke and we haven't had the financial resources to get it fixed."

He turned back to Mom. "We're from Kentucky. We do construction. All the work dried up back home when they closed the coal mine. Got jobs lined up in Florida, nice big condo project."

"This road goes east. Florida is that way," I said, pointing.

He cracked his neck. "Well, now, we're from out of town and don't know our way around these parts."

"Where in Florida are you going?"

He smirked at the tall man. "Inquisitive girl, yessiree."

"Emily, don't be rude," Mom said.

"Tampa area," he said, glancing back at the truck. "Assuming we make it that far."

"Mom," I said. "Me and Becky need your help putting away the groceries."

"Becky and *I*," she said. "Just a minute."

"But we need it now."

"In a minute."

The stocky man wiped sweat from his forehead. "Ma'am, we are proud men and I am embarrassed to tell you we are on hard times. If you could see fit to let us have a little gas, God bless you, and if you can't, bless you just the same. I'm sure we'll find another way."

Biting my lip, I watched Mom's mushy heart give in. Jesus Mary, she even apologized.

"I'm sorry. Of course. Take as much as you need."

I knew it was a mistake, but couldn't say exactly why. More than the stocky man's black clothes, which made his pale skin seem to glow in the sun, more than the tall man's zombie tattoo. Something out of place.

"You need a hose to siphon gas," I said. Dad taught me how. Called it *a useful thing to know.*

The tall man pulled a piece of green garden hose from the orange bag and held it up. "Nots da first time she run out."

The stocky man gave a little bow. "Thank you, ma'am. May the good Lord reward you and your beautiful family for your kindness. Please thank your husband for us as well."

The remark jolted me. Mom too, a slight jerk of a head as the hawk circled above.

The man saw it. "Didn't mean nothing personal. Just figured it was your husband's truck because you don't see many ladies driving F-150s."

"Alright, then," Mom said. "Get your gas and good luck to both of you."

As she turned to climb the steps, the tall one's mouth curled up. He laughed about something before the stocky man poked him in the ribs with a pasty arm.

His skin. He said they did construction. He should be baked brown, like everyone who works outside, like Dad. He had three skin cancers cut out before the accident made it all pointless.

Mom reached the deck, blocking the view. I backed up to let her in, stepping on Becky's toe. She cried *Owee* and hopped around the kitchen on one foot.

"Those poor men," Mom said as she crossed the threshold. "Becky, what's wrong with you?" She closed the door, but didn't lock it.

"*Mo-om,*" I said. "Who works outside and has skin like a vampire? Or carries around a hose to siphon gas?" I moved to the door, but it was too late. The knob was already turning.

1

I LOOK UP from the sketchpad and stare out the window, cows in green fields zipping past like a slideshow filmed with a shaky camera. There *blink* gone. There *blink* gone. Like me. Sometimes I feel I'm not here at all, like I am no one.

I pass time drawing and twisting my hair, waiting for the next stop, the next obstacle, trying to plan for all of them.

Bone-tired. The sky was still dark when I left Chicago. The train's soothing *clickety-clack, clickety-clack* has me nodding off. I chase it away.

"Natalie, are you sure your parents will be waiting for you in Memphis?" says the gray-haired woman sitting next to me. Her name is Mrs. Draper. She's wearing a sky-blue dress and pearl necklace.

Natalie is my name today. Memphis is today's destination.

"Yes, ma'am," I say. "And I can't wait to see them!"

Artificial sparkle. It works on almost everyone. The entire world apparently loves *effervescence. Vivacity, enthusiasm, a merry state.* To get my allowance, Mom, a middle-school teacher, made me look up five words every week and use them in sentences.

"And thank you again for letting me travel with you. My parents will be grateful too. We didn't know about the age limit for unaccompanied minors."

Lies. I know every regulation for unaccompanied minors doing anything, including all forms of transportation. I never used

7

to lie, not about big things. I told my best friend Meggie Tribet I liked her puke-yellow sundress, stuff like that. Now? I only tell the truth when it suits my needs, almost never.

I spend a lot of time outside train and bus stations, avoiding surveillance cameras while checking out passengers. I always pick a woman traveling alone, someone who looks like a mom or grandmother. When they hesitate I pretend to call my parents on my burner phone, but just as I'm about to hand it over, the call gets disconnected. "Not again," I say. "We live out in the country. No cellphone towers."

It doesn't always work. That I've been able to stay on the run for a month is almost a miracle.

Memphis is the first place I'm going to for a reason. At an internet café in Chicago, I got a lead to a place selling fake driver's licenses. A clerk helped me access the dark web on a computer with Tor. He got me to a search directory and the rest was easy. I'm good with computers and figuring stuff out. Got it from my dad. We were always building and fixing things.

At least a hundred websites advertised fake documents. Some were scams and most were in other countries. Then I came to *Best Fakes, USA*. It said *Serving Veterans* next to a fluttering American flag. I sent a message saying I'm a disabled veteran who the government won't give a driver's license to because my eye got shot out in Iraq. They sent me the price, seven hundred dollars in cryptocurrency.

Seven hundred. I agonized about it for two days. Almost a quarter of what's left. Grabbing Dad's hidden cigar box with the five thousand dollars from the garage was the only smart thing I did that day.

This is for an emergency, Emily, only to be used if the shit hits the fan. If I'm not here, we both know you're the only one strong enough to keep this boat afloat. I'm depending on you.

He made me swear to never tell anyone about the money, not even Mom. I took it and ran.

I finally wrote back and agreed to the seven hundred, but said

I can only do cash and in person. After a few more messages, they sent a Memphis address and code to use when I arrive.

Last night, in a clump of trees at a Chicago park, I counted the money, then took out seven hundred. It felt like cutting off an arm. I won't last long when the money runs out, but need the license. Using a fake ID will be dangerous, but not more dangerous than what I do now, and a lot easier. It's hard work convincing an adult stranger to vouch for a young girl traveling alone.

Mrs. Draper is asking about my trip to Chicago. I explain I went there to help my aunt take care of my new baby niece. She asks if I enjoyed it and I say everything except changing her diapers.

She laughs. "Aren't you the nice young lady, helping your aunt like that? What about school?"

They always ask the same questions. "It's already out for summer."

"Do you have brothers and sisters?"

An image of Becky's terrified face breaks loose from one of the black boxes stacked in my dark warehouse of a brain, ricocheting like an out-of-control rocket, leaving dents in the raw walls.

"No, ma'am. I'm an only child." I pull my hoodie around me. I wear it always, with my long pants and double tees, even in the dead of summer.

"Natalie, you're trembling. Are you okay?"

"Just a little cold in here."

Becky's face. So real, like she was suddenly here ... or I was there, like everything was happening all over. But what?

I know the results, from the internet, but the memories are locked away somewhere in the black boxes. *Put your worries in a box.* One of Mom's favorite happy sayings. Maybe that's where it came from. I remember that morning, Mom taking me and Becky to the drugstore soda fountain for milkshakes before we went grocery shopping. The next thing I knew I was sitting on a bus, all alone.

I lean against Mrs. Draper. "Thanks again for being so nice."
Sometimes I act touchy with the women strangers. It wards off
attention by making people think we're related, but it's also my
only human contact that's not one-hundred percent fake. Only
ninety.

She puts her arm around me. "You're quite welcome, dear."

I catch myself snuggling and pull away, grabbing my backpack from under the seat. I angle it to the window and unzip it.
Everything in it except the cigar box is stolen.

At night I prowl for unlocked cars. That's how I got my stun
gun, folding knife with the saw-toothed blade, sunglasses,
makeup, Chicago Cubs baseball cap, a Stephen King book and
the backpack. Three backpacks actually. The one I kept is olive
green. Before the day everything ended, I never stole anything
in my life.

I pull out a deck of cards, swiped from the front seat of a con-
vertible. "Mrs. Draper, would you like to play cards?"

"That's a fine idea," she says. "These train rides seem to take
forever, don't they?"

I nod wearily.

"What game?"

"Poker?"

"The only poker game I know is twenty-one," she says. "Do
you know that one?"

"Um-hm." I know every poker game. Dad taught me. We
used to play for fake money.

I see her looking at my wrists as I shuffle the cards. The
marks are faded, but still visible. I shake my bead bracelets to
cover them.

She's sniffing again, no doubt because I stink like a dog. Once
a week I buy a set of clothes at a thrift store and throw the old
ones away, except for the athletic shoes I ran away in and my
hoodie, which I wash in bathroom sinks. I smother myself in
deodorant, but it can only do so much. It's time for a new set.

My stomach gurgles as we play. The last food I ate was a bag of cheese puffs at the Chicago train station. Mrs. Draper must hear it because she puts down her cards and says, "I'm famished. How about you? Would you like to go to the dining car with me?"

I say yes and hoist my bulky backpack.

"That looks awfully heavy. I'm sure it would be safe here. This meal is my treat."

"I like to keep it with me," I say.

I order a cheeseburger and fries. I'm gnawing on the burger like an animal when Mrs. Draper leans across the table and whispers, "Natalie, I don't know if you're aware of this, but they have public showers on this train."

I get the hint, but there's no way I'm being separated from my backpack or taking my clothes off on a train.

"That's good to know!"

Back at the seats, I try to nap. I hardly slept last night knowing I had to get from the park to the train station before dawn. I wrap my arms around the backpack, curl up and pray. *Please don't let me dream.*

* * *

It's late afternoon when the train chugs into the Memphis station. Aluminum parentheses on poles provide shade for happy people waving at their loved ones. I hate pulling into train stations.

I couldn't sleep, couldn't escape the picture of Becky's face. Why Becky? She was still learning to add and subtract. She hadn't even lost all her baby teeth. *I don't understand, God.*

"Do you see your parents?" Mrs. Draper says.

"Um, hold on a sec, my phone is vibrating."

I pull out the burner. "Hi Mom! Mm-hm, just pulling into the station. ... Oh no, I told him that truck needed work. Sure, no problem. Can't wait to see you either." I disconnect the fake call.

"That was my mom. They couldn't get to the train station because my dad's truck broke down. I'm going to take a cab."

"Nonsense. My husband is picking me up and we'll be happy to give you a ride home."

"That is so nice, but I live really far away."

"End of discussion. It is my responsibility to get you home safely. I won't let you out of my sight until I meet your parents."

This hasn't happened before. "Well, that won't be possible," I say.

I know from her pursed lips she's about to ask the question she's been wanting to ask the entire trip. "Are you in some kind of trouble, Natalie?"

How many kinds are there? "No, I'm not in trouble … but my family is. My dad had a stroke. He's paralyzed. That's the real reason I'm coming home today."

Lately I've been getting confused about what's real and for a microsecond wonder whether I may really have a sick dad.

"I was always planning to take a cab. I'm sorry I lied. I didn't think you'd help me if you knew my parents wouldn't be here. Dad's practically in a coma and my poor mom's a basket case. She won't want to meet anyone. Nothing personal."

"But the phone call, about the truck breaking down."

"Oh, that?" I hunch my shoulders with my sorriest smile.

"Natalie—"

"I take cabs all the time." That's true, unfortunately. They're my only option with a dumb phone and no credit card. "It's no big deal. Really."

"Do you have money for a cab? You said it's far away."

I tap my backpack. "Sure do. Know the exact fare. Forty-two dollars, including tip."

Just in time, the whistle blows and the train screeches to a halt. Mrs. Draper reaches into her purse, slipping me cash as she clasps my hand. Not long ago I would have felt bad taking it.

"This is for your taxi. I've enjoyed our trip together."

All sunshiny, "Me too, so much!"

"Natalie, I'll pray for your father tonight, but also for you. I want you to know that if you need help, I'll try to help you."

"Don't worry about me. I'm fine. Nice meeting you and thanks again for everything!" Slightly dizzy, I squeeze around her and hurry down the aisle.

2

"**BECKY!**" I bolt across the pavement, lean down and wrap her in my arms. "It's gonna be okay, Bec. Everything's gonna be okay. Don't cry." I stroke her silky hair.

Something's wrong. These are my hands. Those are my feet. But nothing happened on pavement. We were inside the house.

"Hey!" A beefy, red-faced man shoves me to the ground. "Get your cotton-picking hands off of her." He helps the crying, brown-haired girl to her feet. "What the hell is wrong with you?"

"I–I ..." The girl doesn't look anything like Becky. "She cried for help." *She did.*

"Bullshit," the man says. "You knocked her down. Ran right into her."

"No, I didn't." *Did I?*

Exiting passengers gather in a circle, including Mrs. Draper.

"Go find a cop," the man says to an overweight woman in a glittery *Elvis* top.

"It was a mistake," I say. "I'm sorry."

"Let it go, Hank," the woman says. "We're gonna miss our shuttle to Graceland. Angel's fine."

"Fucking nutcase. You should be locked up somewhere," he spits, tugging Angel away by the arm.

"I tripped," I hear her say.

Mrs. Draper is talking urgently into her phone. I flee to the parking lot, to a cab idling with the windows up. The air is hot and steamy, like everywhere in the South in late June.

I pound on the window. The startled driver checks me out before unlocking the doors. I jump in and read the address. "I'm in a hurry," I say, in case it wasn't obvious from my flushed face and jerky glances back at the platform.

"Wrong address," he says in an accent I've never heard.

I study the paper where I wrote everything down. "No, it's right." I repeat it.

"You no want to go to this address."

I insist I do and the car peels out, doors locking.

The surroundings deteriorate quickly, block by block, until we're passing buildings with windows covered by bars, bricks and sheets of wood. Some are just gaping holes. At a stoplight I study a wall mural of a red gun painted over a white background. Uneven letters say, *Don't Let Violence Ruin Your Life.*

The driver glances at the rearview mirror and I scoot out of view. We pass a light pole with three teddy bears hanging on it. A few blocks later we come to another teddy bear, nailed to a tree with plastic lilies next to it.

I replay the scene at the train station—not normal even by my low standards. Have I been acting that weird for a month without realizing it? My head's not right. Obviously. As usual, I decide not to think about it.

Think about the driver's license. Stay on mission. Sixteen or eighteen? Being twelve, both are a stretch. At sixteen I could take trains and buses by myself. Eighteen would be life-changing, the minimum age to stay at a hotel, where I could take a shower and sleep in a bed. I bathe with garden hoses in dark backyards and sleep in parks or city hidey-holes on mattresses of leaves or cardboard.

I'm tall for my age, five-three. I can talk like an adult. Mom called me an *old soul*. Adding makeup makes me look at least a little older.

The cab brakes in front of a corner building, two stories of brownish-orange brick. The ground windows are painted black and covered with bars. The second-floor windows have plywood nailed over them, also black. There's no sign, but the street number above the door matches the one I wrote down.

"You think twice about this address?" the cabbie says.

"Is this South Fourth Street?"

He nods.

"Then this is it."

"I mean you think twice about going to this place?"

I look around. Graffiti. Barbed-wire fences. Tall weeds growing out of the sidewalks.

"Yeah," I admit.

I pay and the cab takes off in a hurry. The block is deserted. I cross the sidewalk to a security door and push a button on an intercom. The buzzing inside is loud, but there's no response. I push it again. Nothing.

Everything is eerily quiet until a gray car comes around the corner pumping rap music at a million decibels. *You all alone in these streets, cousin ...* I'm pressing myself into the door frame, watching the car pass, when a voice rips through the speaker.

"Who dere?"

"Um, Roscoe Pallatin." The name I used in the messages.

"Who?"

"Roscoe Pallatin. I came here for a business transaction. I sent you some messages."

"Don't do no business here."

I lean into the speaker and whisper the code from the slip of paper. "B, P, two, nine, seven, hashtag, *eight!*" I yelp. Something is yanking me from behind. I turn to face a wiry man with no front teeth, clutching a can in a brown-paper bag in one hand and my backpack in the other.

I pull away. "What did you say?"

"I said come walk wit me."

"No, thanks."

"Come walk wit me."

"I can't. Actually, I'm really busy right now."

I meet a lot of weird people on the street. Most are harmless.

The only time I react is when someone tries to touch me, which the wiry man is doing right now, crusty fingers reaching for my face. I whirl, face-first into the thick vertical bars of the swinging security door.

An enormous, dark-skinned black man with a shaved head stands in the threshold. He's like a giant, biceps bigger than cantaloupes and a chest that sticks out a half-foot in front of his shoulders. The handle of a black gun rises from his waistband. He shoots me a look of disgust.

"Get the fuck outta here," he says to the man holding the can.

The man raises his hands and backs away with a mumbled apology.

"You. Get your skinny ass inside."

I squeeze past him, hearing the doors lock behind me.

We're in a cavernous room with a high ceiling of peeling paint and rusted pipes. A battered restaurant counter runs along the back wall.

"So you Roscoe Pallatin," the man says. I have to tilt my head back to meet his smoldering eyes. "Disabled veteran of the *EYE-raq* War with his eye shot out."

Clenched-toothed smile, "Well, you see—"

"I was a fuckin' soldier in Iraq. I took a chance on you 'cause your story sounded exactly like somethin' our government would do. Send a man to war to get his eye shot out, then tell him he can't drive 'cause he got his eye shot out."

He looks through a peephole at the top of the door. "At least I know you ain't the *police*. Even they ain't stupid enough to send a little blonde girl into this zip code. So the question is, who the fuck are you and what the fuck you doin' here?"

I clear my throat. "Sir, I am *so* sorry I pretended to be someone else, but I really am here to get a driver's license. I brought the money. Seven hundred dollars."

"You carrying around seven hundred dollars? You fuckin' stupid?"

"I'm not stupid."

"Runaway?"

According to the internet, there was nothing left to run away from. "Not the normal kind," I say.

He dismisses me with a wave of a hand as big as my softball glove. "I don't do business with no kids. Get the fuck outta here."

"I won't tell anyone, if that's what you're worried about. Definitely not the police. I'm keeping secrets way bigger than this."

He points to the door. "Git."

"But we had a deal," I plead.

"I had a deal with Roscoe fuckin' Pallatin."

I close my eyes, so tired. "I don't get it. Why won't you help me? I'm here and you can."

"I ain't got to give you no reason."

"But just *why*? I'm not a bad person ... even if I am, why?"

Neck bulging, "*Why why why*? You sound like a fuckin' broken record. Why the fuck should I?"

"Because I came all the way from Chicago, and I brought the money, like I said I would. It wasn't easy getting here ... and I need help ... and don't have any other place to go."

He walks to the restaurant counter. "Git over here and sit."

The counter is lined with round chrome stools bolted to the floor, just like the ones we sat on at the drugstore the morning the two men came. The early internet stories had a phone video someone took, a panorama of the soda fountain that captured a few seconds of us at the end. *Last Pictures of Family Alive.* I could never watch it.

I plant myself on one of the stools, feeling it turn. Nerves or habit, I take a wobbly spin around, coming to rest where I started, the giant's dark eyes fixed on me.

"How old are you?"

"Twelve."

A half-laugh, half-snort with a shoulder roll. "And you here for a driver's license? How 'bout a library card? Twenty dollars."

"I need an official ID. I travel a lot and it's risky."

"You doin' somethin' risky? I'm fuckin' shocked. What's your name?"

"Natalie."

He slams the counter so hard the stool shakes. "We both know that ain't your name. You wanna do business with me? Don't you dare fuckin' lie."

"Emily. My name is Emily."

"Emily what?"

I hesitate, tightening the hair twirl on my finger.

He points to the door. "Truth or you gonna be back out on the sidewalk."

"Calby. Emily Calby."

"What happened to your eye?"

"My eye?"

"Yeah, one of them holes in your head you look outta."

"Just purple blush. I'm not very good at makeup yet."

"Bullshit. I know a bruise when I see one. One more lie, you out. Last warning."

Like the marks on my wrists, fading, but still there. I don't remember how I got it, so I couldn't tell the truth even if I wanted.

An air conditioner mounted high on the wall starts rattling like the motor's about to fall out. He punches the wall and the noise stops. "Where you family?" he says.

"I don't have one."

A simmering look.

"I'm not lying. I had a family ... but they're gone."

"Gone fuckin' where? Fishin'?"

"Dead."

Something in his eyes. Not softer or harder, just different. *The eyes tell all*, Mom used to say.

"Your parents pass?"

"And my sister. I'm the only one left."

I meet his stare until he breaks away. He goes behind the counter and pulls a can from a humming refrigerator, takes a sip and sets it down hard. A dust explosion reveals a green tile countertop.

"You want a drink?" he says. "In the children's department, we got water and water."

"Water would be good."

He tosses me a bottle. "The fuck you doin' to your hair?"

"Huh?"

"You been twistin' it in knots since you walked in."

For better or worse, my sheeny blonde hair has defined me since I was born. It took until last week, looking in a mirror at a bus station, for me to realize I had turned it into a rat's nest.

"Um, it's a bad habit I have."

"Quit doin' it. It's annoyin' as fuck."

I untwine my hair and shake the loose strands on the floor until I see him glaring. I stoop and pick them up. "Um, do you have a trashcan I could borrow?"

Me holding the golden tangle out like an offering. Him continuing to glare, muttering curse words, until his puffed-up chest deflates.

"Lucas," he says. "Some people call me Big EZ. You call me Lucas. You tellin' the truth about the money?"

"It's in my backpack. I can show you."

"I take you word. Follow me."

3

HE LEADS me down a hall to a metal door and presses his thumb on an electronic keypad. Next to it is a cracked, yellowed light switch dangling on green-crusted wires. *Incongruous.* I earned fifty cents looking it up in the fourth grade. *Now use it in a sentence. That high-tech keypad looks incongruous next to a hundred-year-old light switch.* The door unlocks with a clank.

We enter what looks like a laboratory. White walls, bright lights and techie-white furniture covered with electronic equipment. He bolts the door behind us.

"Driver's license," he says. "Anything particular?"

I'm still taking in the surroundings. Computers, printers, copy machines, even a microscope. The biggest monitor I've ever seen hangs from the ceiling on brackets.

Nonchalantly, "The way I travel, I'd prefer to be eighteen."

"Get fuckin' real."

"What's the highest you think I can go?"

"You pressin' you luck at sixteen, but you gotta be sixteen for a license."

"Sixteen then. Can you make a good one?"

Deep snort.

"I mean, will it be good enough to get me on buses and trains? I need that."

"Makin' a fake driver's license is easy. Makin' a good one ain't. You lucky you stumbled onto Lucas. Driver's licenses shit fulla security these days. Holograms, micro-text, but if you serious about avoidin' detection, you got to have the bar code on the back. Someone scans your driver's license and the information on the back don't match the information on the front, you fucked."

"I definitely want the bar code."

"Adds to the price. I do it for a thousand since you already here."

"Seriously? Shouldn't the bar code be included in the price? Your message didn't say anything about paying extra for a bar code."

"My message said seven hundred dollars for a *basic* license. Basic don't include the bar code."

"Well, how about seven-fifty?"

"This ain't a negotiatin' session. The product costs a thousand dollars with the bar code. Take it or leave it."

I need the license and it has to work. "Alright."

"Over here." I follow him to a computer, where he lights up the jumbo monitor while explaining that the only way to get the bar code is from real licenses and people.

He points me to a chair.

"Tell me who you wanna be, but don't take all fuckin' day." He opens a file and starts scrolling through pictures of driver's licenses. All of them belong to girls with a birth year four years before mine.

"These are all real? Where'd you get them?"

"Trade secret."

"How about that one?" I say. "Sandra Pro-sh-sh-chevsky. I like her hair."

His chin falls to his chest. "It ain't gonna be her hair on the license and you damn sure ain't from Trenton, New Jersey. You got a accent." He moves on. "Here we go. Rebecca Stanley. Raleigh, North Carolina. Looks like a nice girl."

"No," I say quickly. "I can't be Rebecca." That was Becky's name.

He grumbles.

"There's one," I say. "Alice Miller."

Alice in Wonderland was Mom's favorite book. She read it to me a hundred times when I was growing up, always comparing me to Alice. When I asked why, she gave a sly smile and said, *Who in the world am I? Ah, that's the great puzzle.*

Now more than ever. "Yes, definitely that one," I say.

"Even has blonde hair and blue eyes. Alright, Alice Regina Miller from Chattanooga, go behind that curtain and pick out a shirt, the most respectable *I ain't a fuckin' runaway* shirt you can find."

Undress? "What's wrong with these clothes?"

"Other than you stink like a dead body? Suppose you boardin' a train and get stopped. They wanna see identification. You show 'em your driver's license, which you got ... let's see, four months ago, and you wearin' the exact same clothes. What a fuckin' coincidence. I know what I'm doing. Go find a new shirt."

He keeps sending me back until I come out in a white blouse with a navy jacket over it.

"That's better."

"The jacket's too big."

"Only the neck shows," he says.

"Kids don't dress like this."

"That's the point. Now I gotta cut that hair."

"Cut my hair? You?"

"That blonde hair shines like a fuckin' beacon and it's all tore up from you yankin' on it."

"No offense," I say, "but do you know what you're doing, cutting hair?"

"I got skills." He clicks the scissors in my face. "Got to in my business."

I close my eyes and he starts snipping. Twenty minutes later he hands me a mirror. My hair has shrunk from halfway down my back to a shoulder-length blunt cut, and he was right, it looks a lot better with the abused ends gone. "Huh, that's not too bad."

"Damn right it ain't." He holds up his hands. "Check it out. My fingers too big to even fit through the scissor holes. Imagine what I could do with a proper pair."

He announces makeup comes next and wheels over a metal table piled high with cosmetics. He tears wet wipes from a box and starts scouring my face.

"*Ow ow ow.*"

Scrubbing harder, "Ain't my fault. You a fuckin' cake face. Only people wear this much makeup is whores and kids, and I doubt you a whore."

"Gee, thanks," I say.

"Pay attention here. You got to go easy. Start with a light foundation, like this here. And no more glossy orange lips. Use real lipstick, but not too much. For them blue eyes, something copper, like this. Again, easy on the touch."

"Is this why they call you the *Big EZ*?" I ask, but he doesn't smile.

He hands me a pair of tortoise shell glasses. "Put these on. Glasses make people look three years older. They did a study." He holds up a mirror.

"I look like a total geek."

"You look passable for sixteen, all that matters. Fifty dollars for the glasses and that's a fuckin' deal."

I react like he slapped me. "Fifty dollars? No way." I yank them off. "I'll take my chances without glasses."

"You got no room for chances," he grunts. "Put 'em on. We consider 'em a loan for now. Go sit in front of that screen."

* * *

Two hours later I'm holding a driver's license with my new picture next to *Alice Regina Miller* and a Chattanooga address.

"It looks so real," I say with wonder. There's even a state seal over my face. "I can finally take trains and buses by myself."

"Fuck trains and buses. Drive a car. You got a license." He laughs.

"I know how to drive. My dad taught me to drive his truck starting when I was ten."

"Congratulations. You owe me a thousand dollars."

I turn around and dig into the backpack, counting bills from the cigar box. So much money.

I stick it out. "Here."

"What's with the fuckin' look?" he says. "I did you a favor 'cause I thought you was wounded veteran Roscoe Pallatin. I can get five, ten thousand dollars for a license like this."

"Then you should tell people five or ten thousand. Not seven hundred. Anyway, I have to go. It's a nice license. Thank you for helping me."

The metal door stops me. "Can you unlock the door, please?"

"You ain't goin' out that door."

I stiffen. "I appreciate your help, but I need to go," I say without turning around.

"Do I need to talk louder? I said you ain't goin' out that door."

This can't be happening. I never let myself get trapped. Why did I let down my guard?

"It's gettin' dark. You go walkin' around this neighborhood at night, you ain't gonna need no driver's license. You gonna need a Glock. Where you stay at night?"

"Wherever I can. I feel safest in parks with lots of trees."

He breaks away and circles the room, shutting down lights and computers until we end up face to face again.

"You want, you stay here tonight. Extra bedroom upstairs. Got its own bathroom. That's another thing. You gonna get arrested just for smellin' so bad. I'm making gumbo for dinner, best in Memphis. You welcome to share."

I'd be a sitting duck. "That's nice of you," I say, "but I really need to go."

"Is that right? You really need to go find a place to sleep in the dirt? Look me in the eyes. *Do I trust Lucas?* That's your question." He points to a metal door on the back wall. "Answer's no, we go out that door and I give you a ride to Overton Park. They got some thick woods. Find a spot and stay quiet, you probably safe for one night."

He leans his big head in, gold-flecked black eyes tunneling into my pale blue ones. "If I was gonna hurt you, you'd know it by now. I've hurt people, plenty, but they all deserved it. I got no reason to hurt you."

Shower, bed, home-cooked meal. I haven't had even one of them in a month.

"How much would you charge me?"

"Five hundred dollars."

My jaw drops. "What the—"

A booming laugh. "Just fuckin' kiddin'."

4

I SIT at a long table of glossy black wood, sketching on my art pad. Two burning candles stick out of bulbous holders carved like skulls. Like the document room, the kitchen's been renovated, with black and white cabinets and countertops and a shiny concrete floor. A pot boils on a stove with two ovens and eight burners. Loud rap music plays through speakers built into the walls.

Lucas is searching for something in the double-wide refrigerator, hidden by an open door. He's been poking around in there for a long time. A cloud of skunky smoke hovers above him.

"Is the refrigerator on fire?" I ask suspiciously.

He coughs. "Everything fine," he says and goes back to cooking.

He's in a much better mood, singing and dancing to the music as he adds spices and sips from a yellow plastic cup, something he mixed up with liquor. A red-checkered apron emblazoned with *Mr. Good Lookin' Is Cookin'* barely reaches around his barrel chest.

"What you smilin' at, blondie?"

"Nothing. Can I help?"

He shakes his head. "Secret recipe. What you working on there? You an artist?"

"I guess. I like to draw." Random pops punctuate the night. "Why are there so many fireworks? Is it already Fourth of July?" I lost track of days, but thought it was still June.

"Not fireworks," he says, forming his hand in the shape of a gun.

"Oh."

He scoops gumbo with a ladle. "Come try this. How is it? Good?"

"Yum."

"You better fuckin' believe yum."

We eat sitting across from each other. The gumbo really is good. I'm scraping the bottom of my second bowl as he lectures me about using fake documents.

"It ain't just about havin' a document. It's how you present it. Like you bored or bothered, anything but nervous. You know the details like you know your own life. They ask if you an organ donor—which you is, by the way, to your credit—you better know."

"I understand."

"Get used to being Alice Miller. Think of a history. Keep it close as possible to your real life. Less chance to fuck up. And don't get sloppy with that makeup. It takes time to put on, but if you hope to stay on the roam, you got to be perfect."

I stir one of the waxy skull-brains with my finger. "Why are you helping me like this? Somehow I don't see you doing this for all your customers."

"Last thing I need is you gettin' arrested usin' my product. Bad for business."

"Is that the only reason?"

He puts down his spoon. "Hand me that bread." He picks up a sharp knife and points it at me. "You say you family dead. What happened?"

I hold my finger over the flame, watching the wax sizzle. The smell of burning skin more than the pain makes me pull away.

"Quit fuckin' with my candle. I asked you a question."

"I don't want to talk about it," I blurt. "It was my fault. I was supposed to protect them. I failed, okay?"

"Gimme that butter." He takes his time spreading it. "Aunts, uncles, shit like that?"

"My mom had a sister but she died of breast cancer."

He bites off a chunk of bread, chewing in slow motion. Blasting from the speakers, *Cane slanger, bitch banger ...* He picks up a remote and lowers the music, taking another swig of his drink.

"I ain't got no people either," he says. Whatever's in the yellow cup must be strong because his words are slurring. "My dad, he dead. No matter. Never met 'im."

I'm about to ask how it's possible for someone to have never met their own dad, but figure it out. "What about your mom?"

"Mama tried. Had the monkey on her back."

"Monkey?"

"Drugs."

"Oh. I'm sorry."

"Why?"

"I don't know. I just am."

"Don't be. Ain't your responsibility." He stares at the flickering candles.

"Do you have brother or sisters?"

He takes another swallow. "Jarrett. Wanted to be a big-time gangster like his brother. Gangs is a way of life here. Joined one without telling me. Two weeks later, he dead. Three boys in one gang shot him in the front yard just 'cause he in a different gang. No other reason."

I start to say I'm sorry again, but hold back. He murmurs something.

"What did you say? I couldn't hear you."

"Shondra too. My little sister. Only one in the family who took the right track. Worked hard in school, stayed outta trouble."

He smacks his lips.

"Motherfuckers sprayed almost a hundred bullets that night. Went through the walls and killed Shondra in her bedroom while she was doin' her homework."

"How old was Shondra?"

He drains the cup and claps it on the table. "Twelve."

He picks up the knife and weaves it in circles. "I tell you what though. Them pieces of shit that killed Jarrett and Shondra? They never hurt no one else. I see to that. Justice. Always comes too late, but it's still justice."

The music ends and the only sound is the knifepoint tapping on the lustrous tabletop. "Yeah," he says. "They another reason."

In the silence, I have plenty of time to think about what to say, but it still comes out wrong.

"I know you don't want to hear it, but I really am sorry. Thank you for being my friend."

A mocking laugh. "Friend? We ain't no friends. Get straight on that. You just a fuckin' pity case."

"Pity case!" I jump up, grabbing the backpack. "I'm not anyone's pity case. You're a pity case. I didn't want to be your friend anyway. I was just trying to be nice. How do I get out of this place?"

He holds up his wide hand. "Go take a shower. You smell like shit."

I insisted I was leaving unless he took back I'm a pity case, but moved him only as far as *I didn't fuckin' mean it like that.* After a stalemate, too tired to search for a place to sleep and craving a hot shower more than anything I could think of, I relented and followed him up the stairs.

* * *

The second floor looks original, like the front room, but a lot cleaner. He leads me to a small bedroom with a dresser, twin bed and nightstand set up on a dull, scratched wood floor. The windows are boarded up. He points to the bathroom and walks out.

It's small, with black-tiled walls and a green tub and sink. I try to lock the door but it's an old-fashioned skeleton key lock with no key. I stuff toilet paper in the keyhole and plug my stun gun in to charge. Pink, with a flashlight at the business end. That's what I thought it was when I found it under the seat of a car.

The shower is a hose attached to the faucet. *Hot water. OMG.* I stay until it runs out.

I'm drying off with a frayed green towel when a thunderous knock sends flakes of paint drifting from the tall ceiling like snow.

"Don't come in," I shout, tightening the towel around me. "Who is it?"

"Who the fuck you think it is?"

I crack open the door and there's giant Lucas holding out a tiny blue sundress.

"Laundry's downstairs. Wash them nasty clothes. You can keep the dress. Come from a small lady used to work for me."

"Doing what?"

"You don't wanna know."

In the blue dress, towel bundled around my head, I find a washer and dryer in a closet near the kitchen. First time in a month I've been able to recycle a set of clothes.

I wait at the kitchen table. Except for the skull candles, there's not a single clue about who lives here. No pictures on the walls, no knick-knacks on the counters, not even a refrigerator magnet. Back home, you couldn't even see our refrigerator, wallpapered with everything from Becky's *Best Citizen Award* to my detention notice for talking in class. Something about the emptiness makes me sad.

I find Lucas upstairs in a large room at the end of the hall, stretched out on a bed in boxers and a t-shirt watching a theater-sized TV mounted on a crumbling red-brick wall. More incongruity.

"Is it okay if I go to bed?"

"You say prayers?"

"Um, yes ... why?"

"Pray the FBI don't pick tonight to raid Big EZ and his false document enterprise. Havin' a twelve-year-old white girl in here'll get me a fuckin' life sentence." He holds out a bag. "Take it."

"What is it?"

"The makeup you need to not look like a cake face. Throw that other shit away."

"Okay. Thanks. Good night."

The lumpy mattress is like a cloud compared to my usual beds. I get out the stun gun. I test the charge every night before I go to sleep. The zap crackles off the ceiling like a lightning bolt.

Footsteps pound down the hall. The door flies open and Lucas comes in waving a big gun. I'm holding the stun gun in both hands like a flower bouquet.

"What the fuck? Jesus-fuckin'-Christ. I *know* that sound. I thought someone was in here." He lowers the gun.

"Sorry."

"Jesus-fuckin'-Christ."

"You shouldn't, um, use the Lord's name in vain."

"*Pfft*. Lemme guess. You a little goody two-shoes."

"I was brought up to have faith in God and be a good person if that's what you mean ... but not anymore."

"No more faith in God?"

"No more good person." A pathetic liar and thief who runs away.

He starts to say something but stops. "You ever need that stun gun, aim here." He draws a circle on his stomach. "Solar plexus. Bundle of fuckin' pain nerves."

5

I TURN OFF the light and pull up the comforter, plunging my head into the pillow, all soft and mushy, bleachy smelling. *Umm.* So good ... too good, almost like a trick.

A tingly sense and I'm suddenly afraid to close my eyes. When I do, there they are. *The two men. The gas can.*

I sit up, holding the comforter to my throat. What's happening? It's the same tug between then and now I felt at the train station. Until today *then* has been limited to the internet stories, murky nightmares and a bitter taste of doom in every breath.

Even the days since I barely remember. Why did I go to Chicago? Where was I before that? A robot on auto-pilot. *Shelter water food. Shelter water food.*

Then the fog started clearing when I got the idea—an actual *idea*—for the driver's license, like I could see a few steps ahead ... and behind, the memories I run from so hard catching up, widening jaws preparing to chop me in two.

Now the two men, breaking through the deepest, darkest boxes of all: standing right there at the beginning, a movie waiting to start.

Why now? Maybe it was Lucas bursting in with the gun. There was a gun that day. I hear it shooting in my dreams.

I tuck the comforter around me. *Covered*, with walls and a ceiling—and Lucas outside. He's not going to hurt me. I believe that. I'm not sure why, but I do. And I'll bet nothing could hurt him. Not the two men, probably not ten men.

That's probably it, the explanation. *Safe*, for the first time. I need to let myself remember.

I close my eyes and there I am, at the kitchen door, watching the stocky man talking to Mom in the yard. The tall one is holding the gas can, eyes flitting back and forth, acting twitchy.

Mom being nice to them, too freaking nice. I will *never* be that nice.

The doorknob turning. The cramp in my stomach even before it burst open.

Everything breaks free, like a video that's been hung up buffering.

The stocky man tells the tall man to close the blinds. We're in the kitchen.

"Y'all listen up," he says, waving a gun. "Everybody follow instructions and no one gets hurt." He makes Mom dump her purse on the table, taking her phone and the cash from her wallet.

"Any more money around here? Little hidden stash?"

Mom shakes her head.

"Don't fucking lie to me. Everybody's got one."

Dad's cigar box with the five thousand dollars. Should I tell them?

"We don't," Mom says.

"Who else got a phone?" He points at me. "You got a phone, blondie?"

"No."

"Ain't a girl your age in America don't got a phone."

"I don't."

He puts the gun to Mom's head.

"I have one!"

I pull my phone from my back pocket and hand it over as the tall man comes back in the kitchen. "Da blinds closed." The strange accent.

The stocky man points to Becky. "What about you, sweet pea? You got yourself a little iPhone?"

I push her behind me. "She's only eight. She doesn't have a phone. Leave her alone."

"Where's the alarm?" he says.

Mom and I glance at each other. We both wanted one, but Dad said it would be a waste of money out in the country, said the cops would never get to us in time and he'd be here to protect us.

"There is no alarm," Mom says.

"Landline?"

She points down the main hall to the master bedroom.

"What say we take a family trip? Mom, lead the way."

In the hallway we pass pictures of Mom and Dad getting married, me and my softball team, Becky in her Brownie uniform ... At the end is a gauzy photo in a thick frame that we took at a studio, the whole family smiling, dressed in our Sunday best. It's the last thing I see before being hustled into the bedroom.

Stocky man grabs the phone on the nightstand and rips it from the wall. "Girls, I don't think we met properly. What's your names?"

I stare and he starts to raise his hand.

"That's Emily," Mom says. "And Becky. They're good girls. They won't tell anyone. None of us will, if you'll just leave."

A whimper from Becky, a tiny bird chirp.

"Keep her quiet."

I rub her back. "It's gonna be okay, Bec. Everything's gonna be okay. Don't cry." ... Same words I said to the brown-haired girl who fell at the train station.

"Ronnie," the stocky man says. "Get the ties."

Ronnie. He called the tall man Ronnie.

He pulls a bag of plastic straps from the orange sack, clear, like the ones Dad and I used to reattach the gas tank to the lawnmower when it broke off.

"Take 'em," the stocky man says to Mom.

"What for?" she stutters.

He nods to me and Becky. "Can't have loose girls runnin' around. Bind 'em. Ankles and wrists."

She shakes her head. "That's not necessary. I assure you. Take whatever you want. We won't bother you. I'll give you my pin number for my bank card. Anything."

"Anything? Well, we're reasonable folks. Least I am. Can't say the same for my friend here. I suppose we can work a deal. But you still gotta bind the girls."

"I can't do that."

He grabs her by the waist and yanks her close.

I erupt. "Let her go! You heard her. Take what you want and get out."

"Don't worry, blondie. We're gonna take what we want," he says.

Tall man laughs.

Mom tries to pull away. He squeezes harder.

I charge him. ... *That's* where the eye bruise came from. Before I got there tall man's fist hit me from the side.

... I fall to the floor, senses filled with flashing lights and Mom's cry. When I open my eyes stocky man's gun is pointed at my face.

"Everybody just calm the fuck down," he says. "We can do this the easy way or the hard way. Mom, if you can't bind the girls, my partner's gonna do it, and fact is, he really wants to. I'm just trying to help. Honest and true."

Mom doesn't move. He shrugs and says to the tall man, "Looks like they want you to do it."

Mom snatches the bag and motions for me to sit on the bed. She kneels on the beige carpet and wraps my ankles with the ties, way too loose. Even I can see that. Stocky man grabs her hair. "Do it fucking right."

The anguish in her eyes when she looks up tears my heart apart.

I smile and touch her face. *Keep the boat afloat.* Her eyes flick to the nightstand.

"Now the little one," the stocky man says.

"No, no, no," Mom says, shaking her head. "She's just a baby. She can't hurt anyone."

I'm opening my mouth when the tall man butts in. "No need to tie up da little one, boss man," he says.

"Listen to him," Mom says.

"I juss got to cut dem off when I ... ya know."

Seeing Mom's face, watching it turn from non-comprehension to horror, as if her soul died in the space of a second, made everything sink in. It was never really about money.

The movie blows a fuse and everything goes dark. From somewhere, a scream. Lucas runs in again.

"Now fucking what?"

Fists spindled with hair, mouth open, but no sound coming out—until I break down for the first time since the day everything happened. Shriveling like a dying flower, I bury my head between my knees, sobbing.

Lucas sits on the bed. He doesn't speak or try to touch me, just lets me cry.

6

WE'RE ON a blanket having a picnic, the sun reflecting Mom's hair like pure gold. Becky has grape jelly smeared on her face and we're laughing. Then Mom turns to me and everything changes. Her smile, the one that brightened the day of every person she met, transforms into a screaming hollow. *Please! No! Mom! Mom!*

I wake up in a cold sweat, trembling with my head under the covers until Lucas shouts from downstairs, "Get your ass out of bed."

I get up and wash my face and put on the makeup like he taught me. I make the bed and check the backpack, three times, like I always do before I leave a place. My entire existence is in it, including the new license.

A wistful last glance at the room. Man, even laundry. "Bye, bed," I say.

Lucas is at the kitchen table reading on a computer. "Look here," he points. Over his mountainous shoulder is a picture of a smiling black boy. "Shot last night a few blocks from here. Fourteen years old. You be fuckin' careful out there."

"I will."

A plate of bacon, eggs and grits sits in front of my chair.

"Breakfast?" The last person to make me breakfast was Mom. "You did this for me? Because you pity me, right?" After I cried myself out last night, I told him what happened.

"'Cause I like to cook. You wear a bra?"

38

Crossing my chest, "What in the world? That's personal."

"Just fuckin' tell me."

"Of course I do."

"You need to stuff it. You sixteen now."

I look down and nod.

"What's your address?" he says.

"Huh?"

"I said, what's your address, *Alice*?"

"Oh. I didn't get a chance to study it last night, but I will."

"You fuckin' better. Where you headin'?"

I thought about it last night, but didn't come up with an answer. "Not sure yet," I say. "I have some things to figure out."

After breakfast, I stuff toilet paper in my bra and ask directions to an internet café.

"I give you a ride. Back door," he points.

We go outside and get into a gleaming black SUV with fancy chrome wheels. He puts on rap music as we pull away.

"Tell me," he says. "You runnin' from somethin' or to somethin'?"

"Both ... but I'm not sure what or what." The answer doesn't make sense, even to me.

"Better start figurin' it out. You got to have goals in life."

I almost laugh because it sounds like something my dad would say.

"You ever think about going home, to the authorities?"

"No. Never."

"They got foster families."

"Would you be in a foster family?"

He doesn't answer.

"Besides, if I ever turn up alive, it will be all over the news. I'll never be safe from the two men."

We pull up to the internet café. He sticks out his hand, which I shake, or try to. It swallows mine completely.

"Goodbye and thanks again," I say. I exit the SUV without looking back.

The internet café is sketchy, like most. They're hard to find except in big cities, but I prefer them to library computers, which I also use a lot. Too many people and you get more questions. Some libraries have surveillance cameras pointed straight at the computer screens.

A sign says *Payment Required In Advance.*

"How much for thirty minutes?" I ask the clerk, a skinny white guy with a neck tattoo.

"Five bucks an hour."

Ripoff. Except for splurging on the driver's license, I'm cheap. The money has to last.

"Thirty minutes and a small coffee, please." I pay from the bills in my front pocket.

Before everything happened I only tasted coffee once, a sip from Mom's that I spit in the sink. Now it's all that keeps me going sometimes. I have a taste for the good stuff. The muddy liquid in the foam cup he hands me is not in that category.

I tear open a pack of sugar, feeling the clerk giving me *the look*. I've been noticing it for the past year, but didn't understand what it meant. I get it now. I imagine ramming the stun gun in his solar plexus, but smile instead. I stay polite always, even to people who don't deserve it. I can't risk public confrontation.

I go to the back corner and sign onto a computer. I open a browser and type *Calby Murders*, bracing for the results. Usually I just stare, anesthetized. I think I still have feelings, somewhere, but I don't feel them anymore. I worry today might be different. I press enter.

Georgia Family Brutally Murdered
Mother, Two Daughters Killed in Home Intrusion
Month Later, Town Still Reeling from Savage Attack

Only the last story is new. I haven't let my brain roam anywhere near my town, or my friends or teachers or anyone. There's just no room. It's easier to pretend I never lived there. Did they interview Meggie Tribet? What would she say? No one's honest when talking about a dead person. *She was an angel on earth,* instead of, *OMG, that girl could nag you to death.*

I'm staring at the link, hand dangling above the mouse like a spider when a loud sneeze at the next computer startles me. My hand hits the mouse and the screen scrolls down ... *no-no-no.*

For the first couple of weeks I expected it every time I turned on a computer. When it didn't happen, I started to let myself believe it never would. The article is from the Atlanta newspaper.

Home Invasion Shocker:
Victim's Remains Missing from Burned Ruins

I click on the link:

> *For a month law enforcement agencies have operated on the assumption that Theresa Calby, 37, and both of her children, Emily, 12, and Rebecca, 8, were killed in the May 23 invasion at their rural home.*
>
> *But today at a press conference, Dilfer County Sheriff Lawrence Timmons made a chilling announcement in disclosing the results of a forensic investigation. No trace of remains was found for 12-year-old Emily at the fire-charred site.*

This is bad news. Horrible, terrible bad news.

> *The report concluded the assailants poured gasoline throughout the house and disconnected natural gas lines before setting off a blast so powerful it registered on earthquake monitors in Atlanta.*

Before this everyone thought I got incinerated in the fire. Now the sheriff says that's *highly unlikely.*

> *"The remains of the mother and youngest child were intact," Timmons said. "Medical examiners were able to identify specific injuries inflicted prior to the fire."*

Remains ... mother and youngest child ... specific injuries inflict-ed. Poison gas fills my brain. I fight it, but just like last night, I spiral down the dark chute, landing again in that day, except now the movie has skipped to the end.

I'm climbing out the bathroom window, stocky man grabbing at my feet and cursing. I hit the ground next to the stack of firewood Dad cut before he died, rotted because we never wanted to use it. Worm-holed scraps of decaying pulp. That's how desperate we were for something to hang onto.

Stocky man, too big to fit through the window, is shouting. "I'm coming to cut you into pieces."

I run into the woods. I know every inch of them, including that leaves gather several feet deep at the bottom of the shallow coming up. I make a running leap so there are no footprints, burying myself in musty leaves just before pounding footsteps arrive.

"Fuck!" Stocky man. His rage seems to rattle the forest before I realize it's my own panting moving the leaves. I hold my breath and visualize a girl turned to stone.

In the distance, "Come on, boss man. Place about to blow to Kingdom Come. Got to go."

In a regular voice, like he knows I'm there, "Little girl, if I ever get my hands on you, you're gonna wish you died with your mama and sister."

When he's gone, I scramble out, brushing leaves from my face and hair—just before the forest shatters. An explosion. I run back to the house, bits of glass and brick and insulation trickling through the branches.

At the edge, I freeze. The top half of the house I grew up in is gone. What's left is on fire.

I run into the smoke, stumbling over something. It's Pooky, Becky's stuffed dog, melted eyes oozing onto the grass.

I climb through a hole where the kitchen wall used to be. "Mom! Becky!" A coal sizzles through my shoe. My pants leg catches fire. *Can't breathe.* I weave back outside, coughing and smothering my pants, burning my hands.

I round the house, still shouting for Mom and Becky, but I already know they're gone. I come to the F-150, windows shattered, gas cover open, cap off.

The garage is smoking, but intact. *The garage.*
This is for an emergency ... if the shit hits the fan.
I retrieve the money box from the hidden drawer Dad and I
built in the workbench and race into the woods. I run for miles,
until dusk, when I come to a train stopped at a farm. I climb
into a car full of bleating sheep and ride the train all night.

In the morning, I tore my burned-up jeans into shorts and
told my first lies, to a nice old man at a bus station who believed
I was going to visit my cousin. I don't remember where I went.

A tap on the shoulder brings me back. It's the scruffy man at
the next computer, dressed too hot for summer in a plaid wool
coat. "You 'kay?"

I realize I'm bent over, sweaty forehead pressed against
the edge of the monitor. "Uh, yeah, just thinking. Thanks for
asking."

Pull it together. I scroll past the terrible words.

> Asked if Emily could have been taken by the assail-
> ants, Timmons said, "I do not want to raise false hopes.
> Even if that happened, the FBI profilers do not believe
> she would be kept alive for a month."
>
> Timmons said it was unlikely Emily escaped. "If she
> had, we would have heard from her."

My shoulders bow.

> Timmons expressed irritation when pressed about
> the lack of progress in the investigation. He said the fire
> destroyed most of the physical evidence and the only
> witness was a neighbor who passed a blue pickup truck
> parked on the street before the explosion.
>
> He announced one new piece of evidence, a gas can
> found some distance from the house. He said it "pos-
> sibly" could have been thrown there in the explosion.
>
> Timmons urged anyone with information to come
> forward.

The article ends with a phone number and email address to a tipline.

Across the top is the picture I've seen a hundred times, stolen from Mom's Facebook page. Last Fourth of July at the lake. Me and Mom yellow-haired bookends to Becky, who's waving a sparkler in one hand and an American flag in the other. Dad had only been gone a few months and all the smiles look forced, but Mom liked it.

A second picture shows a gas can resting in a patch of weeds. Definitely the same red can with the slanted yellow lettering that the tall man was carrying.

I turn away. Not only did I run, I never went back. Double fail. In the beginning it was fear of the two men. I spent weeks looking over my shoulder, so much my neck hurt. Then one afternoon on a bus ride to who knows where, locked inside my head, I saw the real fear. The blankness, the *nothingness* of nothing to go back to.

When Dad died I didn't think it was possible for things to get worse. His job working with combines was dangerous. We both knew something bad could happen. "Take care of your mom and Becky," he said every morning when he left for work.

"I will, Dad."

He said it the last day, when the owner and foreman from the farm came to the house late afternoon to tell us Dad was dead, killed in an accident. Now he's gone, they're gone, everything *gone-gone*. Not even a house left.

Foster family? I'll jump off a building first. But with new clarity, I know I'm done wandering with no purpose. Mom and Becky deserve better. First I need to help the police. I don't remember everything, but I have information no one else has.

But that's not enough. *Them pieces of shit that killed Jarrett and Shondra? They never hurt no one else. I see to that.*

I can't rely on the police. They haven't done anything. And even if they find the two men, they'll get to lead long healthy lives, in air conditioning, with three meals a day cooked and served to them. I researched it. Prisoners can even get *conjugal* visits. I couldn't believe that one when I looked it up. Becky won't get to watch *Frozen* again, but prisoners get TVs. Mom won't ever read another book, her favorite thing in the world, but rapists and murderers get their own libraries.

Justice. Always comes too late, but it's still justice.

7

STARING AT the Fourth of July picture, noticing for the first time the tips of Becky's top teeth coming in, I make a decision. A longshot. More than that. Crazy. But as Lucas said, *You got to have goals in life.* Haha.

The clerk's standing next to me. I minimize the window. "What do you want?"

"You on drugs? I said your time's up. You only paid for a half hour. Two-fifty for another half hour."

I hand him three dollars from my front pocket and go back to the computer.

"Oh boy. Is this a tip?"

"No. You owe me fifty cents." Meanie.

I go to a free email anonymizer and set up a burner account for *Robert Williams*, entering the tipline address and subject line *Calby Murders*.

> *Dear Sheriff Timmons:*
>
> *I have information about the murders of the Calby family. I have not written before because ...*

I pause. Because?

> *... I've been out of the country.*

LAME. I delete the message and pinch my lips. Why would someone wait?

Dear Sheriff Timmons:

*I have information about the murders of the Calby
family. I have not written before because I am afraid.*

Anyone who knew anything about the two men would be
afraid.

*After reading about your press conference, I knew I
could not live with myself if I did not tell what I know.*
True.

*This information is from a conversation I overheard
in a bar between two men on May 23, the day of the
rape and murders.*

I evaluate the sentence. Sounds plausible, but I delete rape.
The police refused to comment about it. I know it happened.
Somewhere I hear the sounds.

*I did not think much of it at the time, but later that
night I heard about the murders on the news.*

*This is what happened. I was sitting at the bar next
to two white men. One was short and stocky and the
other one tall.*

Short and tall don't mean anything. How tall was stocky
man? Mom was five-seven and they looked about the same
height in the kitchen. Tall man? More than six feet. I revise the
descriptions, adding every detail I remember.

*This is very important: the stocky man called the tall
man RONNIE.*

*I heard them talking about a woman and two children
and a fire at a house. The stocky man told Ronnie he
was stupid for leaving the gas can behind.*

The gas can is crucial. It could have fingerprints or DNA on
it. They need to test it.

They left the bar in a blue pickup truck with a crook-
ed camper-top.

I plan to draw sketches of both men and will send
them to you.

I pause. One more thing.

I am sorry to say your experts are right. Emily Calby
is dead. I heard the stocky man say, "Good thing we
got rid of the witnesses."

I go back and add *probably* before dead, sign the message *Robert Williams* and hit send. I confirm it went through, clean the browser and turn off the computer.

Walking out of the café into the bright sun, I reach in my backpack for my stolen sunglasses and pull out an envelope that's not supposed to be there. Inside is three hundred dollars and a sticky note. *Paid in Full $700.*

I stash it and wave at a taxi that keeps going. A man in dirty clothes approaches me, muttering words I can't make out. I walk the other way.

I'm glancing back to make sure he's not following me when I run into a wall. But it's not a wall. It's massive, solid as a wall Lucas.

"What are you doing here?" I say.

He motions to his SUV, parked at the curb. "Get in," he says.

My door's still open when we speed away. "You supposed to be dead," he says. "You left out that part of the story."

"How'd you find out?"

"Secret computer trick called Google. I searched your name and the monitor lit up like Christmas."

"Are you mad at me?"

"Nah. I ain't tell anyone that fucked-up shit either."

I sink back into the leather seat. "The latest news is the police figured out I didn't die in the house. They think the killers took me."

"Saw that too. Glad you ain't dead."

I start to say, *That's makes one of us,* but instead, "Thanks for the refund."

He nods. "Past is past. Got a plan for what you doin' in the future, where you goin'?"

"Not really ... no. I have an idea, but no plan."

"You interested in going back to Lucas's and tryin' to figure one out?"

"For real? Sure!"

"Alright. First we need lunch."

We drive to a neighborhood with signs for *Abogados* and *Lavanderías.* I recognize most of the words from Spanish class.

"Bad news for your life plan if the police think you survived," he says. "Only thing explaining how you got this far is no one's been lookin' for you."

"I know. The good news is the FBI profilers think I'm dead."

A knowing nod. "Never keep a prisoner alive."

"I sent the police an email telling them what I remember. It's the first time I contacted them." My voice cracks. "I waited too long ... but I just started remembering things."

"It cool, it cool," he says.

I explain how I faked the message to sound like it came from someone who overheard the two men talking in a bar. "I said I heard the stocky man say they got rid of the witnesses."

"Smart. Maybe no one's searchin' for you."

"Except the killers. More memories came back," I say, skin tingling. "I remember climbing out a window after everything happened. One of them was chasing me. I never knew how I got away, or that they knew I got away. I think all my memories might be coming back. They scare me."

Sweating and starting to hyperventilate, I roll down the window.

"Relax and put the fuckin' window back up. Large black men can't be ridin' around with skinny white girls without beggin' to get pulled over by the police."

Swinging the SUV into a parking spot at a *Taqueria,* he says,

"I think them two men is long gone and I wouldn't say it if I didn't believe it. Stay here."

* * *

I like this seat. Same one from breakfast and last night's gumbo. I drink iced tea and munch on a taco. The air conditioners grind in the background. I don't know how we got on the subject, but Lucas is giving me a rundown on the state of the Memphis Grizzlies basketball team. I listen impatiently, shooing a buzzing horsefly.

When he pauses for a breath, "Thanks for coming back to get me. I really appreciate it."

"You welcome."

"It was super nice of you. ... So, you know, I hate to be a pain, but—"

"You gonna be one anyway."

"Remember I said I had an idea? I need your help again."

"Lemme guess, you want a passport now. Gonna fly to Russia, hide out."

"Too much security at airports."

"That was a joke."

"Oh, sorry." It's hard to tell with him. "Can I ask a question? Are you still in a gang?"

There's a piece of tomato on his face next to his nose. "Um, right here," I say, touching my cheek, but he ignores me.

"Why you wanna know?"

"Just curious."

"Curious. That should be your middle name." He shakes his head. "I give that life up after Jarrett and Shondra passed, long time ago. Decided to make a respectable livin'."

"Forging documents?" I say.

He flicks the tomato off his cheek like he knew it was there all along. "That's right."

"Last night you said you hurt people."

He scoops salsa with a jumbo corn chip and puts the whole thing in his mouth. "Sometimes. Not 'cause I liked it."

"I know. Because they deserved it."

"That's right." He's eyeing me, crunching the corn chip, trying to figure out where the conversation is going.

"Did you kill them?"

"Fuck's wrong with you? You don't ask a man questions like that."

He unwraps the last taco. I cross my arms, watching his thick fingers struggle with the tiny salsa packet. He takes his time squirting it in a swirl, picks up the taco and sets it back down.

"You and that fucking look. I bet you annoyed the fuck outta you family when they was alive."

The horsefly lands on the table and he smashes it with his fist. "It's possible," he says.

"You killed the men who shot Jarrett and Shondra, didn't you?"

"Possible."

"They deserved it."

"Just tell me what you tryin' to say."

"Just wondering ... could you teach me how to do it?"

8

LUCAS CHEWS on the taco, shaking his head the whole time.

"Are you shaking your head no?"

"Just shakin' it. You somethin' else, Alice. You ever even been in a fight?"

"One time I pushed a boy who teased Becky ... and I tried to fight the stocky man the day the men came. That's how I got the bruise on my eye. I just remembered it."

He's thinking. I can tell. His chewing slows down and he studies the ceiling, like there's something up there, maybe a spaceship or birds flying by. I lock my teeth on the edge of the glass to keep quiet, suctioning a steady stream of tea.

"I understand where you comin' from," he says. "But you got to leave things to the police."

"Why didn't you leave things to the police when the men killed Jarrett and Shondra?"

"Different."

"How?"

"Lotsa ways."

"Like what?"

"What the fuck? No one ever teach you to talk without puttin' a question mark at the end?"

"I just want to know."

His neck veins swell. "I know you just wanna know. That don't make it right. Fuck it. Jarrett and Shondra was blood. Enough said. Retaliation. Code of the street."

"Mom and Becky were blood. What else?"

"I ain't got a lot of confidence in the police."

"Why should I?"

"'Cause you ain't a black man."

"Well, I don't. It's been a month and all they have is a gas can. What else?"

"How many fuckin' reasons you need?"

"One *effing* good one, excuse my language. Why did you kill them?"

Our eyes lock.

"I had to," he says evenly.

I throw my arms up. "*That* I get."

He pinches the bridge of his wide nose. "Let's assume I could teach you to kill a man. You got two big obstacles. One, you got no idea where the men is. Two, you can't be like me just 'cause you wanna be, just like Jarrett couldn't. Look at me. I'm six and a half feet tall. I weigh two hundred and sixty pounds. You just a—"

"Skinny white girl. I know, I know."

"Bad news. That gonna be a factor when it comes to fightin' grown men. Another thing. It's terrible shit what happened to you, but you just a kid, still got a chance at life. Once you kill a man, you never the same."

"I'm already not the same. I think you know that. As for finding the men, when my memories come back, there might be clues."

I think he's used to backing people down with his mean stare because he gets frustrated when I don't look away. Dad used to joke I have motor oil in my eyes because I can outstare someone forever without blinking.

"So can you teach me?"

"I think on it."

He says he has work to do and heads for the document room. I clean up lunch and go upstairs to start my sketches of the two men, stocky man first. I work intently for an hour. The room is quiet and peaceful. I never realized how exhausting it is to stay on high alert around the clock, on the streets, in the buses and trains.

A buzzing makes me start. I was never a jumpy person. Now I am. I hate it. *Bzzzzz.* The front door.

I stalk down the stairs. Lucas is in the document room. Can he hear it? Too short to see out the peephole drilled at the top of the door, I go to the window and look through a scratch in the paint, but the angle's bad.

The thick metal door to the document room swings open and Lucas comes trotting out, alarmed.

"What's wrong?" I say.

"My girlfriend."

"Oh, jeez. That's all?"

"It ain't good."

"Why? Oh, me. How are you going to explain having a young white girl in here, right?"

The buzzer again. He pushes the intercom button, "Just a second."

"I could be selling Girl Scout cookies."

"They ain't no Girl Scouts 'round here."

"I could be a Jehovah's Witness ... but I don't have any magazines. I know, how about a fake-document trainee, like an intern?"

"This ain't fuckin' Silicon Valley. She ain't stupid. Just let me do the talking," he says, pulling on the door.

"Hey, baby."

"What took you so long?"

"I was in back."

"Well, are you going to invite me in?"

"Yeah, course, come on in." He unlocks the security door.

In struts a statuesque black lady with muscles like a man, wearing a tight pink fitness top, black leggings and athletic shoes. "You ready to work out?"

"Not quite. I got a little behind today."

She sees me, trying to melt into the wall. To say she's surprised would not capture the look on her face. "Who. Are. You?"

I look to Lucas.

"Oh, her?" he says. "Just some person I was tryin' to help."

"Trying to help? You opening a preschool for troubled girls, Lucas? You better start explaining."

"Kiona, this is Alice. Alice, this Kiona."

"Hi!" I say.

She ignores me. "Lucas—"

"Let's everybody sit down."

He leads us to the kitchen table. While Kiona tosses one of the skull candlesticks hand to hand like a baseball, Lucas explains about me coming to get a fake driver's license and him not knowing I was a kid.

"When I found out she got nowhere to go, I let her stay here for the night."

"O-kay," she says. "The night's over. Why is she still here?"

"It's my fault, ma'am. Lucas was just being nice. I asked him to let me stay. It's time for me to go now."

"Ma'am? I ain't no damn ma'am. How old are you?"

"Um, twelve."

"Twelve? Oh, I see, Lucas. This is all about Shondra, isn't it?"

"No," he says. "Nothin' like that."

"And a white child? Have you lost your mind?"

"Kiona, listen. You got no people left and I got no people left. Turns out she ain't got no people and she only twelve. We all in the same shit-storm."

"I see," she says more calmly. "Alice, I think it's wonderful that Lucas was able to help you, but I believe you said you were about to leave."

I stand up.

"No," Lucas says. "She gonna be stayin' a while. I ask for your support on that."

"Staying? What's a while?"

I'm wondering the same thing.

"One month."

My eyes pop, Kiona's blaze. "I don't think I heard you right," she says. "I couldn't possibly have because it sounded like you said one month."

He nods. "Take us that long to train her."

"Us? Train her? For what?"

"Kiona here's a personal trainer, also a boxer," he says. "That's where we met, at the boxing gym. Kiona, I'm asking your help to train Alice, so she can protect herself. You know the street. All alone, she's gonna get eaten alive."

"Then call social services. Call the police. It's not our job. She's better off not being on the streets."

"She's got to stay off the grid."

"I'm supposed to train a skinny little child to protect herself on the streets, in one month?"

"No, your job is to get her in shape by working her hard every day. Mine is to teach her how to defend herself. But she needs to get stronger first."

"Lord have mercy," she says and stomps out of the kitchen and up the stairs. The door to Lucas's bedroom slams.

"She got me at a disadvantage," Lucas says. "Only person I don't intimidate."

"You don't intimidate me," I say.

The half-laugh, half-snort.

"Kiona said this was all about Shondra. Is that true?"

"She say that all right."

"Am I anything like Shondra?"

"No."

That conversation is over. "Are you serious about one month? You're really going to train me how to kill?"

"Did I fuckin' say that? I said I'm gonna teach you self-defense. You ain't never gonna find them two men. Just accept it."

"But you can use self-defense to kill, right?"

"Legally?"

"No, for real. Will I be able to kill someone with what you teach me?"

"You ain't got to worry about that."

"I'm ready to learn. When do we start?"

"Don't get too excited. You ain't gonna be no Avenger in one month, but if you willin' to do the work—and you better not let me down on that—you will be lethal when you leave here."

I cross my heart. "I won't let you down."

"Alright," he says. "I'll go talk to Kiona. Here's something to know about her. Show her appreciation. Butter her up. She likes when I tell her she's smokin' hot."

"I'm supposed to tell her she's smoking hot?"

"No, no. Just an example."

From above, "Lucas, I'm waiting."

"One more thing. You *Alice Miller*. Don't ever make the mistake of feeling all warm and fuzzy and tellin' anyone who you really are. Don't look at it like lyin' to Kiona. We protectin' her. She's better off not knowin'."

He walks to the foot of the stairs and hesitates. "If I don't come down alive, lock the door behind you on the way out."

9

THE THREE of us are in Lucas's basement, a moldy cavern converted into a fitness museum. Rusty dumbbells, lumpy punching bags, benches and mats with yellow foam bulging out from torn covers. The only exercise machine is a stationary bike that looks like something the antique pickers on TV would find in the back of a barn. There's a dirty sink and toilet in the corner and a blotchy mirror covering the back wall.

I don't know what Lucas said to Kiona, but she's here. Not happy, but here.

"You ever train?" she says.

"No, ma'am," I say. "I mean, no."

"Get on this scale."

I do.

"Lucas, this girl only weighs ninety-six pounds."

"Don't surprise me. That's why I call her—"

"Stop! I get it. I know I'm a skinny white girl. I–I used to weigh more." I lower my head so they can't see my eyes tearing. "Sorry. I'm just stressed."

Lucas says, "Alright, no more skinny white girl for Alice."

"Then get ready to prove you deserve a different title," Kiona says acidly. "You have two goals. Building muscle mass and cardio endurance." She pauses for a sarcastic laugh. "So Lucas here can turn you into his little warrior princess."

She looks at Lucas. "You're paying for this, right?"

"I can pay," I say.

"We worry about that later," Lucas says.

"And what about my time? If I'm training her every afternoon, I'll be missing sessions at the gym."

"We take care of it. Don't worry," Lucas says.

She has the same *I can't believe it* look as when he first told her. She points to a bar. "You know how to do a pull-up?"

"Grab the bar and pull?"

She drags over a stool, leaving tracks on the grimy concrete floor. "Climb up and do exactly what I say." Grip the bar, palms out, hands wider, not that wide, thumbs over the bar. "I said over." She pries my thumbs loose and presses them into place.

"Get ready to let yourself down, slow and *all the way*. Then pull back up, *all the way*, chin over the bar. Ready?"

"I think so."

"This oughta be good," she snickers and jerks the stool from under me.

It isn't easy, but I manage one.

"Nice," Lucas says.

Kiona shoots daggers at him. "Do it again."

I don't get even halfway back up. Arms on fire, I let go and drop to the mat. "Sorry."

"Quit apologizing. You're gonna do pullups every day. They're one of the best ways to change body composition."

"I'll bet you can do a lot of pullups," I say.

Lucas winks. "I'm gonna excuse myself," he says. "You in good hands, Alice. You spend two weeks gettin' physical with Kiona, then we start our part."

As soon as the upstairs door shuts, she sticks her finger in my face. "Don't you *dare* try to flatter me. You think I don't know Lucas?"

She asks if I've heard of *high-intensity interval training*. I shake my head. "You're gonna wish you never had. No Daddy Lucas to protect you now."

* * *

I'm on my hands and knees, throwing up in the toilet. I don't know how much time passed. Everything turned hazy after the first wave of dizziness hit.

There was a lot of yelling. *Beast it up! Beast it up!* I remember asking questions at the beginning, wanting to do things right, until Kiona threatened to rip my tongue out if I didn't shut up. When we finished, she left without a word.

Wobbly, I climb the stairs, steadying myself against the wall and massaging cramps from cable-tight muscles. Lucas is in the kitchen. I'm about to go in when I hear talking.

"You tricked me, Lucas."

"Baby, I never trick you. What you talkin' about?"

"How'd you know?"

"Know what?"

"I practically tried to kill that girl."

"Why you do that?"

"Because I wanted to show you what a stupid idea you came up with, trying to turn a little girl into a fighting machine in a miracle month."

"I didn't say that. I said—"

"I'm talking."

"Go on."

"I was putting her through intervals. I don't know how, but she's already in good cardio shape. But I kept pushing her, until she fell down. I started her again and she fell down again. It kept going like that."

"Damn, why you treat her that way?"

"To make her quit. But the girl wouldn't quit. Grown men with muscles as big as yours quit. I've brought trained boxers to their knees with tears in their eyes. She had the tears, but got up every time."

"That good. What's the trick?"

"I respect the girl. You knew I would."

"I hoped you'd see somethin' in her. That mean you do it? Train her?"

"Only because it's so important to you. Assuming she keeps up her end, I will train her for exactly one month. That is it. After that, she is gone. You promise me. She is gone."

"Fair enough," Lucas says.

"Fair enough? You're supposed to say thank you."

"That too. Course."

I bound up the stairs.

* * *

Kiona stays for dinner. The few sentences she directs my way all start with *You will. You will* ... eat chicken, fish, steak, eggs, veggies, nuts, yogurt. *You will* ... drink three of her custom creatine shakes a day. *You will* ... appreciate and respect them. When she goes to the bathroom, I ask Lucas what creatine is.

"Do I look like a fuckin' chemist?" Flexing a bicep as thick as a tire, he assures me it works to build muscle.

We're almost finished eating when Kiona asks where I came from. Lucas's eyes dart to me.

"Chattanooga," I say confidently.

She looks surprised. "I went to the University of Tennessee at Chattanooga for two years. Where did you live?"

Lucas's jaw tightens.

"Montview Drive." The address on the license.

"Really? That's close to the university."

"Mm-hm. My softball team played a tournament there once. We lost five to three. I got a hit, a walk and hit by a pitch. Oh, and struck out, but the ball was high and outside. It was a hideous call. I almost got thrown out for arguing with the ump."

It works. She gives me a *TMI* scowl and changes the subject to a boxing client she thinks can turn pro, then says she has to leave for a five a.m. training appointment.

Lucas and I do the dishes together. "I forgot Kiona went to college in Chattanooga, but you handled it. You a good little liar."

"Thanks." It's true, but I wish he knew me for something better than that. There used to be a nice girl who went to church and was a good daughter and good sister and good person.

He's washing, I'm drying, but I'm behind. "Pick up the pace. You movin' too slow," he says.

"Sore."

He laughs. "Kiona say she kicked your ass. How you doin' otherwise?"

"My brain's starting to work again. I think it's because I'm here, safe. I guess it's a good thing, but being a robot was a lot easier. Now it's like I have all these things crawling through my veins trying to bust out."

"Maybe you comin' to terms."

"Maybe. Do you ever cry, Lucas?"

"No."

"I didn't before, but since yesterday I feel like crying all the time."

"You entitled."

"So are you."

"But you ain't me. That's the part you keep fuckin' missing. And you don't wanna be like me. I was bad the day I was born."

He gives me the last dripping plate. Taking it, I keep hold of his hand. "You're not bad, Lucas."

He jerks away. "We done here. Kiona say we got to buy you some workout clothes in the morning."

I insist he let me pay.

"We figure it out. I'm a successful criminal."

"You mean you're rich?"

"Let's just say while other drug dealers was wasting money on jewelry and shit, Lucas was buyin' mutual funds. How much money you got, if you don't mind me asking?"

"Twenty-four hundred and thirty-two dollars and sixty cents." I explain about the cigar box.

"You lucky to get this far carryin' that much cash. What you gonna do when it runs out?"

"I haven't thought that far ahead."

"Didn't think so. Speakin' a money, I got a client coming. Go upstairs and stay there. He don't need to see you and you don't need to see him. You welcome to watch TV in my room. Just don't touch no firearms. I put a couple shirts in your room so you got somethin' to sleep in."

My room. I like the sound of that. I go take a shower. Two days in a row. I could totally get used to it. I put on one of Lucas's t-shirts. It says *Yo Gotti* on the front and hangs below my knees.

I take the Stephen King book into Lucas's room. I used to read almost every day. Mom made me. She was such a bookworm. I grew up with more books than toys. But my concentration these days is almost nonexistent.

There's a handgun on the dresser and a pump-action shotgun on the floor, like the one Dad used for duck hunting, except this one has the barrel cut off. Propped in the corner is an assault rifle.

I find the TV remote under the pillows, along with another gun. I haven't watched a television since the night before everything happened. I flip channels and come to the Disney network. I used to like it … a million years ago. In the high numbers I come to something called the *Tactical Shooting Championship.* A clock runs while a woman with a pistol runs around shooting at pop-up targets. She never misses. Amazing.

I mute the sound. Half watching, half reading, my eyes get heavy quickly.

10

WE'RE DRIVING to the mall, Lucas complaining he had to sleep in my *tiny piece of shit bed* because I fell asleep in his. Rap music drowns out a thunderstorm that leaves the streets steaming by the time we pull into a place called Oak Court.

"Can you go in there and buy some workout clothes?" he says.

"Sure."

"You need anything else?"

"Not that I can think of."

"Kiona remind me you a woman. You covered in that department?"

"Yep."

"She also say you need a new bra. Yesterday when you was workin' out, she say one of you breasts was in the middle."

My face turns red. "The toilet paper I stuffed in there kept shifting."

"I told her we was tryin' to make you look older. She say to get a gel-bra. You know what that is?"

"I can guess."

"She say go to Victoria's Secret. You know what that is?"

"Lucas, I'm twelve, not five. I can handle finding a bra."

Raising his hands, "Just tryin' to help."

* * *

I return a half hour later carrying a bag. Lucas is standing outside the SUV with his arms crossed. "Get what you need?"

"*Ye-es*. In fact, I got two. They were on sale, two for one. I got one white and one black. You want to see them?" I hold out the bag.

He waves it away. "I take your word for it."

A security cop pulls up in a golf cart. It's a white guy with a thin angular face covered with acne scars, wearing aviator sunglasses. He looks at Lucas, then me.

Lucas mutters, "You about to see racial profilin' in action."

"How are we doing today?" he says to me.

"Fine," I say.

"Is this man a friend of yours?"

"Why are you asking? Because he's black?"

Lucas groans.

"If you must know, he's my bodyguard."

Another groan. Towering next to the shiny black car in his skin-tight black tee and wraparound sunglasses, sculpted arms folded across his wide chest, he totally looks like a bodyguard.

"You have a bodyguard?" the guy says skeptically.

"Have you ever heard of Miller Combines?"

"Can't say that I have."

"We're the second biggest manufacturer of farm combines in the world. I'm Alice Miller. My dad's the president. He's a billionaire. He could buy this mall if he wanted to. I've had a bodyguard since I was born. Is there anything else we can help you with today?"

"I guess not," he says, driving off.

Lucas is shaking his head as we get in the SUV. He asks how I know about farm combines and I tell him Dad worked on them as a mechanic starting when he was seventeen until one killed him.

"Creative," he says, "but fuckin' stupid. Don't call attention to you-self. An invitation to disaster. And especially don't antagonize the authorities. Even a rent-a-cop can ruin your life. All they got to do is push a button to bring the police."

"I know you're right. I couldn't help it. It just gets my back up when people insult my ..." I almost say *friends*, but leave the sentence hanging.

We drive back to his neighborhood, but when we get to his building, we pass it by.

"Where to now?"

"Errand."

We turn down another barren block. A weathered teddy bear is tied to a utility pole. "What are the bears for?" I say. "I've seen them a few times."

"Death bears. Where people got shot. Family, friends put 'em up as memorials."

"It's sad driving around this place."

"Sadder livin' in it," he says, making a sharp turn into a driveway.

We come to a stop in front of a tall fence topped with razor wire. He honks the horn until a skinny black guy runs out and unlocks a chain and rolls the gate back.

Lucas pulls a gun from his waist and sets it on his thigh.

"I didn't know you were left-handed," I say. "Me too."

"Just a precaution. Always expect the worse. The worse don't usually happen, but it only takes one time."

We pull into a compound, some kind of car lot with a mix of junkers and souped-up models in bright colors with fancy wheels. In the side mirror, the skinny guy is relocking the gate. Lucas swerves in a sharp semicircle. "You know why I just did that?" he says.

"If the shit hits the fan, you can bust through the gate."

"Shit hits the fan? Fuck, I'm a bad influence."

"You are, but my dad taught me that one."

Two scary guys, one black, one white, come out of a long rectangular building of garage bays filled with cars barely visible through the smeared windows. The black guy's wearing a backwards cap with no shirt and pants that sag below his butt. The white guy has three silver rings piercing one eyebrow. Both of them are covered with tattoos.

Lucas rolls down the window.

"Yo," he says, as they both lean in.

"What up, cuz?" the black guy says with a grin. Weird. His teeth are solid gold. One even has a diamond in it. They do a black handshake. "Long time no see."

The white guy reaches in and does the handshake too. "*Big EZ*," he says with emphasis.

"What you need, EZ?" the black guy says. "Whoa, what we got here?"

He's looking at me. I shrink into the seat.

"Didn't know you was back to pimpin', EZ. I take a piece a dat. How much?"

Lucas's neck muscles tighten. "She's an associate of mine," he says.

"Fuck yeah, I need an associate like that," the white guy says.

"Don't talk like that 'bout her. We good?"

"We good, we good," the black guy says. "Big EZ just don't wanna share his young ho with us. Understandable."

They're both laughing when the door of the SUV blows open and knocks them down.

Lucas climbs out, gun at his side. Sprawled on the asphalt under his shadow, the men don't look scary anymore. The window frame gashed the white guy's forehead. He's wiping blood from his eyes, staring at his hands. "We was just playing around, EZ," he wails.

Lucas points the gun at one, then the other. "Either of you mention or even think about this girl during your livin' and breathin' days, you die. I prove it right now if you want."

He leans down and presses the gun against the black guy's ear.

"Lucas!" I shout. "It's okay."

"Get up. I come here to do business. You stay here," he says to me.

The men climb to their feet and he waves them inside with the gun. Ten minutes later he comes out carrying a brown paper bag tied with twine. He slides it under the seat. The skinny guy runs out to open the gate.

After a few blocks, "Just in case you wonderin', I wasn't plannin' to shoot them men. I'm mean, but not crazy. Better to let fear do the work. Fear is a powerful weapon. Stronger than bullets. Can get people to do anything if they afraid enough—and they a lot more afraid before they dead, than after."

"Makes sense. Do you think I could ever get people to fear me? I would *love* that. I'm sick of being the one who's always afraid."

"Well, you ain't big and got no reputation for shootin' people, so that make it hard. One thing is people got to believe you gonna do what you threaten to do. Say you tell a man, *Don't move or I'll shoot*, but he thinks he can move and you ain't gonna shoot. You ever see that knowledge come into a man's eyes, you shoot right then, 'cause he's about to come git you."

"You should write a book. Seriously. You're an expert."

"Author. I like that. *How to Fuck People Up*, by Lucas Jackson."

"Well, maybe we can work on that title. *Jackson*. I didn't know your last name. *Lucas Jackson*. It fits you."

"I got a middle name too."

"What?"

"Confidential, 'tween us?"

"Sure."

"Ellington."

"Ellington? *Bwah*. I mean ... sorry, you just don't strike me as an Ellington."

"My grandpa loved Duke Ellington, a blazin' black bandleader back in the day. Named me after him. How 'bout you? You got a middle name?"

"Yes, but I hate it. Blair. *Blech*."

"Blair ain't too bad. What about nicknames?"

"Just *Em*, really," I say, sparing him my history of dorky nicknames. OMG, Mom called me *Pinkie* when I was little because my pale skin burned so easily in the sun. Meggie Tribet called me *Rocket Girl* for a year after I tried to build one and it exploded in the backyard. My favorite was Becky's. *Luv,* like she was from England or something. *Good-night, luv.* It always cracked me up.

Lucas's ringing phone rescues me from the memories.

"Kiona on her way. Time to go to work again. You ready?"

I rub my aching arms. "I guess."

11

KIONA POINTS to the scale and I step onto it. "Ninety-seven," she says. "Congratulations. You gained one pound."

I can't tell if she's congratulating or mocking me, but I clap anyway. We start the workout with pull-ups. I almost make two, but fall short again.

"Over here." She leads me to a punching bag hanging from the ceiling on a chain and hands me a pair of old boxing gloves. "Put these on. Hit this bag, three punches. Jab, jab, cross. Jab, jab, cross," she says, demonstrating. "You a righty?"

"Lefty, like Lucas."

"Go the opposite of me. Jab with your right, cross with your left. Start out easy."

The first punches are fun, but my arms wilt quickly. Still, I keep flailing.

"Hold it." She grabs my wrists. "Don't swing sideways. Do it with me. Jab, jab, cross. Jab, jab, cross. Keep your hands flat when they hit the bag."

Five minutes later, I can't even feel my arms.

"Alright, stop."

I bend over, grabbing my shorts, drops of sweat spattering the blue mat.

"Working the bag builds your core. People think strength comes from their arms and shoulders, but overall body strength comes from your core. We'll do the bag twenty minutes every morning."

70

She takes me over to the loose weights. "Lay down on this bench. See the bar above your head?"

"Isn't it supposed to have weights on it?"

A sarcastic laugh. "Maybe someday, honey. This bar weighs forty-five pounds. Good luck finishing one set."

I lift the bar off the catches.

"Whatever you do, don't drop it on your face. Lucas will never forgive me if his little project loses all her teeth. Lower it. *Slow.* All the way down. That's it. Up again."

She was right. Even cheating by arching my back and using my shoulders, I can only do five before she has to rescue me.

She explains that ten is a set and my goal is three sets of each weight exercise every other day. "Lifting rips muscles apart, resting repairs them. Normally we'd take two days off, but we don't have time to spare. You are gone from here in twenty-nine days unless you give up sooner."

Such a confidence builder.

"Pick up these dumbbells."

We run through a bunch of weight exercises, her criticizing me the entire time, then go to exercises she says I can do without equipment. "You know, for when you're *gone.*" Push-ups, squats, burpees (pure torture), planks, dips, sit-ups.

Then she excuses herself, saying she'll be back. I pick up my towel. The punching bag hangs next to me. I liked hitting it. It felt like real fighting.

I give it a few bare-handed punches. Jab, jab, cross. Jab, jab, cross. Light—then hard—then harder, until the bag swings back and hits me in the face, right on the eye bruise I got from tall man.

Effing bag! I shove it. It comes back and almost knocks me over. I explode, kicking and punching the bag like it's trying to kill me. My surroundings change with each furious hit. The cracked concrete becomes beige carpeting, the dankness smells like Mom's potpourri.

… I hear her begging, saying do anything they want to her,

but just leave me and Becky alone. I'm stuck in the master bedroom on the bed, tugging against the ties, but the harder I pull, the deeper they cut into me.

Tall man says to Becky in his strange accent, "Come, sha ti bae." *Sha ti bae.* What language is that? When she doesn't move, he walks over and picks her up.

"Put her down!" I yell.

"Shut ya mout."

"No! Leave her alone. Take me. Please."

"Don worry. I be back for ya."

I let out an ear-splitting scream and keep it going like a siren. He dumps Becky down and walks to the edge of the bed.

"I say shut you mout." I pull my knees back and try to kick him in the crotch, but he's too close. I keep the wail going. The stocky man is shouting from somewhere, *Shut that bitch up.*

"Where da tape?" tall man shouts back. He points at Becky.

"Ya don move," he says and leaves the room.

"Becky, lock the door. Hurry."

Becky runs to the door, but he's already back with the orange bag, pulling out a roll of gray duct tape ...

"Alice. Alice." Faint, from behind a wall of glass. "Alice!"

The glass breaks. It's Lucas, shaking me. I'm on my knees, still throwing wild punches, knuckles raw and bleeding. He holds me still.

"We done for today," he says.

Kiona is standing next to him, clicking her tongue.

"No, we're not. We haven't even done intervals, right Kiona?"

She looks at me with disgust.

"We pick it up tomorrow," Lucas says.

"It won't happen again. I swear. Please, Kiona? I'm ready to *beast it up.*"

"You want intervals?" she says fiercely. "Fine. You got 'em."

* * *

She tried to kill me again, but that only made me more determined to survive. I'm in the kitchen, cooling down and mixing up one of her shakes. One teaspoon creatine, two scoops vanilla protein, six ounces water and a half-cup of ice cubes.

I sip through a straw while I search my backpack for the magnet I bought at the mall. It's a picture of a smiling puppy that says, *I Love Dogs, It's the People that Annoy Me.* I stick it to the refrigerator. Lucas's first decoration.

His footsteps clomp down the hall. He notices the magnet the second he walks in.

"What's this?"

"A magnet, for decoration. I bought it for you."

"I hate fuckin' dogs. Nasty, smelly things, always tryin' to bite my black ass."

"Oh ... well, you can also use it to hold things up, like bills and pictures and stuff." Nothing. "Or, um, I can just take it down." I reach for it.

He grabs my wrist. "Leave it. I agree with the last part. People annoy the fuck outta me. What happened in the basement?"

"I'm not sure. Another flashback. Third one since I got here. They seem so real. I can see and hear everything. It's like watching a scary movie I can't turn off."

"You learnin' anything useful from 'em?"

"The stocky man called the tall man Ronnie. And in the one I just had, tall man was leaning right in my face. I could see him perfectly. Something else was there too, but the glass broke before I figured it out."

"You broke my glass? Where?"

"I didn't break any of your precious glass. What I meant was inside my head ... oh, never mind."

"Your little freakout didn't help with Kiona."

"I know," I say, rinsing the shaker cup. "I'm sure she thinks I'm a crazy person. Do you want me to start dinner?" Even I can cook bare chicken breasts, the house favorite whenever Kiona's here.

"Come over and sit with me," he says, going to the kitchen table.

I get a bad feeling as I follow him to our usual chairs.

"Me and Kiona was talkin'. You got to know I trust that woman's opinion. Got a shitload of common sense. She say you traumatized and need help, belong in some kind of home or hospital. You know you was screaming the whole time down there? Maybe Lucas didn't have such a good idea."

A vise squeezes my gut, a swampy, swelling cramp that's been happening more and more. I hold my side, voice rising, "What are you saying?"

"I ain't sayin' nothin'. We just talkin'."

"But it is a good idea. It's just my second day."

"First, you got to get straight on this training. I'm talkin' self-defense, but I know what you thinkin'. I understand revenge, no one knows it better, but it ain't the right road for you."

"Not revenge. Justice. *Justice. Always comes too late, but it's still justice. You* said that. Those were your exact words."

"Fuckin' profound, but even settin' aside you got no fightin' ability, you got no way to find the two men."

"I might figure out a way. My memories could bring more clues. I already have tall man's first name. Or they might find me first. And like you said, it's dangerous out there. There are other bad men. I see them in the bus stations, parks, wherever I go."

"No way I can talk you into callin' the authorities?" Already knowing the answer, he doesn't wait before adding, "Just remember. Self-defense. That's it. You hear?"

"Self-defense," I echo with a thumbs-up.

12

A WEEK passes without another flashback. I just finished my training for the day. Making progress! I gained three pounds and did three pullups, and not the fake kind where you jerk yourself up or don't go all the way down. Kiona doesn't let me slack on anything.

I'm at the kitchen table eating a buffalo chicken burrito. I eat five times a day, plus the creatine shakes, but Kiona and Lucas keep nagging me to eat more because my training burns calories as fast as I can consume them. I'm pouring hot sauce on my plate, careful not to get it on my art pad, when Lucas comes in.

"Kiona say you comin' along."

"That's good to hear. I can never tell what she's thinking."

"Me either. More art? Why you like it so much?"

I never really thought about it. "Maybe because I can make my own world, escape the one I'm in whenever I want—except right now." I hand him the pad. "I've been working on sketches of the two men. What do you think?"

He studies them. "I think they look like somebody."

"They do? Who?"

"Just somebody. They don't look like Mr. Potato Head or a smiley face. You really is an artist. So these the men that hurt your family?"

"I think so. A chunk of my memory is still missing, but I can picture their faces as clear as anything."

"You gonna send these to the police?"

"That's my plan."

"Whatever happened to that message you sent 'em?"

"I don't know. I've been so busy training, I haven't been back to the internet café to check."

"Why you need an internet café?"

"I buy cheapie dumb phones. No internet. Figure they're harder to track."

"That's true. You said you told the police you overheard two men in a bar. Who do they think their mysterious informant is?"

I explain about *Robert Williams* and the anonymized email account.

"Not bad, but the government can track anything if they got enough motivation. The burner account might slow 'em down. Meanwhile, I can help with these pictures."

"How so?"

"What is Lucas's life?"

"Um ... violent?"

He frowns.

"Exciting? ... I don't understand the question."

"*Faces* is my life. Follow me."

I do, to the document room, where he fires up the computer and explains that we can turn my memories into real pictures of the two men with facial composite software.

"Your job is to keep talkin'," he says. "That's one thing you good at. *Wider, darker, thicker.* Piece by piece."

And that's what we do. Starting with head shape, I talk him through the pictures burned into my brain: eyes, nose, mouth, chin, ears, hair, skin tone, everything.

"You ever wonder why these two men come to get your family?" he asks as he works.

"Of course. I think about it every day."

"And?"

"And nothing. We were just regular people."

"Maybe your daddy was a drug dealer and you didn't know it."

A high-pitched laugh. "My dad? If you knew him, you would know how funny that is. But there has to be some reason. Everything happens for a reason."

He shrugs. "Not always. Sometimes shit just happens."

I wonder if he's thinking about Jarrett and Shondra. *Three boys in one gang shot him in the front yard just 'cause he in a different gang.*

I stare at the monitor, bone-rigid, as the men who murdered my mother and sister materialize in full color.

An hour later, he says, "They look just like your drawings. That's a good sign. You alright?"

"Yeah," I lie.

He saves the images on a USB stick and prints copies for me.

"Where'd you learn so much about computers?"

"Video games, then the army. Got assigned to sig-int in Iraq. Tested out high aptitude in computers."

"What's sig-int?"

"Signal intelligence. Usin' technology to violate the privacy of every motherfucker in the world."

"It's hard for me to picture you in a uniform, following rules."

"The army loved ol' Lucas 'til I got arrested for sellin' weed. Risked my life for my country and got run out just for raisin' troop morale."

"My dad always said marijuana is bad for you."

"That's complete bullshit, no disrespect to you dad. Anyway, I got no hard feelings for the Army. Helped me refine some of my best life skills."

"You did a good job on these," I say, gripping the pictures so tightly my fingers cramp.

"You did the hard work."

"So I guess I'll send these to the police."

"No. Send your sketches. I put 'em on the thumb drive."

"But these look so real."

"Think about it. You supposed to be a man who overheard a conversation between two strangers in a bar."

I nod. "Robert Williams wouldn't be sending professional facial composites. What can we do with them?"

"Probably nothin' right now. Be different if we knew where
the men was. I got a whiz-kid hacker friend who does special
projects in the neighborhood for extra cash. Last week he stole
some facial recognition software from a tech company. If we
knew the vicinity of the men, we could try to hack into nearby
security cameras and match faces to the composites."

"I love that! Do you think it would work?"

"Don't matter 'cause we don't know where they is."

Deflated, "Can we check my burner account to see if the
sheriff's department replied to my email?"

Headshake. "Like I said, give 'em enough motivation, the
government can track anything. You big news. If they think
you sent the email, they ain't gonna spare no cost findin' you.
Imagine that. Lucas Jackson in possession of the missin' victim
in the Calby case."

"I'll go to the internet café in the morning before Kiona gets
here."

"I got to work in the morning."

"*Hel-lo-oh.* Did I ask you to take me? I can get there on my
own. I don't need a babysitter."

He laughs, reaches out and musses my hair. "Emily Blair
Calby, you one tough little motherfucker."

13

IT'S A different clerk at the internet café, a black kid with a thick gold earring who doesn't leer at me. I pay for a half hour, log-in and do a news search for the *Calby Murders*.

Nothing. I expected to see my descriptions of the two men plastered everywhere. I switch to the burner account for Robert Williams. There's a message.

> *Thank you for your hotline tip to the Dilfer County Sheriff's Department. We will review it and contact you if we believe it warrants further investigation.*

Unbelievable. I start typing:

> *Dear Sheriff Timmons:*
>
> *Last week I wrote you about a conversation I over-heard between two men talking about the Calby murders. I am shocked to not see any news about the information I sent. I thought you might be keeping it private, but now I see all I got is a form reply.*
>
> *I am attaching sketches I made of the two murderers. These are real. They look just like the men I over-heard in the bar. You need to take my information seriously!*
>
> *Robert Williams*

I plug in the USB stick and upload my sketches as attachments.

Guess I don't have to worry about the police tracking my message. Looks like they didn't even bother to read it.

Back out on the street, I call a cab, still fuming about the form reply, not noticing the bedraggled man cuddling up to me.

"Hey, hey, sha ti bae."

I back against the wall. *That accent. Those words.*

"Ya got some spare change to help a mon out?"

The man keeps talking, but I'm not hearing as everything around me dissolves in a blur.

There's tall man, up close, holding me down on the bed, trying to tape my mouth. I bite his hand. "Do dat again I knock ya teet out." He stretches the tape across my mouth and around my neck.

Hyperventilating through my nose, I start to panic. *Slow. Breathe slower.*

His shirt is hanging open. I'm staring at a chest covered with tattoos, a scorpion on the left and a snake wrapped around a knife on the right. In the middle, gloating at me, inches from my eyes, is a hag with a wicked smile, holding up a glass. She looks like a witch, with rotted teeth and a wart on her nose. Spelled in gothic letters above her is *Durty Delphine*.

The man's waving in my face. "Hey in dere, girly. Ya alright?"

Shake it off.

"Ya help me eat launch?"

"I–I will ... but back away first."

The man bows and takes a step back. I fish in my front pocket. "I'll give you three dollars if you'll answer some questions."

"Ya, ya. Watever you want, sha ti bae. Money first."

"After. What is *sha ti bae*?"

"Little darlin'. It's a nice ting."

"Hold on." I get out my pencil and pad. "Can you write it down?"

He writes, *cher t' bébé*.

"Where is your accent from?"

"Cajun."

"Where's that?"

"Wat, not where. Louisiana. All Cajuns from Louisiana. We get blown here by Katrina."

"Do you know a Cajun named Ronnie?" He looks confused. "Never mind." I give him the money.

"Ga' bless," he says as my cab pulls up.

I jump in, rattled, but buzzing with the rush of discovery. The driver looks at me funny when I give the address, but doesn't say anything. He lets me out at Lucas's building. I run around back and push the buzzer.

"You?" he says, baritone voice distorting through the tiny speaker.

"It's me," I say.

An electronic lock clicks. I look behind me before pulling on the security door. Lucas told me to do it, but didn't need to. Since that day, I spend almost as much time looking behind me as in front.

When I tell him my big discovery, he's not excited.

"Don't you see? Now I have a lead to one of them."

"What lead?"

"Tall man's Cajun, from Louisiana. The man said all Cajuns are from Louisiana. You could get your whiz-kid friend to hack into the surveillance cameras in Louisiana and we could try the facial recognition software using the composites you made from the drawings. Yes!"

"It don't fuckin' work like that. Ain't like the movies where you push a button and everything in the world magically appears. Every security system's got its own network, probably more than a million of 'em just in Louisiana."

I sag. "What about the tattoo?"

"What about it?"

"It said *Durty Delphine*, except whoever did it misspelled dirty, D-U-R-T-Y. She must mean something."

"Probably a girlfriend."

"I doubt it. She was an old witch."

"Maybe his mama. Time to eat lunch and get ready for Kiona."

"Can you please just look up Durty Delphine on your phone, in case she is someone?"

"I will."

"Now?"

"Later. I got work to do."

"*Please.*"

"I said later."

"Fine!" I stomp up the stairs.

14

I'M COOLING down on a mat at the end of another torturous workout, the official end of my second week of training.

Kiona snaps, "Pick up your towel. In fact, why don't you make yourself useful and actually wash the damn towels?"

"Okay," I say.

"I'm out of here," she says. "Tell Lucas I'll call him later. Only fourteen days left for you," she says.

Not that she's counting.

I pick up the towel basket and glimpse myself in the mirror. Definitely a difference. My biceps have bulges. I weighed in at one hundred and two pounds, six more than when I started, all of it muscle. I did five pullups this morning. My shoulders look like a boy's.

But I'm so ready for something new. Tomorrow I start learning how to fight. Freaking finally. Workouts switch to mornings. Afternoons are for whatever Lucas has planned. He still hasn't told me. Without being specific, he's said from the beginning I need more *heft*.

Nothing else has happened. Nothing in the news about new evidence in the Calby case. I expected my sketches to be everywhere. I haven't been back to the internet café, but the lame Dilfer County Sheriff probably sent another form reply. Nothing new in the way of memories. I asked Lucas if he did a search for *Durty Delphine*. He nodded and said, "Nothing."

I load the towels in the washer and go in the kitchen to make

83

a shake, grabbing a chicken breast from the fridge that I eat by hand. *Chicken, chicken, chicken.* I never want to see another chicken. A piece falls on the floor and I curse it.

I feel like I'm going to detonate, spontaneously combust. Every day, cooped up, in the basement, the kitchen, my room. I rinse a coffee mug, staring at a brick wall. I've never washed a dish in my life where I wasn't looking out a window, except at this place, *because there are no windows.*

Lucas is in the document room. Business must be grand because he stays there all day. I'm under strict orders not to disturb him. I go to the front window and peak through the scratch in the paint. The rain passed and the sun is shining.

The door keys hang on a hook next to a floppy felt hat that must be Kiona's. Lucas would kill me for this, but he doesn't have to know. Just a short walk. Not a matter of just wanting. I need it. I'm suffocating in here.

I pull the hat on, all the way down to my ears. Making sure the security door locks behind me, I pocket the keys and head down the sidewalk.

Keeping my head down, I stay on the main street. The air is sticky hot, but nourishing. Not many people are out. An old man sitting on a window ledge in the shade gives me a friendly smile. I say hello and relax.

I come to an intersection. A guy with multi-colored braids is leaning against a pole. The light turns and I stop for the cars.

"Hey-hey," the guy says.

"Hi," I say, not looking.

He tears away from the pole. "I think I know you."

"I doubt that." The light changes and I hurry across the street. He stays with me.

"No need to run. I ain't gonna hurt ya. I'm friendly. What, you too good to talk to me? Stuck up white girl?"

I stop. "Okay, but I only have a minute."

"I can do magic in a minute. You my kinda girl."

"Oh, really? What kind is that?"

A car pulls up and slams on the brakes. A woman jumps out. "What the hell you think you're doing?" she says to the guy.

"Just talkin' to a friend."

"Liar, you tryin' to pick her up." She swings her purse at him.

"No, baby, just being friendly. You my queen, you know dat."

She turns to me. "And you, little ho, comin' into my neighborhood to make time with my man."

"I was just taking a walk. That's all. Really."

She drops her purse and comes at me. Not much taller, but thicker. I crouch in my boxing stance. *Jab, jab, cross. Right hand, right hand, left hand.* While I'm thinking about it, she grabs my hair and slams me to the sidewalk, punching me in the face.

I roll up like a snail. She lands a couple more punches that hit my arms before the guy's able to pull her off of me. "Go," he says.

I run for Lucas's building, three blocks at full speed, falling against the wall when I reach the back door, bass drum thumping in my chest. I touch my face and get woozy when I pull my hand away and see all the blood. I press the buzzer. No response.

A small red car hides in the shadow of Lucas's big SUV. I push the button again, but again nothing. The third time I keep my thumb on it.

The intercom squawks. "Quit pushin' my fuckin' button. Who is it? Shit, never mind. I can see the top of that blonde beacon."

The door flies open.

"What are you doin' outside?"

He sees my face.

"Motherfucker. Get in here."

He pushes me into a chair. "Don't move." He leaves the room.

"What happened to you?"

It's a black teenager, in the chair Lucas sits in, the command center for all the equipment. I sat in it once and got yelled at.

"Um, I got in a fight. Who are you?"

"James. I know who you are. Alice."

I don't have a chance to show surprise before Lucas is back with a bag of ice, paper towels and a foul look. "Lean back." He holds my head and cleans my face. "What happened?"

"I went for a walk."

Rage-heat pulsates from his fingertips. "Out the front door? Without tellin' me? Who did this?"

"*Oww.* A lady. I was talking to her boyfriend. She saw us and got mad at me for flirting with him. I wasn't though. I didn't want to talk to him, but didn't know what to do."

"Ooh-ooh," James says. "White woman taking away a black man. *Tru-uh-ble.*"

"The man hit you?" Lucas says.

"No. He pulled her away. I knew she was coming. I thought I could fight her, but while I was thinking about what Kiona taught me, she just flew at me."

Lucas laughs. "At least you finally been in a fight. Best thing could happen to you. This ain't too bad. Just a little cut over your eye. Hold this ice on."

He pinches my cheeks in one enormous hand. "Look at me. You know I take you in, right?"

"Yes."

"I trust you with a lot."

I lower my head.

"And you probably figured out that ain't my general disposition."

"I know. I don't know what happened to me."

"Lemme take a guess. You been roaming the country runnin' from your problems. Now you boxed up with 'em, wanna escape. Understandable, but no excuse. This is my house. It ain't up to you whether you feel like taking a walk. Maybe you forgot, you in a dangerous fuckin' situation. Now you got me in your dangerous situation. Where my keys? Give 'em to me."

I reach in my pocket. *Omigod.* My look says it all.

Eyes wide with disbelief, "You lost my fuckin' keys?"

"I—they must've fallen out."

"You lost my fuckin' keys?"

I stand up. "I should probably leave. I just need to get my backpack. I'll put the ice bag in the sink."

"Sit the fuck down."

"I can stay?"

He massages his forehead. "Alice, this here is James."

"We met," I say. "Are you the hacker?"

A shy nod.

"More than a hacker. James is a computer genius."

I study James. Outwardly, there's nothing about him that says genius. He looks like any other teenager, wearing a plain white tee, black shorts, white socks and oversized basketball shoes.

"Now he's gettin' sent to fuckin' Stanford and he only sixteen years old."

"I'm sorry. Is that a prison?"

"It's a fuckin' university," Lucas says. "He got a scholarship."

"Then it's a good thing. Congratulations, James!"

"Thanks."

I peek around Lucas at the computers. "What are you guys working on?"

They look at each other like cats that ate the canary.

Lucas grunts. "Now that you here—uninvited—me and James been workin' on your little problem."

A half-hearted laugh. "Which one?"

"The two men."

I pull down the ice bag. "What about them?"

"Keep that ice on. I searched for *Durty Delphine*."

"I know," I say. "You already told me. You said there was nothing."

"I lied. James, show her."

James expands a window on the big monitor and I flare back. Towering over me in high resolution is the hag with the wicked smile, holding up the glass, exactly like tall man's tattoo. Above her in the same gothic letters: *Durty Delphine's*.

I stammer, "How-did-she-get-in-here?"

"Chill. Just a picture. Turns out you was half-right. Durty Delphine ain't no woman. She's a place, a bar in Lafayette, Louisiana."

I gawk at the witch, torn between wanting to run out the back door and attack the monitor.

15

I'M NOT sure how much time passes before I say, "Louisiana. That's where the man said the Cajuns live. Are you about to tell me you found the two men? Because I can't stand this suspense."

"Fuck no, nothin' like that."

"Oh." I droop.

"If you just listen for a change, we tell you. James, talk to the girl."

James presses a finger to his cheek. "Well, Lucas said you're looking for two men and showed me the facial composites. I've been working with some facial recognition software I recently acquired."

Acquired. Haha. *Stole.* I like his style. "Um, yeah, I heard something about that."

"It's possible the composites could be used to identify someone from images captured on a security camera network." He pauses and gets a nod of approval from Lucas to continue. "So we gained access to Durty Delphine's computer to try it out. They have three cameras. Front door, inside, and back door."

"You already hacked it? How?"

"A phishing email," he says.

"And it worked? Even I know not to click on those."

Lucas says, "The key to all successful fishin' is the bait. Tell her, James."

"I located the owner of Durty Delphine's using public records.

His name's Mike. His wife is Julia. I found her on Facebook."
He looks like a kid, but talks like a professor.

"That's when I got in the picture," Lucas says with a wicked glint. "I wrote the message. You say I should be an author? Listen to this masterpiece. *Dear Mike: I hate to be the bearer of bad news, but have you seen what Julia's doing on the internet?* Ain't no man in the universe gonna resist clicking on that attachment."

"How come? What's she doing on the internet? ... Oh, I think I get it. That's bad. How did you know someone else wouldn't see the email first, like an employee?"

"Even better. Ain't no one click on the boss's wife faster. Soon as they did, James's little virus give us the keys to Durty Delphine's computer."

Fluttery claps. "Sweet!"

"Tell her the bad news, James."

"Bad news?"

"There's always bad news," Lucas says. "You know that by now."

"Well, their system only stores thirty days of video before it overwrites the old footage. Reduces data storage requirements."

"Thirty whole days? That's not so bad. What else?"

"The video is low resolution, and the cameras are mounted high, so not many full facial views. Then add in that we only have the composites to work with, not real photographs." He shrugs.

"So what does it mean?" I say.

"Honestly, with all those variables, I doubt the facial recognition software will work."

"But we can try, right?" I say, looking at Lucas.

"We can try," he says reluctantly.

"Even if the recognition software doesn't work, couldn't someone, like me, study the videos to see if I recognize the men?"

James says, "If someone wants to look at, let's see ... seven hundred and twenty hours of video. Still a longshot with the low resolution."

"But it's possible?"

"Anything's possible." He gets up. "I gotta go."

"We square up later," Lucas says. They do a black handshake as Lucas walks him to the back door.

James says, "I hope everything works out, Alice. Lucas didn't tell me what happened, but I know it's something bad."

"Thanks for helping, and good luck in Stanford Prison!"

I'm relieved this gets a smile even from Lucas. He's pissed.

* * *

He stayed grouchy as he downloaded the video for me onto a stolen laptop, complaining five times about the lost keys. When he finished he yanked out the transfer cable and handed me the computer, grumbling, "You can keep this and obsess about these videos to you little heart's content."

His crankiness faded only after he lit up some marijuana. He stopped trying to hide it from me last week. I asked what it did for him and he said, "Medicinal chillaxin'." I told him it was bad for his lungs and he said, "If Lucas lives long enough to worry about lung cancer, he be thankin' that God you pray to."

He really does seem more relaxed though.

"Now that you're in a good mood again, can I ask why you lied to me about Durty Delphine? You told me you did a search and nothing came up."

"Didn't wanna get your hopes up."

"Well, they are. Aren't yours? I'll bet he's there. Why else would he have the tattoo?"

"See? This is exactly why I didn't tell you. Tall man coulda been a customer or dishwasher from ten years ago. Or he passed through one night and got drunk. Maybe he just found the picture online and thought it'd be a good tattoo."

"Were you planning on keeping it a secret from me?"

He puffs on the marijuana cigarette.

"I'm talking," I say. It works for Kiona but he ignores me. "Why won't you answer?"

"You and your fuckin' questions. Don't you ever run out?"

"So why?"

He bares his teeth like he wants to bite me. "I just told you. I didn't want you gettin' all excited for nothing."

"I don't believe you."

"You callin' me a liar?"

"No. I just don't believe you. I think you were planning something else."

"Like what?"

"Like going to go kill the two men yourself if you found them."

He puts down the marijuana. "You want the truth?" It comes out like a taunt. "Yeah, I thought about it." He grabs a mirror from the makeup table and rolls his chair in front of me. "Look."

I study my battered face.

"You just got beat up by a pissed-off black woman. How you plan on handlin' two vicious killers? Big, tough Emily Calby. All one hundred and two pounds of her, a motherfuckin' fightin' force to be reckoned with."

"I would have found a way. I mean, I will find a way. She caught me by surprise."

Silence for another staredown, which I win again when he breaks away to relight the marijuana.

"Kiona was right," he says, letting out a long stream of smoke. "You being here? I got guilt, a heart full of it. Told Jarrett and Shondra they got nothing to worry about with me around, but it was a lie. Ain't nobody safe around here. Maybe 'cause you the same age as Shondra, I let myself think I could help you, but it's all a joke, like Kiona says."

"It's not a joke. You already helped me in a million ways. You kept me alive when I was hanging by a thread, even though I don't deserve it."

"Why you say shit like that?"

"Because I know guilt too. That's all I feel. I promised Dad I'd take care of Mom and Becky. Becky was little and Mom was soft. He said I was the strong one."

"He got that right."

My belly tightens. "Then I ran. I ran away. I should be dead."

"You got no choice but to run, but I hear you. Called survivor guilt. Maybe we got that in common."

"Maybe that's why we're here together."

"Yeah, that or you needed a forged driver's license."

"Do you believe in God?"

"Do God believe in Lucas?"

"I think so."

The half-laugh, half-snort. It must have more than one meaning. "I fuckin' doubt it," he says.

"God loves everyone. That's what I believe."

"Your family go to church?"

"Every Sunday."

"Then they got slaughtered. How you keep believin' in God after that?"

"I'm not sure," I admit. "I just do. At night, when I'm alone, God's the only one listening. Maybe he brought me here."

"That's called magical thinking. Back to the subject. Fact is, if we knew where the two men was, only logical thing would be for me take care of it and get this shit over with."

"I appreciate that. Believe me, I do. But that's way too much to ask and this is my fight. Joke or no joke. We're just getting to the training I really need. I can't quit now."

He stubs out the marijuana and looks to the ceiling, stroking his stubbly chin. Always so hard to read.

"Alright," he says. "Maybe I got one quality your God like. My word. I say one month, we go one month."

I realize I've been holding my breath. "*Thank you.* You have way more than one good quality. I know I'm a pest and Kiona hates me, but I don't want you to ever hate me, Lucas ... I love you."

My face turns a hundred shades of red. "I mean ..."

"I know what you mean. You love me 'cause I protect and shelter you. It's normal. Hookers feel the same way about their pimps."

"Hookers!"

"Just an example. Point is, no point lovin' me. Anybody ever did is dead."

"I'm not dead." Yet. Maybe I'm not the best example. "Kiona's not dead. She loves you."

"You impressed her with five pullups today."

"She told you that?"

"Not only. Called you the *Cardio Kid.*"

I cock my head. "Are you joking me? She barely talks to me except when she's giving orders."

"Try talkin' to her. Kiona shy. Folks mistake that. She grew up hard, like me, now you. A hard life makes you put up walls. Got to get to know her on the inside."

"Okay, I'll try. In the meantime, is there anything I can do in the next two weeks to be less of a pest?"

"Yeah," he says, standing up. "Don't lose my fuckin' keys." He walks out.

I run upstairs and fire up the laptop. Thirty files, one for each day. The first is 7JUNE. Twelve days after the attack. I open it and push play. It's night. A timestamp starts at 00:00. Zero time?

Three camera angles, like James said: front, inside and back. The place is full, but the lights are too dim to make out many faces. I notice the waitresses are wearing Durty Delphine's t-shirts with the witch on the front. James was right about the low resolution. The front camera has the best view, next to a light and pointed at the sidewalk.

I watch for an hour. I figured out the timestamp. 00:00 was midnight. I speed up, watching the bar empty out and shut down at three o'clock. I push the cursor to the next morning when workers start arriving to set up for lunch.

Yawning, I hit stop and roll on my back. This is going to take forever.

I close the computer and pick up my sketchpad. I've been working on a drawing of Lucas. Because he's always growling and cursing, it's easy to forget what a nice face he has. The picture I'm making is from my first night here, when he was dancing in the kitchen in his *Mr. Good Lookin' Is Cookin'* apron.

I find my soft-leaded pencil, a 6B, perfect for shading his hair, but I'm unfocused and stray over the line. I stretch for my eraser and the facial composites spill from the pad. Stocky man and tall man stare up at me from the floor. I keep eye contact until my pencil snaps in two.

16

THIS IS the big day—Day One of Week Three—when Lucas promised to start my *self-defense* training. I'm in the middle of bench presses, finding it hard to concentrate. Kiona didn't ask why I have a swollen lip and bandage above my eye. I gather the courage to try Lucas's suggestion.

"Do you like being a trainer?" I ask, straining against the bar, which has ten-pound weights on each end for a total of sixty-five pounds.

"It's alright. Don't arch your back."

"What about boxing?"

"What about it?"

"Do you like it?"

"Not when I'm getting hit. I said don't arch your back."

I try a couple more times with the same result. We just don't have anything in common. When the bar hits the catches after the last rep, she grabs her bag and heads for the stairs.

"Bye, Kiona."

She stops. "Lucas told me what happened yesterday. Don't ever make the mistake of thinking I'm teaching you how to fight. This is just strength and endurance training. Fighting's a whole other thing."

"I get that now."

"Well ... take care of yourself," she says and thumps up the stairs.

I make lunch and scan video at the kitchen table. Lucas is

96

late. I drum my fingers. He better not say he forgot. I bugged him so many times he threatened to staple my lips together.

I'm considering pounding on the document room door when the bolt turns and Lucas comes strolling out.

"You ready for somethin' new?" he says.

I close the computer. "It's about time!"

He digs in the refrigerator and comes out holding a bag. "We start in the basement," he says.

*　*　*

The bag's contents hang from the ceiling on a thin nylon rope looped over a pipe. Nothing but an old t-shirt pulled around a lopsided blob the size of a soccer ball. I expected more.

Lucas tugs on the rope. "Been thinkin' about the best weapon for you. We saw yesterday your boxin' skills ain't gonna do it."

"Yes, weapons. I like that idea a lot."

"We got two choices. Guns or knives."

"What about my stun gun?"

"Fuck my ass with a stun gun. They worthless. This is about puttin' a man down for good. Ain't no second chances. Like I was just saying before you interrupted, again, we got two choices, gun or knife."

"I want a gun, a big one."

"You would. Guns is useful, but got downsides. One, they loud. Two, carrying 'em is dangerous by itself. Knife might be overlooked, but you get caught walkin' around with a gun, your run is done."

"But it's got to be easier to kill someone with a gun than a knife."

"Not necessarily. Most people can't shoot straight, especially up close and under stress. Even the police miss most of the time. Black men thankful for that at least. Your most likely situation is close combat. Knives ain't perfect, but in my opinion, they best for you."

My doubt must be obvious.

"Here's why. Bein' young and a girl, you gonna have the element of surprise every time unless you fuck up. If Lucas walks up to a man, that man's gonna be grabbin' for a fuckin' bazooka, but no one's gonna expect you to fight. Up close, you got the advantage. We start with knives."

"I have one, in my backpack, in my room."

"Go get it."

I fly up and down the two flights of stairs, not even breathing heavy when I land back in the basement and hand Lucas the knife with the serrated blade. He asks where I got it and I say I *acquired* it from a car.

"First thing to know about knives is using 'em is as much psychological as physical. Comes down to one question." He unfolds the knife and holds the jagged blade up to my eyes. "Can you cut a man? Can you stick this into livin', breathin' flesh?"

"Yes," I say.

"That so? 'Cause when you do, you gonna feel tissue rippin' and bones crunchin'. Shit gonna be spraying. Blood and guts, the stink of death, all over you. You can do that?"

"If it were the two men, definitely."

"We see about that." He waves the bundle in my face. "This here is the heart of the stocky man who killed your mama and sister and tried to kill you." He hands me the knife and lets go of the rope.

"Kill."

"Uh, how?"

"Raise the knife like you fuckin' Jason and stab that piece of shit. Once you start, don't stop."

He steps back. "Go."

I lunge, barely nicking the edge. The bundle spins like a piñata. I wait for it to stop, concentrating on the center, and strike again. This time the blade sinks in with a satisfying sucking sound—until the package bursts, spraying me in red.

Mouth gaping, I stare at my dripping arms.

"Game over. You dead," Lucas says.

"What?"

"I said to stab and keep stabbin'. While you was standin' around lookin' shocked, your enemy just stabbed you back five fuckin' times. Do it again and don't stop."

I attack the package again, getting soaked by more bubbly red juice. Picturing stocky man, I keep going, lost in hate, until the rope breaks and the blob sails against the moldy wall with a thud.

"Better," Lucas says. "How that feel?"

"Good," I say, panting. I point at the bloody lump on the floor. "What is that thing?"

"You just killed a flatiron steak wrapped around two shook-up cans of cherry soda. Passed your first test."

He tosses me a towel. "Now you need a new knife."

Drying my face and arms, "What's wrong with this one?"

"Clean the blade and put it where you usually carry it."

I tuck the knife in the front pocket of my backpack.

"Pretend you're walking down the street and a big bad man— that's me—come up and wanna hurt you. Ready?"

"Well ..."

He raises his arms with a scary roar.

"Um, wa—"

He grabs my shoulders. "You dead. And please—whatever the fuck you do—do not tell me you was about to say *wait*. See what I'm getting at?"

"The knife isn't going to help if it's in the backpack. I could carry it in my pocket."

"Same thing."

"Hm. I can't carry it in my hand all the time."

"Wouldn't matter. No criminal's gonna wait around for you to open it. I trade ya," he says, holding out a black thing on a lanyard. "Take it. It's called a neck knife. Pull it out of the sheath, but be careful."

The sheath is rubbery plastic, wide and flat. I tug on a black handle and the knife snaps free. "That's it?" I say. "It's small."

"This here's a four-inch blade. Other one's six inches."

"The handle's smaller too."

"Supposed to be. Made to be concealable. That's the whole idea. Element of surprise. Fit your hand better too. Trust Lucas. Size ain't gonna matter. You sink that blade four inches into a man, you gonna win the fight. Snap the knife back in and put the cord around your neck."

"It's upside down."

"That's so you can grab it from below. Put it inside your shirt. That's where you wear it. Remember, element of surprise. Now you gonna practice pullin' it out and puttin' it back in, but be fuckin' careful. Slash you-self and the enemy ain't got to do nothin' but step over your body."

Lucas has a way of making his tips easy to remember.

A hundred repetitions later—he makes me count—I say, "My arm's tired."

"Quit fuckin' whinin'. Now we switch to tactical training."

* * *

I'm in the basement at the bottom of the stairs. When I get to the top Lucas—the big bad man—is planning to surprise me. I'm supposed to react with the knife *without fuckin' killin'* myself.

I flex my fingers and head up the stairs. I slit the door open and peek out.

"Stop," Lucas says, stepping out from the hallway. "You ain't poppin' out at a surprise party. This is real life. Go back and do it again."

This time I enter the kitchen with my head on a swivel, which *is* how I act in real life. Lucas jumps up from behind the kitchen island.

I whirl and reach for the knife but it's not there. The cord swung around my side. I'm feeling inside my shirt when Lucas says, "Never mind. You dead again. This time I'm goin' upstairs. When you get there look for me standing at the end of the hall."

"That sounds too easy."

"We see."

On full alert, muscles tensed, I reach the landing. There's Lucas, standing where he said he'd be. I yank out the knife. The blade slashes through my shirt. My face turns ashen.

"Good thing that ain't your stomach," he says. "Your guts would be ruinin' my nice floor. You left-handed, right?"

"Like you," still staring at the lustrous jag poking through the cloth.

"Do this." He shows me how to press the sheath against my chest with my right hand and reach for the knife with my left. "Goal is to be smooth and consistent. Make sure the knife's always in the same place when you goin' for it."

"I have an idea." I put the knife cord behind my bra, which not only holds the sheath in place, but makes it almost invisible.

We practice for another hour before he calls a halt. "That's enough, but I want you to practice gettin' that knife in and out one hundred times every day. Keep count and don't cheat."

"I won't. Now do I get to learn how to fight?"

"You is learnin', Patience. Knife-fightin' ain't about dancin' around, dodgin' and blockin' like in the movies. You don't win quick with a knife, you lose. Best thing is to ambush your enemy from behind. Only the stupid and dead try to take someone on from the front with a knife."

"Don't I need to know some moves?"

"We gettin' to it. Tell me this. What's the absolute worst thing you can do in a fight?"

"Not stab hard enough?"

"Was that your problem yesterday? You didn't punch hard enough?"

"I never got a chance to throw a punch."

"Why was that?"

"I froze."

"That's the answer to the question. The worst thing you can do in a fight is freeze. Don't think. Attack. Seize the advantage while the other motherfucker's thinkin'. Don't stop 'til the end. Finish the job. You got that?"

I nod.

"Repeat it."

"Don't think. Attack. Seize the advantage and don't stop until the end. Finish the job."

"You know why most people freeze?"

"They're afraid?"

He nods. "Fear is bigger than your enemy. It will lock you up inside. Since you gonna be in the same situation anyway, might as well make the choice not to be afraid. You always got a choice. You'll come out better for it."

"It sounds so logical when you say it."

"Repeat after me: *I am not afraid. I am Emily-the-Powerful.*"

"I am not afraid. I am Emily-the-Powerful."

"I think your best strategy against freezing is to picture them two men, no matter who your opponent is. Rage is one of the only things that beats fear."

"Picture the two men. Rage beats fear," I repeat. "Good strategy. Now can you please teach me how to fight?"

Twerking neck veins, "Remember you was wonderin' how to be less of a pest? Quit asking the same fuckin' question. This ain't no game. Fightin' with a knife is serious business."

"That's why I need to start learning right now!"

He tilts his head one way then the other, examining me like I'm a species of bug or animal he just discovered. "You a strange little girl, Emily Calby. Gimme the knife. Here we go. Just two moves, thrustin' and slashin'."

He demonstrates each in the air. "See how I'm thrustin' hard? That's what you want. You got to strike with power, which is why we was waitin' for you to gain some muscle and weight. Power's proportionate to body weight."

"Where's the best place to aim?"

"Good thing about knives is they work wherever they land, but try to avoid bone. Bone will stop a knife, not for Lucas, but for you. Anything around the neck is good. You got the carotid arteries up there. You get a chance at the neck, go for it. But like I said, don't waste time thinking. Just go."

I take mental notes. *Neck best, carotid arteries, no bone.*

"All else fails, slash," he says. "Any kind of slashing—arms, legs, anywhere—gonna drain a man of his will to fight."

He drops to his knees on the mat. "For a particularly ugly and disgustin' way to die, if you happen to be in the right position, you can thrust up at the bottom of the crotch." He demonstrates with an upward stroke.

"They a soft spot there. You go right up into the large intestine. Do that to a man and he be wishin' you killed him quick instead."

I cringe.

"Any questions?"

All I manage is, "Wow."

"That's right. Gettin' real now, ain't it?"

"*Real* real."

"We done for today."

* * *

On the bed wearing Lucas's *Yo Gotti* shirt—who I learned is a rapper from Memphis—I watch more grainy video from Durty Delphine's. When the evening crowd arrives, I see some of the same faces from the night before. I pause the video every time a man comes in the front door.

A couple hours later it's three days down and twenty-seven to go. Rubbing my eyes, I close the computer and look around for something else to do. Kiona's staying over. I keep to my room as much as possible when she does, part of my pest-reduction plan, but it's boring beyond belief.

I dump my backpack on the bed and organize my pitiful little pile of life. The stun gun needs charging. Lucas says they're worthless. I drop it in a trash can and open the cigar box to count the money. Just over two thousand. It's going fast.

I draw out my repacking, taking time to polish my phone and clean my hairbrush, but it still takes less than ten minutes.

The empty dresser sits in front of me. Lucas asked why I carry everything in the backpack instead of just using the dresser. I said I didn't know, but I do. Dogging me since the first day is a sense of foreboding that everything's going to fall apart again and I need to be ready when it does.

17

IN FOUR days of knife-training, my skills have advanced. Yesterday I spent an hour in a closet removing and reinserting the knife in total darkness. Each day ends in two parts:

Part I: Stabbing an old punching bag, wearing gloves in case my hand slips, which it does. It's for strengthening, but Lucas let me draw a scale outline of tall man on the bag with a marker, giving me a better idea of where to aim.

Part II: Clinging to a riot shield for dear life while Lucas pounds on it with his fists or a bat. Sometimes he hits lightly, but he also knocks me down a lot. *Desensitization,* he calls it.

"Desensitization is at the heart of every successful killer," he said. "People got to be conditioned to fight and kill. Only psychopaths are natural born killers. The rest of us got to get our brains rewired."

At night, he makes me watch violent movies, saying over and over, "Don't close your eyes." *Cannibal Holocaust* made me throw up on his rug, which to put it mildly, he was not happy about.

I'm in the middle of my morning workout. I started the day at the internet café. What did the brilliant investigators at the Dilfer County Sheriff's Department have to say about the sketches I sent them? Nothing. Not even a form reply this time.

The digital scale registered *103.4* at weigh-in, up seven pounds. I did six pullups for the first time. Kiona raised the weight on all my exercises. I've kept trying to talk to her and it's worked a little bit.

Today I decide to play my ace card, the one big thing we have in common.

"How long have you known Lucas?" I say, grunting through sit-ups with a twenty-five pound weight on my stomach.

"About three years."

"He said you met at the boxing gym."

"Mm-hm," she says.

"Was he boxing?"

"He'd call it that."

"I bet he's a great boxer."

"No, he's not. Lucas is so big and strong he doesn't need a lot of skill to take most people out. He's more of a bruiser than a boxer. He knocked out a man and was prancing around the ring flexing his muscles like he was the heavyweight champion of the world."

I laugh. "I can totally picture that."

"He's yelling, *Who's next? Who's next?* I don't know what got into me, probably his arrogance. So I got in the ring and said *me.*"

"*Omigod.* What'd he do?"

"He said, *I ain't boxin' no woman. You should be home taking care of babies or some shit like that.* That pissed me off. I already had my gloves on, so I said let's go and we started sparring. I should say I started sparring. Lucas just stood there looking at me until I hit him hard in the nose."

"No way!"

"Mm-hm." She smiles for the first time since I met her. "You should have seen the look on his face. Everyone in the gym was hootin' and hollerin'. He got more serious about defending, but still wouldn't punch back. I worked him over until he threw his hands up and declared me the winner. Couldn't hit a woman."

"Aw."

"Even though I embarrassed him in front of everyone, including some rough people you don't want to be embarrassed in front of. I guess that made me kind of like him."

"That is so adorable. What happened next?"

"We had coffee, then just started hanging out."

"Do you love him?"

"Good grief. Lucas warned me you were an interrogator. His exact words were, *I swear, that little girl's worse than the fuckin' District Attorney*," perfectly imitating his fierce voice.

We giggle together and for that second she looks like a completely different person. She catches herself and the smile disappears.

"None of your business," she says. "Get back to work. Curls."

I start a set of bicep curls with fifteen-pound dumbbells.

"He loves you," I say.

"My Lord. What on earth makes you say something like that?"

"I can tell by the way he looks at you and talks about you."

"Time for squats," she says. "Today you're doing them with the bench bar on your shoulders. Let's go."

* * *

I make pasta for lunch. More carbs for more weight. Chicken added, of course. Lucas is convinced I'll let everything shrink away once I'm back on my own.

"I'm gonna be majorly pissed off if you let all this hard work go to waste," he said. "Kiona? She probably burn down my building."

"I won't let you down. I'm going to keep my weight on and keep working out. Kiona taught me how to do most exercises without any equipment. Don't worry. When I'm back on the streets, I'm gonna stay *one tough little motherfucker*."

I expect a laugh, but get nothing. Expressionless, he says, "You do that."

The postman just delivered the mail. Lucas greeted him like an old friend and they did the black handshake. I'm probably the only person in this entire zip code who doesn't know how to do it.

"Lucas, can I ask another favor?" I hold up pinched fingers. "A really itsy-bitsy one."

"Now what?"

"Can you teach me the black handshake?"

"Later," he says, grabbing his keys. "We got business. Goin' for a ride."

"Where to?"

"You see."

"Let me get my backpack."

"You and that fuckin' backpack. It's safer here than carrying it around."

"I know. I just like having it with me."

Fifteen minutes later we're on I-40 going east. Hip-hop music shakes the windows. The bass is making my right ear ache.

"Lucas, can you please turn down the music?"

"What?" he shouts.

"I said can you please turn down the music?" I shout back.

He lowers the volume.

"*Phew*, thank you."

"You don't like hip-hop?"

"Not really. I like country, but I don't like loud noise in general."

"You high maintenance."

We drive for an hour before exiting onto a divided highway. We're out in the country, nothing but trees and farmland. Not many cars. Reminds me of home ... I mean, Georgia.

Without warning, Lucas swerves to the shoulder and stops.

"What's wrong?" I say.

"Switch seats."

"What? Why?"

"You drive."

"Yeah, right." I still can't tell when he's joking or serious. This time I guess it's a joke but I'm wrong again.

"You say your daddy teach you to drive."

"Some."

"You got a driver's license, right?"

"Yeah."

"So drive."

"If you say so." I know better than to argue with him. He's as stubborn as I am. We change seats and I'm staring at the middle of the steering wheel.

Lucas laughs. "That seat may need adjustin'." He reaches for a button and I start growing. "I got to keep it low as it goes or my head hits the fuckin' roof."

"A little forward too, please. Actually, a lot."

"That better?"

"Much." I put my seatbelt on.

"You know how to put it in gear?"

"I think so."

"Let's go."

I slide the gearshift into drive and ease back on the highway. I'm glad there aren't many cars.

"You can go faster than fifteen miles an hour," he says.

I speed up. "Am I doing okay?"

"You fine."

"Why are we doing this?" I say, eyes glued to the road.

"Suppose you can't get no bus or train. What do you do?"

"Wait until I can."

"What if you got no time to wait?"

"Hitchhike?"

"Dangerous, unreliable."

"Ah, I know. Steal a car."

"There you go. Cars the best way to travel, by far. You got complete control."

"One problem. I don't know how to steal a car."

"When you was breakin' into cars, you ever find keys?"

"As a matter of fact, yes. A couple of times under the seat and one time they were right in the ignition."

"There you go. Never overlook cars."

We continue for several miles. I'm doing okay until I almost go through a red light while pointing out a dead raccoon on the side of the road. I prepare to get yelled at, but Lucas says peacefully, "Don't crash my fuckin' car."

A mile later, "Slow down. Turn left, there, at the sign." He's pointing to a weathered piece of plywood that says *Odom Pork Farm.*

I drive down a narrow road until we come to a barn with a much larger sign on the roof. *Odom Pork Farm. Best in Tennessee since 1945.*

"This is it," Lucas says. "Pull up over there."

An old black man in overalls comes out of a cabin that says *Office.* I can hear the pigs grunting and squealing even before Lucas opens the car door. I follow his lead.

"You Mr. Odom?"

"I am. Mr. Jackson?"

"Lucas Jackson," he says. They shake hands, a regular shake. "Pleased to make your acquaintance, sir. We appreciate you helpin' us out."

"This must be the girl," he says, looking at me.

"This here is Alice Miller."

"Nice to meet you," I say, surprised to learn the visit is about me.

"Hello, young lady. Understand this gonna be your first pig-killin'."

My head snaps back. "My first what?"

Mr. Odom looks at Lucas. "Oh, well, Mr. Jackson here said …"

Lucas jumps in. "Excuse me, Mr. Odom. I was just about to explain it to her. Hold on."

He leads me away. "I shoulda told you sooner. Was planning to ease you into it."

"Kill a pig? Why do I have to kill a pig?"

"Remember what I said when we started? Pushing a knife into a man is more psychological than physical. It's easy to stick a knife in a steak or a punching bag, but like you said, this gettin' real."

Stricken, "I really have to kill a pig?"

"How many times have we talked about desensitization? You got to be able to kill when the time comes without stoppin' for a moral conversation with you-self. You don't wanna figure out you can't do it when your life depends on it, do you?"

"I guess not," I murmur.

"Don't worry. This pig scheduled to die today no matter what you do."

I follow him back to Mr. Odom, standing in the sun wiping his brow with a bandana.

"Sorry for the confusion," Lucas says, handing the farmer some cash. "We all straight now. Where's the pig?"

We follow Mr. Odom into a barn filled with grunting hogs and an overpowering stench. He leads us to a pen holding a solitary pig and reaches for a dagger hanging from a hook, a sword compared to my little neck knife. He hands it to me and picks up a thin rod with prongs at one end, the other end connected by a cable to a metal box.

"This here is the stunner," he says. "Electric shock to the brain. She won't feel no pain. I do that part. When I stun 'er, you finish her with the knife. Pull back on her ear and cut the throat, all the way, like this." He demonstrates an ear-to-ear cut.

"You got to cut down to the bone. I'll be standing by in case you can't finish the job."

Eyes wide, I stare at the wedgy sword blade, dark under layers of dried blood.

Mr. Odom pats my arm. "Missy, this been happenin' 'round the clock, 'round the world since the dawn of time. *Every moving thing that lives shall be food for you.* God's will."

I look at the pig, fat and gray, contentedly vacuuming food pellets off the dirt.

"Does the pig have a name?" I say.

"We don't name 'em, we brand 'em. See that tattoo on her shoulder?"

"How old is she? You said it's a she?"

He nods. "Yeah, she a gilt. These bacon pigs. This one here, about six months."

"Six months old? That's all?"

Lucas interrupts. "Mr. Odom, could you give me one more minute with Alice?"

The old man nods.

Lucas leads me away. "What's it gonna be, Alice? You been dyin' to kill. Now's you big chance. What you waitin' for?"

The knife grows heavy, like it's going to pull me through the dirt to the center of the earth. "I–I don't think I can do it," I say.

He spits. "You think you can kill a man, but can't even kill a fuckin' pig?"

I look back at the pig, wagging her curlicue tail. "The pig didn't hurt me," I say.

"That pig gonna die today anyway."

"Then it should get to live until then."

He paces. "You know that bacon you love every morning? Where you think it comes from? You a hypocrite."

"I'm not going to eat any more bacon."

"You a killer or not? This is your moment of truth." The look in his eyes, like everything depends on my answer.

"Okay. I'll do it."

He propels me back to the pen with a hand in the center of my back. "Remember, the pig ain't gonna feel nothin'. Mr. Odom's been doin' this for fifty years."

I tighten my hands around the killing knife.

"Do just like Mr. Odom say. Slit the neck all the way through. Just like with men, you got to go deep. Only humane way to finish the job."

I swallow, forcing down the acid bubbling up my esophagus.

He says, "We ready, Mr. Odom."

Mr. Odom throws the switch on the electrical box and the stunner starts humming. Unlooping a lasso of rope, he opens the gate.

"Go on in, missy, she won't hurt you." He follows me. The pig doesn't even look up.

"Get ready now," Mr. Odom says. "I'm gonna stun her." He grabs the pig by the ear and lowers the buzzing prongs.

"No!" I drop the knife, open the gate and run out of the barn, vomiting before I make it to the grass.

*   *   *

We drive back to Memphis in silence. Lucas doesn't even turn on the music, just stares ahead, thumping his fingers on the steering wheel. The car stinks from the puke on my shirt.

A half hour passes before I say, "I know you don't believe me, but I could have done it to someone who deserved it."

Not a word.

A few minutes later, "I failed. I'm sorry."

Still nothing.

Twenty more miles, coming into the city, he speaks. "You got a major flaw for a killer."

"I know. I froze. I didn't seize the advantage."

"Worse. You got a heart."

Another mile, "That pig dead by now."

18

I'M CLEANING my room in the dark. I want it to look nice. I'm leaving.

Things were never the same after the pig farm. Lucas lost faith in me. He didn't say it in so many words, but didn't have to. When I used to talk about finding the two men, he'd scoff and say it will never happen, but at least he'd respond. Now he just turns and walks away, which is worse.

Then yesterday, near the end of knife-training, I stabbed the punching bag so hard the handle went through the cover and the knife got stuck. "Lucas, look! Emily-the-Powerful," I boasted. No response. He doesn't even act like Lucas, no laughing, growling or gazing at the ceiling.

I should have killed the pig.

The nightstand clock says five-thirty. Before I went to bed, I laid out my clothes and makeup and wrote a goodbye note, using a blue pencil, Lucas's favorite color:

> *Dear Lucas –*
>
> *Thank you for EVERYTHING—the driver's license, food (I'll miss your gumbo!), knife and knife-training, pictures of the two men, videos from DD, makeup and tips and haircut (haha), bed, shower ... SAFETY. A million things.*
>
> *I know you don't believe in God, but I still think we*

met for a reason. But I am a pest and it is time for me to go.

Even though I let you down in my moment of truth I want you to know my training was NOT wasted. I am a completely different person now. STRONG, and I will STAY that way. Tough little mother-effer. All because of you and Kiona. Marry her!

I will find those men some day and when I do I will make you proud of me. I apologize for leaving without saying goodbye in person, but know you would try to talk me out of it to be nice.

This is a picture I drew of you. I hope you like it.

Love, Emily

p.s. You may not want to know it, but you have a heart too.

I tiptoe downstairs and fasten the letter and drawing to the refrigerator with the *I Love Dogs* magnet. The new keys to the front doors hang on the same hook as the ones I lost. Lucas had to get the locks changed. It's a miracle he let me stay this long.

Everything is dingy gray in the breaking light. I replace the keys and pull the inside door shut. The security door will lock automatically, cutting off any chance for second thoughts.

I blow a kiss and let go ... and the world implodes. I grab the door-edge just before it latches, using it to hold me up.

Cold sweat, tightening throat, the terrifying *I can't breathe* feeling. I wobble back inside and lower myself to my hands and knees.

Slow deep breaths. Wait it out. You know the drill.

The first time it happened I was curled in the corner of the train car with the sheep, the day the two men came. I thought I was having a heart attack and dying. This many panic attacks later, you'd think they'd get easier, but the opposite is true. Knowing one's coming makes everything worse.

Pathetic coward, once and forever. Going back on the streets all alone? I'm not sure I can do it ... I mean, I can and will, I just need to prepare better. That's all. Unless Lucas kicks me out early, I have one more week to get ready.

I gather myself off the floor and go to the kitchen. I tear up the goodbye letter and hide it under the other trash, leaving the drawing stuck to the fridge.

I make a creatine shake and take it upstairs. With nothing else to do, I watch surveillance videos, doing a lot more skimming.

12JUNE, midnight. The bar is full. Must be a weekend. Even in the dim light, it's easy to read people as they get drunk. The ones who like each other laugh and touch a lot.

The bar begins clearing out. I study people as they leave through the front camera. It's the closest, best-lit view, but I can only see their backs. A short man, a fat man, a guy in a wheelchair, two women holding each other up laughing.

A tall guy leaves alone. Brown curly hair, tall and thin. I back the video up. Tattoos on his arms. I lean closer. Is that a zombie?

Tall man? Can't be. I'm fantasizing but ... something about him. I make a screenshot of the best frame. To walk out the man had to walk in.

I open the file from the day before, which ended at midnight. How did I miss him? Too much skimming, or more likely the guy doesn't look anything like tall man from the front.

I start at seven p.m., when the night people start arriving, forcing myself to go slow.

Lucas's heavy steps pound down the stairs as the time stamp passes 21:30. Nine-thirty at night, Durty Delphine time. Still no sign of the man. Lucas hollers for me to come downstairs. I take the computer with me.

"You did this?" he says, admiring my sketch in one hand and eating Cheerios with a soup spoon in the other.

"You like it?"

"I really do. Shit, I'm even better-looking than I thought, 'cept I never smile like that."

"Oh yes you do. That's the way you looked my first night here, when you were cooking gumbo and singing and dancing."

"Musta been high. Anyway, this is good. Where you workout clothes? Kiona on her way."

I forgot all about my workout. I'm still in my running-away clothes—jeans, double t-shirts and hoodie, neck knife underneath.

"I was just getting ready to change. Can I show you something first?" I open the screenshot. "Look at this. I think it might be tall man."

"How you figure? Can't see nothing but his back."

"He's tall and thin and has curly brown hair. And look, see that tattoo right there? I think it's a zombie, like the one tall man had."

"All I see is a blob."

"Still ... something about him. I've got a feeling."

"You 'titled to believe what you believe."

"So you don't think it could be him," I say, not hiding my irritation.

"No. I think you desperate."

"You're not even willing to admit it's a possibility?"

"No."

I slam the computer shut. "You *never* believe in me. It doesn't matter what I try to do. Why do you always have to rain on my parade?"

"Rain on your parade? Fuck is that?"

"I don't know," I say, shoulders sinking. "My mom used to say it."

"Well, sorry to rain on your parade, but I got bad news. James already run all seven hundred and twenty hours of video through the recognition software using the facial composites and nothing came up."

I slap my forehead. "Oh, nice! Don't you tell me anything anymore?"

"He just called last night."

"Well, it doesn't mean anything anyway. James—who you love and adore so much—said based on all his *variables*, the software probably wouldn't work with the composites."

He gives me a crooked look. "I'm just the messenger. Kiona almost here. Go get ready."

"*Kiona almost here*," I mock. "It's supposed to be *Kiona's* almost here, a contraction of *Kiona* and *is*. You're leaving out the verb. You said last night we're doing something new today. Would you mind clueing me in for a change? Do I have to chop off the head of a cow? Strangle a cat? I'm sick of your *fucking* surprises."

"That's right," he says mildly. "Something new."

* * *

Kiona lifts the bar off my shoulders after a set of squats. My muscles are screaming, but today is one of the sick days I enjoy the pain.

"I saw that picture you made of Lucas," she says. "You have real art talent."

"Thanks. He said he never smiles like that."

"You know Lucas, always has to keep up his badass image. Pick up those twenties for curls. You're ready to move up. Congratulations. Big day for you."

"It is?"

"July fourteenth. Three full weeks of training. We started June twenty-third."

"Oh, right. Only seven more days before you're rid of me."

She puts her hands on her hips. "That's not what I meant. I was trying to congratulate you for lasting three weeks of hard training."

"Wait, did you say July fourteenth?"

"I'll be honest," she says. "I didn't think it was possible."

"Today is July fourteenth?"

"Yeah, what's wrong?"

"Oh ... nothing. It's my birthday." I pick up the weights.

"Your birthday? No kidding?"

"Not if it's July fourteenth. I lost track of the calendar a long time ago."

"Well ... happy birthday."

"Thanks."

"So you're ..."

"Thirteen. These twenties are definitely a lot heavier."

"Two sets, then push-ups. Don't overdo it. I'm going upstairs to use the restroom."

She returns to find me on my stomach, panting. "I did twenty-five push-ups. Five more than I've ever done."

"Not bad. Hey, I got a call from one of my clients who I can't afford to lose. I forgot to change his appointment. Can you keep going without me?"

"Sure. I know the routine."

"Don't cheat," she says and walks out.

I don't cheat. When I climb the stairs a half hour later, Lucas is sitting at the kitchen table. I wave as I go by, headed for a shower.

"Hold on. Come sit with me. Got something to talk about."

I never like the way that sounds. It's always bad news. The front door buzzes as I collapse in my chair.

Lucas gets up and punches the intercom button. "Yo."

"It's me."

Kiona. He goes to let her in. I hear them whispering behind my back as they come back down the hall. The cramp in my gut starts again.

They're getting ready to tell me to leave. I know it. My instinct to run away was right the whole time. *Always trust your instinct.* Lucas's own words. He said it during training. I stare at my morose reflection in the glossy table until Lucas's wide shadow makes me disappear.

"Alice," he says.

"Yes?" I say without turning.

"We got to ask you to move."

"I know," I say, burying my face in my hands. "I understand. Would it be possible to wait until morning? I'll stay in my room for the rest of the day so I won't be a pest. I–I know I can do it, I just need to get myself ready."

"The fuck you babblin' about?" Lucas says. "You got to move over so I can put this down." I turn to see him holding a cake with burning red numbers on top: 13.

He sets it down and they start singing. "Happy birthday to you, happy birthday to you." Lucas is terribly off-key. "Happy birthday *dear Alice*, happy birthday to you."

They start clapping. I start crying.

"Whoa, whoa," Lucas says. "Ain't no cryin' allowed on your birthday. Blow out the candles."

"What's wrong?" Kiona asks.

So much. I cried at my last birthday too, the first one without Dad. Mom and Becky sang *Happy Birthday* to me then. "I'm just so happy," I say. "Thank you." I give them both hugs.

"Cheer up. You a fuckin' teenager now," Lucas says. "Think of all the mayhem you can cause."

Leaden laugh. "Yeah."

"Even got you a present," he says, dropping a brown paper bag tied with string onto the table. It lands with a clunk. "Ain't had time to wrap it properly."

"Ooh, presents," Kiona says. "Open it."

The package looks familiar. I pick it up. Solid. I tear off the twine, reach in and pull out a gun.

"Lucas!" Kiona says, slapping his arm. "A gun?"

"Don't worry, baby. It ain't loaded."

"That's not the point. You don't give a girl a gun for her thirteenth birthday. What's the matter with you?"

I turn the gun over. Bluish-black. I'm surprised how small and light it is. Not much bigger than my hand. It almost looks like a toy.

"Just a coincidence," he says. "Was plannin' to start training her with it today."

"A gun, Lucas? A gun?"

"I know what you sayin', but a knife ain't gonna be enough to protect her."

I know he's thinking about the pig farm, but if he's giving me a gun, maybe he hasn't given up on me.

"Thank you for the present," I say. "What kind is it?"

"This what you call a pocket rocket. Three-eighty semiautomatic. Holds six cartridges in the magazine and one in the chamber. Made to be extra-concealable."

"What's this thing on the end?" I say, looking into the barrel.

Lucas rips the gun from my hands. "Don't ever point a fucking gun at anything or anyone you don't intend to shoot. Rule number one."

"You said it wasn't loaded."

"You hear me? Rule number one. Say it."

I make a face. *"Don't ever point a fucking gun at anything or anyone you don't intend to shoot."*

"Shit, you already sound like a teenager and it's only been a few hours."

"That does it. I am gone," Kiona says and walks out.

19

"KIONA GOT the cake," Lucas says. "Felt sorry for you."

The candles are still burning. Streams of red wax flow across the white icing like molten lava across tundra. I blow them out without making a wish.

"Back to your question. This thing on the end is a laser sight. Might help you shoot a little better. Works like this."

We spend an hour in student-teacher mode. I practice loading, unloading, gripping and aiming through the tiny sights with the help of the red laser dot. He shows me how to take it apart and reassemble it.

He pulls out the magazine. "Loaded or unloaded," he says.

"Unloaded," I say.

"Safe to put the barrel to your head and pull the trigger?"

"Don't point a gun at anything or anyone you don't intend to shoot," I recite.

"Yeah, that good, but this is a different lesson. Safe?"

It feels like a trick, but I saw him take out the bullets.

"Safe."

"Wrong." He pulls back the top of the gun and a bullet pops out. "Six cartridges in the magazine *and one in the chamber.* Never forget it."

"You got this gun from the men at the car lot that day, didn't you? The ones who said the nasty things about me. I remember you coming out of the garage with it."

He nods. "They gun-runners, along with a lot of other nefarious activities."

"Were you planning on giving it to me the whole time?"

"Goin' back and forth. You was doin' good with the knife, but ..." His voice trails off.

"I know. I couldn't kill the pig. Are there more bullets?"

"They comin', Patience. First we eat lunch."

I force down a shake, but just pick at my other food. What a day. From the beginning, everything has been *off*. My aborted runaway attempt, yelling at Lucas, now the gun and Lucas and Kiona getting in a fight, because of me. And I forgot my own birthday!

"We have to eat some birthday cake," I say. "After the trouble Kiona went through."

"You right."

I cut a small slice for me and a fat wedge for him.

"Ready for some shootin' practice?" he says when he finishes.

"Sure," I say, although I'm not really sure. I wanted a gun at the beginning but then I got comfortable with the knife. The gun scares me. Locked up somewhere in my memory is another gun going off.

I go upstairs to change, coming down in the clothes I started out the day out with, backpack in tow.

He gives me a *You and that fuckin' backpack* look and hands me the gun. "If you gonna haul that thing everywhere, might as well get used to illegal gun carrying."

* * *

Our first stop is in the neighborhood, at a small well-kept house with a chain-link fence marked by *Beware of Dog* signs.

"This where James stay. We got to talk business. Wait here." He gets out and locks the doors.

He comes out a few minutes later palming a small package that he slips into the console. We drive north to Summer Avenue. Sounds like a street in Florida, but it looks like another rough part of town.

We pass pawnshops, nail salons and used car lots before

coming to a gun store. Lucas pulls into the parking lot and tells me to stay put. He goes inside and returns with six boxes of bullets.

"Let me pay you for those, and for the gun." I unzip my backpack.

"You don't pay for birthday presents."

We go east until the city fades behind us and we're back out in open country. Please, not another pig farm.

"Could you tell me what I'll be shooting at?" I say politely. "I just, you know, want to be prepared."

"Don't worry, killer. Just paper targets. You good with that?"

I say yes and relax for the first moment since I woke up. "It's okay to turn on the music if you want."

"Don't need no music. Always better to talk, ain't that right?"

"I'd say so."

"Complete honesty. That's the best way, ain't it?"

I sense a set-up. "Mm-hm."

"Tell me then, where you plannin' on goin' when you leave here?"

I wonder if he somehow knows I tried to run away this morning, but nothing on his face hints of secret knowledge. "No real plan yet," I say.

"You just agreed complete honesty is the best way. Now you backin' out on your word. I thought better of you."

"You already know where I'm going. Lafayette, Louisiana. I know you think it's stupid, but I think tall man could be there, maybe both of them."

"It ain't stupid to believe the tall man's from Louisiana. From what you say, I believe he's Cajun. But you bettin' everything on one little bar."

"If he's in Lafayette, I'll find him, even if it's not at Durty Delphine's."

"Tell me how you plan to do that. Lafayette's exactly the wrong city for you. I looked it up. One hundred and twenty thousand people. Not big enough to hide in, not small enough to find a man in."

My only plan is to show the facial composites of the two men around and hope someone recognizes them, but I don't dare tell him. He'll say it's stupid, because it is. I think of another answer that's just as honest.

"I'm going there because I don't have any better place to go."

"That's where you thinkin' wrong. You got plenty of places, all of 'em better. Places to start a new life. It ain't got to be your destiny to chase down them two men."

"Why don't you start a new life?"

"It's too late for me. I got no choice. You do."

I turn on the radio. "Can I pick some music?" He doesn't object until I land on a country station which he turns off.

"You can't make me listen to that shit. I got to draw the line."

"It's not shit. I could say the same thing about rap."

Out the window a hawk glides in and out of cotton-ball clouds. It reminds of the red-tailed hawk the day the two men came. I watch it with envy. Predator, not prey.

We pass a hardware store with a sign advertising hunting permits and bibles. Lucas takes the next turn, onto a dirt road, ignoring a *No Trespassing* sign pocked by bullets. We twist through patches of meadow and woods before the big tires grind to a halt in a clearing.

Ten minutes later I'm pointing my birthday gun at a paper target of a man's head and torso tacked to an oak tree, listening to more instructions: top finger flat on the side, arms straight out, feet not wider than my shoulders, right one a little in front of the left. He adjusts my thumbs on the grip.

"How's that feel? You wanna be nice and stable."

"Not bad."

"Alright, aim at that target."

"From this close?"

He laughs. "We see. Turn on the laser. That might help a little."

I tap the laser button.

"It must be broken. I can't see it."

"That 'cause you aimin' at fuckin' Mars. Lower the gun. There you go."

I see the red dot, but it's bouncing around like Tinkerbell. "Why won't it hold still? In the movies, it stays where they point it."

"'Cause that peashooter ain't no sniper-rifle and you ain't no marksman. You ready? Shoot."

I pull the trigger. Nothing happens.

"Huh, a dud."

"No dud. Think."

"Oh. No bullet in the chamber."

He nods.

I pull back the slide, re-aim and pull the trigger. Even though I'm expecting it, the loud pop makes me jump. I study the target.

"Missed."

"Try again."

I miss again.

"You pullin' to the left. Calm your breathing. Steady, steady."

This time I hit the edge of the target. He tells me to keep going. Three shots later, the gun is empty. Only the one hit.

"I stink."

"Reload and move closer. I wanted you to know you can't be shootin' at people from a distance. You gonna practice at three feet, six feet and nine feet."

"You're kidding. That's like practically nothing."

"Real shootin' ain't like a video game. It happens up close, where people usually miss. Your best chance is to set up an ambush from a defensive shootin' position."

"Like what?"

"Behind somethin' solid where you got a clear field of fire. A car, concrete wall, heavy furniture if you inside."

I shoot for an hour. At nine feet, I manage to hit the target most of the time. At six feet, I do a pretty good job of hitting near the center. Surprisingly, three feet is the hardest of all. You can't stretch out your arms.

He stops me. "We save seven cartridges. Full magazine and one in the chamber, only way to carry. Tomorrow we reload and find a holster you can conceal. Just like the knife, gun ain't gonna be no help in a backpack. Wanted to see how you take to it."

"Shooting's fun," I say. "But neck knives will always be my first true love." I fake swoon.

"Whatever. Let's go home."

20

HEAT WAVES shimmer off the interstate like a mirage as we close in on Memphis. I wrangle out of my hoodie and toss it in the back seat. We're back to rap music. From what I can make out, it's a song about gunning someone down in traffic. And I thought country music was sad. I reach over and turn down the volume.

"Lucas, I have to tell you something. A couple things actually. First I want to apologize for yelling and saying those mean things earlier. I didn't mean them."

"Fury got its place."

"I don't know why I blew up like that. I think it's because ... I'm just so ashamed I couldn't kill the pig. I never wanted to fail you because you *did* believe in me ... and because I've already failed everyone else."

"I rushed you. Ain't easy puttin' a blade in a livin' creature. Been speedin' everything up since we only got one month. What else?"

I hesitate. "Well, we were talking about complete honesty, but I haven't been completely honest today. I planned to leave this morning. I even started to, but chickened out."

"What the fuck? Leave where?"

"Memphis ... you."

"We got one more week."

"I thought you wanted me to go and were just too nice to say it."

"You worry too much. I ain't that nice. When I want you to go, I'll tell you."

"Then how come you've been acting weird?"

"What you mean?"

"You know, not joking around and stuff. Being quiet all the time. I figure I'm the reason."

We're inside the city limits. He stops at a light, looking out the side window, but the only thing out there is a carwash. When we start moving again, he says, "Alright, since we gettin' to the heart of the matter, you right. I probably have been different and, yeah, you the reason."

I knew it, but didn't really expect to hear it. Be careful what you ask for.

"When I opened my door three weeks ago expectin' Roscoe Pallatin from the Iraq war with his eye shot out and saw that skinny blonde girl, I never guessed I was meetin' the Amazing Emily Calby. Well, you ain't my houseguest no more. Ain't my trainee. You my friend."

It's been such a roller-coaster day, I almost start bawling.

"Picturin' you out on the streets again, wandering? It makes me worry ... and sad."

"That's all it is? This whole time I thought you were counting the minutes to get rid of me. Don't worry about me, I'll be fine," I say with manufactured confidence. "So, we good?"

He makes the deep, warm chest laugh I love so much. "Yeah, we good. Here, lemme teach you that handshake. 'Cept it ain't called the black handshake. Called the dap."

I give it a couple tries.

"You need more snap pullin' away. Try again. There you go, there you go. You gettin' it. Look here. I got somethin' for you." He opens the console and pulls out a small box, crookedly wrapped in green paper with a gold bow.

"What's this?"

"Another birthday present. Open it."

"Aw, you didn't need to get me another present."

"Even wrapped it myself."

I tear into the package expecting some kind of gun or knife accessory. If I had to list a hundred guesses, jewelry would not have been on it, but inside the box is a beautiful bracelet, thin strands of black leather held together by silver rings with a thick silver medallion in the middle.

"This is for me? *Omigod, omigod.*"

"See, the thing is—"

"Thank you!" I kiss it. "*Mum, mum, mum.*" I snap it to my right wrist.

"The thing is about that bracelet—"

"I'll never take it off. Notice how I didn't put it on my dominant hand? I always keep that hand free in case I need it, just like you taught me. What were you saying about the bracelet?"

"... Try not to get it wet. Ruins the leather."

"I'll take perfect care of it." I lean my head against his shoulder and keep it there. We pass through downtown and into Lucas's neighborhood. The surroundings decay so fast, two different worlds a mile apart.

A red light stops us at an intersection. I point to an abandoned fast-food restaurant with a parking lot of tall weeds. "What's that graffiti over there mean? I've seen it before. I assume it's some kind of gang sign."

Before he can answer, a dark green car pumping a window-rattling beat pulls alongside us. "Man, that is loud," I say, holding my ears. "I thought yours was bad."

The car's windows are tinted black. The back window is cracked open, smoke pouring out. The front passenger window lowers. A man waves.

Lucas rolls down his window.

"'Sup, Big EZ?" the man says with a grin. I recognize the gold teeth with the diamond in it. It's *grill-man*, the guy from the car lot where Lucas bought my gun. That's what I've called him since I asked Lucas why the man had gold teeth and he said they were *just a grill.*

"Not a lot," Lucas replies.

"You enjoying that little pop gun?"

Lucas doesn't say anything. Instead, he pulls his big gun from his waist. "No worries," he says softly.

"I ain't hear ya," the man says. "I ax if you enjoyin' that little gun."

The driver is looking straight ahead.

"I don't talk fuckin' business on the street."

"Just thinkin' if you liked that one, your motherfuckin' black ass gonna love this one."

I see a thin black metal rod poke out the rear window.

"Lucas!"

But it's too late.

Bap, bap, bap. Bap, bap, bap. Bap, bap, bap. Bap, bap, bap.

Everything seems to happen in slow motion. Glass explodes, bullets thud and grill-man's gold mouth gleams in the sun. The gun keeps shooting, like a machine gun, barrel flashing with each shot. Then just like that, the shooting stops and the car squeals away.

"Lucas!" He's slumped in the seat. I get out my phone and call 911.

"Memphis nine-one-one, what's the address of your emergency?"

"A man just got shot! He's bleeding everywhere."

"What is your location?"

I look around. "There's a street sign that says Crump something, and a building on the corner. Latham Terrace. Hurry! A man is dying."

She tells me to hold and comes back a few seconds later.

"Stay calm. Help is on the way. What's your name?"

"My name? Um." I hang up and take Lucas's face in my hands. "Lucas? Lucas?"

His eyes flutter. "Run," he breathes.

"No."

Wheezing, "I *orderin'* you to run. Police be here soon. You ain't no doctor and you ain't gonna help me by gettin' caught."

"I'm not leaving," I say.

Sirens in the distance.

His chest starts convulsing. In a fading voice, "Emily Calby, if you truly my friend, you will honor my dyin' wish and get the fuck outta here."

His eyes roll back and he goes still.

21

"LUCAS, LUCAS." The voice is muffled through the wall of glass. I watch as a calm girl who looks like me, but older, holds his wrist. She can't feel a pulse. She presses her head against his chest, painting her face in blood, but hears only her own pounding heart.

Someone's knocking on the window. A man, yelling. What's he saying? Two other men on the corner, pointing.

Don't know what to do.

The sirens get louder. *Honor my dyin' wish and get the fuck outta here.* I kiss his cheek and jump out, running into the man tapping on the window. He's talking as I run away, but I hear only the roar between my ears.

I don't look back until I reach the alley. Through a veil of tears, I watch blurred flashing colored lights converge on the SUV.

I run and pray at the same time, staying in alleys, heading north to downtown. When I stop to catch my breath, I see a reflection in a window. It's a girl with the entire front of her body covered in blood. She's familiar to me, but I don't quite recognize her.

I smack my cheeks. *Come back. Come back, now.* The sun is setting, but it's still light. Can't run around like this.

I find a dumpster, empty except for a few newspapers and bottles. I climb inside, close the lid and curl in a ball. The smell of coppery blood and rotted food make me start to throw up. I swallow it and close my eyes ... ending up in a worse place.

Mom's bedroom, bound by the ties, hopping to the night-stand, where she pointed with her eyes.

She's crying somewhere. I can't hear Becky.

Nothing in the nightstand except books and a pair of nail clippers. I thought there'd be a gun. Dad used to have one. What good are books and ... nail clippers?

A minute later my legs are free, but the clippers won't reach my wrists. I'm straining for a better angle when a loud bang echoes through the house.

The gun in my dreams. Mom's crying stops. *No!*

Steps in the hallway.

"The fuck you do dat for?" Tall man.

"She pissed me off. Wouldn't quit crying about the damn kids."

"Why you got to be such a hothead?"

"Let's get out of here. It's all gone to shit. Spread the gas. I'll pull the lines. Follow the plan."

"But I ain't done," tall man whines.

"You are now. Remember, no evidence."

"You don worry about me. Just be sure dey dead-dead. Don want dem comin' back to life."

"Spare me your hoodoo voodoo and spread the fucking gas."

I run into the bathroom and lock the door. Gotta get free, find a weapon, *find Becky.* Dad's barber scissors, still in the medicine cabinet. I use them on the wrist ties, but my hands are numb and they slip free, clattering onto the ceramic tile. I freeze, but the men continue arguing in the hall.

When the last strip falls away I tear at the tape on my mouth, sucking for air, trying not to gasp. Want to just breathe, but no time. Need more weapons. Under the sink I find the spray-bottle Mom used to clean the shower. We always complained about the smell, but she insisted only pure bleach works. The bedroom door opens.

"Hey." Stocky man. "Where'd you put blondie?"

"She in dere."

"Fuck, she ain't. Keep working. I'll find her."

I slide open the bathroom window. The backyard looks like paradise. A bird soars against the bright blue sky. I want to be it, but don't let myself think about leaving.

Stocky man is searching the bedroom closets. I step into the bathtub and close the shower curtain.

Footsteps. The doorknob wrenches back and forth. "Cutie-pie? You in there?" He pounds on the door. "She locked herself in the bathroom."

"Finish her off. We got to go."

"Open the fucking door!" *Boom. Boom.* The door splinters on the third hit.

"Fuck, she climbed out the window. We gotta find her."

I don't breathe or even blink.

The bathroom gets quiet. The gas smell is getting strong.

Silence. Did he leave?

The shower curtain flies open. Face to face, stocky man's spattered with blood. *Mom's blood.*

We reach out at the same time, me with the bleach bottle, pulling the trigger as fast as I can, until he stumbles back against the broken door clawing his eyes.

I boost myself into the window frame, feeling his hands grabbing for my ankles. Kicking like a mule, I push through, landing next to Dad's woodpile. Stocky man is screaming he's going to cut me into pieces as I race into the woods.

Through the trees, into the ravine, tunneling under the leaves … then the explosion.

A sound outside. I pull out the neck knife and crack open the lid. A cat skitters away into the dark. How long have I been in here?

Mom, shot. And Becky, oh, Becky. I drop to the wobbly floor and weep, trying to do it silently, but discover it's not possible as I start to choke. The calm girl in my head, the older one who looks like me, tells the crying girl she has to go away and hide for now. She doesn't want to go, but the calm girl's soothing voice insists she must.

Need to get out of this stinking *coffin*...

I make my way down the alley, spooked by every sound. Are the police looking for me? I crashed right into the guy knocking on the window. But I remember what Lucas said when I asked why he never got caught for killing the men who shot Shondra and Jarrett.

"People must have known it was you," I said.

"Folks 'round here don't talk to the police."

"Even when someone gets shot?"

"'Specially when."

Car lights at an upcoming intersection trigger images of the flashing gun barrel. *Lucas cannot be dead.*

Still need to get rid of the blood. I find a faucet on the back of a building and use a sock for a washcloth, swapping the bloody clothes for my only other set which—*ugh*—includes my work-out shorts. I hate being uncovered.

I put makeup on in the light of my phone, thinking about the day I met Lucas. He called me a *cake face* and gave me makeup tips. Every day I knew him, the funnier that got. I put on the nerd glasses, stuff the soiled clothes under some trash and look for a place to call a cab.

*   *   *

Pacing under the awning of a print shop, I make myself stop tearing my hair for the third time. The cab is taking forever.

My phone rings. Lucas is the only one with the number. "Hello, hello!"

"This is Officer Rogers, Memphis Police Department. I'm following up on a nine-one-one call placed from this number earlier. Who am I speaking to?"

"That's actually a really good question," I say and disconnect. Lucas said they can track 911 calls even on dumb phones by triangulating the signals from cell towers. I remove the battery and toss the burner in a garbage can just as the taxi rounds the corner.

"Bus station," I say, jumping in back.

Ducking behind the seats, I forage for the driver's license and one hundred and fifty dollars, enough for cab fare and a bus ticket. The gun rests against the cigar box. *You get caught walkin' around with a gun, your run is done.* The only time anyone's looked through my backpack was at a store where I almost got caught shoplifting a flashlight, before I was an illegal weapon carrier.

We're on the interstate. The driver's weaving in and out of cars, tilting me back and forth like a metronome.

"Are you sure this is the way to the bus station?" They're usually downtown.

"Sure."

He exits at the airport and pulls up to a green-glass building with a sloped roof. No hoodie to hide my white hair, I snug down the Cubs cap before opening a door with a sign that says *NO WEAPONS.* A huge round clock says it's almost midnight.

Not many people. There's a diner on the right. My only fuel today was the two shakes and sliver of birthday cake. I have no appetite but promised Lucas I'd keep my weight on and stay in shape. It's a promise I'm going to keep no matter what, but first I need a ticket.

My shoes squeak against the green-speckled terrazzo as I cross to the ticket counter.

Remember, it ain't just about havin' a document. It's how you present it. Like you bored or bothered, anything but nervous.

An unsmiling woman says, "Can I help you?"

"I need a ticket to Lafayette."

"Indiana or Louisiana?"

Who knew there was more than one? "Louisiana. What time does the next bus leave?"

"Three-twenty."

"Day or night?"

"In the morning," she says crisply. "Three hours from now. Are you traveling with someone?"

Bored or bothered. "Just little ol' me."

"You got to be sixteen."

"Perfect because that's how old I am."

She holds out a palm. "ID."

I give her the driver's license, ready to recite Alice Miller's life story, but she just scans it and hands it back. *Thank you for the bar code, Lucas.*

"Bags?"

"Just this carry-on."

"Eighty-seven dollars."

I pay and cross back to the diner. Nothing healthy. I order a fried chicken sandwich. Six dollars. I get a cup of water and take them to a round café table.

A man at the next table is talking to himself as I study the ticket. Fourteen hours. *Freaking long.* Two transfers. Texarkana and Shreveport. No idea where those places are.

I force down the sandwich and go to the waiting area, unable to turn off the horror show playing in my brain. Dead bodies everywhere. Mom, Becky, now Lucas.

22

NAVIGATING to the back of the bus, I concentrate on looking old. Straight posture, sullen face. I find two open seats, taking the aisle and guarding the window with my backpack. I once saw two guys get in a fistfight over a seat, but the bus is only half full when it pulls away, a light rain coating the windows.

My first trip without a travel companion feels lonely. I never realized how much comfort I got from the Mrs. Drapers of the world.

I push the seat back and close my eyes, still getting beaten up by the grisly images. I need a diversion. If I had the laptop I could search the video for the man leaving the bar. I could probably watch all thirty days of video on this long trip.

It must be four a.m. by now. Before everything happened, the latest I ever stayed up was at Meggie Tribet's slumber party. We made a sworn vow, eight girls, to stay awake until morning, but no one lasted past one.

The droning motor and pattering rain sooth my jangled nerves and I catch my chin dropping. Need to stay awake, alert . . .

I'm walking in a field with Lucas. It's like the meadow where we went shooting, but not the same one. I know we're here for something important, but don't know what. I'm clutching his hand.

"Where are we going?"

"You'll see."

"I don't like surprises."

He smiles. "I know."

"Don't let go of my hand. Okay?"

"No worries."

A blank-faced man comes out of the woods and calls to Lucas. "I got to go talk to that man," Lucas says. "You stay here. It'll only take a minute."

"But I'll be all alone again."

"I'll be right back."

But the moment he lets go of my hand I already know he's gone forever. Sure enough, when he reaches the woods, he vanishes, just as a shadow attacks me from behind.

My eyes blink open. The bus, the bus. Only a dream ... then something touches my back and I see the shadow of an outstretched hand on the seatback in front of me. I grab for the neck knife, but the cord is twisted under my armpit. *Fail. Always.*

Wrenched sideways, fists raised, "Get away!"

The shadow tips a cowboy hat. "Sorry to frighten you, young lady." He points to the window. "Is that seat taken?"

We're stopped. More people are getting on the bus. The sky is lightening.

"Where are we?"

"Little Rock, Arkansas."

"Arkansas?" I say, suspicious. "I thought this bus was going to Texarkana." *Did I get on the wrong bus?*

"I sure hope so," the man says. "That's where I'm heading. Texarkana's in Texas and Arkansas."

"Oh."

I realize he's holding a bag and waiting for my answer about the seat. "Um, yeah, sure. I mean, no, it's not taken." I stand to let him in. He's tall with a silvery mustache, wearing turquoise jewelry around his neck on a leather thong.

"Sorry I was rude," I say when he sits down. "I was asleep."

"Quite alright."

I reach for my backpack before remembering I threw the burner in the trash. "Sir, do you know what time it is?"

He looks at a watch that matches his neck jewelry. "Six on the dot."

"Do you know how long we're going to be here?"

"Not long, I hope. We're supposed to depart at six on the dot."

"How long it is to Texarkana?"

"You are a girl with a lot of questions."

"People tell me that." *I swear, that little girl's worse than the fuckin' District Attorney.*

"Three-hour trip. Make it every week."

The man unfolds a newspaper as the bus grinds out of the station. I ask if I can look at it when he's done, but there's no news about Lucas.

I get out my pad and pencils. Need to think ahead, plan for Lafayette, but the list I come up with is all about Lucas:

—*Buy phone WITH data and check for news.*

Tracking's still an issue but I might have to start taking some risks. A crazy-person laugh erupts from my throat. The man looks over and I disguise it as a cough. I mean *more* risks.

—*Find Kiona.*

Three weeks in a basement together and I don't even know her last name. I add *Find boxing gym.*

—*Call hospitals.*

—*Call police about grill-man?*

The pencil lead breaks. I can't believe it took me this long to realize it. It's my fault Lucas got shot. Why would grill-man want to kill Lucas? Obvious. He stood up for me at the car shop, knocked grill-man on the ground and embarrassed him. Retaliation. Code of the street. If it wasn't for me we wouldn't have been there in the first place.

He's dead. I know it. He even said his dying wish. But I also know he's not dead. He's *so* not dead at all. ... I really don't know anything. Two hours wasn't enough sleep. The man in the cowboy hat is reading a book. He seems safe enough. I curl around my backpack, making sure I know where the neck knife is.

* * *

The bus horn, long and mournful, wakes me as we pull into the transfer station in Texarkana, a convenience store and gas station. My seatmate tips his cowboy hat and wishes me a good day as I step onto the pavement, already radiating summer heat.

Fifty minutes until the next bus. I go inside and ask the woman behind the counter about prepaid phones. She's wearing a black Iron Maiden shirt and sucking on an unlit cigarette. "Ain't got nothin' like that," she says.

I look for healthy snacks. All I can find are a granola bar and bag of dried apricots. Five dollars. Ridiculous.

I avoided paying for food whenever I could on the road. Sometimes I shoplifted it, sometimes I ate it right in the store. Then a homeless man in Baltimore, or maybe Cincinnati, taught me an easier way. Knock on the back door of a restaurant looking pitiful and ask for it. *Ain't no one gonna turn down a kid, especially a girl.* He was right, but the thought of returning to that life pushes me to the edge of a bottomless pit of blackness. I lock it in a box.

I board the transfer bus as soon as it arrives, impatient to get underway to my *penultimate* stop before Lafayette. One of my weekly look-up words from Mom. *Second to last. Shreveport is my penultimate destination.*

Forever or just this bus trip I don't know.

23

WE PULL into the Shreveport station at noon. All I can think about is that I should be getting ready to have lunch with Lucas, my favorite part of the day. When Kiona joined us, we were like a little family.

The bus to Lafayette doesn't leave for an hour. I jog to a Subway, gobble down a chicken sandwich with every possible free topping and hurry back. *I will not let you down, Lucas.*

There's a flat space across from the station, a plaza in front of a curvy white building. All I need. No time for warm-ups, so I launch straight into intervals, five lunges out, five back. Repeat. I'm five outstretched steps away when I hear a sound and turn to see a man in a dark uniform holding my backpack.

"Hey, that's mine!" I run over and try to grab it, but he hoists it above his head.

"This is yours?"

"Of course it's mine. I just said so."

"Miss, this is a United States Courthouse. See that sign? All unattended packages will be confiscated, order of the Department of Homeland Security."

"It wasn't unattended. I'm right here."

"Well, I'm going to have to search it."

"Go right ahead, Officer …"—I lean in to see his nametag— "*Freemont*. If you want to lose your job and ruin your life."

Lucas's voice. *Attack. Seize the advantage while the other motherfucker's thinkin'.* I don't know if it translates here. He also said not to antagonize the authorities, but I've got nothing to lose. If he opens the backpack and sees the gun, it's all over.

"Excuse me?"

"My personal things are in there, including my panties." I start to call them underwear, but panties sounds creepier. "Do you know what they do to men who like to play with girls' panties? My parents taught me to watch out for people like you."

A short standoff before, scowling but flustered, he hands over the backpack. "Leave it unattended again and I *will* confiscate it."

Breathing relief as he marches away, I cross the street berating myself for being careless. I wouldn't survive five minutes without the backpack. Beyond the bus station is a blank wall abutting the sidewalk. I wedge the backpack against it and resume my workout. When anyone gets close, I stop and guard it.

I'm sweating through a set of burpees when a runner comes down the sidewalk. Tall guy, shirtless, in black jogging pants with white stripes down the sides. I lean against the wall, cradling the backpack behind my legs.

I expect him to step out around me, but he doesn't. No chance to react before he runs into me, knocking me down.

Pulling out an earbud, "Oh, shit, sorry. Was in the zone."

I'm sprawled on the sidewalk, rubbing my scraped elbow. "You should be more care—" I never finish because he grabs my backpack and starts running.

"Hey!"

No. Effing. Way. I take off after him. At the first corner he looks back, surprised I'm right there, and picks up the pace. His legs are longer, but he's carrying the backpack. Another block. This time he turns around with a *WTF?* look. He doesn't know it, but I could run like this for another mile. With what's at stake, more than that.

We're approaching a river the color of rust.

"Stop!" I'm hoping he'll decide the backpack isn't worth this much trouble and drop it. I'd yell more but can't afford official attention any more than he can. He's heading up the long ramp of a bridge. It's a climb and he's wearing out by the time we're over the river. I give an extra kick and close to ten yards when he stops and turns.

Finally.

He holds out the backpack. *Thank you.* I must smile involuntarily because he smiles back and waves—then tosses my backpack off the side of the bridge.

No!

I lean over the railing in time to see it splash in the red water. The man resumes jogging across the bridge at a normal pace. I want to chase him down and stab him, but don't dare take my eyes off the backpack as it begins sailing downriver with the current.

My first instinct is to dive in after it, but reason wins out. I race back to the foot of the bridge and run like fire along the bank to catch up with the backpack.

"Hey, watch out!"

I look down in time to avoid a baby stroller, but not the curb next to it, landing on the grass with a somersault.

"Pay attention to where you're going," the mother scolds, but I'm already back on my feet, running and scanning the water. Where is it? *There.*

I come to a swirling eddy where the river bends. The backpack could get caught in it, maybe even get swept ashore. I descend to the water's edge, fingers on both hands crossed as the backpack reaches the eddy, bobs once, twice—and vanishes. I wait for it to pop up again, but it doesn't.

I gallop into the water, instantly realizing my mistake as the muddy bottom swallows my feet. The more I struggle, the farther I sink. The Cubs hat falls off and gets swept away by the current, which is threatening to tear me in two.

My fear turns to terror when the mud reaches my knees. I look around for help, but there's no one.

The worst thing you can do in a fight is freeze. Lucas Jackson.

A log juts from the bank behind me. I have to twist ninety degrees to reach it, abs and shoulders burning, reminding me of Lucas's basement, which helps calm me. *All in the core.*

The log's slippery, but the wood is soft. I dig my fingertips in and pull. My arm muscles look like thin bands of steel ready to pop out of my skin. I feel my legs rising inch by inch until they break free, shoes and socks left behind in mud graves.

I wrestle my way to the shore and collapse on a bench, staring at the one-square foot of the universe where my life sank. I picture my backpack on the river bottom, all alone, like me, being devoured by the mud, like I feel.

Gone. Everything. The cigar box. My sketchpad. The gun. The pictures of the two men ...

The bus to Lafayette is about to leave. Doesn't matter. The ticket was in the backpack.

I should have jumped off the bridge. The worst that could have happened was drowning.

24

I STAY on the bench a long time, drying in the sun. The rays are blinding. I reach for my nonexistent sunglasses in my nonexistent backpack.

My last lifeline gone, I consider surrendering, eyes flitting back to the bridge. The voices in my head are competing. The hiding girl from the dumpster says she wants to jump off, but the calm girl tells her it wouldn't help anything and reminds her, not in a mean way, that she's too chicken.

Meggie Tribet and I used to play a gruesome game. *Would You Rather?* Would you rather be locked in a room filled with rattlesnakes or slide down a hundred feet of razor blades? I picked any option that didn't involve not being able to breathe, my worst fear.

That day, on the bed with the tape on my mouth, I wasted precious seconds panicking about suffocating while stocky man was hurting Mom. This thought saves me. *You haven't suffered anything like Mom and Becky. Effing do something! You're a waste of space.*

I push off the bench and head back to downtown, cataloging my belongings as I go. The neck knife's still in place, and the bracelet. Lucas said not to get it wet. I fish some napkins out of a trash can and buff it dry. In the zippered pocket of my workout shorts, I find the fake driver's license and fifteen dollars.

Lucas asked what I planned to do when the money ran out. I said I hadn't thought about it. I should have. *Two thousand dollars.*

My travel choices have evaporated. Lucas talked about stealing a car. I'm not sure if he was joking but it doesn't matter. It could take weeks to find a car with keys in it. And it's a long way to Lafayette.

Hitchhiking is the only idea that comes to me. I've thought about it before but always had the money for trains and buses. Dangerous, like Lucas said. I've seen hitchhikers, but don't even know if it's legal.

The sidewalk scalds my bare feet. I enter a discount drugstore where the cool tiles feel like an ice rink by comparison. I find a rack of Louisiana roadmaps, locate Shreveport and trace I-49 as it follows the Red River all the way to Lafayette. Two hundred miles. Even farther than I thought.

Without a smart phone, I'll need the map, and I gotta have shoes, and something to carry stuff in. Everyone on the road has some kind of luggage. Need a story people will buy.

Runaway? No. My parents are big believers in growing up strong and independent. Everyone in my family hitchhikes.

My grandmother has cancer. She lives in Lafayette. I'm the only one in my family who can take care of her right now. We don't have a lot of money so sometimes I hitchhike.

It's kind of a desperate situation. My mom's boyfriend is hurting her. My brother's the only one who can help. He lives in Lafayette.

The last one would work best, but someone might call the cops, trying to help. Grandmothers are always getting sick and people love them. The first one is lame, but isn't subject to follow-up questions like, *Where in Lafayette does your grandmother live?*

I find a yellow plastic backpack on sale, a piece of junk, but it'll work for now. With the map that leaves six dollars. I track down a pair of sneakers. The only ones that fit are pink, but even on sale they cost fifteen dollars.

Getting arrested for shoplifting would be a disaster, but I'm not going to get far in bare feet. Maybe no one noticed me coming in. I tear off the price tag, put them on and go to the register to check out.

Behind the counter is a display of prepaid phones. I look up into the harsh fluorescent lights. *Thank you for being so smart to hide the money, Dad. It kept me going a long time. I'm sorry I lost it. ... I'm sorry for everything.*

On the way out, I hear a "Hey!" and take off down the sidewalk, rounding the first corner into an alley. When I'm sure no one's coming after me, I stop to catch my breath and study the map. I need to start on I-20, which merges into I-49. Just a few blocks away, crossing the river not far from where the backpack sank.

I'll need a sign, which reminds me of my pad, with the sketches and facial composites. The whole plan in Lafayette was to show the pictures around. Add *No plan* to the list of things I can't think about without my head collapsing.

I dig a piece of cardboard out of a garbage can and start my walk to the interstate. Passing a donut shop, I force on my bubbly teenager disguise and burst through the door.

"Hi! Our high school is holding a carwash. I was supposed to make the sign. *Du-uh*, the blonde forgot. Do you happen to have a marker I could borrow? Thanks so much!"

LAFAYETTE

"Thanks again! God bless."

* * *

I stand at the entrance ramp next to a line of orange cones guarding a bulldozer parked on the shoulder. Drivers look at me and some cars slow down, but no one stops, until a green car with a crumpled bumper pulls up with two men in the front seat.

"Hey baby, get in," the passenger says.

"You're going to Lafayette?"

He looks at the driver and says, "Yeah, sure."

"Um, no thanks. I'll wait."

"Bitch," he spits and they speed away.

Nice! Great form of transportation. I seethe about my back-pack until I notice a highway patrol car coming down the side street with its blinker pointed at me.

Frizzy blonde hair. A lady cop. It doesn't matter whether hitchhiking is legal or not. She's not going to pass me without stopping. Probably has kids herself. Here I am, all one-hundred and three pounds of me, standing on the road for the taking. I can hear her now. "Do you want to end up one of those kids on the side of a milk carton?"

I dash behind the bulldozer, crouching beside the tread and thumbing the license Lucas made for me. My only weapon against a cop. I'm Alice Miller from Chattanooga, just a regular girl on my way to kill two men.

Too many accelerating motors to distinguish them. Did she pass already?

I pop my head up in time to see her disappear beneath an overpass. Need to get moving. Can't be too picky. I step back out onto the shoulder and stick out my sign.

A beat-up Honda Civic passes, stops and backs up. I can't see through the tinted glass. The passenger window goes down. A skinny young driver with wavy black hair and skin so white his dragon tattoos glow like neon.

"You want a ride?" he says. "I'm going to Alexandria."

"How close is that to Lafayette?"

"About halfway."

"Are you safe?"

"You want a ride or not? Hurry up. I'm gonna get hit by a truck out here."

"Okay." I get in.

"I'm Alex," he says.

"Alex from Alexandria?"

"Shreveport. Got invited down there to jam at a party tonight."

I see the instrument cases piled in the backseat. They relax me.

"I'm Alice."

"Alex and Alice and their Amazing Adventure to Alexandria. Must be karma."

He sounds nice, but I don't trust anyone unless I have a reason to.

"What kind of music do you play?" I ask.

"Bluegrass."

"Seriously? I would have guessed punk rocker."

"Ah, fair Alice. Looks can be deceiving," he says. "I'm in a bluegrass band with my girlfriend, but she's got a solo gig tonight. What's your story?"

"Super-boring. Tell me about your girlfriend. What's she like?"

Jackpot. He's still talking about her an hour later as we approach a green sign announcing the Alexandria exit.

"Sounds like you two were meant for each other," I say. "Where do you think would be the best place to catch a ride?"

"Same as Shreveport, at the entrance ramp, but don't take a ride from anyone not going all the way to Lafayette. There's nothing in between but farms and bayou."

"What's bayou?"

"Swamp, basically."

We're on a long circular exit road when I see the big sign. Alex says "Uh-oh."

Louisiana State Police.

"Looks like a headquarters," he says. "That's where the entrance is back onto I-49 South. Bad luck."

I almost laugh. Luck? I forgot what it means. "Is hitchhiking legal in Louisiana?"

"I've heard it's legal if you stay off the roadway, but I wouldn't chance it here. If you want, you can hang with me tonight. In the morning, I can drop you off at the exit outside the city."

"Could you possibly do that now?"

"Sorry, already running late. I'm sure people would be cool with you coming to the party. Free food and drink."

The sky is turning orange. If I don't get a ride fast, I'll be stuck here in the dark with no place to go. If I do get a ride, I'll be stuck somewhere else in the dark, all assuming I don't get arrested first. A free meal and place to stay for the night isn't the worst option in the world, but it means taking a chance that Alex isn't evil. I study him: dreamy-eyed, sweet laugh, lover of his girlfriend.

"Okay," I say.

* * *

Such a weird feeling, being *out*. The only humans I've socialized with in two months have been Lucas and Kiona. I find a cushy chair in the living room and camp there. Everyone is nice. No one hassles me.

I had no idea how many people in the world smoke marijuana. The living room is clouded with it. Maybe it's my imagination but I think I might be feeling the effects. The food is super-good. Jambalaya, with chicken—haha, of course.

The party goes late. I dose off in the chair before Alex wakes me and says it's time to go.

We drive to the bass player's house. No one's mentioned sleeping arrangements. They'd better not have any funny ideas. But I worry for nothing. We enter a dark house and the bass player points me to a couch as he and Alex stumble off to other rooms.

I twist and turn to get comfortable. The couch isn't very wide and the fabric smells funky, but at least I don't have to worry about my backpack getting stolen while I sleep. The joy of silver linings.

When the house gets quiet I practice pulling out the knife, counting to one hundred.

25

"**BE SAFE,**" Alex says the next morning as I'm climbing out of the Civic at the interstate exit north of Alexandria. I wave goodbye and walk to the entrance ramp going south, parking myself on a sun-burnt patch of grass off the roadway and holding out the sign.

A woman in a small car approaches. I put on my sweetest smile, but she doesn't stop. Neither does anyone else.

Thirty minutes later I'm getting nervous about being stranded in the heat in the middle of nowhere when a nice silver car slows down. A Lexus. The dark passenger window lowers.

"You need a ride to Lafayette?"

It's a man with thinning brown hair and wire-rim glasses. He reminds me of my science teacher. Maybe in his forties, but I'm terrible at guessing ages.

"Uh, yeah." So hard to evaluate people on the spot. Khaki dress pants, tucked-in polo shirt. The inside of the car is immaculate. "Are you safe?" I ask.

He laughs. "Yes, I promise. That's why I stopped. I have a daughter about your age."

"Okay."

I get in. The air is nice and cool. Taylor Swift is playing at a low volume as we cruise onto the interstate.

"I'm Jim," he says. "Would you mind putting on your seatbelt?"

"Oh, sure. I'm Alice. Thanks for the ride."

"No problem. Going there anyway."

"You like Taylor Swift?"

"It's my daughter's CD, but I'll make a confession and say, yes, I actually do like her. Don't tell anyone." He chuckles.

"You live in Lafayette?" I ask.

"Just go there on business. I've been driving this route for years. From Lafayette I go on to New Orleans. I'm in sales. What's there for you?"

"Going to visit my grandmother. I'm from Chattanooga."

"How'd you end up in Alexandria?"

I tell him I rode there with a musician friend, but that's as far as he was going. "How old is your daughter?" I ask, trying to deflect the conversation away from me.

"Seventeen. Already applying to college. That'll make a dad feel old in a hurry. How old are you?"

"Sixteen."

"Really? You look younger."

"I know. How long does it take to get to Lafayette?" I ask as we pass the exit Alex took yesterday.

"About an hour and a half."

A tractor trailer blows past us. "Damn, I hate those trucks," he says. "Death on wheels. You hitchhike much?"

"Not much. Too dangerous."

"Good. If I found out my daughter was hitchhiking I'd ground her for a year. Worse, I'd take her phone away." He chuckles again. "What grade are you in?"

"Going into eleventh," I say. I hadn't calculated it. I think that's right.

"Do you like school?"

"It's fine. Hey, you can turn up Taylor Swift if you want. I like her too."

"I can listen to her anytime. It gets boring on the road. I enjoy having someone to talk to."

Great.

"Are you thinking about college yet?"

"Nope. What do you sell?"

"Business software. I'd tell you all about it, but it's as boring as sin," he says.

I believe it, but ask what kind before he can force in another question.

"*CRM*, customer relationship management. Like I said, boring."

"Where are you from?"

"Illinois."

"Is that a nice place?"

"Not bad. So what do you want to be when you grow up? Not that you're not already grown up. My daughter would lecture me for that one."

"I don't know."

He keeps talking and I switch to robo-mode. Yes, no, maybe, gazing out the window. Alex was right. Nothing out here but baked farmland and swampy woods. Every so often we pass an exit with the name of a town, but I never see one.

Jim finally shuts up to hum along to Taylor Swift. I concentrate on what to do when I get to Lafayette. First I need access to a computer, then money.

"You hungry?" Jim says. "I need lunch and a driving break. My treat."

"Um, I don't see anything around here."

"At the next exit there's a family restaurant with real home cooking. It's a couple of miles off the interstate, but a thousand times better than a truck stop or fast-food. I spend most of my time on the road and just can't eat that stuff anymore."

I'm not thrilled about getting away from the interstate, but Jim's driving so I don't feel like I have a choice. I am hungry and another free meal will save me from having to spend my last six dollars.

"Homemade apple pie to die for," Jim says.

"Alright."

We veer off an exit with a green *Saint Landry* sign onto an empty highway. Same landscape of farms and marshland. We drive several minutes before another sign announces we're entering a town, but it's so tiny we pass through it without even coming to a stop sign. When we get to the next town I'm sure it's been more than a couple of miles.

"Is this where the restaurant is?"

"Just on the other side. I guess I underestimated the miles a little. We're almost there."

This town has one stoplight. We leave it in the rearview mirror.

"I think we might be lost," I say. "We should probably go back."

"We're not lost."

"I'd really rather go back."

"Too bad this isn't your car and you're not driving," he says.

"What?" The change in his tone is so sudden I'm not sure if he's joking.

"Alice, admit it. You're a runaway."

The friendly dad voice is gone, the new one cold and dark.

"No, I'm not. I'm on my way to my grandmother's."

"Bullshit."

"I appreciate the ride, but I have to insist we go back now."

"Oh, you insist." He laughs and swerves off the highway onto a dirt road lined on both sides by green water with moss-draped cypress trees growing out of it.

"There's no restaurant here," I say.

"No. There's not."

Rocks bounce off the chassis. He curses them but doesn't slow down. The doors are locked and the dang seatbelt has me pinned to the seat. The hiding girl starts to panic, but calm girl says take deep breaths and think.

"How do you make enough money to live as a runaway?"

"I told you, I'm not a runaway."

"And I told you that's bullshit so quit saying it. Believe me, I know runaways. I've picked up plenty of them. One thing you all have in common is you need money and I'm going to give you some because I'm a nice guy, but you have to do me a little favor."

"What kind of favor?"

"Oh, come on. You seem like a bright girl. I'm sure you can figure it out."

We drive another mile in silence before he pulls the car off the road onto a splat of dirt next to the marsh. "What's your answer?" he says.

"I still don't know what you're talking about. I thought we were going to lunch."

"Think real hard." He releases his seatbelt and starts unbuckling his pants. "You get ten bucks and we finish our ride to Lafayette. Win-win for everyone."

"What if I say no?" I stare out the windshield. Can't look at him.

"There was a girl who said no a few months ago. You could dig her up and ask her."

"Make it fifty dollars."

A disgusting snort. "I knew it. All runaways are sluts, but most aren't half as pretty as you. Ten bucks."

"Forty."

"Ten."

I clear my throat. "Alright. Can we do it outside?"

"Suits me," he says, unlocking the doors.

I get out. Water on both sides. Nowhere to run. Somewhere nearby a barred owl is howling. We had them in Georgia. They sound more like wolves than owls.

"I'm not really an expert at this," I say, staring at the ground.

"Get on your knees. I'll talk you through it."

I kneel down and make myself look. I don't have any choice. "Are you sure you want to make me do this?" I say.

He laughs. "Very sure."

I don't think he understood the question.

Being young and a girl, you gonna have the element of surprise every time unless you fuck up.

"What if I told you I'm really only thirteen?"

"I'd say it's my lucky day. Let's get going."

For a particularly ugly and disgustin' way to die, if you happen to be in the right position, you can thrust up at the bottom of the crotch. They a soft spot there. You go right up into the large intestine.

"I have a question. Do you really have a daughter?"

"Why do you wanna know?"

"I feel sorry for her."

In a move made smooth by thousands of repetitions, I slide the neck knife out and, using both hands, rip upward with every fiber of my being, from my core to my fingertips. *Just like with men, you got to cut deep.* The pig farm.

A wrenched look of disbelief before he screams and starts to topple. I jerk the knife out and move out of the way. A polluted sewer smell makes me gag as he hits the ground. He's thrashing, clutching his groin, continuing to scream.

Finish him! Finish him! A new scary voice. Where did she come from?

I raise the knife and slash the side of his neck. Carotid artery. Blood sprays like a fountain. He gurgles and jerks before falling silent and still. I'm drenched in blood for the second time in two days.

The whole scene feels like I'm watching a movie starring someone who looks like me. There's even a soundtrack, the barred owl's forlorn yowling.

Can you cut a man? Can you stick this into livin', breathin' flesh?

Yes, I can, Lucas. So there.

I drag him by the ankles to the water's edge. He must weigh two hundred pounds. No way could I have done it three weeks ago. *Thanks, Kiona.* In his pockets I find a nylon wallet, keyring and a phone. The phone's locked. Using it would be stupid anyway. The police will try to track it for sure. I throw it in the water. Any location signal shouldn't last long.

The wallet has almost two hundred dollars in it which I stuff in my pocket.

A driver's license. Not Jim. *Scott Brooker.* But he really was from Illinois. Champaign. There's a picture of his wife and daughter. The daughter looks like him. He has credit cards, but I can't use them. Like the phone, too easy to track. My first thought is to scatter them in the water, but they probably float. The longer it takes the police to identify Brooker the better off I'll be.

I roll his body into the pond, hoping it will sink but it doesn't. His chubby white butt pokes up like an island. His blood blooming against the green algae reminds me of Christmas.

I just killed a man. I turned thirteen two days ago and I'm a killer. *Happy birthday to me, happy birthday to me,* sings the new scary girl. She's wearing a purple gown and drinking Champagne, *not* from Champaign.

A crazed laugh from somewhere silences the owl. Startled, I look around but there's no one there.

I'm not sure what I feel. I don't feel bad about Brooker. I don't really feel anything. But I'm going to hell for sure now and that bothers me ... or maybe I'm already there. It doesn't seem like I'm really here.

My head's buzzing, too full, like it's counting down to an explosion. I rinse the knife in the pond and hold it to the sun.

"To good times with knives, Lucas," I say and press the blade against my forearm. As the crease fills with blood I imagine a silver submarine slicing through the Red River in search of my backpack.

At first it doesn't hurt. When it does the pressure in my head pops like a balloon. *I exist,* but who am I? Calm girl is shaking her head, dismayed. The scary girl looks impressed. Hiding girl is nowhere to be found.

I still hear buzzing, but it's only the flies gathering on Brooker.

Lucas didn't teach me what to do after a killing, but I'm sure it doesn't include hanging around the crime scene. I drag over an enormous branch to hide the body and jump in the car.

A droplet of my blood falls to the floorboard and disappears in the black carpet. I grab coffee-stained napkins from the drink tray and stick them to the cut.

Why did I do that? *Stoo-pid.*

A button on the dashboard says, *Engine: Start Stop.* I push it. Nothing happens.

Now what? I push buttons on the remote. The doors lock and unlock and the trunk pops open. I push a red one that sets off horn blasts and flashing headlights. *Jeez.* I hold it until the sound dies.

The car was working fine when we got here. Has to be something simple. The manual in the glove compartment is a freaking encyclopedia, but there's a quick-start guide at the front. *Start the engine: Push the Start/Stop button while depressing the brake pedal.*

That's all? The car comes to life, dashboard shouting, *Make a U-turn. Turn right on Highway 106.* I turn down the volume and adjust the seat. In the mirror I see the hollow-eyed, blood-stained face of a girl I used to know, and the trunk lid sticking up. Everything's *such a pain.* I get out and close it.

Now all I have to do is turn a car to go in the opposite direction for the first time in my life in a tiny space with water on both sides. *Alrighty then.* One of Mom's favorite expressions. Foot welded to the brake, I ease the car into reverse.

It takes ten minutes but I manage to get the car pointed toward the highway. I creep down the rocky road, scanning for a place to stop and get my head together.

I find one, a grassy clearing guarded by pine trees. I coast behind them and shut off the motor.

Calm girl says THINK. No one saw me with Scott Brooker. We didn't stop anywhere so I'm not on any surveillance cameras. *Clean yourself. Clean the car.*

I wade into the swamp, fully dressed, gripping a branch in case the bayou starts to swallow me like the Red River. Slimy plants whipsaw me, but the algae is so thick I can't see them.

So much blood. No choice but to go all the way under. I close my eyes and hold my nose. When I climb out I'm tinted green.

* * *

Erasing Scott Brooker's life is taking too long. I'm waiting for his suitcase and briefcase to sink. I filled them with his every trace, including the wallet, even the car manual, then added rocks and cut holes in the sides with—*ta da!*—a multitool. I found it in the console. Pliers, screwdrivers, scissors, all kinds of great stuff. So many times I could have used it.

He had a laptop I was tempted to keep, but like the phone, password-protected and too easy to trace. I whirled it into the bayou like a discus.

All I keep are the cash, multitool, a stash of protein bars and two clean t-shirts. The thought of Brooker's shirts against my skin makes me itch, but mine are soaking wet and still show blotches of blood. I make the switch, wrapping my shirts around a rock and sinking them.

I check myself in the mirror as I crank up the car. The blood's gone, but I look like a drowned rat—make that a drowned mouse, way too young to drive. Need to upgrade my appearance as soon as possible. I raise the seat to look taller, put the car in reverse and back up.

Wham.

Oops. A tree. *Easy, easy.*

I start out shaky but get more confident as I close in on I-49. Then I see the monster trucks. Brooker was right about them.

I remember to use the turn signal when I get to the ramp. I accelerate, feeling like I'm in a NASCAR race until I notice the cars behind me jamming on their brakes and switching lanes. I edge up to fifty-five.

The car's easy to drive. Just point it where you want it to go. I roll my shoulders, stress bones crackling, and turn on the radio, scanning until I find a country station. Waylon Jennings is singing that being crazy kept him from going insane. Haha, I don't think it's working for me.

Another green sign. *Lafayette 50 Miles*. I don't let myself think there's nothing there for me. I can't.

26

AI YAI YAI. I just side-swiped a Toyota pulling into a parking space at a drugstore in Opelousas, outside of Lafayette. I back out and hurry to the other side of the store.

Carrying a shopping basket, I use Scott Brooker's cash to stock up on the cheapest versions of everything I need: hygiene stuff, makeup, antibacterial ointment and bandages for my stupid arm, pocket-sized notebook, three-pack of pencils, world's ugliest sunglasses (but only $1.99!) and wet wipes to clean the car.

In the hair product aisle I hear Lucas's voice. *That blonde hair shines like a fuckin' beacon.* I pick out a color called *Pecan Brown.*

Back in the car I tend to my cut. I'm disgusted at myself, but why did it feel good? I bandage it and roll deodorant up and down my arms and legs to hide the rotten-egg smell from the bayou.

I study the Louisiana map and eat one of Brooker's protein bars. The map has insets for major cities, including Lafayette.

Where to sleep? One of the first things you learn on the street is the need to figure out a place to sleep way before you actually want to go to sleep. There's a park called Acadiana in the northeast corner. Hard to tell how big it is from the little green trapezoid.

The public library is downtown. I'll start there. Need a computer more than anything.

The traffic as I come into Lafayette winds me tight as a rope.

Has anyone found Scott Brooker? How fast can they identify him? Probably depends how long it takes for someone to report him missing, unless they find his stuff. Once they figure it out, they'll be looking for his car. The navigation system is off but it might still be tracking me.

If the police find the Lexus in Lafayette, they'll be looking for his killer here. The best thing would be to give the car to someone leaving town, or let them steal it. I could leave it on the interstate but the police would probably find it first. People are driving on the interstate, not walking.

Two months ago my biggest worry was whether a cool kid at school liked me.

I end up driving to a mall and backing the car up to a wall to hide the license plate. I use the wipes to clean everything I touched, scrutinizing every inch of the interior for stray blonde hairs. It's taking too long, but I force myself not to rush. Can't leave any clues behind.

My last job is to disconnect the battery cable with the multitool to cut off any GPS. I close the hood, wipe my fingerprints and walk away. Down the street, I use the last of the wipes to clean the remote and bury it in a garbage can.

The heat and humidity bear down on me as I walk to downtown. Hard to believe I'm actually here. A sign says *Welcome to Lafayette, Home of the Ragin' Cajuns*. The streets are kind of pretty, with tall trees lining wide sidewalks.

I study the face of every man I pass. My plodding steps remind me my only food today was the protein bar. I go into a pizza place and order the cheapest thing on the menu, a plain, personal-sized pizza. Scott Brooker's money is already disappearing.

"I think I have a coupon for thirty percent off in here," I say to the girl behind the counter, rummaging through the yellow backpack. "Dang, can't find it." She says no problem and gives me the discount.

The library is a red-brick building with an artsy round front.

I pull on the door but it's locked. I try a different door, same result. No way. It's only five o'clock. The sign says it's open until nine. I bang on the glass until a tall woman with red hair in a ponytail comes out.

"Hi, I need to use a computer."

"We're closed."

"The sign says you're open until nine."

She points to the bottom. "Um, it's Saturday."

"Already?" The last few days have seemed like one long one. "Oh, right," I say. "I've been taking care of my grandma and the days kind of run together. She doesn't have a computer so I thought I'd try here."

She tells me to come back tomorrow. They open at noon on Sunday, first-come, first-served.

"Is there an internet café around here?"

"With computers? Not anymore. Free wifi," she shrugs. "Sorry."

"It's fine. I'll be back tomorrow."

Back out in the heat: *Of course it's not fine.* I'm frazzled, fried and my damp shorts are rubbing my legs raw. I get out the map and look for the park I spotted. Acadiana. Looks like about a three-mile walk. Kiona was surprised by my cardio stamina. One day back on the streets and I remember how I got it.

* * *

Sweet! The map inset did not do justice to Acadiana Park. Way bigger than I expected with thick woods and even a campground. I enter from the side to avoid the office in front, almost getting hit by a mountain bike with fat tires when I step onto a trail.

The woods are moist and mossy with a pungent musky smell. A bird that looks like a sparrow trills an *ooh-ooh-ee-oh* song that doesn't sound anything like a sparrow. I go off trail in search of my version of the perfect hotel room and find it, a leaf-covered patch of dry ground encircled by thicket. *Shelter.*

I slip the backpack off. It lands on a rock that tears a big hole in the cheap plastic. Of course. I sit down and get comfortable.

It takes five minutes before I'm fidgeting. How did I possibly do this for an entire month? It's only dusk—I'm here for twelve hours.

In shrinking light I get out my new pencils and mini-pad to make a list of what I need to look up on the computer, pausing to smash a fat mosquito digging into my writing hand. It bursts with blood like a tiny water balloon and I have to chase away a picture of Scott Brooker's exploding carotid artery.

Darkness finds me stalking in circles around the mouse-house, but it doesn't calm my electrified brain. *Need something.* Cutting comes to mind. *No.*

I spot a branch in the shadows above me, which turns into a pullup bar which turns into a full workout, after which I plunk onto the mat of leaves, gassed, sponging sweat from my face with Scott Brooker's shirts.

A half-moon is out, but I can only catch glimpses of it through the branches. I need a candle. I had one before, I'm pretty sure. Pixelated memories of the robot girl, sitting alone in the woods, warming her hands on a tiny flame.

Using the backpack as a pillow, I eventually fall asleep but it's a restless night of slapping mosquitoes and adjusting my body around knotty tree roots.

I pack up early in the morning and make my way to the campground, lurking in the trees at the perimeter, sizing it up. A few tents but mostly RVs on asphalt pads, air conditioners churning.

I zero in on a faucet. *Water.*

I'm alternating between drinking long slurps and rinsing algae and dirt from my face, arms and legs when a noise from behind makes me start.

An older woman, short and rosy-faced with a hairdo of brown ringlets, is holding a bucket. "Sorry to sneak up on you," she says.

"That's okay."

"I'm Darla," she says in a Southern accent. Sounds familiar, but I can't place it. Definitely not Georgia.

"I'm Alice."

Something intense going on behind her brown eyes. "Are you staying at the campground?" she says.

"Yes, ma'am. I'm here with my aunt. She's a big camper. *Huge* camper."

"You know there are showers, right?"

I'm dripping like I just stepped out of a carwash. "Just freshening up a little."

"How long are you and your aunt here for?" she says.

"Not really sure. I just go wherever she goes." I move my hand like a bird flying.

Another woman approaches, taller and older, with glasses and gray hair. "Darla, did you say you wanted bacon or sausage?" she says in a stronger accent. She notices me. "Well, hello there."

"Alice, this is Peggy, my wife."

"Oh, hi," I say.

"We both just retired in Arkansas and decided to see the country. That's our little home over there." Darla points to a cute pink camper. A picnic table sits beneath a blue awning extending from the side.

"You just drive around and stay in campgrounds?"

"That's the plan," Darla says. "We're just getting started."

"Sounds fun." It really does. I always loved camping with my family. Maybe that's how I could spend my life.

It hits me why their accents are familiar. Same as the man with the cowboy hat on the bus to Texarkana. *Arkansans.* Another allowance assignment from Mom. Memorize the nicknames for the people of every state. *Floridians, Michiganders …*

"So far, so good," Peggy laughs. "We haven't killed each other yet."

"Notice she said *yet?*" Darla gives Peggy a nod. "Alice, are you hungry? Peggy here is one heckuva breakfast cook."

"She ain't lying about that," Peggy says. "I run with the big dogs when it comes to breakfast."

Shelter water food. Trifecta. "Sure!"

"Do you need to ask your aunt?" Darla asks.

"Oh, she won't mind. She's still sleeping."

Peggy's breakfast is to die for, no disrespect intended to Scott Brooker. Yes, an insane joke, but that's just because I'm going insane. Scrambled eggs, hash browns, biscuits, even fresh strawberries. I skip the bacon.

When they turn down my offer to help clean up, I sling on the backpack. "I should get going. My aunt is probably up by now. Thanks again for the meal." I need to get to the library early in case there's a line for the computers.

"What's your aunt's name?" Darla asks. "In case we run into her."

This one's sneaky. I know sneaky. "Kiona. Well, bye." I stroll back past the faucet and veer into the woods.

27

WAITING FOR the library to open, I chew on my hair and go over the list I made last night in the woods. Scratched out at the bottom is *Search Scott Brooker murder.* Not a good search trail to leave behind.

I'm first in line when the doors open. The inside is bright and airy with wavy walls and ceilings like a spaceship. A sweet old lady with a silver perm, someone's grandma, greets me from behind the counter. I fill out a form as Alice Miller and go to the last computer, scanning the ceilings for surveillance cameras. Don't see any, one advantage of a small city.

I open a search engine and type *Lucas Ellington Jackson Memphis*, pausing before I hit enter. If Lucas is dead I'm dead, or might as well be.

When I push the key my breath catches. I'm not sure what to feel. Being happy seems obscene. It's at the top of the list. I click on the link.

Man in Critical Condition after Shooting
Memphis police are investigating the shooting of a 32-year-old Memphis man yesterday afternoon. Lucas Ellington Jackson was shot while stopped in his vehicle at a light in South Memphis.

An ambulance took Jackson to the Regional Medical Center where he is listed in critical condition.

Critical condition, but *alive.* Dated two days ago. I'm shocked there aren't more details. I expected a big story, but remember a conversation we had about the teddy bears, the *death bears*.

"How can so many people get shot and nobody does anything?" I asked.

"Nobody gives a shit about black men gettin' shot. Barely makes the news. If it was white people they'd call out the fuckin' National Guard."

Speaking of white people, no mention of one running from his car. I guess he was right about folks not talking to the police. I search for more, but that's all there is.

I just *knew* he was alive ... that's not true. I thought he was dead. I find the Regional Medical Center and write down the phone number.

Kiona could tell me everything, if I knew how to find her. I don't know the name of her gym, but from the way she came and went, it can't be too far from Lucas's building.

I search *Memphis boxing gym*. A map icon shows a Max's Gym in South Memphis. Boxing and martial arts lessons. No website. I write down the number, clean the browser and turn off the computer. I need a phone now.

"Back in a few," I chirp to the gray-haired librarian. "I have to go make lunch for my memaw. Tuna salad on toast. Her favorite." She looks like she wants to adopt me. Such an effing liar.

I find a drugstore and buy a dumb phone with talk and text for one month, cheapest one they have. Can't afford a smart phone now and have more reason than ever to worry about being tracked. My first call is to the hospital.

"Regional Medical Center. How may I direct your call?"

"I'm trying to reach a patient, Lucas Jackson."

The phone starts ringing again.

"Patient information."

"I'm looking for a patient named Lucas Jackson."

Pause. "No Lucas Jackson."

"No, I'm sure he's there. The newspaper said so. Lucas Ellington Jackson."

"Alright, I see we did have a Lucas Jackson, but he checked out yesterday."

"Checked out?"

"Left the hospital."

"I thought he was in critical condition."

"I don't have that kind of information."

"Can I talk to his doctor or nurse?" But she already disconnected me.

I punch in the number for Max's Gym.

"Ya."

"Hi, I'm trying to reach a friend of mine. She works there. I mean, I'm pretty sure. Her name is Kiona."

"Kiona?"

"Yes! You know her?"

"Ya, know Kiona. She work here."

"Can I talk to her?"

"Not here. Friend got shot."

"I know. He was my friend too. That's why I'm calling. Do you know anything about him? I called the hospital and they said he left."

"If you find Kiona, tell her she's missing her appointments and pissing off clients." He hangs up.

People! I jam the phone in my backpack and tromp back to the library.

"Me again," I say brightly.

I go to a different computer and type in *Durty Delphine's*, immediately confronted by the witch's face. I scroll past her, suppressing the twitch of a trigger. Basic website. Hours, menu, a few pictures. I know the interior from the videos, but never saw the front, mustard-yellow with a multicolored Durty Delphine's neon sign. Some of the letters are out. At night it looks like *Durt_ Delp_ _ ne's*.

It's in the middle of a block, across from a bank, not very far from the library. There's a craft store on the corner called Mary's Maybes.

But now what? Everything depended on having the pictures of the two men. With no ideas I move to the last thing on the list. *Calby Murders.*

Nothing new. I shake my head in disgust. What is wrong with the police down there? There should be a hundred news articles with my sketches of the two men by now.

The sketches!

Du-uh. I sent them as email attachments. All I have to do is find the email and print them. I go to my burner account for Robert Williams, but can't remember the password. I wrote it in my sketchpad.

I try *lucas, becky,* even *mrsdraper* before the computer threatens to lock me out. Then it comes back. Of course. My purpose:

justicecomeslate

I'm surprised to see a new message in the inbox with the subject line *Calby Murders.* Don't tell me, the police are so lame that now it takes a week just to get an automated reply. I click on it.

Dear Emily:

An earthquake starts at the top of my head and cracks every bone in my body. Impossible. My first thought is I accidentally logged onto my old home account but the header shows I'm in the burner account.

> *First, I am very glad you are alive. My name is Jeff*
> *Forster. I'm the FBI agent in charge of the federal side*
> *of the investigation into the terrible crimes committed*
> *against you and your family.*

Cannot be. I sent those messages from the internet café in Memphis. The most they could have done was track the IP address to the café. Must be some kind of trick.

> *Our handwriting analysts have determined that you*
> *are "Robert Williams."*

I typed those messages. Definitely a trick.

> *Because you were trying to protect your identity, I know receiving this message must come as a surprise and I apologize for that. I have been studying you for several weeks. I know you to be a highly intelligent and inquisitive young woman, so let me explain.*
>
> *In addition to handwriting, the FBI has "text analysts" who examine the content of writings and compare them to other writings by the same person. Doing that in your case, with the help of your teachers, gave us some hints, but were not conclusive.*
>
> *However, the sketches you sent were. Mr. McKennan, your art teacher, recognized them immediately. He loaned us one of your drawings for comparison. It was still hanging in his classroom, a compliment to you.*

A drop of drool rolls down my chin. Mr. McKennan taught me art for three years in elementary school. He was the first person who said I have art talent. I know the picture the FBI guy is talking about: a portrait of Mr. McKennan I drew for his birthday.

> *Our experts confirmed his opinion by matching characteristics such as stroke angle, pencil pressure and overall style.*
>
> *Mr. McKennan did not know the reason for our visit and was only trying to help. Everyone in your community is devastated by what happened. We all are.*
>
> *Which brings me to the point of this email. We need to find you and get you to come in quickly. First and foremost, we are worried about your safety. How you managed to survive this long is a mystery we are all anxious to learn, but you are in a dangerous situation.*

Same words as Lucas. *Maybe you forgot. You in a dangerous fuckin' situation.* As if I needed constant reminding.

> *We also need your help to prosecute the men who hurt you and your family. We are in possession of new evidence, but without you—the only eyewitness—it will not be sufficient to arrest or convict.*
>
> *I am sending this from my personal email account.*

I check the sender line: *jaforster@fbi.gov.*

> *It is vitally important you contact me without delay. You can email me or call my personal cell number.*

He gives a number, which I write down in my pocket pad.

> *I can't imagine what you've been through and the last thing I want is to send you running again, but you need to know there are people in my office urging me to put out a nationwide alert for you.*
>
> *I want to help you stop running. I am on your side. Please contact me.*
>
> *Jeffrey A. Forster*
> *Special Agent*
> *Federal Bureau of Investigation*

The old lady who checked me in is trolling behind the line of computers, examining the screens with stooped shoulders. Low-tech surveillance. I ask if I can print something. She points to a printer in the corner and whispers, "Dear, a library patron has complained that your body odor is ... offensive."

"Do I have to leave?"

"No, no. I just wanted to let you know, in case you were unaware."

"Don't worry. I'm aware. I'm almost done."

She pats me on the shoulder and moves on. I find my email with the sketches and print the attachments. Image one: stocky man. Image two: tall man.

I wave to the librarian on the way out. "I'll be sure to smell better when I come back." I'll definitely need to come back.

"Thank you for being so understanding, dear."

"No problem!"

Time for a clothes switch. I've stunk before, but no one's ever filed an official complaint. I despise wearing Brooker's shirts anyway. I'll buy another set of clothes and go back to Acadiana Park, use the campground showers to clean up and dye my hair.

One important thing to do first.

Contradictions punch it out in my head as I walk. In this corner, Lucas alive. In that corner, Lucas in critical condition. Nothing better, nothing worse. Same with the sketches and the FBI. The sketches pick me up—on track again with a plan—but Special Agent Jeffrey Forster's email knocks me back down.

It has to be real. No one could have made up that stuff about Mr. McKennan. I'm tempted to ignore it, put it in a box with the rest of my problems, but if he's telling the truth about a nationwide alert, the best thing might be to write back and try to buy time.

Three blocks south, turn left, four more blocks and I come to Mary's Maybes, the craft store. In the window is a life-sized doll, a skeleton of white bones on black fabric, wearing a wig the same color as my hair. It weirds me out. A faded sign says, *Mardi Gras is coming. Let us help you plan ahead.*

I hang a left and Durty Delphine's pushes away all other thoughts.

I lean against the side of the bank across the street to study who comes and goes, but no one does. There's no movement at all behind the windows. Then I see the *Closed* sign, which doesn't make sense. I checked the hours on the website and ... oh, jeez, it's Sunday. Have to start keeping track.

Just as well. Need to clean up and make a plan.

28

THAT BIRD again. *Ooh-ooh-ee-oo, ooh-ooh-ee-oo.* My ears hear, *I can see you, I can see you.* Late afternoon and I just finished making a new bed in my sleeping spot at Acadiana Park, stuffing dry-cleaning bags with leaves.

I spread my shopping haul on top. From a thrift store I got long tan pants, two white tees, and a black canvas backpack. Stuff kept falling out the hole in the plastic one. The dry-cleaning bags were piled in a corner. The clerk said take as many as I want. At a dollar store I got socks, underwear, a votive candle and a lighter. I bought apples, almonds, peanut butter, crackers and bug spray at a grocery store.

I sink into the new bed and lean against the tree. A butterfly with blue wings trimmed in black floats to a rest on a bush. Becky would be able to tell me what kind it is. That girl *loved* butterflies. Her entire room was covered with pictures of them.

Pulling off my shoplifted shoes, I wiggle my gummy toes and bite into an apple, the juice running down my chin. A breeze picks up and something like contentment fills me, just for a second. No walking, drowning or stabbing. Just eating an apple in the woods.

Dark clouds move above the branches. I wish I could see them better. I love sky, any kind, sunny or stormy, except when it's raining on me. Sometimes I wish I could be sky.

Mom, I miss you so much. I wish I could take back every time I was a brat.

Becky, I hope heaven is filled with butterflies.

Dad, I'm so, so sorry.

A tear leaks, but I refuse to let it take control of me.

What should I do when I get to Durty Delphine's? I need a plan for showing the sketches around. Have to go inside, can't just stop people on the street asking, *Have you seen these men?* Also need to be careful. It's a longshot, but if tall man or stocky man are around, they'll try to kill me. Obviously.

I need a story:

I'm looking for my cousin. His name's Ronnie. I think he might have worked here. I have a picture of him. Well, it's not exactly a picture …

My mom fell on the sidewalk and a nice man named Ronnie helped her. My family wants to thank him. He had on a Durty Delphine's t-shirt. I have a picture of him. Well, it's not exactly a picture …

I met a rapist-murderer named Ronnie and I'm here to slash his throat to the bone with my neck knife. I have a picture of him. Well, it's not exactly a picture …

I swallow another maniac laugh, having narrowed their source down to the scary girl. Need to stay hidden. Slapping at mosquitoes provides a distraction. They've always loved my juicy blood and the ones in Louisiana are no exception. I coat myself with bug spray and tear open the bag of almonds.

A sound in the brush freezes me. I reach for the neck knife, but it's only a mutt scooching through a hole in the bushes, wagging his tail.

"Hey, fella," I say, scratching his neck. "Where'd you come from?"

"Buddy! Buddy!"

A man.

"Go, go," I whisper to Buddy, pushing him away, but he just licks my face. The man is crashing through the bushes.

"Buddy! Buddy!"

At the last second Buddy snorts and runs back through the

hole he came in from. I sigh and lie back. I forgot how exciting life on the road can be, just the ordinary stuff.

* * *

I head for the campground after dark, lighting the path with the new burner phone. Unfortunately, I never charged it and the light dies halfway there. Cocooned within the canopy of trees, I can't even see my feet. I trip along, using the smell of grilling hamburgers as a homing point until I emerge from the woods.

As I make my way along the asphalt road, people wave or say hi. Campers are friendly people. I don't think I ever met one who wasn't nice.

The park office is dark and empty. Moths crowd a yellow light above the door of the women's restroom.

Act like you belong. Bored or bothered. Take that bathroom like you own it.

Empty, a relief. I despise public showers, but at least these have curtains.

Thirty minutes later I'm in my new pants and tees, staring at a stranger in the mirror. A brunette. Weird, but I like it. Different inside, different outside. It also hides the torn ends. I feel almost like a girl. *Ha.* Funny-funny and funny-strange. I'm not sure what I am now, but it's definitely not a girl. I hide my trashed clothes at the bottom of a garbage can.

Even with the brown hair, I feel exposed outside with nothing covering my head. I miss my hoodie, a faithful pillow, blanket and invisibility cloak almost from the beginning. I'd spend more time missing it, but a man in a khaki uniform is blocking my path.

"Good evening," he says.

"Hello."

He flashes a badge pinned to his shirt. "I'm Officer Talley, Lafayette Parish Parks. We had a report of a young girl wandering around the park alone."

"So?"

"*So* is you happen to be a young girl wandering around the park alone."

"I'm not wandering and I'm not alone. I was just using the shower." Counterpunch: "Are you stalking me in the bathroom? That's pretty creepy." I skirt around him and continue walking.

"Young lady, I would advise you to stop." A cop voice.

"Seriously?" I say, but I can tell from his look it's the wrong strategy. It worked with the security guard in Shreveport, but it's usually smarter to be compliant. *Yes, sir. No, sir.* I'm wearing the neck knife, a murder weapon.

"I'm sorry, I didn't mean to be rude," I say. "You caught me by surprise."

"Are you a guest here?"

"Yes, sir."

"Where are you staying?"

"With my aunt."

"Not with. Where?"

"Right over there." I do a half-wave, half-point.

"What say we go meet your aunt and clear this up?"

"No problem."

I'll lead him to the last campsite and take off into the woods. It's dark as coal out there. If I get a head start, maybe I can lose him.

We stroll side by side down the paved road that loops the campsites, passing Darla and Peggy's trailer. We're at the end when Officer Talley says, "Did we miss it?"

"You know, sometimes I get lost in this place. I think my aunt's on the other side. Over there," I point. I wait for him to look, but he keeps his eyes fixed on me.

He air-pokes me with a finger. "You are coming with me. What's your name?"

"Alice!"

A flashlight in the distance weaves back and forth. "Alice!" The light gets closer. A silhouette begins to take shape, short and squat.

"Alice, where have you been?"

It's Darla.

"You know this girl?" Officer Talley says.

"I should hope so. She's my niece. What are you doing out here?" She sees my wet hair. "You were supposed to be taking a shower."

"Well," I say. "This man—"

"Ma'am, I'm Officer Talley. We had a report of a girl out here by herself. We get runaways sometimes. My mistake," he tips his hat.

"Well, thank you for looking out for her, Officer Talley. Right, Alice?"

"Yes, sir. Thank you for looking out for me."

He wishes us a good night and walks away.

"Thank you, Darla," I gush.

"You're welcome, but we need to talk. Now." She points to their camper and starts marching. I follow.

Peggy's sitting under the awning, which is strung with pretty white lights. "Hey there," she says, cheerfully hoisting a tall beer can in an Arkansas Razorbacks coozie. I know all about SEC sports. My dad was a huge Georgia fan even though he never went to college.

"Hi, Peggy!" It feels good to be back under the awning. They have citronella candles burning and music playing on a Bluetooth speaker.

Darla points to a folding camping chair. "Sit," she says. She plunks herself down opposite me in a pink chair that says *No One Fights Alone* on the back. Pink camper, pink chair, even her face is pink.

"Alice, which I'm guessing isn't your real name, I'll get to the point. I know you are not here with your aunt. In fact, I can state confidently you are not here with anyone. And yet, you are here."

I nod. "I am. Here, I mean."

Peggy laughs and Darla shoots her a look.

"What gave me away?"

"Oh, little things, like your evasive answers to questions, inhaling breakfast like it was your first meal in days and sneaking out the side of the park when you said you were going back to your aunt's."

I thought I was being so clever.

"But more than anything else, I can tell when people are hurting. It's written all over your face, honey."

I blink.

Peggy pipes in. "Darla here was one of the best psychologists in Little Rock."

"Was? I only retired a month ago. Don't go putting me in the grave. So I take it the officer was right and you are a runaway?"

Maybe it's her eyes or voice, both soft, but I'm going to have a hard time lying to her. No point anyway. She's already figured me out.

"Yes," I say. "But not a regular one. I mean, not for the usual reasons."

"Can you tell me about it?"

"Anything you tell her is confidential by law," Peggy says.

"Confidential?"

"By law," Peggy says.

"It's not quite that simple," Darla says.

Peggy cackles. "Well, unless you killed somebody or something."

"Peggy, will you please be quiet for a minute and let me talk to Alice?"

Peggy gives a fake look of being offended. The Indigo Girls are singing in the background. Mom loved them.

Darla says, "I don't expect you to tell me all your secrets."

I spew relief. "Thank you."

"But I do need to know some basics. I told that officer I was your aunt and assumed a responsibility from that. I didn't do it lightly."

"Believe her," Peggy chimes in. "She does not do things lightly."

"Peggy, please shut up."

Peggy makes a zipper-lip motion.

I take a deep breath. "Well, I guess you could say ... do you happen to have a glass of water by any chance?"

Darla pours a cup of water from a pitcher on the table. I drink the whole cup and she refills it.

"The thing is," I say, "I can't tell you the truth, but I also can't lie to you. It's a compliment, I swear. I lie to everyone. All day long. That's all I do."

Peggy slaps her knee. "I do believe the girl's telling the truth."

"Do your parents know where you are?" Darla asks.

I look out at the black sky. Orion's sword dips below the awning. "Um ... I think so."

"Okay, so the basics of why you're out here alone would be?"

"Well, in terms of basics ..."

You Alice Miller. Don't you ever make the mistake of feeling all warm and fuzzy and tellin' anyone who you really are.

"I come from a very good family, but ... things just didn't go right. Actually, they went really bad. I didn't have any choice but to leave."

"What happened?"

"Well, sometimes in a family, everything just falls apart." A picture of stocky man grabbing Mom's hair sears my brain.

"So you're not willing to tell me about it."

"I can't. I wish I could."

"Okay. I respect that, but we can't shelter you under those circumstances. It would be unethical on my part. I was hoping to talk you into letting me call your parents. I'm sorry."

I stand up. "I understand. You already helped me." Without thinking, I reach down and hug her. "Thank you."

I wave goodbye and walk into the dark.

29

RAISED VOICES at my back as I head into the woods. I got out of a jam but won't be able to come back. That ranger will be watching for me. Lucas told me Lafayette would be too small for me. I haven't spotted a single other place to sleep. Big cities have a ton of them.

I'm disappearing into the trees when a flashlight beam crosses me from the edge of the campground. Officer Talley already? I'm about to hightail it, but hear my name and recognize Darla's voice this time. I run to her.

Panting, "Yeah?"

"Your friend Peggy persuaded me to let you spend the night with us. But just one night."

"Are you okay with that?"

"No, but I'm more not okay watching you walk into the woods in the dark." She holds out her hand. "Come back with me?"

As if that would take a lot of convincing.

Back at the camper, we sit outside watching baseball on an old-fashioned TV with an antenna on top. It's the same night air as in my little sleeping spot, but it tastes different, like there are colors in it.

Peggy jumps up. "Whoo hoo. Base hit. Now we're talkin'." She digs into a cooler and pops open another beer can.

"As you can tell, Peggy's a big baseball fan. Do you play sports?"

"I used to."

"What sport?"

"Mostly softball."

"Were you on a team?"

"Mm-hm. Hey, would you mind if I plug in my phone charger?"

"There's a plug right there. I'm glad to see you have a phone. We noticed you colored that pretty blonde hair of yours."

"Yeah." I can usually talk forever, but once I ruled out lying, I have nothing to say. "Does it look okay?"

"Very nice. You seem to pull on it a lot. Have you been doing that for a long time?"

"Not really," I say, embarrassed.

"Did you know there's a medical name for that? Trichotillomania."

"Tricho ..."

"Trichotillomania. Obsessive hair-pulling."

"Huh." I wonder if she's putting me on, sounds like a made-up word. "What causes it?"

"Can be a lot of things. Sometimes it's triggered by stress or trauma."

I recognize my cue. She's waiting for me to confirm or deny. Peggy rescues me. "Back up, back up! Right over his head." She skims the top of her hair.

"I like Peggy," I say, changing the subject.

"Me too."

"She's funny."

"She certainly thinks so."

I can tell Darla's trying to be nice and not interrogate me, hoping I'll spill my guts on my own. I'll bet she was a good psychologist. She gives up and offers me dinner. I scarf down leftover barbecue chicken and green beans while Darla settles in next to Peggy, holding hands.

We go inside the trailer after the game and they show me to a bunk. Darla and Peggy settle into a wider bed a few feet away. It's dark except for a nightlight. I feel guilty. Darla was right,

Peggy wrong. It's risky keeping a fugitive minor, as Lucas reminded me every other day. No reason to take a chance on me. A killer and a liar. Can't undo the killing.

Maybe I got one quality your God like. My word. I say one month and we go one month.

"Darla?" I say through the dark.

"Mm-hm."

"I lied to you."

"What about?"

"Alice isn't my real name."

"I guessed that."

"But I can't tell you my real name."

"Then why'd you tell me?"

"I just wanted to tell you it was a lie, because I said I wouldn't lie to you and wanted to keep my word."

"Thank you for telling me."

"There's another thing."

"Oh boy, here we go." Peggy.

"You asked if my parents knew where I was."

"Mm-hm."

"And I said they did."

"Don't worry. I already guessed that was a lie too."

"No ... not as much. I was thinking about it in a different way. My parents, they're ... they passed. Sometimes I keep myself going by thinking they still know where I am, like, from another place, but I knew what you meant, so it was a lie."

Silence until Darla says, "I'm sorry about your parents. Would you like to talk about it?"

"No. That's all I can tell you."

"Okay. Goodnight."

Something about Darla makes me want to talk to her. Probably because she doesn't try to force me. Like right now. I have so many secrets I'd like to tell.

The next morning I'm Peggy's breakfast assistant, cleaning up behind her. The kitchenette inside the trailer is like a dollhouse, no place to put anything except exactly where it goes.

We eat outside at the picnic table. Darla said only one night, so I decide to make it easy on everyone.

I snag my backpack. "You guys have no idea how much I appreciate everything, but it's time for me to move on."

"Where to?" Darla says.

My mind starts concocting before I remember my word. "I thought I'd hang around here for a little while. In Lafayette, I mean. Not the park."

Darla gives me a hard look. "Peggy and I talked and agreed you could stay with us for one more night, if you'd like."

Head bobbing, "Um, yeah, if it's, you know, okay."

"But it really is just one more night. We're leaving in the morning for North Carolina."

"Oh. Well, that should be a fun trip. Thank you ... I gotta go now. I have a lot of stuff to do. I'll be back later."

I break away, mad at myself for the tears welling in my eyes. I went a whole month without even one. *They're just strangers. Get over it.*

30

THE SAME grandma from yesterday does a double-take and sniffs when I reach the library counter. "Welcome back, dear, but didn't you have blonde hair yesterday?"

I give a goofy shrug. "You know teenagers. We love to change our hair. I almost went with purple!"

I sign in for an hour, but all the computers are being used. I fan myself with a magazine while I wait.

On the way I stopped at a high school athletic field and did a full workout. Seven pullups for the first time. I fist-bumped Kiona in the air. My muscles have already saved me twice, from the Red River and Scott Brooker. It takes a lot of strength to ram a knife blade four inches up a man's intestines without leverage.

When a computer opens up, I log on and go straight to the burner account for Robert Williams. I reread Special Agent Jeffrey Forster's email and click reply.

> *Dear Agent Forster,*
>
> *I knew the police were stupid in this case, but nothing like this! I sent you important information based on something I heard in a bar and now you think I'm the dead girl? I am sad about the state of our government.*
>
> *Please stop chasing fantasies and do some justice by catching the men who did these terrible crimes.*
>
> *Robert Williams*

I reread it. As Lucas once said, *The more desperate the truth,
the more desperate the lie.* Sounds exactly like Emily Calby. I'm
sure a text analyst would agree. I delete the message and lean
back.

He already knows it's me. Need to stall ... and get information.

> *Dear Agent Forster,*
>
> *Just suppose I am Emily Calby.*

Ha, yeah, just suppose.

> *I'm not saying I am.*

Oh no, not at all. I hiccup.

> *I have some questions. I need to be careful. As you
> said in your own words, I'm in a dangerous situation.
> Please do not put out a nationwide alert on me. You
> are right. I will run. I will run until I die. Do not
> worry. I am fine.*

The last three words propel me into a giggle-fit, bringing a
nasty look from a bearded man at the next computer. I've told
a billion lies since that day, but that one always takes the prize.
I'm fine! Better than fine. GRRREAT. Haaaa.

> *Here are my questions:*
>
> *1. How do I know you are who you say you are?
> Please provide proof.*
>
> *2. You said you have new evidence. Please provide
> proof.*
>
> *Unless I have proof you know where the two murder-
> ers are, I will not "come in" because I will never be
> safe.*
>
> *I will keep checking this email account. If I think you
> are trying to find me, I will disappear forever, any
> way it takes.*

I read it over. It's not very nice. If everything Jeffrey Forster said is true, he's trying to help.

> *Thank you for trying to catch the two men and not wanting me to run anymore. Honestly, I do not care what happens to me. All I want is justice for my mother and sister—that is, if I really was Emily Calby.*
>
> *Sincerely,*
> *Robert Williams*

I send it and turn my attention to Lucas. I'm desperate for information about him, but have no clue how to find any. On the way to the library, I called the hospital again and got the same answer. They "had" a Lucas Jackson, but he checked out two days ago.

I type *Lucas Jackson* in a browser, not expecting anything new. His shooting only got like three sentences. Nobody's going to write a story about him getting out of the hospital. When results flood the screen, I'm momentarily stunned before I realize I screwed up. I left out *Memphis*. The world is filled with Lucas Jacksons.

M-e-m-p-h-i-s

They have fast internet speed here. The sound, something between a squeak and dying breath, escapes before I can lift my finger off the enter key.

Obituary — *Lucas Ellington Jackson, Memphis*

Today's date, a link to the Memphis newspaper and part of a sentence:

> *Lucas Ellington Jackson, Memphis, passed away yesterday at the ...*

The hiding girl crawls out of her cubby, already breaking down. Calm girl shoos her back in. She can come out later, maybe, she says, and clicks on the link.

... age of 32. Born and raised in Memphis, Jackson served in the U.S. Army, where he was deployed to Iraq. He leaves behind no surviving relatives. Mr. Jackson will be cremated under the direction of Green & Sons Mortuary.

I close the window and stare at nothing.

"My dear." It's the librarian.

"Yes," I say without looking.

"Your time is up. We have someone waiting for this computer."

"It's been an hour already?"

"I'm afraid so."

I would have sworn it was only a minute. "Um, just one more thing, real quick." I search *green sons memphis* and write down the funeral home number.

I stumble out of the library like a drunk person. *Desolation, noun: state of complete emptiness.* All alone again. Lucas made me feel like I wasn't. I never would have believed that was possible after my family was gone. I enter the funeral home number on my phone as I walk.

Honk, honk.

A man is jawing at me from behind a windshield because I stepped in front of his van. People get upset over anything. I keep walking.

"Green and Sons," says a deep voice. "Mr. Green speaking."

"Hello. I'm calling about someone who died. It's an emergency."

"I regret your loss. You have come to the right place. We are here to help you with all of your virtuous needs. Do you require body removal?"

"What?"

"You mentioned it was an emergency."

"That's not what I meant. I'm calling about an obituary I saw for Lucas Jackson. Lucas Ellington Jackson."

"Yes, Mr. Jackson. Such a tragedy. Still a young man. ... Hello?"

"I–I'm here. What did he die from? I mean, I know he got shot, but the hospital said he checked out."

"Who are you?"

"My name's Alice. I'm one of his best friends." I look at the bracelet, medallion reflecting the sunlight like a starburst.

"It appears brother Lucas checked out of the hospital too soon. The doctors say he wasn't ready to leave, but he insisted."

"Has he already been ... cremated?"

"The arrangements are private, but, well, yes."

Silence.

"Remember what the bible says, child. *The righteous man perishes while no one understands, but he enters into peace and rests in a bed of uprightness.* Isaiah, chapter fifty-seven."

"Is that supposed to make me feel better?"

"Do you believe in the Lord?"

I pause. It's getting harder. "Yes."

"Then listen again. Lucas was a righteous man. Not free from guilt or sin, far from it, but he lived by a righteous code few men could honor. Do not weep for Lucas Jackson. He is at peace, resting in a bed of uprightness."

"Okay," I say, not completely convinced. I mean, he did kill people.

The phone disconnects as two girls zip past me on bikes, all flying ponytails, pointy elbows and breathy squeals. I remember when Meggie Tribet and I were like them ... in a different lifetime.

I find the number for Max's Gym in my recents.

"Ya."

"Hi, I called yesterday looking for Kiona."

"Ya, Kiona."

"Is she there?"

"No."

"Have you seen or talked to her?"

"Ya, talked."

"Do you know when she'll be coming in?"

"Not coming. Friend die."

"Do you know how I could reach her? It's an emergency."

"No."

"I'll pay for information," I say desperately, but he already hung up on me.

I melt onto the sidewalk, clenching the bracelet. Lucas. *Gone.* But where? It can't be *the end* of Lucas, just like it can't be *the end* of Mom or Dad or Becky. I'd believe in God just for that because I couldn't face the alternative.

Lucas is good, Lord. Look into his heart. He only killed people who deserved it.

The concrete is burning my knees like a stovetop, right through my pants. That's probably where I'll end up. Down there.

People are staring. I get up and walk. No destination, but the mind is a trickster. We think we control it, but it's the other way around. Within ten minutes I'm standing in front of Mary's Maybes, the craft store. The skeleton doll who looks like me is still watching from the window. I wave to her and turn the corner.

31

NO PLAN. Beyond stupid. *Insane*. But there's nothing left to lose except this worthless life. Any last hope it could offer more than misery left with Lucas.

I unfold the sketches as I approach the door. If tall man's inside, I'll seize the advantage, kill him with the neck knife before he has time to react. *Hi, Ronnie! Remember me? THRUST, SLASH.*

A painting of Durty Delphine on the glass smiles maliciously. *Bitch*. I yank the door open, strut inside and freeze like a deer in headlights, staring at the video camera before dropping my head. *Dumb*. I move behind a brick column and scan the room.

Tall man's not here, of course. Hardly anyone is, just a few people eating lunch.

A polished-wood bar runs along the back wall, empty except for a hunch-backed old man with hair like a wire brush sitting at the end drinking beer from a glass. Behind the bar is a stringy young guy with slicked-back black hair.

Bartender. I studied them on the security videos. They're the center of attention. Everyone talks to the bartender. Keeping my head down I walk to the bar and take the middle stool. He comes over and nods.

"Hi, I'll have a whiskey!"

Blank look.

Chill. "Just kidding. I'm looking for a man who comes here. I wonder if you've seen him. I have a picture of him. Well, it's not exactly a picture ..."

I lay the drawing of tall man on the bar. I think I see a flash of recognition but it could just be wishful thinking.

"Who are you?"

"*Who in the world am I? Ah, that's the great puzzle.*" Control yourself.

"What the fuck?"

"Sorry, just something from *Alice in Wonderland*. My name's Alice." I stick my hand out to shake, but he leaves it hanging in mid-air.

"Why you looking for him?"

"It's kind of a long story, but we met and one thing led to another and … well, I'll just say it. I'm pregnant!"

I can't believe I said it. Either can the bartender, who steps back like I just turned radioactive.

"Don't know him." He turns away.

"Over here, sha."

It's the old man at the end of the bar. Cajun. I recognize the accent now. It has a pretty sound, but I can't separate it from the nightmare.

"Lemme see dat picture. I know everyone. Been sitting in dis seat for twenty years." He pats the stool next to him. "Sit."

I scoot down and hand him the sketch. He takes a long look and lays it on the bar.

"Well? Have you ever seen him?" Patience.

A guttural laugh. "Never in my life."

"Oh."

"'Cept maybe a hundred times."

"Huh?"

"Dat Ronnie."

I struggle to hide my excitement. *Ronnie.* "Is he here?" I say, heart pounding.

He looks around. "Ya a blind girl?"

"I mean is he here in Lafayette?"

"Ronnie blow in and out, like da wind." He waves his glass to the bartender for a refill.

"Do you know how to find him?"

"Like I say, in and out, but he always come back."

Tall man is here. Or will be. I pull out the sketch of stocky man.

"What about this man? Do you know him?"

The bartender comes up. "Are you gonna buy anything?"

"Just water, please." I smile. He scowls.

I turn back to the old man. "Dat Ronnie's friend," he says.

Act normal. "Do you happen to know where *he* is?"

"Don tell me dey bote make you pregnant. I lose my fate in God."

"Um, no. I'm just trying to get any leads I can." A jukebox starts up. I recognize the song, my dad used to play it on a CD in his truck. The singer's pulling into Nazareth feeling half past dead.

"He blow in and out wit Ronnie. In and out."

"I know, like the wind," I say, frustration slipping.

"Ah, bright girl. Someone be pleased to got ya as dere daughter."

"Thanks. When's the last time you saw Ronnie?"

He takes a drink of beer and wipes his mouth with the back of his wrinkled hand. "Who keeps count? Don look so lost, sha. Ronnie's people come here even when he away."

"What people?"

"Family, friends. I bet dey know Ronnie get ya pregnant, dey take care a ya."

"When do they come?"

"Like everyone, dey come when dey get here."

"If I give you my phone number, could you get one of them to call me? I'll pay you."

He waves his hand, dripping beer on my leg. "No need to pay. Happy to help."

Digging out my pad and phone, I double-check my new number and print it under *ALICE.*" I tear out the sheet. "Here. You swear you'll do this? It's super-important."

He kisses his fingertips and touches my belly. "Wat more important don a bébé?"

I push his hand away. "You're not just saying that? You'll give them the message?"

"Not just saying. I see Ronnie's people, I give dem da message."

The bartender is back with the old man's beer and my water. He sets them down and turns his back.

I take a sip and stand up. "Thank you, sir," I say.

"Call me Sam," the old man says.

"Thank you, Sam. I'm Alice, like it says on the note. I'll be waiting for that call. You're really going to do it, right?"

"Toast to it!"

He holds out his beer. I pick up my water and we clink glasses.

Backing away, "Okay, so I'll be waiting for the call."

He raises his glass again. "Toast!"

32

NOTHING TO DO but wait and see if someone calls. I pass a copy shop on the way back to the campground. If I don't hear anything by tomorrow I'll make copies of the sketches with something at the bottom like *If you've seen these men call* .... Tape them up around Durty Delphine's.

Desperate? Yes. Semi-suicidal? Possibly. Out of options.

My last night at Acadiana Park, so I stay alert for a new place to sleep. I pass a golf course but it's too wide open.

A sweet, buttery smell stops me at a bakery. Peggy has a sweet tooth. I go inside and buy three cupcakes. The lady behind the counter is Cajun. "Lagniappe," she says with a wink, slipping in an extra one for free. Every Cajun I've met has been super nice—except tall man.

Back outside, I stop and gaze at the old church across the street. I've passed it a bunch of times. I doubt if it's by accident. So pretty. Made of irregular white bricks with pointy archways and real stained-glass windows. Not an *ersatz* church, one of Mom's words I always liked just because it sounded weird.

The last time I was in a church was the Sunday before the men came. Before that, almost every Sunday since I was a baby.

Hiding girl asks if we can go inside.

Cool and dark, so quiet I can hear my breathing, but not my steps, which get swallowed by the deep blue carpet. I go to the sanctuary and kneel at the altar.

Please, Lord, forgive my sins and spare my wretched life. I came

197

here to pray for a miracle, even though I don't deserve one. I need a miracle to ...

"Hello."

It's a man with chestnut hair in jeans and a blue button-down shirt, entering through a door behind the altar. I unclasp my hands, lowering my left one to my lap.

"Forgive me for interrupting your prayers. I didn't know anyone was in here. I'm Reverend Campbell, the pastor."

He sees my doubt. "Yes, I really am the pastor. We dress like normal people during the week. Can I help you with anything?"

"No," I say, embarrassed my first reaction was to stab the preacher.

"Very well. I'll let you resume your prayers." He starts to leave.

"Well, maybe you can help me," I say. "Do you have time for a question, about God?"

"Certainly. He is my specialty, after all. Follow me. We can talk in my office."

He leads me down a short hallway, past a colorful sign, *WHAT A FRIEND WE HAVE IN JESUS*, with Jesus nailed to the cross at the bottom. We come to a door with the preacher's name painted in gold on frosted glass. He waves me in. I let him go first and sit in a scarred leather chair as he settles behind a desk cluttered with books.

"What's your question?"

"Is it a sin to hurt someone who's about to hurt you?" I maintain an expression of youthful inquisitiveness as I see my knife ramming upward into Scott Brooker's guts.

"You mean, in self-defense?"

"Exactly."

He tilts his head. "Is this a personal question?"

"Oh, no. Just research for my summer church school project, back home in Chattanooga. I'm here for the summer taking care of my grandmother."

"Ah, good for you. If more young people would pitch in to assist our elders, the world would be a better place."

"Definitely. So what about self-defense? How does God feel about it?"

"It's an interesting theological question. The bible does not speak directly to self-defense, but contains several passages that appear to approve of it. In the Old Testament, Exodus says, *If a thief is breaking in and is struck so that he dies, there shall be no bloodguilt.*"

"Seriously? You can kill a thief?" If you can kill a thief, you've got to be able to kill a rapist.

"Again, that was the Old Testament, which leaned toward the unforgiving side. However, even in the New Testament, in Luke, Jesus tells his disciples ... hold on, I need to look this up."

He picks a well-worn bible off the desk and thumbs through it. "Here it is. Jesus said, *Let the one who has no sword sell his cloak and buy one.* That would suggest that even deadly self-defense is justifiable, at least in some circumstances."

Good news. "What about revenge? Is it a sin to get revenge on someone who hurt you?"

"Revenge is an entirely different proposition. God does not approve of revenge." He flips through the bible. "Romans. *Never avenge yourselves, but leave it to the wrath of God.* And in the New Testament Jesus tells his disciples, *Whosoever shall smite thee on thy right cheek—*"

"*Turn to him the other,*" I finish. "What if it's something a lot worse than a slap on the cheek?"

"Such as?"

"Murder."

His face screws up. "God does not sanction revenge. Plain and simple."

"Then how come some criminals get the death penalty?"

"That's a thorny issue," he says, continuing likes he's teaching a bible study class. "The Old Testament approves of punishment by death in many passages, but most theologians believe Christ's messages of forgiveness and mercy are contrary to the death penalty. If capital punishment is proper under any circumstances, it is not for revenge, but only to achieve justice."

"So if you call it *justice*, it's okay?"

"Not quite that simple. The line between revenge and justice depends on several factors."

"Like what?"

"Well, motivation for one. Is the motivation to right a wrong or to be vindictive?"

Mom and Becky are dead. Stocky man and tall man are alive. That is WRONG. "What else?"

"Justice is about achieving a fair and just result for society. Revenge is personally motivated."

"So it's fair and just for society to kill criminals who do horrible things, but not for the people they did them to?"

He turns up his palms. "You got me there. To be honest, I believe capital punishment is rooted in revenge, which is one reason I oppose it. Most clergy do."

"But not all?"

"Not all. Some believe in what they call *just revenge*, showing how difficult it is to separate the two concepts. Death penalty supporters also argue it's necessary to deter future crimes."

I have no doubt stocky man and tall man are committing more crimes. They might be wiping out the preacher's family right now.

"But studies show capital punishment is applied discriminatorily, with minorities being sentenced to death at higher rates than whites."

Stocky man and tall man are white.

"Still another issue is that the criminal justice system sometimes makes mistakes by convicting innocent people."

Stocky man and tall man are guiltier than anyone who ever breathed.

"You can see why it's such a complicated issue."

Seems simple to me. Killing tall man and stocky man would be justice.

"Thank you so much," I say. "That helps a lot with my research. Could I ask a different question? A personal one."

"Of course."

"Do you believe in miracles?"

"Certainly. Don't you?"

I puff my cheeks. "I guess. Do you think you could possibly pray for a miracle for me?"

"Certainly. Tell me your name and what it is you are seeking and I will be sure to say a prayer for you."

Giving a fake name in church when asking for a miracle is probably a reason to go to hell all by itself.

"Just pray for the girl with the brown hair who stopped by today. He'll know who I am. Pray that ..."

I'm still not sure what my miracle is. For my family to be alive? For Lucas to be alive? Those are past. Impossible to change. For strength? Killing ability? Something to save me? From others or myself, I'm not sure.

"Is someone sick?" he prods.

Yeah, me. Scary girl wants to laugh, but hiding girl says not in a church.

"Just a general miracle would be great. Any help at all. Thanks for answering my questions." I try to muster my usual artificial enthusiasm, but can't do it.

"Bless you, child. Come back any time if you'd like to talk more, or come join us for worship."

I nod and exit into the fierce afternoon sun.

33

I'VE KEPT my phone in reach since I got back to the campground. Is Sam for real? The question's been swirling in my tornado brain since I left Durty Delphine's. He might have just been playing me and was probably drunk, but he looked at the sketch and said right away, *Dat Ronnie.*

Peggy appreciated the cupcakes. "Only four?" she said. "You didn't get any for you and Darla?"

It was funny, but my laugh was hollow and listless.

"What's eating you, Squirt?" she said. She refuses to call me by a fake name so she made up her own. "I don't need Darla's psychology degrees to tell me something's wrong."

My last friend just died. It was my fault.

"Just tired, I guess."

I helped her make dinner, short-rib stew, one of her specialties. It was delish. After dinner we lit the citronella candles, made popcorn and turned on a TV movie.

The movie is half over. My mind is a million miles away. Peggy goes inside.

"You're awfully quiet tonight," Darla says.

I'm twisting my hair so tight my scalp is on fire. I let go when I realize how good it feels. "Just thinking," I say.

In the movie, a man asks a woman, "Do you think there's hope?" She assures him everything's hopeless.

"Darla?"

"Mm-hm."

"When you were a psychologist, did you ever have patients who thought they were, you know, cracking up?"

"Many." She nibbles popcorn, eyes glued to the movie.

"Were they? Cracking up?"

"Some. Most just felt overwhelmed."

"By what?"

"Depended on the person. Lots of things. Jobs, relationships ... loss."

The man in the movie insists he can change, but the woman says no one ever can.

She puts another piece of popcorn in her mouth. "Do you feel like you're cracking up?"

"Me? Oh, no." *Don't lie to Darla.* "I mean, well, maybe sometimes. Did you ever have a patient who lost everything, like *everything*?"

"Your parents?"

"More."

"You lost more than your parents?"

I nod.

"I'm not going to guess, so you'll have to decide if you want to tell me."

"My little sister," voice barely a whisper, "and my best friend." *Today.*

She mutes the TV and turns her chair to face me. "Honey, that's called grief."

"You don't think I'm going crazy?"

"I think you're suffering."

"What if I did crazy things?"

"What kind of crazy things?"

I cough. "Bad."

She lowers her head. When she looks up, her eyes are wet and blazing.

"You listen to me. It's everything I can do to restrain myself from calling social services to get you help. I should have done it at the beginning, but somehow I let you convince me, against all logic and common sense, that you're better off out here on your own."

"I am. I swear. I wouldn't last long in … captivity." One way or another, I know it's true. "I don't lie to you."

She tightens her lips. "You can tell me anything, but do you remember what Peggy said about confidentiality?"

"By law, right?"

"You never got the complete version. If your *crazy things* include anything that shows you're a danger to yourself or others, that isn't confidential. You need to know that up front. Do you still want to talk?"

I shake my head as Peggy barges out of the trailer. "What are you gals gabbing about?"

"Oh, just this and that," Darla says.

Peggy claps her hands. "I say it's time for cupcakes."

We each have one, settling in to watch the rest of the movie. I expect the man and woman to get back together at the end, but she pushes him off a building. *Nice.* The news comes on after the credits.

Darla stands and yawns. "We have to hit the road early. Time to pack up."

"How long is the trip?" I say.

"Eleven hours to Asheville. Fortunately, Peggy here volunteered to drive the whole way."

"What? I did no such thing. Hey, look at this," Peggy says, pointing at the TV.

Breaking News. A pretty black woman is talking into a microphone. The mossy trees and green water behind her look familiar. Peggy turns up the sound.

"Police in Saint Landry Parish are investigating a homicide after a body was discovered floating in the bayou near Chicot State Park. We're live at the scene, about to hear from the state police."

The camera switches to a grim-faced man in a blue uniform and Mountie hat reading from a piece of paper. On the ground behind him, covered by a white tarp, is a lump. Scott Brooker.

"At this time, we are working to identify the victim, a white male estimated to be in his forties. The cause of death appears to be multiple stab wounds, but we will not know for sure until an autopsy is completed. We ask that anyone with information contact us ..."

Peggy turns off the TV. "We drove right by there on our way here."

"My goodness," Darla says, shaking her head. "Sometimes I think this whole world is going insane." She climbs two steps and disappears into the trailer.

I stare straight ahead without a twitch until Peggy says, "Help me pack up, Squirt?"

* * *

When we get everything squared away, Darla insists I take a shower in the trailer. I'm sure I reek, but can't smell myself anymore. The shower stall is the size of an airplane bathroom, but I like it. Feels safe. Darla gives me a nightshirt to wear with a faded Scooby-Do on the front.

I plug my phone in and stash it under my pillow. Darla hands me a piece of paper with their contact information, making me memorize her cell phone number. "Just in case you lose this," she says. "And if you ever come to Arkansas, you'd better let us know."

"I totally will."

"I hate leaving you here by yourself. We both do. I wish—"

My phone hisses from under the pillow. I pounce on it. *Unknown Caller.*

"Um, I'm sorry, but I have to answer this."

"You go right ahead," Darla says, not happy.

"Hello."

"Is this Alice?" A man.

"Mm-hm. Who's this?"

Peggy and Darla are three feet away. The man has a loud voice. I'm sure they can hear everything.

"Friend of Ronnie's."

"Hold on." I cover the phone. "I have to take this outside. Sorry." Darla turns up her palms.

Standing under the stars where the awning used to be, "So you say you're a friend of Ronnie's?"

"That's right. I heard Ronnie got you in a ... predicament."

"Yeah. How did you hear about it?"

"At Delphine's, from old Sam."

"Why are you calling?"

"On behalf of Ronnie's family. They want to help."

"Help how?"

"First, they want to meet you, make sure you're not making this shit up or have the wrong dude. If things check out, they'll do right by you. Good people."

"Thanks, but I'd rather deal with Ronnie directly."

"Ain't gonna happen. No one's giving up their kin to some girl from nowhere. Ronnie's been in trouble for something like this before. He's always been a mess, but he's their mess. Family, you know? That's why they want to help."

Not like I have a choice. "Alright. How do I contact them?"

"Meet me at Delphine's tomorrow at eight."

"In the night?"

He laughs. "Yeah, the night."

"Who are you?" I say.

"My name's Albin."

"How will I recognize you?"

"Don't worry," he says. "I'll recognize you. Sam said you look fourteen."

"That's not true."

"Whatever. Won't be a problem. See you tomorrow."

He disconnects.

Back in the trailer, Darla and Peggy are already in bed. Neither of them say a word. I know they're waiting for me to go first.

"That was, um, Albin."

"Lemme guess, friend of Ronnie's," Peggy says, but she's not smiling.

"Yeah."

The air weighs a ton when Darla turns out the light. I lie awake for a long time. The air conditioner covers the snapping sound of the knife going in and out of the sheath.

34

"WE'LL MISS you, Squirt," Peggy says with a hug.

"You too, so much."

She climbs in the driver's seat as Darla comes around the front of the camper. We're parked a few blocks outside the park. It was Peggy's good idea to not have me walk out of the campground alone after my "aunt" drove off and left me.

Darla puts her hands on my shoulders. It's a tie which of us looks sadder. "Well, I guess this is it, kiddo. Sure you don't need anything?"

"I'm sure. Thanks again for everything." They tried to give me money, but I turned it down. I already took advantage of them. I also have a feeling I'm not going to need money after today.

"What's my phone number?"

I recite it.

"You know it's not too late for me to get you help. I'll do all the talking."

It's way too late, but I just say, "Don't worry so much. I'm great. You guys have an awesome trip."

She gives a last exasperated look before walking away. I wave as they drive off, not stopping until the last bit of pink disappears around the corner.

I check my phone. Eight o'clock. It's going to be a long twelve hours until I meet Albin. I begin my haul to the library.

Darla knew I was faking. I'm as empty as I've ever been. I

wish I never met them. Feeling even a little bit is dangerous, much worse than not feeling at all. I vow to never make another friend.

I slap my face, harder than I mean to. Stop the pity party. In case this is my last day on earth, I'm going to spend it thinking about happy things. My brain lets loose a memory of my family's vacation to North Carolina. We started in Asheville, same as Darla and Peggy, before going to the Outer Banks.

Mom wanted to stay in a beach cottage, but Dad insisted we had to rough it and camp at a place called Ocracoke. OMG, the sand! In our eyes, noses, everywhere. I remember me and Becky having a giggle fit as we held up beach towels to keep it from blowing into the hamburgers Dad was cooking on the Coleman stove, but it didn't work. Every bite was like chewing sandpaper.

The day our house exploded, I still had a pink t-shirt in my dresser. *I Survived Ocracoke.*

Terrible idea. There is no such thing as a good memory anymore. The better the moment, the worse the memory. Never again.

* * *

A balding man with a bow tie welcomes me to the library with an enthusiastic "Good morning!" Everyone here is so friendly. Mom would be glad I'm spending more time in libraries. I ask for a computer.

He lays the sign-in clipboard on the counter alongside the morning newspaper. I print my name: *A-l-i-c-e M-i-l-l-e-r* ... *Police Identify St. Landry Homicide Victim; Killer Could Be in Lafayette.* Across the top of the newspaper in bold letters.

"Excuse me. Can I look at your newspaper?"

"Not my newspaper," the man says. "The people's newspaper. This is a public library and it's excellent to see young people like you taking advantage of it."

I just say, "Uh-huh."

> The body found yesterday floating in a pond near
> Chicot State Park has been identified as Scott Brooker,
> 43, Champaign, Illinois. His abandoned car was dis-
> covered last night ...

I stop reading. No point. Nothing I can do about it. Just another reminder time is running out. *Put your worries in a box.*

At the computer, I log onto the burner account. There's a new
message from FBI agent Jeffrey Forster.

> *Dear Emily:*
>
> *I was very happy to receive your reply. Now my job is
> to convince you to let me arrange for your immediate
> return to Georgia.*
>
> *You asked for proof of two things. Am I who I say I
> am? I've attached a picture. As you can see from the
> caption, it is a photograph of me at an FBI banquet.*

I open the picture. He's handsome, tall and tan with short-
cropped salt and pepper hair and a smooth face. The photo
caption says, *Special Agent Jeffrey Forster receives Certificate of
Merit for distinguished service.*

> *I'm sure you also noticed my emails are coming to you
> from fbi.gov. Only someone affiliated with the FBI
> would be able to send an email from this address.*

I'll bet Lucas or James could spoof it.

> *You can also call the Atlanta FBI Office and ask
> for me by name. I trust this is sufficient proof of my
> identity.*

I already knew Forster was real, but it would be logical for
any scared girl on the run to ask and it stalled him for at least
one day.

*Your second question is more problematic. I cannot
share case details with you because FBI investigations
are confidential by law.*

*I can say that with your testimony and the new evi-
dence I mentioned, I believe there is a strong chance
we could successfully prosecute the two suspects.
Candidly, however, there is never a guarantee in a
criminal prosecution.*

I appreciate him being honest and for sending the picture. Lucas
said never trust the cops, but maybe Agent Forster is alright.

*I have kept our communications private, but will not
be able to do so for much longer. That is not a threat,
just a fact. To repeat from my last email, my cell
phone number is ...*

I hit reply and type.

Dear Agent Forster,

*I believe you are the FBI, but I need proof you know
exactly where the two men are. Once I have that, I
will call you and "come in." I promise.*

*Sincerely,
Robert Williams*

I send it and log out. Can't think of anything else so I shut
down the computer.

"Have a nice day," says the cheerful man with the bow tie.

"I'll try."

I sit on a bench and check my phone. Not even ten o'clock.
Since I can't stay still, I do what I always do to kill time: walk.
A guy setting up a window display at a clothing store waves like
he knows me. Have I been here that long?

Focus. There's work to do. I'm not going to be stupid and go to
Durty Delphine's again without a plan. Two possible situations:

Situation 1. Albin is for real and telling the truth about tall man's family wanting to help me.

Situation 2. It's a set-up. Tall man and stocky man might be waiting there to kill me.

Situation 1 depends on having a believable story about— DESPICABLE!!!—getting pregnant from tall man. *We met in Georgia two months ago.* Can't be contradicted because he was there.

How long does it take for a woman to know she's pregnant? I'll go back to the library later and look it up. What if they want proof? I've seen commercials for home pregnancy kits. I'll look that up too. They might offer money to make me go away, but that's not going to help.

I need to find him to see if he really loves me like he said.

I need to find him so I can tell him in person that he's going to be a father.

I need to find him because my lawyer said he has to pay child support.

The pregnancy story is nauseating, but it packed a punch. I saw it on the bartender's face. Some of my best lies are the unplanned ones.

Hard to predict the odds of *Situation 1.* Albin sounded believable on the phone. *He's always been a mess, but he's their mess. Family, you know?* He also said tall man's been in trouble for something like this before. Wonder what that's about.

Situation 2 is impossible to plan for. Obviously, if tall man is there, I'll try to kill him. If Albin or anyone else is with him, I have to be sure to finish the job before they stop me.

I decide to treat myself to an early lunch at a Chinese buffet, gorging on cashew chicken and spring rolls. Last supper?

Stuffed, I walk to a movie theater the size of a shopping mall and buy a ticket to a romantic comedy. That I'm wasting money on lunch buffets and movies is not a good sign about my confidence in the future.

The theater is dark and empty. I lose track of the plot quickly.

Darla and Peggy should be halfway to Asheville. I get out my phone and put in Darla's number. It goes to voicemail.

"Hey there, you have almost reached Darla and Peggy." Peggy. "Leave a message and Darla will be sure to call you back." Darla's laugh in the background makes me smile.

I click off the phone. A mistake to call. I feel worse again.

I trek back to the library after the movie, realizing I have no clue what it was about.

The air is so thick it's like breathing water. A bank clock says the temperature is ninety-eight. I've covered at least ten miles today. My big toe is already poking through one of the cheap pink sneakers.

The man with the bow tie is still behind the counter. "Well, hello again," he says. "Back to resume your quest for knowledge?"

"You can never have enough. That's my opinion."

"Indeed. But I'm afraid there's going to be a wait."

"No problem. I have all day."

* * *

How long until a woman knows she's pregnant? After she misses her period. That makes sense. So two months works. *How long before a woman looks pregnant?* Twelve to sixteen weeks. That works too. I search for home pregnancy kits. Ninety-nine percent accurate. Interesting.

I check the burner account. Nothing back from Agent Forster, but I didn't expect anything so soon. I also don't expect anything new when I search *Calby Murders*, but I'm so wrong:

House of Horrors Bulldozed

The link leads to a picture of a rectangular grave of freshly turned dirt where our house used to be.

I stare at the picture for what seems like a long time before closing the window and going to YouTube. *No Sound* signs are posted above the computers. I just mouth the words, blinking away tears. Carrie Underwood. *I will see you again ...*

When my time's up, I go to the restroom to clean up. Usual routine: brush hair and teeth, plaster on deodorant, fix make-up. Gazing deep into the mirror, dusting on copper eyeshadow like Lucas recommended the first day, I blink and jerk away.

I thought I saw someone else. I'm afraid to look again, so I turn out the light and open my phone. Six o'clock. Two hours until *Situation 1* or *Situation 2.*

35

DUSK—FINALLY. Stars are showing. The Big Dipper reminds me of a summer night on a blanket in our backyard when Becky was little. I was trying to explain constellations.

"So if you look at them right, the stars form beautiful pictures. Do you get it?" I said.

She bobbed her head. "Just like your drawings."

"Well, not exactly."

"Yuh-huh. They're so beautiful they *zoomed* into the sky and became stars."

Instead of locking the memory up, I let it feed me as I do final breathing and stretching exercises. I'm at the corner, in the shadows outside the glow of a streetlight. I spent the last hour in an alley practicing with the knife.

Five minutes to eight. Time to move. I reach for my hair, but calm girl says, *Easy does it.*

Halfway down the block, Durty Delphine's comes into full view. Two more letters are out on the neon sign. Now it says _urt_ _elp_ _ ne's.

I see *Hurt Help Me.*

A wall of noise greets me when I pull open the door. *Hurt Help Me.* Music blaring, people yakking and laughing. I don't see old Sam or the bartender, but I spot a man waving from a corner table. I wind my way to him, dodging a dancing woman in a red Ragin' Cajuns t-shirt. *Hurt Help Me.*

215

"Alice?" he says. He's young, maybe early twenties, with dark hair and green eyes and a rattlesnake tattoo running down one arm.

"Albin?"

"Told you I'd spot you," he says amiably. "Have a seat."

He kicks a chair from the table. I sit down, backpack on my lap. He calls over a waitress and orders another beer.

"You want anything?" the waitress asks. She's wearing a sky-blue Durty Delphine's t-shirt with the witch stenciled on the front.

"Just water, please."

"So how old are you?" Albin says when she walks away.

"Sixteen. Is Ronnie's family coming? What's the plan? What's Ronnie's last name?"

"Whoa, whoa. Slow down."

"Sorry. Just trying to ... find the father of my child. I'm desperate to know anything."

"First tell me this. Are you crazy? Clovis said he thinks you're a crazy girl."

How do you know I'm mad? You must be, or you wouldn't have come here. Alice and the Cheshire Cat.

"I just act that way sometimes," I say. "I'm under a lot of stress. Who's Clovis?"

"The bartender."

"You talked to him too?"

"Small town. Everyone talks. So Ronnie really knocked you up?"

"I don't like that word."

"*Impregnated* you?"

I swallow hard. "Yes. So what's the plan?"

"I'll take you to 'em. No hurry. First we need more information about you. Where'd you meet Ronnie?"

"It happened in Georgia, but please, I can't talk about the details. They're personal." I choke up, half fake, half real.

"Lemme see these pictures I heard about," he says.

I hand him the sketches. The waitress returns with his beer and my water. Nodding, he hands back the drawings and takes a steep drink from the beer.

"Alice is your real name?"

"Mm-hm."

"What's your last name?"

"Miller."

"You have ID?"

I get out the driver's license and show it to him. "Your hair color is different."

"I dyed it."

"How come?"

"Because I'm embarrassed to be a pregnant girl going into places like this trying to find the person who got me this way."

He seems satisfied by that answer. "What about you?" I say. "What's your last name?"

"No last name."

"Not very fair. I told you mine."

He laughs. "Who said life's fair?" He drains the rest of the beer and drops bills on the table. "Ready?"

Am I ready to get in a car with another stranger, one who claims to be a friend of the man who killed my mother and sister? Not really.

"How do I know you're not trying to trick me?"

"Fuck, you're wasting my time." He stands to leave.

"Wait. I'll go."

Walking next to him on the sidewalk, I notice Albin is about the same height as Scott Brooker but with more muscle. Brooker was flabby, at least he looked that way floating in the water with his pants down.

He stops at a pickup truck and unlocks the doors with a remote.

"Get in."

I hesitate. "How far did you say they lived?"

"A couple of miles."

It's a couple of miles off the interstate, but a thousand times better than a truck stop or fast-food.

I open the passenger door, but wait until he's settled in the driver's seat before getting in. I don't put on my seatbelt. *Sorry, Mom.* Albin doesn't put his on either.

The doors lock as we pull out. He lights a cigarette and holds out the pack.

"No, thanks," I say.

Expecting *Situation 2,* I'm on the verge of surrendering to paralyzing fear before remembering what Lucas said.

Fear is bigger than your enemy. It will lock you up inside. Since you gonna be in the same situation anyway, might as well make the choice not to be afraid. You always got a choice.

That was one of his main philosophies of life. We always have a choice.

People get scared or lazy, think "Poor me. I ain't got no choice." But you always got a choice. How should I react? A or B. What should I do next? A or B. Sometimes you get lucky and got choices all the way to fuckin' Z. But you always got at least A or B.

Lucas was wise. He really could have been an author.

Repeat after me: I am not afraid. I am Emily-the-Powerful.

I am not afraid. I am Emily-the-Powerful.

Eyes adjusting to the dark, I glance sideways at Albin. Hands on the wheel, his entire side is exposed. *So easy.* Slip out the neck knife and ram it below his ribs. Once we leave the truck, I lose the advantage.

The street lights end as we reach the edge of town. We're whooshing down a dark two-lane highway lined by woods and occasional houses, isolated, like our house was.

"How much farther?" I ask.

"Not far."

Homemade apple pie to die for. ... Is this where the restaurant is? ... We're almost there.

"Which of Ronnie's family members are we going to meet?"

"Cousins, I think."

"Boys or girls?"

"Not sure. Maybe both."

"You said Ronnie was in trouble for something like this before? What did that mean?"

"Let's just say Ronnie has an appreciation for youth."

I'm about to complain it's been more than a couple of miles when he pulls off the road into a long lane-like driveway. We stop in front of a gray house with peeling paint, missing shutters and a broken gutter in the front yard. A dingy porch light is on. Two cars are parked in front, but no blue truck with a crooked camper-top.

"This is it? This is where Ronnie's family lives?"

"This be the place," Albin says, climbing out.

Walls of darkness and cicadas in full chorus surround the house. Albin waits for me on the porch before knocking.

"Who's there?" A man's voice.

"Albie."

A nickname. Huh, Albin must be his real name. That's a surprise. I thought for sure it was made up. Maybe the whole thing is legit and I've been expecting the worse for nothing.

The door opens. In the threshold is a white guy with a shaved head and bushy beard.

"You must be Alice," he says with a friendly smile. "I'm Otis, Ronnie's cousin. Nice to meet you. Y'all come on in."

Situation 1. Who would have thought? My brain races to fabricate plausible conversation about pregnancy. I spent the day fixated on killing and dying.

Albin waves me in. "Go ahead."

"That's okay. You can go," I say.

"Ladies first."

"No, you go."

He shrugs and steps inside. I follow him into a living room that looks like a garbage dump. Cans and bottles, ashtrays overflowing with cigarette butts, empty fast-food bags. The only furniture is a bulky TV, a table with two chairs, one of them missing a leg, and a pair of dirty mattresses on the floor.

The door closes behind me and I turn to see the bartender from Durty Delphine's, looking wired.

"So you're the famous Alice," Otis says.

Albin says, "Alice Regina Miller according to her driver's license."

"She's a pretty little thing. I can understand why Ronnie went astray."

I say, "Are you really Ronnie's relative? And what's he doing here?" I point to the bartender.

"Prepare yourself," Albin says. "She's a fucking question-machine."

"I see," Otis says.

He's in charge. That's obvious.

"Ronnie's my first cousin. Clovis over there is a friend. And you already know Albie. So I hear you're spreading rumors Ronnie knocked you up."

"Fact. Not rumor."

"Where did the blessed event take place?"

"Georgia."

"When?"

"Two months ago."

"Can you prove you're pregnant?"

"I took a pregnancy test. They're ninety-nine percent accurate."

Otis turns to the others. "Either of you know where Ronnie was two months ago?"

Shrugs.

"He was in Georgia," I say. "With his friend, a stocky man with black hair."

"Maybe so," Otis says. "They say you got a picture of Ronnie."

"And his friend. Drawings I made." I pull the sketches out of my back pocket and unfold them.

"I'll be damned. That's Ronnie alright. Spittin' image. And that sure looks like Ben. You're a damn good drawer."

Stocky man's name is *Ben*.

He tears the sketches into pieces and sprinkles them on the soiled carpet. That's when I notice the scattered needles.

"Hey, those were mine."

"And now they ain't."

Situation 2.

"Gentlemen, what do you suggest we do now?"

"Get rid of her," Clovis says. "Now. She's dangerous. I felt it the second she walked in the bar with those pictures."

"That's the fucking meth talking. Don't start tweaking on us. What about you, Albie?"

"We don't need to get rid of her. Just make her promise to go away. I didn't sign up for killing no one."

Otis says, "Let's see what Ronnie wants. Tell you the truth, I thought she was making it all up 'til I saw the pictures. Lemme call 'im."

I could save him a call. Ronnie will want me dead.

"If you want me to leave, I'll go. I didn't mean to cause this much trouble. I was just looking for a little help."

"Can't do that," Otis says.

"Albin said you wanted to help me."

"Albin lied. You are here to pay a debt to Ronnie. I gotta find my phone and take a piss."

He tells Clovis and Albin to *secure* me so I can't escape. Albin doesn't move, but Clovis picks up a roll of black electrical tape from a pile of junk in the corner.

Ain't gonna happen. I give Albin a *Help me* look and he turns away. Otis comes back with his phone and a large pistol grip sticking out of his pants. No way I can win three against one, but the first person who lays a finger on me is going to regret it.

Clovis moves in closer with the tape. I pull out the neck knife. "Back off."

He stops, raising his hands. "I told you. She's a fuckin' little ninja."

Otis slides out his big gun and thumbs back the hammer. This is where a gun definitely beats a knife.

"Drop the knife."

I screwed up. *You don't win quick with a knife, you lose.* And lost.

Otis says, "Albie, get your thumb out of your ass and do something."

Albin picks up the broken chair leg and raises it like a club.

Since there's no way I'm putting down the knife, I guess this is it. Strange. I really did make the choice. I'm not afraid to die right now. It's not really me inside anyway. My only regret is I never got justice.

I point the blade at each of them. "Don't make the mistake of thinking I'm a harmless little girl. I was trained to kill by an expert. I killed a man just last week. The only way you're going to stop me is shoot me and that's going to make a big fat mess. The police are already looking for me."

"Temporary truce," Otis declares. "Nobody fucking move until I straighten this out. Especially you." Keeping the gun pointed at me, he pushes a button on his phone.

"Ronnie. It's Otis. ... No, we ain't got the money yet. That's why I'm calling. We wanna pay our debt a different way. ... Hear me out. We got a little package in our living room. A girl. Name's Alice Miller. Claims you got her pregnant in Georgia. ... She said two months ago."

He looks at Clovis and Albin. "Ronnie says he don't know no Alice Miller from Georgia. ... Mm-hm. Okay."

He pulls the phone away. "How old are you?"

I don't answer, in part because I'm stunned that tall man's on the other end of the phone call.

"Sixteen, according to her driver's license," Albin says.

"Her driver's license says sixteen, but she looks younger to me. She showed up at Delphine's with a drawing that looks just like you. One of Ben too. ... Brown hair, blue eyes."

He looks at me. "No, I wouldn't call it blonde. Albie, what color was her hair on the driver's license?"

"Blonde."

"You hear that? Albie says her hair's blonde on the driver's license. That mean something? Okay, I'll ask."

He lowers the phone. "Ronnie wants me to ask you a question."

I glare.

"How's your mama and little sister?"

I lunge with the knife, but he's too far away. Clovis grabs me from behind. I swing across my chest and slash his arm.

"Fuck!" He lets go, but Albin grabs my wrist, squeezing with both hands until the knife falls loose. Clovis grabs me in a chokehold, cursing.

"I guess that was the right question," Otis says calmly into the phone. "She just tried to kill me with a knife. ... Sounds good. Then we're square? ... Thank you, my man. We'll take care of it. Don't you worry. Later." He puts the phone in his pocket.

"Good news, gentlemen. Turns out Alice here is a fake, along with her story."

"I fucking knew it," Clovis says, spitting on me.

Pig.

"Relax, I said it was good news. "Turns out this girl is much more valuable than any Alice. Ronnie says if we dispose of her without a trace, we are not only debt-free, Ben and him will pay us a substantial bonus."

"Who is she?" Albin asks.

"Wouldn't say."

"Gimme the gun," Clovis says. "I'll kill the bitch right now. Look at my arm. *Shit!*" He punches me in the back and I fall to my knees.

"Calm the fuck down," Otis says. "We got to do this without a trace, which means not inside. Go wrap your arm. You're bleeding all over the place."

Sucking for air on all fours, my eyes lock on the knife ... until Otis reaches down and picks it up. He pulls me to my feet by the hair. It doesn't hurt any worse than when I pull it myself, but he's gonna pay. I palm one of the needles on the way up.

"Ronnie wants proof you're dead. If you play nice, we'll make it quick and send a few pictures. Don't cooperate, we'll cut your hand off with your own knife and take it to him with a bow on top."

"Fuck you," I say and jam the needle in his face.

Clovis, back with a dish towel tied around his arm, grabs me and pushes me back onto the floor.

"Bad choice," Otis says, pulling out the needle and wiping a drip of blood from his cheek. "I say we let Clovis take that hand off right now."

"Come on, guys," Albin says. "We don't need to kill her."

"Gimme the knife," Clovis says.

Bonk, bonk, bonk, bonk …

"What the fuck is that?"

"Sounds like the alarm on my truck," Albin says. "Raccoon probably jumped in the back again."

"Fuck you waiting for? Go turn it off."

36

OTIS LOCKS the deadbolt behind Albin and orders Clovis to hold my wrists behind my back while he wraps them in tape. *So she don't cause no more fuckin' damage.* Clovis twists my arms like he wants them to hurt, which they do. His stale breath makes me want to gag.

"What's this?" Otis tugs on the cord around my neck. "So that's where she got the knife."

When they finish, I'm facedown, cheek against the filthy carpet, tape over my mouth, breathing through my nostrils and starting to hyperventilate—just like that day. I suddenly realize I'm unable to choose not to be afraid anymore. *I'm sorry, Lucas.*

My brain swirls like a carousel as I suck for air, making everything even blurrier than usual. I try to focus on a sliver of porch light shining through a crack under the front door. Hiding girl wants to wriggle through it and escape. Calm girl says that's impossible and tells her to quit breathing so hard or we're both going to pass out.

My backpack is on the other side of the room. Calling 911 might be my only chance. Can I get to it?

Clovis says, "Where should we do it? Out back?"

"Too close. We'll take her out to the wetlands and sink her."

I worm my way toward the backpack, making it two feet before Otis says, "Where the fuck you think you're going?"

I go back to gazing at the slit of light. It brings back a memory of that day, of looking out the bathroom window at the trees and sky, at freedom.

Then the porch light goes out. I blink, twice, thinking it's my imagination, but it stays out. Maybe it's a message, from the devil or even God, to give up, that there's nothing left for me outside of this disgusting room. Only darkness.

Otis and Clovis are discussing how to make sure my body sinks and stays sunk.

The doorknob starts to turn. No, cannot be. The start of another flashback? Please, not now. But this door doesn't open. *Mom, you should have locked the door.* The knob moves left, right, then stops where it started.

Someone or something starts pounding. *Boom boom boom.*

"Albie?" Otis says.

No reply.

Otis picks up the gun.

"Albie?"

"Of course it's fucking me. Who did you expect? Open the goddamned door."

I forgot all about Albin.

Otis opens the door and says, "What happened to the light?" Albin's standing in the shadows, face hidden. He takes a step and Otis's face changes.

He's raising his gun when a loud grunt sends Albin rocketing into the room, smashing into Otis and knocking the gun loose. They both land on the floor.

A monster fills the shadows, ghostly, with green demon eyes. *The devil.* Then I notice the angel wings. This must be what happens when you die, you don't know which one has come to get you.

The girls in my head get dizzy as the carousal spins faster and faster, until the monster, holding a semiautomatic pistol in a black-gloved hand, steps into the room and says, "Anyone moves one fuckin' inch gets shot."

"Lucas!" It comes out *Ookuh!* through the tape.

He's leaning on a cane. The ghostliness is his sickly pallor, angel wings his long, thick arms. Demon eyes his ... green eyes? Lucas has brown eyes. Is it all a hallucination?

Otis makes a move for his gun.

Bam.

Nope. It's real. Otis grabs his leg and rolls on the floor like a wounded animal.

"I told you not to fuckin' move." Lucas labors across the carpet and kicks the gun out of reach. "You alright?"

I move my head up and down. My eyes must be as big as pancakes.

"Sorry it took me so long."

He orders Clovis to take the tape off me. "Fuckin' now!" Clovis jumps to it. "And don't fuckin' touch her while you doin' it." Clovis unwraps the tape with twitchy fingertips.

"Alice, you remember we was talkin' about how to get people to fear you?" Lucas says, a rasp in his voice.

"Mm-hm," muffled by the tape.

"Remember, I specifically say, you tell a man *Don't move or I shoot* and he moves, you got to shoot. He got to believe you to be afraid. This man with the bullet in his leg didn't believe me. That man undoing the tape did. See what I mean?"

Arms free, I shove Clovis away, tearing the tape from my mouth.

"You need to put that in your book," I gasp.

He holds out his cane. I grab hold of it and he pulls me up..

"You're alive," I say, eyes wet. "And you're here. I can't believe it." I start to hug him.

"No hugs. I got three holes in my side and we got a job to finish."

"But how—"

"Later. Tape them boys' hands up. Gentlemen, you will cooperate fully and respectfully or die."

When I finish, he orders them to sit against the wall.

"Alice, my first question to you is do these men deserve to die?"

I look down the line from Clovis to Otis to Albin. "I'm not really sure. That one choked me and punched me in the back, and volunteered to cut my hand off. Oh yeah, and spit on me!

"That one's the leader. He made the plan to kill me.

"That's Albin. He was the nicest, the only one who said they shouldn't kill me. But he also tricked me into coming and drove me here. What do you think?"

"Why they trying to hurt you in the first place?"

"To pay some kind of debt to tall man, Ronnie. Otis—that one—even talked to him on the phone."

"No shit? You talked to tall man, Otis?"

Otis glares, clasping his leg, bleeding badly.

"Damn, girl, you do good detective work. Fuckin' dangerous, but good. So what is it, deserve to die?"

"I ... don't know. I went to church yesterday and ..."

"Oh, fuck. Here we go."

I think about the pig farm. "Okay, they deserve to die."

"Don't let me talk you into it. We can decide as we go. Let's see what they know about Ronnie."

"And *Ben*. That's stocky man. They know him too."

"No shit? I'm gonna nominate you for the FBI."

Oh, man. I forgot all about the FBI. I wonder what Agent Forster's doing right now.

He points the gun at Clovis. "We start with you, motherfucker who spit on my friend. Tell us what you know about Mr. Ronnie and Mr. Ben?"

"They come into the bar once in a while and I serve 'em drinks. Just bar talk. That's it. I swear."

Bam.

A piece of something hits me in the cheek. Clovis slumps with a hole in his forehead. Calm girl explains to hiding girl that nothing is real. *It's better that way,* she says.

"I made an executive decision," Lucas explains, and points the gun at Albin, shaking like he's freezing cold. "So you're Albin."

"Yes, sir."

"You scared, Albin? Looks like you peed your pants."

"Yes, sir. I didn't mean no harm, sir. I didn't know what I was getting into."

"Why did you transport this girl here tonight?

"We did a drug deal with Ronnie and Ben, a few months ago. They fronted us ten grand worth of meth to sell, but we got ripped off. We were trying to figure a way to pay it back. We heard she was at Delphine's showing pictures around and saying Ronnie got her pregnant."

"So you thought, fuck it, we can kill the girl and save ten thousand dollars. Problem solved."

"No, you heard her. I didn't wanna kill no one. I thought we were just gonna scare her away. Ronnie and Ben said they'd kill us if we didn't come up with the money. Ronnie's a fucking psycho. He'd kill you for five dollars or no reason at all. Ben too. They're not normal, man."

"Chickenshit," Otis yells.

Lucas whacks Otis in the head with the cane. "Shut the fuck up. You get you turn. Ronnie and Ben. Last names."

"I don't know," Albin whines. "They never used last names."

Lucas turns to me. "Alice?"

"I think he's telling the truth. Albin, just tell us how to find them."

Albin starts crying. "I wish I knew."

"You said Ronnie got in trouble before. For what?"

"Sex crime, on a minor. Spent time in prison for it. That's where he met Ben. That's why we believed your story about him getting you pregnant."

"Lucas, can we skip him for now?" I point to Otis. "He's the one. He said he's Ronnie's cousin. He's got Ronnie's number in this phone. We need the password."

"So you're Ronnie's cousin."

"I lied."

"Just a friend then. What is it you admire most about Ronnie as a friend? His child-rapin'? Mother-killin'?"

Otis spits.

Lucas asks for the password and he spits again. *Bam.* Lucas blasts a hole in the wall two inches from his head.

"The password."

Grabbing at his ear, "Fuck you."

Bam. Lucas shoots him in his healthy leg. He howls.

"I got a lot more bullets than you got body parts. Password."

He spits, "Seven, five, seven, six."

"It works!" I say. I search his recents. "I got the number."

Lucas points the gun at Otis's groin. "I'm gonna ask you a question. And I warn you in advance. You got exactly three seconds to answer it or you gonna be dickless. Where is Ronnie? One, two—"

"Florida. Pensacola," he says, sucking air through gritted teeth. "He wanted me to send the money there. Said they was laying low, needed it for livin' expenses."

"Now we gettin' somewhere. He give you an address?"

"No," voice thinning, breath getting shallower. "We never ... never had the money to send. That's why we were trying to make the ... deal."

"Ah, yes. *The deal.* The deal to kill my friend."

I butt in. "I have an idea. Otis could call Ronnie and say he needs the address to bring him proof I'm dead."

Lucas nods, but when we turn back, Otis is still, empty eyes gazing at nothing.

"Two down. About time for us to git," Lucas says. "But we got to do somethin' about Albie here."

"Can we just leave him?"

"Can't leave no witnesses. You know that. No better proof than you."

"I won't tell anyone," Albin begs. "Believe me. Please."

"He sounds sincere," I say.

"They all do when they about to die."

"I'll tell the cops we're drug dealers," Albin says. "It's true. I'll say we got attacked by people who came to steal drugs. It happens everywhere."

Lucas looks at me. "You let this man live, you takin' a big chance for both of us. Ain't no way to guarantee he won't talk."

I fret. "I'm just not sure he deserves to die. ... I have an idea."

Five minutes later we've filled Albin's phone with selfies. He's smiling into the camera while pointing Lucas's unloaded gun at the bloody corpses. If he deviates from the story, we send the pictures to the cops.

I retrieve my neck knife, careful not to step in the spreading blood.

"We done here?" Lucas says.

"I think so." I pat my backpack. "I have their phones and Otis's gun."

"New backpack? I thought you was in love with the old one."

"Oh, brother. We have a lot to talk about."

Lucas opens the front door and nods for me to go first. I run past him, leaping over the steps onto the weedy grass. I twirl in circles, gulping the dewy night air until I trip over the gutter and fall on my butt, laughing.

"I can't believe I'm alive—omigod, I can't believe *you're* alive! And you're *here*. It's a miracle! That's the only possible explanation."

"Shit, I forgot somethin'," Lucas says.

I jump up. "What is it? I'll get it for you."

"I got it. Wait here."

He goes inside and closes the door. I hear a single gunshot. He comes out and slowly makes his way down the stairs, wheezing with each step. "My vehicle's over here," he points.

We begin a slow hike into the darkness, him leaning heavily on the cane. I grab his arm to help, but he pushes me away.

"I ain't no fuckin' invalid."

37

"**LIKE MY** new ride?" he says as a colossal silver SUV takes shape in the shadows.

"It's huge. What is it?"

"Chevy Tahoe. Rental."

"Where's yours?"

"Police impound lot. Evidence."

It hurts my heart to watch him struggle climbing into the driver's seat. "Can I at least hold your cane?"

"I got it."

We roar out of the driveway onto the pitchy highway. I lower the window and stick my head out, letting the rushing air blast away the bloody mess left behind. The stars shine bright as bulbs outside the city lights. The Big Dipper is on the other side of the sky.

Who would have thought the night could end like this? With so much to say, I have no idea why the first thing is, "Your eyes are green."

"Contacts. Needed to change my appearance. Couldn't do much with my hair on short notice like you. That brown looks good on you. Makes you look less white."

"Um, okay. Thanks, I guess. Where are we going?"

"The beach," he says.

"Pensacola?"

"Got no place better to go. I'm on vacation. What about you?"

"Free as a bird. Do you think we can find them?" I cut him

off before he can say it's a stupid question. "I still can't believe you're here. I have a million questions."

"Surprise, surprise."

"Number one is how did you find me? Wait, that's number two. Number one is you're supposed to be dead."

"Legally, I am. Lucas Ellington Jackson has departed this earthly world. You are talking to Joseph Black. You can call me Joe."

"I think I like Joseph. New identity?"

He nods. "With every identification document known to mankind and a whole life to go with 'em."

"Why change?"

"Lucas Jackson was always gonna get shot. Only surprise is it took so long. Hospitals borin' fucking places. Nothing to do but think, so I done some of that."

He catches me looking out the side mirror. "Hey, you listening?"

"Yeah. Just checking to make sure no one's following us."

Softer, "We good, we good. Chill. Got some drinks in a cooler in the backseat."

I reach back and retrieve a bottle of icy water.

"Anyway, I did a lotta thinking. Course my first thought was to kill them men that shot me."

"Obviously. They deserve it. I'll help. When are we going to do it?"

He's quiet, thinking of a plan.

"Suppose I did?" he says. "Suppose I kill 'em. Then what? Somebody else come to kill me, I go kill them. Ain't no end to it. So I decided to make my own end. Remember when I said you always got a choice?"

"As a matter of fact, I was thinking about it earlier tonight."

"I called you a hypocrite that day at the pig farm, but in the hospital, I realized I'm the hypocrite. I once told you to go start a new life."

"I remember. I asked why you didn't."

"I said it was too late, that I got no choice. My second night in that room, alone in the dark hooked up to all that shit, I realized I do got a choice. Stay in the hood, keep killin' and tryin' not to get killed, or move on."

"A or B."

He laughs. "I guess you do listen. I chose B."

"I saw your obituary."

"They even had a funeral for me. Mr. Green made me a video."

"I talked to him on the phone. He said you were *righteous*."

"That some bullshit, ain't it? I've known Mr. Green since I was a little kid collectin' cans to sell. Trust him like a real dad. He helped me set the whole thing up, did all the paperwork."

Back in Lafayette, we pull onto the interstate. A green sign says we're heading to Baton Rouge. The first billboard we pass warns, *Someone will pay for your sins. Will it be YOU or JESUS?*

"That funeral video was really something," he says. "Hearin' people talk about me like they loved me, for real, not just saying shit 'cause they at a funeral."

"Of course people love you. Didn't you know that? Mr. Green obviously loves you. James, a million people. Kiona, she adores you, and you know I love you. I already told you that. I love you to death."

He drags a hand across his face. "Change the subject."

"Who knows you're alive besides Mr. Green?"

"Kiona and James."

"Is Kiona doing okay? I've been worried about her."

"She's happy I'm alive, but that's about it. Definitely ain't pleased I'm leaving Memphis."

"You are?"

"Can't change your identity and stay in the same place."

"Oh, right."

"And she was pissed off I left the hospital early. Even threw her phone at me."

"I don't blame her. Why did you do it? Mr. Green said it was against the doctor's advice."

No response. I need to be more like Darla, not press so hard, let people talk on their own.

Another billboard approaches. *Pregnant? Need Help?* Was and did. I start worrying the billboards are talking to me personally, especially when the next one that rushes up is just a blank space. I shake off the feeling.

I ask, "Where are you planning to go?"

He swats a mosquito and raises my window. The car gets silent. "Ain't decided yet."

"What about your document business?"

"Portable. Goes where a computer goes."

"I assume you're going to take Kiona, right? If you don't, you're making a huge mistake."

"You know Kiona. Woman only does what she wants. Annoyin' as shit, but probably why I love her."

"I knew it! I told her that, but she didn't believe me. Have you ever thought about telling her?"

"Next subject."

"Okay, but I gotta pee first."

"Now?"

"Yes, right now. That water. Sorry."

He pulls onto a sloped shoulder and I go into the woods. A chill seizes me as soon as the Tahoe is out of sight. I picture coming out of the trees and it being gone, like a scene from a scary movie. I hurry to finish and run back.

"*Phew*, thanks," I say, climbing in.

"No more water for you 'til we stop."

"Okay, *dad*. You wanted me to change the subject. Here's the new one. And don't try to dodge it. It's driving me crazy. How did you find me, out here, in the middle of nowhere? I still say it's a miracle. I prayed for one. I even had a preacher pray for me."

"Sorry, no miracle. You like that bracelet?"

"I love it. I've taken really good care of it. See?" I hold it up. "It has a few scratches, but I couldn't help that. I accidentally got it wet once, but I dried it right away. Look how shiny I keep the medallion."

"It's a pet tracker," he says.

"What?" I study the bracelet in the flashes of passing street-lights. "GPS?"

"You registered with the pet-trackin' company as Alice the Pit Bull."

"Pit bull!"

Lucas laughs so hard he grabs his side. "Couldn't think of a more appropriate beast."

"*Grrr.*" I growl and pretend to bite his arm, which keeps him laughing. "How did you get it in such a pretty bracelet?"

"Courtesy of James and a drug dealer who got arrested." He explains that James, *bein' a fuckin' genius*, put the electronics from the pet tracker into the medallion. He wove antennae wires into the leather straps to save space.

"What does that have to do with a drug dealer who got arrested?"

"Man can't build somethin' like that overnight. Took James a month. I told you he does special projects in the neighborhood for spendin' money. A drug dealer who wanted to keep an eye on his woman hired James to design a tracker disguised like jewelry."

"Yuck. That's creepy."

"Then the drug dealer got arrested. Meanwhile, James already made the bracelet."

I hold the medallion to my face, catching a reflected glimpse of my disappointment. "Then it wasn't really for me."

"I fuckin' gave it to you, didn't I? It was for you. I bought it from James."

"Why didn't you tell me what it was?"

"I planned to when I give it to you, but you was so excited I didn't have the heart to tell you it was just a dog tracker. Then I was gonna tell you before you left, show you how to charge it and all, but I got shot."

"You knew where I was the whole time?"

He shakes his head. "Saw you was headed to Lafayette, but I already knew that. GPS sucks power when you use it. Had to save the battery for when I needed it."

"How did you know to come tonight?"

"I'm tired of talking. Let's talk about you." We slow down entering Baton Rouge. Not much traffic. A clock at the top of a towering truck-stop sign says *12:01*. A new day. I never expected to see one.

"Anything interestin' happen since you been gone, other than almost gettin' you-self killed by meth addicts?"

"Interesting?" I laugh. "Yeah, I think you could say that, but it's a *lo-ong* story."

"Long drive."

I'm not sure where to start. "Well, the first thing I did when you got shot was run—as usual," I say, face flushing.

"I ordered you to run."

"Then I hid in a dumpster ..."

As the words tumble out, even I can't believe everything that's happened in the last week. Lucas raises his eyebrows at the mention of Scott Brooker and the FBI, but listens without interrupting, grimacing each time he moves.

"Do you want me to drive? I can. I drove fifty miles between Alexandria and Lafayette in the dead guy's car. I forgot that part."

"I'm good. Finish."

"That's about it. Tonight I went to Durty Delphine's to meet Albin. He took me to the house, saying we were going to meet tall man's family."

"Ronnie."

"I call him tall man. He's not human to me. Doesn't deserve a name. The last thing that happened was Clovis volunteered to chop my hand off. Then the horn went off in Albin's truck. I assume that was you."

"You lead an excitin' life, Emily Calby. No fuckin' doubt. You ever go back to school and write about your summer vacation, you guaranteed to win first prize. So back up. You killed a man? What was that like?"

It felt like *everything* and *nothing* at the same time. How do I explain that?

"I'm not exactly sure. It wasn't like the pig. Brooker deserved to die. He was going to rape me, maybe kill me. I thought about the other girls he picked up hitchhiking, the ones who didn't have a neck knife … and about Mom and Becky. I didn't even have to picture the two men like we talked about in training."

"I guess you got the killer instinct after all."

"I *told* you." I don't mention that at the time I felt like I was watching someone else do it. "Then I started feeling bad. Thought I was going to hell, but the preacher said self-defense isn't a sin."

"Good to know a preacher's right about somethin'. Course it ain't no sin. Self-defense is a fuckin' constitutional right, though covering it up and fleeing the scene ain't. Did you really do that uppercut through the intestine? Don't lie."

"I really did it. Had perfect positioning, unfortunately. I had to look at his … you know, to make sure I didn't miss. That was the worst part."

"Damn, girl. I taught you that move, but never knew anyone who did it in real life." He fist-bumps me.

"Alright, now back to you," I say. "I have to know the rest of your story. How did you know to come get me tonight?"

It was the videos from Durty Delphine's. He got Kiona to bring my laptop to the hospital, reminding me that hospitals are *borin' fucking places.*

"First thing I see when I turn it on is your screensaver," he says.

I made it from the screenshot of the guy leaving Durty Delphine's, the one who looked like tall man from behind. Lucas studied the facial composites and saw a similarity in hair and head shape. He went back to the video from the night before.

"Figured that to leave, the man had to arrive."

"I did that too, but didn't get a chance to finish because ..."

"I got shot with a fuckin' assault rifle. You can say it. Well, what to my wonderin' eyes should appear but a tall man who looked a lot like your drawing, strollin' in the back door like he owned the fuckin' place."

"*Ah*, the back. That's why I missed him. I focused on the front. Hardly anyone came in the back."

"The whole time I thought you was chasing a fantasy."

"Believe me, I know. Why didn't the recognition software pick him up?"

Like James said, low resolution cameras, tall man never looked in the camera and they only had the composites to work with.

"That's why you checked out of the hospital early, isn't it? To come help me."

He doesn't answer, eyes fixed on the spot-lit asphalt rushing under the wheels.

"You shouldn't have done that ... but I'm glad you did."

"Believe me, I was ready to get outta that place."

He and James hacked back into Durty Delphine's security cameras and used my high-resolution driver's license photo with the recognition software to keep an eye out for me in real time.

"Yesterday it started alertin' like a motherfucker. I hardly believed my own eyes when I looked at the screen. Thought it was the pain narcotics. There you was, starin' straight at the fuckin' camera."

I wait for a lecture about how stupid that was, but he keeps going.

"Tall man and Emily Calby in the same place. Dangerous combination for someone. I made a plan to leave for Lafayette and here I am."

A muted "Yay." I rest my head on his massive forearm.

"Once I got to Lafayette, the bracelet brought me straight to you. Well, not quite. I scared the shit outta some family down the street before I found you. Let's talk about this FBI shit. The fuck you thinking, tellin' some FBI fucker you alive?"

"Agent Forster. I didn't have a choice. He already knew it was me. They analyzed my sketches. Compared them to a picture I made for my teacher."

He nods appreciatively. "That's why they in the FBI 'steada drivin' a golf cart around a parking lot."

I yawn and rub my eyes. "He said they have new evidence about the two men. I think he's trying to help. He said people in the FBI want to send out an alert for me and he's been holding them off because he knows I'll run. I thought by playing along I could stall him." I nestle into the crook of his elbow.

"That makes more sense. Your free roamin' days is over if every police department in America got your picture. We talked about that. Where'd you leave it with FBI man?"

Closing my eyes, "I said I wanted proof where the two men are. That was yesterday. No, wait, today, I think."

"You can't trust the FBI. They probably sending a SWAT team to Lafayette right now."

My eyelids flutter. "Huh? What'd you say?"

"I said goodnight."

38

A RATTLING air conditioner wakes me. I'm on a bed in a dark room. The air tastes like salt. There's a giant hump on the bed next to mine. Lucas. *Miracle,* no matter what he says.

No idea how I got here. The last thing I remember we were driving. I get up and peek through the curtain to see a green blur behind a salt-caked window. The gulf! We made it to Pensacola.

Tiptoeing so I don't wake Lucas, I figure out how to work the coffee maker and carry a foam cup through a sliding glass door onto the balcony.

Beautiful. I love everything about the beach. The smell of salt-water and garlicky seaweed, the forever water and the whooshing surf, which right now is competing with angry sounds in my stomach. My last meal was yesterday's Chinese lunch buffet. I see a coffee shop and decide to serve Lucas breakfast in bed.

On the way out I ram my bare toes into a black duffel bag parked in front of the door. I have to bite my fingers to squelch a yelp. Lucas grumbles and turns over. It takes all my strength to move it. The bag weighs as much as Scott Brooker.

I hit the ground running, straight across the white sand down to the water. I roll up my pants legs and let the foamy swash lick my ankles. A seagull drifts across the blue sky. I sip coffee as a sailboat joins my postcard view. Still seems so unreal, impossible.

At the coffee shop, I use the last of Scott Brooker's money to load up on pancakes, hash browns, fresh fruit, orange juice, and bacon for Lucas. Eggs would be nice, but I don't know when Lucas is waking up and cold eggs are gross. He needs to sleep as much as possible. I'm going to take good care of him.

Sneaking back into the dark room I stumble on the bag again, losing my grip on the door which slams with a bang.

"Why don't you just light a sticka fuckin' dynamite under my ear?" Lucas growls.

"*Sor-ry*. Go back to sleep."

He sniffs. "What you got there?"

We eat on the beds, me facing him cross-legged. He explains how I sacked out in the car and he carried me up the stairs. We catch up on the details we didn't get to last night.

"So what do we do now?" I ask.

"Holy shit, Patience, can I at least finish breakfast?"

"Oh, sure … are you almost finished?"

He looks like he wants to dump the plate on me. "You ain't changed a bit."

"You wouldn't want me to. Admit it."

He eats in slow motion, just to be stubborn. "Now I'm finished," he says, setting down his fork. "What we do is figure out a way to track down the tall man in Pensacola."

"*Obvi*. But how?"

He wags his finger. "I take it back. You have fuckin' changed. Whatever happened to that polite, demure girl from Georgia?"

"She's *go-one*."

Ceiling look. Sometimes I think a part of him, only a small part, but it's there, would like to strangle me. "Here's how," he says. "Go find Otis's phone. Soon as you turn it on—"

"I know. Turn off location services and wifi. But can't the police still track us by triangulating the signal?"

"Possible, but I doubt they gonna waste a lot of time on dead meth dealers. Probably glad they gone."

He zeroes in on the bandage on my forearm. "What happened there?"

"Oh, that? Just a little cut I got." I type in the password. "*Omigod*, there's a text from *Ronnie*."

"Open it."

"*You take care of it?* Huh. I guess I'm the *it*."

"Turn it off and take out the battery. Fact, take out the batteries in all their phones."

The phones are all different. I have to find instructions online with Lucas's burner and use the multitool. "Why take out the batteries?" I ask as I work. "You just said the cops probably won't waste their time on meth dealers."

"Be careful as possible under the circumstances you stuck with. In a perfect world, you right, we don't use a dead man's phone, but I'm sure you noticed, this ain't no perfect world."

"Got 'em. Now what?"

"Now we got the basis for a plan."

* * *

Two hours later, I'm dead, sprawled on the worn hotel carpeting, ghostly pale, chest soaked in blood. I stare into space through glazed eyes, lips contorted in pain.

"Close your fuckin' eyes and stay still," Lucas says. He's taking pictures with Otis's phone.

"I'm acting."

"Yeah, well, quit."

We went shopping earlier. Lucas bought me new clothes and shoes. We also got dark corn syrup, flour and red food coloring to make fake blood, and talcum powder to dust my face and arms. I already had the gray eyeshadow.

"Wow, these look so real," I say, flipping through the pictures. "I'm going to dress like this next Halloween. Hey, here's a good one. See how my neck is twisted? Looks like somebody snapped it. Adds a nice touch."

"Nice touch?" he says with a funny look.

"Yeah, like someone grabbed my skull and tried to rip it from my body."

His eyes peer into me like he's searching for something. "You doin' alright?"

"Mm-hm. Fine." Except for the voices in my head, cutting myself and a few other things.

The plan is to reply to tall man's text pretending to be Otis. I told Lucas everything I remembered from last night, including that tall man promised Otis a bonus if they got rid of me.

Lucas hands me Otis's phone. "You type. I'll dictate. My fingers too big to text. First message. *Took care of it.*"

I send it. We wait ten minutes before the phone pings.

"*Need proof,*" I read. "You were right. Good thing we took the pictures."

"Send your favorite. No message."

I send it as Lucas taps the air with a stick of cold bacon.

"What's the matter?" I say.

"Hope it don't scare him off. A smart man would kill Otis for sendin' a picture like that."

"He said he wanted proof. Maybe he's using a burner."

Ping.

"Motherfucker," I mutter.

"Uh-oh, little goody two-shoes is cussin'. What's the problem?"

I hold the phone to his face. "Look at this! He sent a thumbs-up. That's what he thinks about my dead body. Unbelievable!"

"Save it. Tell 'em we need the money."

I read aloud as I type. "*When do we get bonus? Need cash.*"

Ping.

"He says when they come back to Lafayette. Lucas, he said *they.* That means they're together!"

"Calm the fuck down. Write this. *Can I come pick up? Could be there tonight. Need it bad.* Put a *Plz* on the end."

"Drugs, right?" I say.

This time there's no reply.

"Do you think he'll answer?"

"Don't know. He's got to at least be considerin' the possibility

Otis might double-cross him, maybe even snitch to the police. Meth addicts ain't the most reliable people to put your faith in."

Five slow minutes tick by before he says, "No point sittin' here starin' at the phone. He'll get back to us or not."

I spring off the bed. "Can we go to the beach? ... Oh, never mind. You should probably stay in bed."

"You kiddin'? Wouldn't miss it. Ain't never been."

"You've never been to the beach? Seriously?"

"I might even go surfin'."

I laugh. "I would love to see that, but they don't have very big waves in the gulf."

"Hey, don't rain on my fuckin' parade."

"Hardy har har."

He digs into the duffel bag.

"What's in that thing? Bricks?"

"Just some household items."

"Like what?"

He pulls out a huge gun, like something the army would use.

"Like this fifty-caliber BMG sniper rifle."

"That's a *household item?*"

"It is in my household. Here. Hold it." He hands it to me.

"Man, this thing is heavy. I could use it for bench presses. What's it for?"

"Shootin' accurately at long distance, shootin' through walls, shootin' incendiary rounds, all kinds of useful shit."

"Is it legal?"

"Fuck, yes. This is America. Not sure about the incendiary rounds."

"What are they for?"

"Startin' fires."

"Why did you bring that thing? We're not going to a war."

"Never know what you gonna need out in the cold, cruel world. I told you before, expect the worst and be happy when it don't turn out that way."

He pulls a shaving kit from the bag and goes into the

bathroom, leaving me holding the sniper rifle. When he comes out, he checks Otis's phone and says, "Let's go to the beach."

* * *

He rents us a cabana with two comfy lounge chairs and orders a margarita from a guy in a white shirt and shorts. I get a lemonade. I made a comment on the way about wishing I had a bathing suit and he insisted on buying me one at a beach shop.

"Lucas, are you sure you can afford all this? I still feel bad about you spending so much money on me." I start getting mad about my backpack all over again.

"I told you, I invested my criminal proceeds. Set for life. Money might be the only problem you ain't got."

The guy brings the drinks. Lucas licks salt from the rim of his glass and takes a slurp.

"Are you supposed to drink alcohol when you're recovering from major surgery?"

"Mm-hm," he says, taking another swallow. "Doctor say it good for me."

"He did? ... Liar." I punch him on the arm.

He lays back in the shade and chills, which he needs to do. I try to keep my mouth shut, which is always hard.

I scoop up a towel. "I'm going swimming and then do some exercises. I've been keeping my word about staying in shape."

"Good. Be careful in the water. Might be a shark, or a jellyfish."

I groan.

The water is smooth so I decide to try swimming parallel to the beach. It's not easy going against the current, but still a nice change from doing intervals in the heat. I go about a quarter mile before a lifeguard whistles at me to come in. I trudge back to where I started and collapse on the sand. After I catch my breath, I do sit-ups. In my bathing suit, I can see the definition in my abs.

Back at the cabana, Lucas is looking at Otis's phone.

"Did he write back?" I say.

"Nope. I just sent a message to speed things up. *Cops asking around town about missing girl. Want to talk to me. Need bonus.*"

"Make him nervous, right?"

He nods. "Get him thinkin' he better start treatin' ol' Otis right—or kill him."

Ping.

"You got his attention."

"*Product stead of cash?*" he reads and hands me the phone. "Tell him yes and say, *Can be there tonight. Address?*"

I send it, frowning when I get the response. "He says, *Text when you get here.*"

"Then that's what we do. Turn it off and take the battery out."

When we get back to the hotel room, I help Lucas change his bandages, trying not to look grossed out by the three purple holes in his side, which still have stitches in them. I take a shower and put on my new clothes: jeans, double tees, one white and one purple, and a pair of crispy-clean Nikes. I trash the smelly shoes I shoplifted in Shreveport.

"Can I get rid of the stupid gel-bra now that I'm with you?"

"Keep it. Never know when you might need to be Alice Miller."

Poking around in the duffle bag, he pulls out a handgun and lays it on the dresser.

"Ooh! Do you happen to have an extra gun for me?"

"No."

"But I need one."

"Quit losin' 'em in the river. Guns don't grow on fuckin' trees."

I leap up. "I just remembered. Otis's gun. I can use that."

"Lemme see it."

I get the gun from my backpack. It's a lot bigger and heavier than the pocket rocket.

"Browning Hi-Power," Lucas says, turning it in his hands.

"This here is a legendary handgun. Got to be stolen. No way that fuckin' tweaker owned a nice gun like this legit."

"Can I keep it?"

"It's big for your hands." He pulls back the slide, studies the chamber, lowers the hammer, pushes a button on the side and takes out a loaded magazine. "Here you go. Pull the trigger."

I take the gun. "Excuse me. Aren't we forgetting something?"

"Like?"

"One in the chamber?"

"Pull the trigger."

"You're sure you're not joking? Remember, I can't always tell."

"Go on."

I point the gun at the ceiling, at least we're on the top floor if it goes off, and squeeze the trigger, one eye closed, head back. "Nothing. How come?"

"First, this here is a single-action gun. Means you got to pull back the hammer to make it fire the first time. Most semiautomatics are double-action, like your pocket rocket, or striker-fired. Same difference. Pull the trigger, they go boom. Go ahead and pull the hammer back."

It takes both thumbs to do it.

"Now pull the trigger."

"Are you—"

He stops me with a look.

I pull the trigger, but it doesn't budge. "I give," I say. He loves toying with me.

"Browning Hi-Power's got what's called a magazine disconnect safety built in it. Gun won't fire without the magazine in it even if there's a cartridge in the chamber. Safety device. Gimme it."

I hand him the gun, which he disassembles. "Where's that tool you was usin' on the phones?"

I hand him the multitool. He uses the awl to tap out a pin near the trigger.

"What are you doing?"

"Removin' the magazine disconnect."

"I thought you just said it was a safety device."

"Ain't no self-respectin' gun carrier in America wants a fuckin' magazine safety. Say you in a struggle and accidentally hit the magazine release. Oops. You defenseless."

He pokes around inside the gun with a screwdriver, prying loose a spring-loaded tab, which he holds up like a tooth removed by a dentist. "No more magazine disconnect."

"Thanks, I guess."

He reassembles the gun. "The best way to carry this gun for quick use is called *cocked and locked*. Cartridge in the chamber, hammer back, but with this thumb safety on." He shows me how to use the thumb safety. Up to lock, down to fire.

He looks at the clock. "It's gonna take our dead friend Otis a while to drive here from Lafayette. Let's go find a shootin' range."

39

WE GET some strange looks at the indoor shooting range, where I had to use the driver's license to prove I'm sixteen. Maybe it's the brown hair or because I didn't wear the gel-bra, but the guy looked at the license three times before handing it back.

I'm standing in one of the stalls, wearing ear muffs and safety goggles, separated from Lucas by a clear plastic panel. On the other side is a man with a long beard, dressed in camouflage. He has four pistols lined up in front of him.

The Browning is a cannon compared to the pocket rocket, so big I have no choice but to hold it with both hands. Even with the ear protectors I flinch when I pull the trigger.

I feel like a two-year-old, shooting at a paper target exactly six feet in front of me. Lucas's rule: three feet, six feet and nine feet. Some people are shooting at targets so far away they have to look through a scope to see if they hit them.

The man in the camouflage taps on the plastic panel, saying something. I put down the gun and take off the ear muffs. Lucas watches out the corner of his eye, but keeps shooting.

"What did you say?"

"I said nice Browning."

"Oh, thanks."

"Interested in sellin' it?"

"No, we had to kill a man for it," I say. The man laughs and goes back to shooting.

Lucas is an excellent shot, even one-handed and leaning on the cane. I'm getting better. The Browning doesn't have a laser, but it's a lot more accurate than the pocket rocket. I hit near the center on most shots even from nine feet.

When we leave, the sky is ablaze in pastel pinks and purples. We drive to an all-you-can-eat seafood restaurant, where I refill Lucas's plate for him three times. I stare down the people who pause to look at us as they pass our booth.

"Why does everyone keep giving us weird looks?" I say, paranoid. "I guess we do make an unusual couple."

He snorts. "Yeah, unusual. That one word for it."

Back in the Tahoe he tells me to put the battery back in Otis's phone. I'm becoming an expert.

"Tell the tall man that Otis has arrived."

"Already?"

"Meth users don't take rest stops. Drive straight through, speedin' the whole way."

I'm here, I text.

An address comes back, along with *Meet in 30 minutes*. "I'll map it. ... Hm, some kind of industrial park."

"Well, well. Ronnie apparently ain't invitin' his ol' buddy Otis home for supper."

"Maybe he's just being careful."

"Most likely plannin' to get rid of the evidence. Kill 'im. That's what I'd do."

Ping. Another message.

"*What kind car?*"

"Tell him a maroon Buick," Lucas says. "Don't want to get ambushed drivin' up. Ask him the same question."

Maroon Buick, I type. *What about you?*

No answer. Ten minutes later we're on a dark road next to a bunch of warehouses. The phone says, *In two hundred feet, your destination is on the right.* I lower the volume.

Lucas turns off the headlights and takes his gun out. He gives me a nod and I do the same.

"Stay low and keep a lookout. Keep that safety on and let me do any shootin' unless the shit hits the fan."

I slink in the seat, phone in one hand, Browning in the other, cocked and locked. We cruise down a driveway. Security lights on the buildings provide spotty illumination. The only vehicles I see are dark silhouettes locked behind tall fences. I keep an eye on the side mirror for cars coming up from behind.

Lucas says, "For your future information, assumin' we survive, this ain't no way to set up an assassination. We at a big disadvantage, in a place we don't know against a hidden adversary."

"Look at the bright side. At least we know they're really in Pensacola. Otis could have been lying."

"You a glass-half-full girl. Keep on the sunny side. My grandma sang me that song as a baby. *Keep on the sunny side, always on—*"

Otis's phone rings. "Uh-oh." I hold it up. "*Ronnie*. What do we do?"

"Don't answer."

The ring stops. No message comes up. Lucas pulls the Tahoe over, leaving the engine running. "He's gonna get spooked if Otis don't call him back."

A text message pings.

I bite my lip. "It says *Call*. Do you think you could imitate Otis's voice?"

"Mostly I just heard the man gaspin' for air," he says. "Course I can't imitate that cracker's voice. You call him back."

"*Me* me?"

"Mm-hm."

"And say what?"

"Anything to get him to react without thinking."

I take a deep breath. "I'll try." I hit redial and put the phone on speaker.

"Otis?" says a voice tattooed on my brain. I drop the phone. Lucas gently squeezes my shoulder as I pick it up.

"No, this isn't Otis," I say.

"Who da fuck den?"

"This is Emily Calby."

"Who?"

"Emily Calby. You murdered my mother and sister. I guess you forgot our names."

"Bullshit. Dat girl dead."

"I was, but I came back to life. Now I'm the angel of death. And guess who's gonna die? Ronnie and Ben. You can come to me or I can come to you. I'm waiting for you right now." I laugh scary girl's maniac laugh and the phone goes dead.

Two parking lots away a vehicle lights up. "There he is," Lucas says. Tires squeal as the car fishtails out of the lot.

"Hold on." Lucas rams the Tahoe in gear and accelerates across an open field. We jump a curb, then another one, Lucas groaning with each tear of the seatbelt in his side. He keeps his foot on the gas, but when we reach the street, the car is already gone.

Lucas gives the steering wheel a half-hearted punch. "Shit. Did you see what kind car?"

"No, but it wasn't the blue truck with the camper-top, that's for sure. Looked like a regular car, dark-colored."

"Call 'im again."

I do but there's no answer. I turn off the phone. "I can't believe he was that close. Why do you think he ran?"

"You said you wanted people to be scared of you. Congratulations. I think you just scared the shit outta tall man. Come back to life? Angel of death? What was all that?"

"Remember? I told you. Before they set the fire, tall man said he was afraid of us coming back to life. Stocky man made fun of him, something about *hoodoo voodoo*."

"Louisiana voodoo. Good thinkin'. What about that fuckin' laugh? Sounded like a crazy person."

"Haven't I told you? I'm going crazy."

He gives me a one-eyed look.

I change the subject. "Do you think we'll get another chance?"

"Can't say," he says. "They might decide to run."

"Why not stay and try to find me? I'm a threat as long as I'm alive."

"For all they know this Tahoe was full of FBI agents."

The FBI. I keep forgetting about them, accidentally on purpose I'm sure.

"That reminds me," I say. "I need to check my email account for Robert Williams to see if Agent Forster put the alert out on me."

"I brought a laptop. We can check it on that. Let's find a bar with wifi to drown our sorrows."

"Public wifi? Is that safe?"

He pulls a USB stick out of the console. "It is with this," he says. "Tails." He launches into a lecture about Tails, a computer operating system using Tor that you can just plug into a computer and become invisible on the internet. Pretty cool, but he's giving me way too much detail. My concentration only works these days when I absolutely need it to.

Mainly to get him to stop talking about Tails, I say "Nice place" when we pull into the dimly lit parking lot of The Diamond Club. *FREE WIFI* is hand-painted on the window in red block letters below *Drinks Music Dancing*. Men are outside leaning on cars, holding jumbo-sized beer cans wrapped in paper bags. Lucas tells me to leave my gun under the seat.

I follow him in, staying close. A man at the door gives me a look. One glance from Lucas and he turns away. Sometimes I forget how intimidating he is, even with the cane.

At a booth in the back corner, Lucas orders a beer and I get coffee. He puts the USB stick in the computer and waits for Tails to load.

"Lemme check something first," he says, typing. "Here we go. Good news."

He rotates the laptop. It's a news story about three meth dealers who got shot in Lafayette, quoting the police saying they think it was over drugs.

"That's great," I say in a monotone.

"What's wrong?"

"Seeing that just brings back how hard it was to get this far. I blew it. I should have said something different to tall man on the phone, something to lure him in instead of scaring him away."

"Ain't your fault. I told you to get him to react without thinkin' and you did."

I squeeze my cheeks. "So close."

A pretty waitress with long purple fingernails brings our drinks. "Are you guys from out of town?" she says.

Lucas laughs. "You mean we don't look like regulars? I'm Joseph. This here's my daughter, Alice."

I give a friendly wave. "Nice to meet you," I say.

Her skepticism is obvious.

With a look of practiced irritation, like *I'm tired of having to explain this to every person we meet*, "Adopted. My mom—his wife—died of breast cancer."

"I'm so sorry," the waitress says. She gives Lucas a flirtatious look and skates her nails down his arm. "Let me know if you need anything else."

"Daughter?" I say when she walks away.

"That offend you?"

"No, but it's not very believable."

He takes a drink of beer and licks the foam from his lips. "Probably not. That cancer shit was a good addition. Good lyin', as usual."

"Whatever." He'll probably put that on my gravestone. *Here Lies A Good Little Liar.* "Do black people even adopt white people?"

"Course they do," Lucas says. "I mean, they must, least sometimes."

"Okay, *father*, how do I log onto my burner account?"

Lucas helps me navigate Tails to the email account for Robert Williams.

"There's a message," I say.

"Let's see it."

I move across the table and squeeze in next to him on the bench. When I open the new email from Agent Forster, I'm surprised by its shortness.

> *Dear Emily:*
>
> *Attached is a photograph.*
>
> *If I do not hear a positive response from you by noon tomorrow, a nationwide alert will be issued to find you.*
>
> *Jeff Forster*

"The man gets to the fuckin' point," Lucas says.

I click on the attachment.

Lucas is bitching that I might have just turned his computer over to the FBI, but I'm not paying attention. The strangest feeling. It probably takes less than a second for everything to sink in, but my molasses-brain seems to glob along in slow motion. First I notice the green grass with the sign in the yard, then the beige house, then the men on the porch.

"*Omigod.*"

40

I JUMP up and smash my pelvis on the table. "It's them," I say, slinking back to the bench, rubbing my side. "That's stocky man on the right, with the cigarette."

"And tall man on the left," Lucas says. "I'll be damned. They look just like your drawings."

"Agent Forster really does know where they are."

"Surprised he sent a picture."

"I promised if he proved the FBI knew their location, I'd come in. I was trying to trick him into telling me where they were, but I guess this is proof."

"Now you got a deadline of noon tomorrow," Lucas says. "You know what that means."

"How bad will it be?"

He types on the laptop. Up comes a picture of a pretty girl named Allison on an FBI webpage, *Kidnapping/Missing Persons*. It's a full-color downloadable flyer with complete details about the girl and her disappearance.

"They send these everywhere. Police, bus stations, train stations."

Blowfish imitation. "I'm toast."

He gives me a sharp elbow.

"Ow, what was that for?"

"What happened to the glass-half-full girl? Just means we gotta find them two men before noon tomorrow and get the fuck outta town."

"Yeah, right. Just like that, by magic."

"You a quitter?"

The growl in his voice gets my attention. "You know I'm not."

"Then quit feelin' sorry for you-self and get with the fuckin' mission. See that swirly spot, on the wall above the mailbox?"

"Yeah. It looks like the FBI blurred the address number. And there in the yard," I point. "The *For Rent* sign too. I guess that's how Agent Forster decided he could send the picture without giving up evidence."

Lucas smiles as he whistles over the lip of his beer bottle. "I guess your FBI friend don't know you travelin' with a former signal intelligence soldier and photographic expert."

He opens an app and drops the picture in it.

"What are you doing?"

"Checkin' for geotagging. Every picture has hidden data showin' where it was taken, longitude and latitude, unless you turn it off on the camera. ... Nothing here. Didn't expect the FBI to be that stupid, but I got another idea."

He gets out his phone and finds a number. "James. Lucas. Call me back, soon as possible."

"What's going on? Why do you sound excited?"

"Deconvolution."

"*Deconvo*-what?"

"Deconvolution, a process for reversing distorted signals and images. When you blur a picture with editing software, you just changin' the data that makes up the picture. Nothin' but math. Match the formula used to change it, you can un-change it."

"We can un-blur the address? That's awesome ... but we still won't know the street."

"Fuckin' baby steps. We ain't got what we need here though. Need James's help. He's stayin' at my building, lookin' after it."

* * *

We're back at the hotel waiting for James to call, sitting on the beds cleaning our guns with a kit from the duffel bag. I love the smell of the oil and gunpowder. *Shrek* is playing on the TV with the sound off.

"Now what do we do?" I ask when we're finished.

"Can we just do nothin' for a while? Just relax?"

"Sure."

He lays back on the pillows and closes his eyes. I twirl my hair and watch the TV for thirty seconds before, "Um, could you tell me how to charge my bracelet?"

I expect an outburst, but he says serenely, "You don't need the bracelet no more."

"*Boys*. You don't understand anything." He wards off more nagging by telling me the charger's in the duffel bag. I discover it under a ton of combat gear and plug it into a port hidden on the back of the medallion.

James calls and Lucas doesn't waste time chatting, diving straight into the problem.

"Hi James!" I yell from the other bed.

Lucas waves at me to shut up and picks up the laptop. "I'm sending the picture right now. Got it?"

I tune out as Lucas talks James through the complicated process of deconvolution, using software on one of his computers.

Shrek is kissing Fiona for the second time, after he knows she's an ogre, and everything ends happily ever after. Just like always. Yeah, right. I tug on Lucas's arm.

"Hold on a sec, James. What is it?"

"Can you ask James to tell Kiona I miss her?" I say.

"This ain't no family reunion," he says and goes back to more *blah blah blah* about deconvolution. I squirm impatiently until he snaps his fingers and makes a writing motion. I grab a pen and hotel notepad from the nightstand.

"Eight, nine, six. What about the *For Rent* sign? ... Janet Brayton Realty. B-R-A-Y-T-O-N. Thank you, my little man."

He sees me pouting. "James," he says. "When you see Kiona, tell 'er Alice misses her."

I do butterfly claps and poke his knee.

"Tell 'er I miss her too," he says.

I give a thumbs-up. "I miss you too, James!"

Lucas pins my lips together. "You gonna be around later? May need you again. ... Same as always, hopin' for the best and plannin' for the worst." He puts down the phone. "James say you welcome."

"Eight-nine-six," I read.

"Question is eight-nine-six what?"

"I have an idea." He used to ignore me when I had ideas. Now he pays attention.

"You a resourceful little fucker," he says after I explain it. "But you do it."

"Me? Don't you think it would be better if an adult called?"

"Lemme ask you this. You think I sound black?"

"You mean, like, when you talk? I guess so. So what?"

"People don't like to rent property to black folk."

"Is that legal?"

"No, but it don't stop 'em."

"That stinks. Alright, I'll call."

I search for Janet Brayton Realty and click on the call link. "It's going to voicemail," I say. "Wait, she's giving her cell number." I write it down and enter it, doodling a picture of a handgun on the notepad while the phone rings. She picks up and I wink at Lucas.

"Hi! Sorry to bother you so late. I'm calling because my family is looking for a house to rent. ... No, I'm not over twenty-one, but I'm here with my dad. He can't talk because he has throat cancer. Thank you, we appreciate your prayers."

Lucas mouths, *Throat cancer?*

"Yesterday we passed one of your houses we liked. I was supposed to write down the address. *Duh,* I wrote down the numbers, but not the street. We wanted to take my mom by tomorrow to see if she likes it. Tour? Um ..."

Lucas is shaking his head.

"We don't want to waste your time in case my mom doesn't like it. *Super*-picky. It's a beige house. The address is eight-nine-six. ... Coconut Drive? Thank you. If my mom likes it, we'll call you back. Hold on, my dad's trying to speak."

"Ask if people already livin' there," Lucas whispers.

"We were wondering if the house is occupied because we saw a couple of guys on the porch when we drove by. ... Perfect. That's exactly when we would need it. Have a nice night and God bless!" I turn off the phone.

Lucas is smiling. "Knowin' you, watchin' you in action, I finally understand how you survived a month on your own."

"I know, I know. I'm a good liar."

"More than that. You smart, strong. A warrior and a survivor." He pats me hard on the back, guy to guy, like my dad used to do.

I blush. "Thanks. Well, it's eight-nine-six Coconut Drive. She said *the two men* are on a short-term lease that ends next week."

"Here's the house," Lucas says, holding up the laptop.

Same house as in the FBI picture. "That's it. We've got to go. Now. Get the guns!"

"Whoa, whoa. Slow down, Patience."

"Don't *Patience* me, not now. You said they might run after I spooked them with the phone call."

"If so, they already gone. You got to have a plan before you go kill two men."

* * *

We use earth view to scope out the neighborhood, a cluster of small houses and lots. The house behind 896 Coconut Drive is an exception, bigger, with a swimming pool. Lucas clicks on it and switches to street view.

"Why are you looking at that house?"

"Just checkin' something."

He uses a stylus to draw escape routes and closes the computer. "We got to get them alone," he says. "Most logical choice is—"

"Inside the house," I say.

He nods. "Two ways in. Fake-in or break-in."

An image of stocky man talking to Mom in the yard about running out of gas assaults my brain.

"Fake-in seems to work," I say.

"Easier in the right situation. Ain't got to worry about alarms or breaking down doors."

I wonder if stocky man and tall man thought about that before they came to get my family.

"But no one's gonna open the door for Lucas in the middle of the night, no matter what the story."

"I'm a good faker," I remind him.

"No doubt, but they already gonna be on alert for you after your phone call. But breakin' in at night? Dangerous. Best time to break in is when no one's home, which is usually the daytime."

I shake my head. "No way. We need to go tonight. If they leave, there may never be another chance. I'd rather die tonight than let them get away. Please, Lucas."

His gaze shifts to the ceiling, but it's not the usual look. If I didn't know him, I'd think he was praying. "Alright," he says, pushing up on the cane.

He drags the duffel bag into the bathroom and shuts the door. When he comes out, he's dressed completely in black.

"Hey, I need black clothes too."

"Don't fuckin' worry about it. You ready?" he says.

"I've *been* ready," I say, snatching the Browning off the bedspread.

41

A DIGITAL clock on a church sign turns to midnight as we drive to 896 Coconut Drive. Why is it always striking midnight? It starts freaking me out until calm girl says, *Midnight comes every night, we're just getting out more.*

The church sign says, *Be Thankful You Don't Get What You Deserve.* I laugh. Lucas asks what and I say nothing.

Hardly any cars out. I'm giving directions from the phone map. Not complicated. Pensacola is even smaller than Lafayette. "This is the street," I say.

Lucas slows the Tahoe. "Keep your eyes out. Just gonna drive by and check it out."

A car turns up ahead, coming our way. It hits a bump and the headlights blind me.

"Fuck, get down," Lucas says.

I slide to the floorboard. "What's the matter?" I whisper.

"Stay down. Your friends are here."

"The two men?" I pop my head up, but Lucas pushes it down.

"The FBI. Don't move."

A car motor gets louder before it passes and fades away.

"How do you know it's the FBI? Can I get up now?"

"Stay."

"Stay? I'm not a dog."

"Let me rephrase. Please remain on the fuckin' floorboard 'til I can be sure the fuckin' FBI ain't coming to git you."

"Why do you think it's the—"

"Because it makes sense they be watchin' the two men, and the vehicle was a black Dodge Charger, common vehicle for law enforcement, and ... shit, it's turnin' around and comin' back our way."

I moan. I hate not being able to see.

"You got to get out in case they pull me over."

"Why would they pull you over?"

"Maybe 'cause they got an all-points bulletin out on you or maybe 'cause I'm black and driving a shiny new Tahoe. Maybe they won't do anything, but you can't take a chance." He swerves around the corner. "Get out. Quick. Take your gun and hide."

"What about you?"

"I'll be back. Wait for me. Go!"

I leap out with my backpack and run behind a clump of hibiscus bushes. Lucas drives off as a black car with two men in the front seat comes around the corner. He puts on his signal and turns down the next street. The black car makes the same turn.

Ten minutes go by. I'm still crouched in the bushes. If they pulled him over, he's got the sniper rifle, fake IDs, probably marijuana and Lord knows what else in the duffle bag. I get out my phone, but realize I never got his new number.

Twenty minutes and still no sign. Did he get arrested? Maybe it wasn't the FBI. Maybe the Tahoe broke down or he decided he needed to buy something for the mission. He said to wait.

A half hour passes and I know he's not coming back. Something happened. I could probably make it back to the hotel. That would be a logical place to meet up if we got separated. But with the two men a block away, I know I'm not leaving. No point wasting time thinking about it.

Staying in the shadows, I prowl along the sidewalk. The only sound is insect chatter. Maybe this is how it was always meant to end.

No need to fake-in. They'd open the door in a heartbeat if they knew I was on the other side. *Knock, knock. Who's there?*

Em. Em who? Em you glad I came to kill you? Scary girl's laugh bubbles up, but I clamp it down. Like Lucas said, after my call, they'll be expecting me, so that option's out.

But breaking in isn't a good idea either. Not only dangerous, but I have no idea how to break into a house. I need to draw them outside, make some kind of diversion. Maybe I can sneak in behind them and find a defensive shooting position. Set up an ambush. Lucas said that was the best way to go.

I step lightly around colorful chalk drawings of flowers and hearts. From a perch, I see a gangly girl with a blonde pony-tail drawing a sidewalk picture of a stick-figure family holding hands. Pink for momma, blue for daddy, orange for baby sister, and purple for her—my favorite color even then.

Across the street is a miniature basketball hoop. It's a quiet family block. Have to get the men to come out the back, not wake up the neighborhood and bring the FBI.

I pass a privet hedge. *Jesus Mary*, the beige house. I jump back. Peeking around the squared-off branches, I'm surprised how small it is, nothing like the fortress I constructed in my head. The porchlight's on, but the curtains are closed. It looks dark inside. A brown car is parked in the driveway, probably the one that sped away.

Standing at the edge of no return. My real moment of truth. *I am not afraid. I am Emily-the-Powerful* ... then why are my legs iron posts? I can't make them go until the scary girl, angry and impatient, tells me to quit wasting time and go kill the fuckers.

I inch along the side wall, picturing *Ben* and *Ronnie* on the other side—sleeping, dreaming, getting to wake up in the morning and eat breakfast. *Rage beats fear.* I pick up the pace. An air conditioner drowns out my climb over a chain-link fence. *Air conditioning.* Mom and Becky don't even have air.

The backyard is dark and empty. No trees or even bushes, just a wood fence separating it from the two-story house with the swimming pool. As my pupils dilate, I spy a shape on the patio, darker than the night itself.

I draw back the hammer and lower the thumb safety on the pistol. Calm girl is thinking she prefers double-action to single-action because a cocked, loaded gun with the safety off makes her nervous. Hiding girl whispers, *Be careful, be so, so careful.*

The shape turns out to be a charcoal grill reeking of recently cooked meat. The smell reminds me of entering our burning house and I have to swallow to keep from gagging. Backing away, my foot hits something metallic. The clang seems deafening. I point the Browning at the back door, but no one comes out.

It's a can of charcoal lighter fluid. Half full. *You a glass-half-full girl.* Scary girl cackles, *Burn them alive!* Calm girl says forget about it because the walls are cinder block and they would just walk out the front door.

* * *

Ten minutes later I'm squirting the finishing touches of lighter fluid on the back fence, making sure the lines connect. I dig out the lighter I bought at the dollar store for nights in the woods at Acadiana Park.

To quote two great men, this—right here, right now—is where the shit hits the fan. I flick the lighter and touch it to the fence, watching the yellow stripes chase each other until the fence is ablaze with *F-E-A-R_M-E.*

The flames won't last long. Running to the house I hurl a rock through a window and jump behind the corner, gripping the Browning with both hands. Only a couple of seconds before the back door swings open and two men run out, heading for the fence. It's dark but I recognize their voices.

"Wha da fuck?" Tall man. "I tell ya she come back from da dead."

"She didn't come back from the dead. It's a trick." Stocky man.

I'm holding the trigger, quivering. I *so* want to start shooting, but they're too far and moving. Lucas told me a million times to never shoot at a moving target. I loosen my finger.

They reach the fence and I run for the open door. Entering a kitchen, I search for a place to shoot from, but the house is dark as a dungeon. I feel along the wall until I come to a doorway, where I make out the shape of a couch against the streetlights filtering through the front curtains. The living room.

A defensive shooting position. Protection and a clear field of fire.

The voices outside get louder. They're on the way back. I size up the room, the width of the doorway and distance from the couch. Best to wait until they're in the room together. Shoot whoever's on the left, then move right. Calm, steady breathing. No wasted shots.

I make for the couch, but trip over something in the middle of the floor, landing on dusty carpet that makes me sneeze before I can stifle it. At first I think it's my imagination, just one more piece of evidence I've lost my mind. Then I hear it again. My name, not even. My nickname: *Em.*

I feel behind me, touching something both hard and soft. It's a person—*Omigod*—a really big person.

"Lucas," I whisper, setting down the gun. "What are you doing here? Are you okay?"

The men are on the patio, arguing about voodoo.

I press my lips to Lucas's ear. "*Loo-cas.* You need to get up. Right now. *Please.*"

He stirs and makes a sound as the ceiling light flares on. I grab for the Browning but a black boot comes down on my fingers. I hear them crunch.

Gazing down I see my worst nightmare, Lucas in a pool of blood. Looking up I see my next one, both grinning.

42

"**WELL, WELL,** well. If this ain't a surprise," stocky man says, still pale-skinned and dressed in black. He points a gun at me while stooping to grab mine. "Holy shit, Ronnie, the girl's packing a Browning Hi-Power."

"Otis got one a dem," tall man says warily.

"You take this from Otis, honey-pie?"

I just stare. You couldn't even call it a glare. I'm stupified. The two men, standing right in front of me. I dreamed about it, prayed for it, gave everything to make it happen ... but not like this.

Stocky man takes the magazine out of the Browning and puts it in his shirt pocket. He lowers the hammer and sets the gun on a table.

"I asked you a question," he says, keeping his gun fixed on me. "What happened to Otis? And who the hell is this big black motherfucker?"

"Don't you dare call him that," I spit.

"I don't think she likes us, Ronnie," he says.

"I hate you. I came here to kill you. Both of you."

They both laugh, but tall man looks spooked.

"I don't think you succeeded, dolly," stocky man says. "Judging by the situation."

"Even if I don't, whatever happens, you're going to burn in hell for eternity."

Twisted grin. "You might be surprised to know I agree with you on that one, but it ain't gonna be for a long time. Get up."

No. I'm not sure if I say it or just think it, but I stay on the floor guarding Lucas until tall man jams a foot into my ribs. "Da mon say get up."

My fingers burn like hot needles, but I'll slit my own throat before letting them see me suffer. I push up with my good hand. At least it's the left one. I can hear my preacher. *Always remember to be thankful for even the smallest of blessings.* He ended every sermon with it.

"I think I liked her better as a blonde," stocky man says. "What do you think, Ronnie?"

"I like 'er fine eeder way." He takes a step toward me and I crouch to a defensive position.

"Keep it in your pants," stocky man says. "We need some answers first. What happened to Otis?"

"I'll answer your questions if you let me help my friend. Deal?"

"I got a better deal. Answer my questions or I'll splatter your friend's brains all over this shitty carpet. Deal?"

"Before you do that, you'd better know he's an FBI agent. Special Agent Jeffrey Forster. No lie. If you let him die, you'll probably get the death penalty."

"Ronnie, see if he has ID."

I seethe as tall man searches Lucas's pockets.

"Nutting," he says.

"Don't matter. We already shot him. Better he does die. No witnesses."

"I'm a witness," I say.

"Correction," stocky man says. "No living witnesses. Little girl, we've been mighty patient for all the trouble you caused us, but that's done. Time for you to die."

"No, *little man*, it's time for *you* to die."

Calm girl says, *What are you doing?* Scary girl says, *Fucking A!* Hiding girl puts her hands over her eyes.

Lucas's breathing is getting raspy. One way or another, I need to speed things up.

"What'd you call me?" His look says, *Surely you didn't really just say that while I'm pointing a gun at you about to pull the trigger.*

"Nothing personal, but you are kind of short, you know, for a man. You're not even taller than my mom was. Not like Ronnie. He's tall." I shoot him a dreamy smile.

Stocky man's face is on fire, but his voice is calm. "Been nice knowing you." He snugs his finger on the trigger.

Tall man jumps in. "May la, boss! I still ain't got my turn. Dat was da point to begin wit. And she *likes* me."

Stocky man hesitates before pulling down the gun and putting it in a holster on the back of his belt. "Make it quick," he says. Then to me, "Just so you know, I don't approve of his youthful indiscretions, or I should say, indiscretions with youth. Now, your mama, she was a different story."

I almost lunge for him, but remember how that turned out in Lafayette.

Tall man draws near, goofy smile spread wide.

I smile back, beckoning with a crooked, bleeding finger. He crosses in front of stocky man, blocking the view. I press my broken hand to my broken heart.

I can't tell which girl's in control anymore. It's like they all became one again for this moment. We all want the same thing.

"Ronnie," I whisper, gazing in his eyes. "There's something I've been wanting to tell you. Could you come a little closer? I don't want *him* to hear."

About ten inches would be perfect.

"Wat is it, sha ti bae?" he says with outstretched arms.

I smile shyly. "You know, it's funny you should call me that because it's actually a message from my sister." I can see stocky man over his shoulder, eyebrows knit, trying to figure out what all the whispering is about.

Tall man looks confused.

"She speaks to me from her grave, you know."

"Wat da?" He ratchets upright, straight as the outline I drew on the punching bag.

"She wanted me to say *bye-ee.*" I flash the neck knife and ram it four inches into his belly, pull it out and do it again.

Dumb-ass. The element of surprise. Lucas was so right about it. Even though they just got done taking a gun from me and tall man already thought I came back from the dead, he reached for me like I was a harmless little lamb ... like Becky. He screeches and falls backward, knife still in his stomach.

Stocky man comes into full view. He didn't see what happened. In the second he's processing it, I jump for the Browning, snatching it from the table and pulling back the hammer.

"Don't move or I'll shoot!"

He laughs, but it sounds more like a pig snort. *Pig.* That's weird.

"Bad news, dolly. That gun can't fire." He takes the magazine from his pocket and dangles it mockingly.

"Didn't you ever hear of one in the chamber?" I say.

The pig snort again. "Didn't you ever hear of a magazine safety, like the one they been building in that gun for a hundred years?" He reaches behind his back.

"Actually, I did," I say, sighting the gun from six feet and pulling the trigger.

The bullet explodes in a place where a human would have a heart. He grabs his chest and collapses.

"I told you not to move," I say.

I run to Lucas, noticing for the first time he's wearing a black coat and gloves. He didn't have them on when we were in the Tahoe. I see holes and unbutton the coat in a panic. Body armor. From the duffle bag. I saw it when I looked for the bracelet charger.

He must have been planning to come here all along. Where's the blood coming from?

I trace it to his upper thigh, a hole that goes clean through his leg. What a mess. Gotta stop the bleeding. I retrieve my knife from tall man's belly and wash it in the kitchen. Returning with clean towels, I set to work cutting off his pants leg.

"Lucas? Lucas?"

No response.

Time slows down. Frame, *tick*, frame, *tock* … I hear the scrape on the carpet behind me at the same instant I'm pressing on the towels and wondering how I can keep them fastened. They happen simultaneously, but distinctly.

Interesting, calm girl thinks as she goes flying backwards. Maybe when you're about to die, life separates into all its parts. As my skull hits the floor, some tiny brain-speck thinks *I'm glad this floor is carpeted*. Good ol' calm girl.

Tall man climbs on me and puts his hands around my throat, disgusting belly blood leaking everywhere. I fight, but my right hand is useless and I can't pry him loose with my left. The look on his face surprises me. Stocky man's was all rage, but tall man is smiling. The tighter he squeezes, the happier he looks.

I close my eyes as I start to choke. My worst fear. It's almost funny, in a mentally ill sort of way. I can't even get a break while dying.

Consciousness slips. *At least I killed one … at least I killed one.* I tell hiding girl she can come out now, that everything will be all right in the next place.

But my trachea suddenly finds air again. I open my eyes. Tall man's still there, but he's not smiling. Big black hands grip his head, twisting it sideways, cartilage ripping, bones popping.

Lucas shoves him aside and starts to fall. I try to catch him, but he tumbles on top of me.

43

DON'T FUCKIN' call for help. That was the first thing Lucas said when he opened his eyes. The second thing was to keep pressure on the wound. Then he fell out again.

I went back to the kitchen searching for something to hold the towels down with. In a pantry I found an orange bag hanging on a hook. Canvas. I never noticed it was canvas. Never saw the words on the back either. *Welcome to Georgia, The Peach State.*

Their murder bag. The aura of a flashback rises like a tide, threatening to drown me. Hiding girl freezes. Calm girl speaks gently, but punctuates each word: *Get the tape from the bag.* Scary girl nags at the fringe that we need to pump more bullets into stocky man and cut off tall man's fingers, the ones that touched Becky.

I unwind the duct tape with my teeth, the sound of the ripping adhesive punching holes in the black brain boxes, images shooting out like beams of light from a projector. There I am. On Mom's bed, mouth sealed, hyperventilating.

Is it the same tape? Did they do it to another family? The thought has haunted me. Well, it won't happen again. *Them pieces of shit that killed Jarrett and Shondra? They never hurt no one else. I see to that.*

* * *

273

With my busted fingers buddy-wrapped in duct tape, it took a while, but I managed to bind the towels around Lucas's barrel thigh.

I wedge a sofa pillow under his heavy head and wipe his face with a washcloth. His pulse and breathing are steady.

"I'll be right back," I say, and run to search the house for more supplies. In a medicine cabinet I find a jar of pills. *Take one for pain every four to six hours as needed.* Next to them is a bottle of rubbing alcohol. I take both back to Lucas.

I'm pouring the alcohol on his wound when he jerks and grabs his leg. Eyes still closed, "What the fuck you doin'?"

"*Sor-ry.* I didn't want you to get infected." It definitely woke him up. "I found some pain pills if you need them."

"What are they?"

"*Hy-dro-co-done,*" I read.

"Gimme three."

"It says you're only supposed to take one every four to six hours."

His bulging neck veins are a good sign. "But I think you could probably take more because you're so big."

He raises himself to his elbows, brushing off my effort to help, chokes down the pills and surveys the room. "I can't fuckin' believe Big EZ had to get rescued by a twelve-year-old girl."

"Thirteen, and I can't believe I had to get rescued again by an *old man.*" I start to hug him, but there's no place left to hug. "I have a million questions"—he opens his mouth and I raise a hand—"but I'm not going to ask them now. Except for one. How did you get here?"

"Not now. We got work to do before sun-up. This ain't over. You about to be on the FBI's Most Wanted list if we don't hurry."

"Most wanted for what?"

"Murder. Your friend Agent Forster ain't stupid. You think he's gonna believe it's a fuckin' coincidence that the day after he sends you a picture of the two men at the beige house, the two men get murdered at the beige house?"

"Why would he assume it's me? How could I possibly pull off something like that?"

"Guess what? You just did. And he don't have to assume. Your DNA and fingerprints are all around us. When he figures out you tricked him, he's gonna be pissed."

"I do feel a little bad about breaking my word to him."

"We talk about that later. Right now we got to work on changin' the future and we ain't got much time."

* * *

Waves of pain from my fingers attack my brain like electric shocks as I pull tall man across the carpet and park him on top of Lucas's blood. I'm wearing cardboard taped to my feet so I don't leave bloody footprints.

Lucas shifts uncomfortably on a chair, giving instructions. He tosses me his latex gloves. "Put these on. Fair warnin'. This part's gonna be hard."

"Oh, good. Finally, a challenge. Everything else has been too easy."

He calls me a smart-ass and tells me to use tall man's blood to write on the wall: *RIP OTIS, CLOVIS AND ALBIN.*

It's a setup to make things look like tall man and stocky man were killed in revenge for killing Otis, Clovis and Albin.

"Make it different from anything you ever wrote. We know your Agent Forster's a fuckin' expert on Emily Calby. No curlicues or shit, nothin' girly."

"Yeah, I'm so girly."

Calm girl holds hands with scary girl as they dip their fingers into tall man's blood.

"How's that?" I say when I'm finished.

"Good. Go ahead and add *Die Fuckers* below it."

"Ooh, I like that!"

Lucas scowls. "It ain't supposed to be fun. Fuck's happenin' to you?"

I shrug. "You desensitized me. You're a good teacher. Oh, and remember, I'm going crazy."

My next job is to search for his gun. The two men took it, but he hasn't said how. I find it in a bedroom.

"Wipe it down and put it in stocky man's hands. Perfect evidence. Same gun that shot Otis and his pals."

"Can the police trace it to you?"

"Course not. Stolen, with an obliterated serial number."

"His fingers won't stay in place."

"Just be sure his prints all over it."

Next I look for tall man's phone, with the texts and pictures of me dead. I find two phones and take both. Then he tells me we need gasoline.

"Gas? Revenge?"

"Destruction of evidence." He points to the carpet. "Like that pint of my DNA. Don't suppose you know how to siphon gas?"

"My dad taught me. It's easy. I even know where to get a hose. I found their murder bag in the kitchen. Same one they used on us."

Lucas goes quiet before saying, "You gonna be able to handle that? I'd do it if I could."

"I know you would. I can do it."

He doesn't look convinced. "Stay outta the light and keep a lookout for the FBI."

I get the hose and go outside, coming back with a pitcher full of yellowish gasoline. It was easy until it occurred to me that one of the two men, maybe both, put their lips on the hose to get the gas to burn our house. I rinsed my mouth out with gasoline when I finished.

Lucas is resting on the cane and measuring the back window with his hands.

"Set that down and come open this window."

I crank open a casement window.

He stares through it into the darkness. I'm too tired to ask why.

"Should I pour the gas?" I say.

He nods. "Start on top of your friends, then spread it around the room."

Scary girl shrieks with delight as the gasoline splashes away the blood on tall man's pale belly, exposing two jagged knife holes. *Nice grouping!* she says. Hiding girl asks her to *please* shut up.

The fumes are burning my nostrils. I don't feel well.

"Hurry. Gonna be light soon."

"I am hurrying," I snap. "Are we almost done?"

"Not quite. You got to soak a rag with the rest of that gasoline and wipe down everything you touched. How you holdin' up?"

"*Fine.*" I go to work, replicating my steps so I don't miss anything. I can't decide if my dizziness is from the gas fumes, exhaustion or the growing realization of what I've become. The last thing I wipe down is the table where I grabbed the Browning.

"I'm finished," I say. "All we need to do is light the fire."

"That's comin'," Lucas says. "We ready to go. You got everything?"

"Yep."

"Everything?"

"I just said yes."

He looks at the ceiling. "You ain't forgettin' fuckin' *nothin'*?"

"Oh, wait, my backpack!"

The look on his face is a classic I will never forget. After all the times I insisted on bringing my backpack.

"Last thing," he says. "Open the front curtains, just a couple inches, and turn out the living room light. Don't leave no more prints."

"I know. I'm not stupid."

Standing in the doorway I absorb the grisly living room for the first time. It looks like a CSI crime scene photograph, something Agent Forster might show me while asking, *Do you recognize these two men?*

Stocky man's open eyes stare at nothing. Tall man's broken

head points at me sideways at a ninety-degree angle. Their skin is getting whiter, blood darkening to a crimson-purple that reminds me of the dress I wore to the sixth-grade *We're Just Getting Started* graduation dance.

Behind me, *cane, step, cane, step.* Lucas lays his heavy hand on my shoulder.

"You happy now?"

"No."

"You get that part now?"

"Mm-hm."

"You regret it?"

"Nope."

"What you thinking?"

"Justice. Always comes too late, but it's still justice."

44

A HUMID breeze with a sweet taste of night-blooming jasmine broke the spell of death as we stepped out the back door. Lucas turned to me, embarrassed. "I might need a little help walkin'."

"Aw, I'll help you walk all the way to the moon." I clasped his arm. "But where are we going?"

He pointed to the two-story house taking shape behind the wood fence in the hint of dawn. "To my house with the swimming pool."

We entered a back gate, his lean on me getting heavier with each step. I almost stumbled into the swimming pool, concealed by a sinking leaf-filled vinyl tarp. The back door was open.

"Go on in," Lucas said like it was his house.

Now here we are. The house is empty except for a few pieces of random furniture and Lucas's duffle bag in the middle of the kitchen floor. He's sitting on a lone kitchen-chair telling me to put on clean latex gloves and change out of my bloody shirts into one of his from the duffle bag. The short sleeves reach past my elbows.

Third time in a week. I could star in a laundry detergent commercial. *Parents, when your kid comes home from her latest bloodbath, only one detergent is strong enough to get out the tough stains.* I offer to help him change clothes but he insists on doing it himself.

He tells me to get the heavy sniper rifle—he calls it *the*

BMG—from the duffle bag and leads me through the steps to attach a scope on top and a suppressor to the barrel.

I keep messing up and calling it *The BFG*, like Roald Dahl's book about the *Big Friendly Giant*, another one of Mom's favorites to read to us. After the third time, Lucas barks, *It's a fuckin' BMG*. I just smile. My own *BFG*. *Big Fucking Giant*.

He finally starts explaining. He guessed the house was empty back at the hotel when he noticed the pool cover full of leaves. The earth view picture was taken last month. He did a search and found it was for sale.

"Be sure that suppressor's screwed on tight," he says, gingerly straightening his leg. I know he's hurting.

"It is. How did you get into this place?"

"It was hard. Had to push a button. Got a device that can hack a garage door code in ten seconds. James builds 'em. Pulled the Tahoe right inside."

"What about the FBI? Did you make that up to trick me?" I say accusingly.

"You saw the fuckin' car. The FBI is real. Only surprise would be if they wasn't around. Course they gonna keep tabs on them men, but they passed me by."

"You abandoned me."

"Didn't mean to. Thought I could kill them fuckers and get back shortly, but they was waitin' in the dark. Ambush. Started shootin' as soon as I kicked in the door."

"My creepy phone call."

"Got the jump on me," he says. "First time in my life. Losin' my touch. *Old man*, like you said."

"I was just teasing. You were on a cane and already had three bullet holes in you so I wouldn't be too hard on yourself. Why didn't you take me? I could have helped. Maybe."

"Tell me you know why by now."

"Shondra?"

"Not Shondra."

A twinge in my heart. "I feel horrible. I keep getting you shot."

"Sun's up," he says. "Got a job to finish. Look through that bag and find the big cartridges with the blue tips."

I pull out a plastic bag filled with bullets almost as long as my hand. "Holy cow. What's the blue tip mean?"

"Incendiary cartridge."

"Now I get it."

* * *

Lucas is standing on a table, aiming the BMG through the scope, barrel rested on the top edge of a window. Satisfied, he hands me the heavy rifle and I help him down.

"Got the perfect angle, right through that window we opened," he says. "Any luck, the bullet starts the fire and disappears in the floor. FBI never even notices it. Sometimes I amaze myself. You ready?"

"Ready."

"You sure you got that new phone down?"

I'm using a new burner from the duffel bag. There are at least a half dozen of them in there. "We just ran through everything. I'm not a baby."

"No, you ain't. Just bein' careful."

"I know. I'm just tired."

"Me too. Almost done, but we got to be at the top of our game. I'm gonna shoot exactly three minutes after you leave the house. Count to ten and call nine-one-one. Can you change your voice?"

"I bloody well can."

"This ain't no time for jokes."

"I'm not joking. That was my British accent."

"Drop it. What else you got?"

"Deep South," I say with a twang.

"Use that. Lower though, chest voice, not head voice. After you make the call, run like the fuckin' wind."

"Why call at all?"

"You wanna burn down a neighborhood full of women and children?"

"Um, no."

"We also need the firetrucks to get there before your blood art gets burned up. Best thing we got to lead the FBI off track."

"Can't we just call from here?"

"Got to assume this is one call the FBI's gonna work overtime to pinpoint later."

I nod. "When the shit hits the fan."

We start our phone timers and I sprint out the back door, past the pool and over the fence, back to 896 Coconut Drive. I stop at the front corner and survey the street. Some lights are on, people making breakfast and getting ready for work.

I duck against the wall as a woman walking a small dog passes on the opposite sidewalk. I check the timer. Thirty seconds. I casually cross the street. At exactly 00:00 I hear a pop and flames shoot up through the gap in the curtains. I count to ten by one-thousands and dial 911.

A dispatcher answers. "I'm out here walking my dog," I say breathlessly. "There's a house on fire." *There's* comes out like *They-yers* in my deep-throated Southern accent. "Eight-nine-six Coconut Drive. Hurry!" I disconnect before she can ask questions, take out the phone battery and run like the wind.

45

THE HORIZON is molten gold under a layer of purple clouds as we back out of the garage. We go only two blocks before I hear sirens coming.

At the hotel, I clean the room while Lucas checks us out. The Tahoe is idling at the foot of the stairs when I come down.

As I wave goodbye to the beach—*I'll be back some day*—Lucas tells me to gather up all the phones. We have a bunch of them. Mine, his, the one we used for the fire call, tall man's, stocky man's and the phones we took from Otis, Clovis and Albin.

"Clothes too."

My feet rest on a plastic bag stuffed with our bloody outfits. "I got everything. What are we going to do with it?"

"Dump it off the bridge back to the mainland."

"Good idea."

"And the gun."

"The Browning?"

"It's a murder weapon."

"Alright," I say. "But when I get my next gun, I'm sticking with Browning. They're good guns."

"You ain't gonna need no more fuckin' guns," he says. "Neck knife too."

"What?" I latch onto it through my shirts. "I can't do that. It's like an old friend."

"Your old friend is linked to three murder scenes."

"Fine." I pull the cord over my head and add the neck knife to the pile.

283

"Get ready," he says as we approach the three-mile bridge. "Lemme know when they ain't no cars."

I give him an all-clear sign at about the halfway point and he screeches to a stop. "Make it quick."

I scatter eight phones, two sets of blood-soaked clothes, four pairs of latex gloves, and one handgun in the blue water. I save the neck knife for last, kissing it before letting go. Lucas honks impatiently.

We head north when we get to the mainland. I don't start to relax until a sign welcomes us to Flomaton, Alabama. Lucas has stayed quiet, me too, head still reeling from the vicious night. He hasn't said where we're headed, but I assume we're on our way back to Memphis to hide out in his building until he recovers and we think of a plan.

I break the silence by pointing to a drugstore and insisting we stop for first-aid supplies.

I load up with rolls of gauze, hydrogen peroxide, the whole works. I pass the refrigerators and gather an armful of sports drinks. Lucas lost a lot of blood so fluids make sense. Before I tossed the phones I searched for how to treat massive blood loss. Google said go to the emergency room.

"Don't worry," I say, climbing back into the Tahoe. "Dr. Calby's going to fix you right up." I hold up the bags of supplies with a big toothy smile. He doesn't smile back, just accelerates back onto the highway.

"What's the matter? Are you okay?"

"Three hours 'til noon. You got to contact your FBI agent. Sooner the better."

"Why do you care so much about him?"

"If he puts out that alert, you gonna get hunted down, which means I'm probably gonna get hunted down too."

"That's a good reason," I concede.

"Here's another one. You said you promised you was gonna come in if he gave you proof of the two men."

"Yeah, oh well."

"No fuckin' *oh well*. That's all your word means? That man trusted you and helped you. He's probably gonna be in a heap a shit. Lemme tell you somethin'. When a man got nothin' left, he got his word."

"So what are you saying? That I should *go in?* Yeah, right."

No response.

"Why are you looking at me like that? Omigod, you're joking me. Stop it. ... You're not joking?"

"Hear me out. You thirteen years old, got your whole life in front of you. You got a choice."

"Yeah, yeah, I know. A or B. *Blah blah blah, tra la la.*"

"Look at me."

I don't, focusing on my shaking hands struggling to tie a knot in a cable of brown hair.

"If God put Lucas in your life like you think, it was to take care of them two men. That part's done now."

I kick the glove compartment and bite my lip, too hard, tasting blood.

"Meanwhile, the FBI ain't gonna stop lookin' for you. So your choice is keep tryin' to survive on these fucked-up streets 'til they find you, which they will, or go in where you ain't got to worry about safety or the FBI. And get help. I believe that man will get you help."

"I don't need any help! I can't even believe this is happening. After everything we've been through?"

"Look, Em—"

"I want to stay with you. I'll be safe that way. I can do a lot more to help. I can take care of you. I can learn to make fake documents."

"Yeah, well."

"I can learn not to be a pest. I know I can if I just try harder."

My eyes follow his down to where the fingernails of my good hand are breaking the skin on his forearm, drawing blood.

I let go and start to cry. The voices in my head are quiet. Calm girl and scary girl have disappeared. The hiding girl is all alone, on her knees, praying.

"Emily, look around you," he says softly. "This ain't no life."

"We could make a life, with Kiona, off the grid. I met these people, Darla and Peggy. They're *so* super nice. They drive around in an RV and camp in all kinds of beautiful places. It's really fun, camping. I–I don't know if you've ever done it."

"You need a family."

"You're my family. *Please*, Lucas."

Stone-faced, "Five hours to Atlanta. There's a fresh burner in the glove compartment. Call Agent Forster. Tell him you be there by two o'clock."

46

I SPOT Agent Forster the second I enter the Mexican restaurant. He looks like his picture, but I would have recognized him even without it. Gray suit, buzzed haircut, clean-shaven, he looks exactly like the FBI. He wanted to meet at his office but I said no.

He stands and smiles. "Robert Williams, I presume?"

"That's me," I say wearily.

He starts to shake my hand, sees the duct tape holding my purple fingers together and pulls back. "How are you, Emily?"

"Good."

"You look tired."

"I am, but I'm good."

"Have a seat. Would you like something to eat or drink?"

"Coffee, please."

He orders it and an iced tea refill for himself while I study the restaurant for signs of other FBI agents in case it's a trap. I don't spot any.

"I have to say you look remarkably fit for someone who's been missing for two months. Except for those fingers. Ouch. How did that happen?"

"Playing softball. Ball bent them back."

"Is that right? You've been playing softball. How about that?"

"Mm-hm. I live a very healthy lifestyle."

I can tell he doesn't believe a word of it. In fact he looks like he's having a hard time keeping a straight face.

"Well, that actually leads nicely into my first question. Where have you been?"

I wave in an arc. "Here, there. I'd rather not get into specifics. I'm a very private person."

"Everyone thought you were dead."

"I know. I read the news."

"Can you tell me how you, um ..."

I stare at him, unblinking. "How I'm not dead? Short version, I climbed out the bathroom window and ran away while the two men killed my mother and sister."

He doesn't turn away. "I know this is hard," he says. "It's hard for me. I'll try to keep this initial interview short. I'm looking forward to your getting help from professionals."

"*What* are you talking about? What professionals?"

"Counselors. People you can talk to. They're trained to help trauma victims."

"Why does everyone keep thinking I need help?" I say too loud. A young couple at the next table stops their conversation.

Forster clicks close-trimmed fingernails on the laminated menu. "Based on what you've been through, I can't imagine you don't. Most victims of violent crime do."

"Maybe I'm not an average victim."

"I'd stake my reputation on it. How about we come back to that later? Let's fill in a little more background, if you don't mind."

Why did I run away? I was afraid. *Where did I go?* Traveled around on buses and trains to different cities. *How did I pay for everything?* I had a box of cash my dad hid for an emergency. *Why didn't I contact the authorities?* I did, that's why I'm sitting here.

"Have you had any help these past two months?"

"Yep."

"May I ask from whom?"

"I have a friend. He helped me a lot."

"What can you tell me about him?"

"Um, he's *amazing*."

"How old is he?"

"Older."

"How much older?"

"Fair amount."

"Sounds like you two are close."

"Very close. I love him."

He pauses to wipe the corner of his mouth with a red napkin. "Love, wow. That's strong stuff. I apologize, but it's my job to ask. Did your friend ever do anything inappropriate around you?"

"He cusses a lot." I leave out the marijuana.

"How about physically?"

"*Gross*, no. He's not my boyfriend. He's like a dad. See, this is why I don't like talking to the FBI. I'm telling you one thing and you want to hear something else."

I lower my voice. "Please hear this. *I am fine.* Like you said, I'm remarkably fit, so I must be fine to be that way." Flipping my palms up, "Logic, right?"

He folds his hands. A thick wedding band shines on his left hand. "I have some news you might be interested in. Something happened this morning in Pensacola, Florida. Ever been there?"

"Nope. My family talked about going there once on vacation, but we voted on Panama City instead."

"The two suspects are dead."

I just look at him before realizing it would be abnormal not to say something. "How?"

"Murdered, last night or early this morning. The crime scene is being processed as we speak."

"Wow. That's something."

"It happened inside the brown house in the picture I sent you yesterday."

"Really."

"You don't sound too surprised."

I shrug. "How am I supposed to act? They were evil. They

raped and killed people. It doesn't surprise me people wanted to kill them." I barely hold back, *They deserved to die.*

"Are you familiar with a process called deconvolution?"

"Whoa, that's random. What is it again?"

"Deconvolution."

"Hm, we studied evolution in school. Does it have anything to do with that?"

A crooked smile. "Emily, I don't think you believe I'm on your side."

"It doesn't matter. Don't you see? I don't want to be here."

"Then why'd you come?"

"One, you threatened to send out a nationwide alert on me and—"

"Alerts are SOP. I stuck my neck out to hold yours back."

"I appreciate that, but I wasn't finished. And I'm sorry for sounding snotty, but I really am tired, like you said. The reasons for the alert don't apply now. The two men are dead. Case over. I'm here, remarkably fit, proof I'm okay."

He starts to speak, but I keep going. "But the main reason I'm here is because my friend—the one you insulted—made me come, because you helped me and I gave you my word. That's the kind of person he is."

"Good to know."

"So can I go now?"

"I'd rather you stay a while."

"Can you make me?" I'm pouring sugar packets on the table, building a crest like the sand in Pensacola.

"I could get a judge to order you held as a material witness until you're willing to talk, but I'd rather talk informally like this."

"How can I be a material witness? You said the criminals are dead. Can you put dead people on trial?"

He leans back and folds his arms. "After all the hours I spent studying you, I should have known to bring a lawyer. There's also an interstate law allowing authorities to take runaways into custody and return them home."

"Aha," I say. "I'm not a runaway. To be a runaway you'd have to have something to run away from, right? And a home to be returned to. Mine's just a vacant lot now."

"Yes, I'm sorry about that." He really does look sorry. "They had to clear the property for safety reasons. You asked a question about the definition of a runaway. Let's look it up."

He pulls up a document on his phone. "Here it is, the Interstate Compact on Juveniles. It defines a runaway as a juvenile who runs away from his or her place of residence without the consent of a legal guardian."

"I don't have any legal guardians. They're dead."

"I had a feeling you might pick up on that. You should consider law school someday."

"Can I leave?"

"There's another issue. We're going to be here a while. You might want to order lunch."

The waitress comes over. "I'll have the chimichanga lunch plate," he says. "How about it, Emily? You hungry?"

I try to remember the last meal I ate. I think it was yesterday at the seafood restaurant in Pensacola, when the sun was setting, but that seems like years ago.

"Do you have chicken burritos?" I ask.

The waitress points to the menu.

"I'll have one of those. Actually, make it two, please. With the whole-grain tortillas ... and rice and black beans ... and a salad with extra tomatoes and the dressing on the side. Thanks." When she walks away, "I don't have any money on me."

"No problem," Forster says.

"You said there was more?"

"Yes. Let's assume—just hypothetically, don't get your hopes up—that you can't be detained as a runaway or material witness. You could still be held for your own crimes."

His hazel eyes are intense, telescopes dialed in on my reaction.

"My crimes? I'm the victim." I start twirling my hair, catch myself and stop.

"You haven't committed any crimes?"

"Okay, so I stole some things from cars at the beginning, when I was on the run before I got settled. You can put me in jail for that."

"That's all?"

"All I can think of." I wonder if he can make me take a lie detector test.

"Where were you this morning?"

"Actually, my friend dropped me off yesterday because I knew I had to meet you."

He starts another question, but I cut him off. "Agent Forster, can I ask you something for a change? Do you have any kids?"

"I do. Two boys."

"How old?"

"Ten and thirteen."

"If something happened to you and your wife, what would you want for them?"

"That's a tough one. I guess I'd say to be happy and safe."

"Anything else?"

"Provided for."

"And you'd want them to be with somebody they loved, right?"

"Of course," he says.

"What if I could *swear swear swear* on a stack of bibles I'm happy and safe and provided for by someone I love? Then could I leave? I'm not meant for foster care. You said you studied me. You should know that."

"I'm sorry, Emily. It's not that simple. There are a lot of pro-cedures involved and several levels of investigation. Local, state and federal."

The waitress brings a basket of tortilla chips. I wait until she leaves.

"But if you turned your head or went to the restroom and I happened to …"

He shakes his head.

The meal comes. With the first steaming bite, I realize I'm famished. Forster stops talking to let me eat. I finish the first burrito before asking, "How did you find them? The two men."

"The gas can. You mentioned it in your first email."

"I thought that was it. DNA?"

"Fingerprints. Touch DNA doesn't last long in the elements. The prints matched those of a convicted sex offender."

Ronnie.

"His parole officer helped us track him down. We found him living in the house in Pensacola with the other assailant, the dark-haired man in your drawings."

Ben.

"They met in prison. I knew they were a match as soon as I saw their photographs. They looked just like your sketches. The agents in Identification were impressed. The FBI could use artistic talent like that."

A weak laugh. "Me in the FBI. Imagine that."

"But the sketches couldn't be used as evidence without you to authenticate them and the fingerprints weren't enough to get an arrest warrant because there was nothing to connect the gas can to the attack. I tried."

I believe him.

We finish the meal in silence. The waitress comes over and asks if we need anything else. Agent Forster and I look at each other and shake our heads at the same time. She lays down a check and walks away.

"You're a good detective, Agent Forster. Thanks for finding the two men."

"Are you trying to butter me up?"

I stretch a single hair until it snaps. Like it was never there.

"No," I say dismally. "Because I know it won't work. You're not going to let me leave here, are you?"

47

AGENT FORSTER didn't let me leave the restaurant that day. When it became clear he wasn't going to, I waited until he looked away and bolted, but two other agents, a man and woman at the bar pretending to be a couple, blocked the door.

They put me in a hospital, where I spent two weeks being prodded, poked and pricked. Blood tests, urine tests, brain scans, even a horrible pelvic exam. Everyone tried to be nice, too nice, like I was a delicate piece of glass that would shatter in their hands. Nobody listened when I said I was fine.

Then I shattered. One morning I smashed the mirror in my bathroom when I didn't recognize my reflection. They found me on the floor, blood dripping from my thigh, where I carved *NO ONE* with a piece of glass.

They transferred me to the psychiatric ward and kept me for two months under a fake name, *Sarah Smith*. I felt more like a prisoner than a patient.

I fought, even had a lawyer. The court appointed her as my temporary guardian to act in my *best interests*. When I told her my best interests were to get out and go wherever the eff I wanted to, she didn't agree and said the judge wouldn't either.

The doctors prescribed me piles of pills. I flushed them down the toilet until I got caught and they started monitoring me. It only took a week for the drugs to change who I was. I'd already lost enough of me. The next time the nurse came with the little plastic cup, I waved her off.

"But you *have* to take these," she said.

"Then you're going to *have* to shove them down my throat." It turned out I had legal rights and they stopped forcing drugs on me.

The day I met my first shrink, Dr. Stone, she announced I'd be spending a lot of time in *psychotherapy*.

"Therapy for psychos? That sounds about right." I started laughing which only convinced her I was nuts. The more she tried to get me to talk, the more I clammed up. I suggested she follow the approach of a well-known psychologist from Arkansas named Darla.

"You need to make people want to talk to you," I offered. Dr. Stone got very frustrated with me.

Then she was gone, replaced by Dr. Townsend, who looked a little like Santa Claus, with rosy cheeks, half-glasses and a furry white beard. He liked to talk about the stages of grief. They don't go in order like people think. *Denial* goes away one day and hits twice as hard the next. *Anger?* I worry it's welded to my heart. When Dr. Townsend asked me about *bargaining*, the only thing I could think of was negotiating the price of my fake driver's license with Lucas.

The last one was a complete joke. *Acceptance.* Accept that Mom and Becky were murdered? That my whole family is gone forever? "No offense, Dr. Townsend, but that's the most ridiculous thing I've ever heard anyone say in my entire life."

"So your approach is working better for you, yeah? You don't let yourself talk or even think about your family."

He said it gently but it landed like boiling water. I was still yelling *That's a lie! That's a fucking lie!* when he walked out.

Of course it was true. I'd spent months holding my family prisoners in the black boxes. When I finally broke through the darkness, I landed in an opposite world. Mom used to joke I only know two speeds: Full and Off. Little Miss Ice Cube turned into Little Miss Chatterbox, talking about my family to anyone who would listen, the nurses, docs, even the guy who came to change the lightbulb in my room.

I loved telling about the time Mom was getting ready for work and Becky said, "You know, Mom, you look a little cute today, but if you'd let me bedazzle you, I think it would help a lot." I still laugh every time I think of it.

I started a journal, writing down everything I remembered, not just the big stuff. Dad taking the training wheels off my bike and letting go for the first time, when it felt like I was flying. Mom bringing cookies to me and Becky in our backyard pirate fort, a blanket thrown over the picnic table. Becky saying I looked pretty as I got ready for my first school dance, when I was so nervous.

I filled three notebooks in a week, afraid my memories could vanish any second. I was already noticing blanks, like parts had been rolled over with black paint. One night I had a dream about someone called the Hiding Girl. She seemed so real, but she was just a dream.

On the twenty-third day of November, the six-month anniversary of the end of everything, I woke up with a memory so clear and alive I thought it too was a dream.

It was the morning of the day the two men came. Mom took us to the drugstore soda fountain for milkshakes. We sat at the red counter on the chrome stools. I was bugging Mom about my allowance, which was a day late. She hadn't given me my look-up words for the week, said she'd been too busy at school.

"Mom, I *need* my allowance."

"Alright," she gave in. "Your first word is *love*."

"Seriously? Isn't that a little easy?" Usually it was words like *incongruous* and *penultimate*.

"What does it mean?" she said.

I shrugged. "Simple. When you love someone ... you just, you know, *love* 'em."

"Hm. That's called begging the question. What does it really mean to you?"

I watched my sweet sister spinning around on the stool. I thought about Dad, his sturdy hugs when he got home from work smelling of sweat and tractor grease. I remembered the time Mom said there was nothing I could ever do to make her stop loving me. "What if I killed someone?" I said. She laughed. "Hopefully it won't come to that, but even then."

"I know the answer," I said. "If you really love someone you'd do anything for them. You'd even die for them. And I can use it in a sentence real easy. I love you, Mom." With watery eyes, she said I earned my allowance.

But I *didn't* die for them, and Agent Forster turned the sweet memory upside down when he finally answered the question that had been torturing me since the moment I ran into the woods with the cigar box. Why did the men come to our house? Why *us?*

The FBI assembled a timeline of their day, showing they did stop and get gas at the Exxon station at the foot of the hill. I never believed their running out of gas story. I should have insisted on looking at their gas gauge, seen if it was really broken. *Should've, should've.*

They put our day together too. The answer came from the drugstore. Security video showed the two men checking out at the cashier. Tall man bought some athlete's foot medicine. Ten minutes later another camera showed them following us into the parking lot.

Agent Forster looked at me unflinchingly. I always appreciated that about him, but knew bad news was coming.

"Emily, there's no good way to say it, but I know you well enough to know you want a straight answer. Your case has been studied from every angle, by dozens of agents spending hundreds of hours. The official conclusion is ..."

He hesitated, maybe to give me time to get ready, maybe he just felt bad. "The official conclusion is that the attack on your family was random. Two sick men spotted you at the drugstore and followed you home. There was no other rhyme or reason ... I'm sorry."

Somehow the pointlessness of everything did make it worse,

which I didn't think was possible. My conversation with Lucas came back to me:

"But there has to be *some* reason. Everything happens for a reason."

"Not always. Sometimes shit just happens."

I talked a nurse into letting me use her computer to search for the video taken that day inside the drugstore by a fan of old-fashioned soda fountains, the one I could never make myself watch. *Last Pictures of Family Alive.* I found it on YouTube. Eight million views.

Just seventeen seconds. The camera pans left to right, capturing the chrome stools, shiny fountain taps and candy jars on the red counter before coming to us. Becky whirling around on the stool with a gap-toothed grin. Me and Mom talking. Was I defining the meaning of *love*? Then it was over. *The End.*

I replayed it again and again. Becky was wearing her favorite dress that day, yellow butterflies over blue sky. I'd forgotten that. I gazed long and hard at Mom's all-knowing eyes, always teaching without telling.

It wasn't until the fifth time through that I saw it. I stopped the video. Behind us, down the aisle. Two blurred shapes. One tall and narrow, one short and wide. Watching us.

It sent me into a tailspin.

* * *

The people at the hospital liked telling me how impressed they were by my strength. "Um, it's not like you have a choice," I said. "You either keep going or die. So the only strength is not dying. Get it?"

Are you suicidal? Over and over. No, I said, my family wouldn't want that. I left out the many long nights in the hospital bed when I wondered if it might be a path back to my family.

One day I asked Dr. Townsend for my diagnosis. He tried to brush it off. "There's nothing to be gained by getting into that."

"It's my diagnosis. I have a right to know."

I guess he knew me well enough by then because he opened a thick file, adjusted his glasses and read in a clinical voice: "*Posttraumatic stress disorder, dissociative identity disorder, depersonalization-derealization disorder, dissociative amnesia.*" He closed the folder. "They overlap, but you meet the diagnostic criteria for each of them."

"That's it?" I laughed.

"No. You're also off the chart on differential diagnoses for major depressive disorder and a cluster of anxiety disorders."

"But except for that I'm perfect, right?"

He smiled. "Right."

He wanted to know why I cut my leg. It was a logical question, but the only answer that came to me was, "It was a way to take the pain out of my head and put it in my skin."

Dr. Townsend agreed with Darla's diagnosis of my hair-pulling. *Trichotillomania* really is a word. He reminded me a little of Darla. Talk if you want, or don't.

"So, Dr. Townsend," I declared one afternoon, breaking a long silence.

"So, Emily," he declared back.

I kicked out my legs, crunched my shoulders and took a deep breath. I started to talk, stopped and did it all over again: leg kick, shoulder crunch, deep breath. Something had been weighing on me. I worried it made Lucas go away.

"There were times," I said. "By the way, don't write this down."

I waited until he set down his pen and pad.

"There were times on my, um, *trip*, where I—" Dr. Townsend offered an encouraging nod. "Where I, well, you know, thought I was going crazy." I laughed it off as I studied his reaction.

"That's not surprising," he said. "Anything in particular?"

I reached for my hair, but he floated my hand down with a wave. "Well, like, for example ... I did some things ... but it was like I didn't do them, like I was watching someone else do them ... like I *was* someone else."

"I see," he said.

"There were other times where a normal person would have been—*should* have been—afraid, like, I mean *really really* afraid. I was, but instead of acting afraid, I acted calm."

He took off his glasses and leaned closer. "Emily, you seem to have a remarkable ability to dissociate. It's a common symptom of the disorders I mentioned."

I brightened. "Ability? So it's a good thing?"

"No. Poor word choice, but sometimes the brain uses dissociation as a tool for self-protection in response to trauma. It's a mental state where a person can separate herself into parts able to function independently. Think of it as an internal detachment from self."

"Like not recognizing yourself in the mirror?"

He arched an eyebrow. "In severe cases. Did that happen to you?"

"No, just curious." I never told anyone why I broke the mirror. I said it was an accident.

He studied me for tells before continuing. "Individuals experiencing dissociation sometimes report what you just described, feeling like an observer of their own actions. They can feel detached from their feelings and surroundings, their entire beings. In some cases they perceive voices."

"Voices, huh. Interesting." I never told anyone about the voices, either. I don't remember much about them, just that they were there.

He bent even closer. "Emily, I don't think you're crazy. Everything you've experienced is easily explained as a response to the extreme trauma you suffered. That's my expert opinion, unless you're leaving out something important."

Important? Oh, just a few formerly alive people named Scott Brooker, Otis, Clovis, Albin, Ben and Ronnie.

"In truth, all of the disorders I listed can be lumped into one diagnosis. *Posttraumatic stress disorder with dissociative symptoms.*"

I repeated it in my head. "Sixteen syllables. I feel special."

"Adrenaline may have also played a role. The body releases adrenaline in response to *fight or flight* situations. For those who choose to fight, it can boost physical strength and mental acuity. Time might seem to slow down. They may feel calm, at peace even."

Every word sounded exactly like me.

I told Dr. Townsend about Darla and Peggy because they were the only topic that cheered me up. One day he let me call them on his phone. I still remembered the number Darla made me memorize. Just hearing their voices put me in a better place. They were on the road, headed to California. I always wanted to go to California.

Peggy grabbed the phone and yelled *Hey, Squirt* with Darla scolding her to concentrate on driving. They were shocked to learn about the *Calby Murders*. Darla talked to Dr. Townsend. We promised to stay in touch.

There were tons of visits from law enforcement people, not just the FBI. I stuck to a simple story, most of it true. I roamed from city to city by bus or train using Dad's money. "I don't remember a lot of the details because I was in a state of dissociative amnesia. You can ask Dr. Townsend if you don't believe me." I honestly answered questions supporting my story and lied about everything else.

As Lucas predicted, some of them thought I was involved in killing the two men. I played dumb and it became obvious as the questioning went on they didn't have any proof. The closest thing was the 911 fire call, which we all sat around listening to in my hospital room, like a campfire circle where I was the fire.

"You think that's me?" I laughed at the end. "That sounds like some hillbilly. I don't talk anything like that. Do I? I mean, you're right here listening to me."

The FBI voice analysis came back *Inconclusive*.

One day three detectives from Florida showed up, two men and a woman. The woman took charge, questioning me with a don't-eff-with-me attitude. She handed me a picture of the crime scene inside the beige house. Tall man and stocky man were pretty much burned to a crisp, but still recognizable.

"What do you think?" she said like a challenge.

Attack. Seize the advantage while the other motherfucker's thinkin'.

"What do I *think*? I think they look a whole lot better in this picture than they did when they were raping and killing my mother and eight-year-old sister. Why do you even care about these pieces of shit? *Why aren't you looking at pictures of my family?*"

They all reared back. The men raised their hands like I was robbing them. Even the woman apologized. Agent Forster sat watching the whole thing from a chair in the corner. I think I saw him smile.

That was the last I heard of that.

As I powered up on offense, my defenses broke down. Under a hundred feet of lead, I discovered a waterfall of tears that had been there the whole time, hidden by my protective, dissociating brain. Painful as it felt, it was a relief to know that part of me still existed.

Every time I started to climb out of the well, I'd fall back down again. Only Agent Forster suspected there might be more to it than the obvious things. I never mentioned Lucas after our first interview. When Forster asked about him, I said he was an imaginary friend.

But as the weeks passed I made slow progress, enough to graduate from hospital patient to *ward of the state*. Impossibly, it was worse than I even imagined. If I was withering before, I disintegrated.

First they put me in a group home, with the same fake identity I got in the hospital. Sarah Smith. An older girl started picking on me the second I got there. It only took one day to snap. *Jab, jab, cross.* I knocked her out.

So much anger. Raw, boiling, stomach-eating. Always *right there* below my skin. At everything and everyone, including Lucas. I waited every day for him to come rescue me, wearing the GPS bracelet. James did such a brilliant job even the FBI thought it was an ordinary bracelet. But Lucas never came.

After the fight I got moved to another group home. That didn't work out either. There was another fight. A couple actually. With my record, it took a while, but I finally got placed with a foster family, a couple who already had three other foster kids. Turns out the state pays foster parents by the kid.

Paid parents, just what I always wanted. I tried, just to see if I could still do it, but even the crazy laugh had been snuffed out of me.

I thought about running away, of course. It would have been easy. I took walks every day, for miles, and was even scheduled to go back to school. An older boy in the house had already run away twice. But I didn't know where to run and didn't have the energy I used to. I felt old.

One morning Agent Forster came to visit. We went for a walk. It was early spring, a bright, chilly day. He offered me his suit jacket. I turned it down.

"How are you?" he said.

"Lovely," I replied, kicking leaves.

"Still mad at me?"

No answer.

"I couldn't let you leave the restaurant that day, even if I wanted to. I think you know that."

He picked up an orange leaf. "Pretty, isn't it?" He handed it to me. It was pretty, but I dropped it.

"Emily, have you ever had an epiphany?" he asked.

"If I did, I'm sure they tested me for it."

He laughed his light, subtle laugh, the opposite of Lucas's deep-chested snorts. "It's not a medical condition. An epiphany is a sudden understanding of something. Like a revelation. Ever had one?"

A flickering slideshow, like the cows in the pastures from the train windows, clackered across my inside eyes. Revelations, about love and hate, revenge and justice ... infinite sorrow.

"A few," I said.

"I had one, about you."

"Like?"

"Like contrary to what I always believed, it might be possible for a thirteen-year-old girl to know more about what's in her best interest than the government and all its experts."

I kicked a rock.

"The attention to your case has died down. People have moved on to other things."

"Must be nice," I said.

"I'm going to tell you something, but we're not having this conversation."

"What do you mean we're not—?" I read his face. "Okay."

"I've been checking on you. Your progress. More accurately, your lack of it."

I aimed for another rock, stubbed my sneaker and almost fell. He grabbed my arm and propped me up.

"You're not the same girl I met at the restaurant that day," he said. "That girl was tired and hurting, but after everything she'd been through—which I'm sure I don't know the half of— there was a shine in her eyes. How was that possible? I've asked myself a hundred times."

I remember that girl.

"About that friend of yours, the imaginary one. What if he wasn't imaginary anymore? Would you be interested in getting to see him?"

I skidded to a stop.

"Um, maybe," I said. By then, I didn't think Agent Forster would trick me, but didn't know what he was getting at. My first thought was they had Lucas in custody.

He said, "Do you know how to contact him?"

Sadness leaked through my armor. "No."

"If you gave me his name maybe I could find him."

Headshake. "Can't do that, but let me get this straight. Are you saying you'd let me leave here?"

We resumed walking. "I thought over your legal theory, about not being a runaway. It makes sense to me. It won't to a judge though."

A jogger came down the sidewalk. Agent Forster stepped aside to let her pass. "I also thought about your question, about my own kids, if something happened to me and my wife. I said I'd want them to be happy. You're obviously not."

"No."

"The clog in the pipe is the law doesn't let minors make those kinds of decisions. That's why we're not having this conversation."

"What conversation?" I said.

"I don't have the authority to let you walk away, but as I see it, the FBI's job is done. We don't control the states, and frankly, they don't have the resources to chase down every runaway foster child. Of course, I'd have to know you were safe. Not just running away to live on the streets."

Dazed, still not sure what he was saying. "Of course," I said.

"The only way I could know that would be to meet your friend, run background checks on him."

A barely contained *Bwah* before, "You know, I just don't see that happening."

"If he's a law-abiding citizen, he shouldn't have any problem with it."

"He's very, you know, private, like me. But there is another way. I could promise to stay in touch with you, let you know where I am and how I'm doing. I keep my word. I proved it."

A week later I was taking another walk and passed a gleaming bus parked on the side of the street. Black and silver, huge, like something a rock star would travel in. The engine was running. I fantasized about jumping in it and just driving away.

The doors parted. "Hey, you seen a lost pit bull? Name's Alice."

After

MY NAME is Alice Black. My adoption became official a month ago. My father is Joseph Black. I kept Alice because I know her. I also have a stepmother, Kiona Shaw. Finally learned her full name. The only one with nothing to hide, she kept it.

The adoption is fake, with lots of beautifully forged documents, a way for us to get around legally, but Lucas and Kiona's marriage is real. We had a ceremony near a waterfall. I got to be the maid of honor.

We're parked at a campground in Northern California. Gorgeous cliffs, clear rushing streams and air that tastes like it's never been breathed before. Lucas's massive bus rests next to Darla and Peggy's pink trailer, a whale swimming with an angelfish. Calling them was the first thing I did after Lucas picked me up.

I'm sitting in a folding chair sketching the landscape, which includes Lucas wedged onto the bench of a picnic table typing on a large-screen laptop. His thick fingers are surprisingly nimble, thanks to video games, he says. A brown and white ground squirrel waits by my side for another handout.

"What's a good word for gettin' the shit kicked out of you?" Lucas says.

Darla frowns. She's wearing cute shorts overalls with orange and yellow flowers. Lucas is writing a book. Not the how-to book on killing we always talked about. A memoir, about a reformed—well, semi-reformed if we're honest—gang member.

"Beaten, brutalized," Darla says.

"*Brutalized*. I like that. Thank you."

"You're welcome," she says. "But I could do without the cursing."

"Right," he says contritely. He's been trying to cut back now that he's a fake father.

The five of us have been hanging out for a month, the plan being to stay together until Darla is convinced I don't need to be reinstitutionalized. That was her condition for the whole arrangement. If she says I need to go back into treatment, I have to go.

The good news is I'm doing a lot better. No voices, no cutting. I still twist my hair, but not nearly as much. It's harder to do because I cut it an inch long after dying it black. Still, when I let myself think about how long the road back to normal is—infinity, basically—I can almost muster the crazy laugh.

Darla and I spend a lot of time hiking. Walking and talking, sometimes just walking. Each trip puts another crack in the walls I worked so hard to build. Lately we've been talking about anger, which won't let go of me. I thought it was all about stocky man and tall man, clueless about how much of it was aimed at *me,* for failing my family.

One day Darla asked if I was mad at Mom or Dad. "Of course not," I said harshly. "What kind of a person do you think I am?"

I fell silent but farther down the trail I started weeping. I never dared let myself think it, but in my deepest well I was mad at both of them. At Mom for being nice to the killers, for turning her back on them and not locking the door; at Dad for not getting an alarm system or being there to protect us like he always promised. The realization brought a tsunami of shame, but Darla said it was a normal reaction to grief.

I told her about the cutting, making her swear to keep it a secret.

"Confidential," she agreed.

I nudged her shoulder. "By law?"

"By law, as long as you're not still doing it."

I expected her to think I was a freak, but she said self-harm is common, especially for girls. I'd heard of it, but had no idea it was *a thing.*

"Why do people do it?"

"Depends on the person. It can be a way to assert control, release pressure or just escape emotional pain."

They all fit. Sometimes I wonder how different my story would be if Darla hadn't gone to get a bucket of water in the early morning at the Acadiana campground.

Lucas is asking her opinion about a book passage recounting his days as a pimp. Darla has an expert poker face, but I know she's cringing inside. While they debate the literary value of a story about Lucas breaking a customer's legs for mistreating a *sex worker*, a term Darla suggested in place of *ho*, I get out my phone and compose a text:

> *Hi Agent Forster! I'm writing from the beautiful*
> *mountains of California, sitting here with my best*
> *friends. Everything is great. I am happy and healthy.*
> *I hope you are too, and your sons and wife. I will keep*
> *my word and stay in touch. Love, Robert Williams*

I hit send as Kiona exits the RV, rolling her eyes. "Do you believe James just called to say he got an A on his first final exam at Stanford?"

"Why you say it like that?" Lucas says. "My little man's a genius."

"Because he got the answers by hacking into the professor's computer."

"Like I said, genius."

It wasn't easy convincing Kiona to join us on the road. "Black people don't camp," she said flatly, but Lucas talked her into giving it a try. She's not a fan of the close living, much more of an introvert than me or Lucas, but she loves the wilderness. Rock-climbing, mountain-biking, kayaking—they were all made for Kiona. She's thinking about starting a business where customers meet up at parks for wilderness training.

I wouldn't say she's exactly thrilled to have me along, but I'm pretty sure she likes me, in her own quiet way. One day when we were having breakfast she looked up from her bowl of muesli and said, "You know, I was wrong about you," then went back to eating.

We picked her up in Memphis after leaving Atlanta. Driving away from the foster home, sitting in the front seat of the bus next to Lucas, rap music playing through twenty-four speakers, was the best day of my post-end-of-life life.

It was a Sunday. We kept passing churches. I felt so much gratitude and wanted to stop at one to give thanks. I tried everything to persuade Lucas, even gave him *that look. No* was all he said.

Then the fuel gauge started flashing. Lucas pulled into a truck stop and got out to fill the tanks. I went back to the kitchen area and kneeled next to a shrunken refrigerator with the *I Love Dogs* magnet. He brought it with him.

Thank you for this miracle, Lord. I know I didn't deserve it. Thank you for Luc—.

A sound made me start. It was Lucas, standing behind me. He went back to the front without saying a word, but when we came to the next church, he veered off the road, grinding the bus to a halt next to a sign. *We Welcome All Sinners.*

The church even looked a little like our church back in Georgia, red brick with a black roof and white steeple. "We can go in?" I said.

He nodded wordlessly, keeping his head down as we crossed the asphalt. I couldn't read his mood because I'd never seen it before. He had a hitch in his step, from all the bullets I assumed. When he wouldn't look at me, I asked what was wrong and he said something about his clothes.

"Oh, don't worry about that. Church people are nice. They won't care. My clothes are a lot worse than yours," I laughed.

He insisted on sitting in the back. I held his arm as I flipped through the hymnbook, buzzed with excitement. "Look! We get to sing this one. It's one of my favorites. Don't worry if you don't know it. Just mouth along and fake it, that's what everyone does."

A jowly man in a flowing black robe, red sash across his chest, moved reverently up the aisle in our direction, head bowed in humility to the Lord. The pastor, coming to welcome us, like our pastor always did when he spotted new worshippers. I leapt up, stretching over Lucas to shake his hand. He stopped but didn't put out his hand.

He said, "You have to leave."

"Leave? Me?" My first thought was I smelled bad again. I even sniffed my armpit.

He cleared his throat, looking only at me. "Both of you. Church policy does not allow mixed families. God's will. Nothing personal."

"Nothing personal?" I said. "Whose God are you talking about? Not mine."

Lucas tugged on my shirt. "Let's just go."

"No." I climbed over his tree-trunk legs and jammed my fingers into the preacher's chest, hard enough to drive him backwards. "How dare you."

I shouted, "Hi, everyone!" Every face in the congregation turned around. "This man says we can't worship here because we're a mixed family. Is that your gospel?"

Most people remained still. A few nodded.

"Seriously?" I was in complete shock, speechless until, "You call yourself Christians? You're a bunch of fucking hypocrites!" Lucas grabbed me by the collar and started pulling me out. "You don't even deserve to *be* in a church. I hope you all burn in hell, you fucking mother*fuckers!*"

In the parking lot I broke down sobbing. "I'm so sorry, Lucas. My church wasn't like that. I didn't know."

"Ain't worth gettin' upset over," he said. "Let's go."

I kept my faith—it belongs to me—but it'll be a long time before I step inside another church.

Kiona is saying she's going for a run. "Join me, Alice?" After a month she has me in even better shape than before. And she's teaching me real boxing—*offense*, not just exercise. No more victim. *Never.*

"You wore me out this morning," I say.

"No pain, no gain," she says and trots down a trail into the woods.

Peggy comes out of the trailer waving a phone. "Darla, it's your sister. The one who's mad at your other sister."

"Oh my, this is going to take a while," Darla says, going inside.

Just me and Lucas. I get a chill as the sun dips behind a spindly ponderosa pine. The long shadow makes me think of tall man. Like I said, still a long way to go.

I join Lucas at the picnic table, covering the scar on my forearm with my left hand. I made the mistake of telling him I did it on purpose when he asked about it. Now he looks upset whenever he sees it. Because I only wear long pants, he's never seen the NO ONE scar on my thigh. I think he'd freak.

Sitting across the picnic table brings back good memories of the kitchen table in Memphis. "Can we talk?" I say.

"Like my answer's gonna make a difference," he says.

"I'm serious."

"You know we can."

A snapping tree branch makes me jerk. Lucas's reassuring nod says if the tree becomes a threat he'll make it into toothpicks.

I start, stop and start again. "Okay, yeah, so ... what it is ... is that I've been wanting to ask you something. Since the day you picked me up in Atlanta."

He looks surprised. "Never knew you to hold back a question."

"I guess I've never been afraid to know the answer before. When you left me that day, it broke me. I would have sworn on a stack of bibles you would never abandon me like that." I promised myself in advance I wouldn't let it happen, but tears leak down both cheeks.

He pushes the computer aside. "That was my bad and I am truly sorry I didn't handle it better. It broke me too. I cried soon as I drove away."

"For real?"

"Bawled like a little baby. Didn't know no good way to do it."

"Why did you?"

He puts his big hands on mine, railroad spikes locking with bicycle spokes. "Sometimes you got to fight for what you love. I tried my best that way."

I reflexively glance down to where four bullet holes are still healing under his clothes.

"Sometimes you got to push away what you love. I wanted you to have a life, a real one. And to get help."

"What made you change your mind?"

"How you think I found you that day?"

"The GPS bracelet, of course," I say, holding up my wrist. "Tracking your registered pit bull, Alice."

He shakes his head. "Battery died not long after they put you in the hospital."

"Then how?"

"I guess you stopped checkin' the news about your case."

"There was no case anymore."

"I checked it. A few days before I came to get you there was a interview with your friend, Agent Forster. The reporter asked him how you was doin'."

Peggy comes out of the pink trailer. "Lucas. Are you still cooking gumbo tonight?"

"You better believe it. And it's gonna be good."

Nancy gives a thumbs-up. She loves Lucas's gumbo.

"Forster told the reporter you wasn't doin' too good, was havin' a hard time adjustin'. Said you seemed happier the first day he met you. Called it one of the big mysteries of your case. That got my attention."

Mine too. "I'm surprised he said all that. He's usually pretty tightlipped."

"Not only. He said your condition might have something to do with the loss of a good friend you met on your journey."

"Omigod. *You.*"

"Sounded like he was sendin' a message, so I took a chance and called him."

My mouth gapes like a fish. "You called the FBI? No way."

"For real. Course I used a fresh burner and spoofed number. We had a nice, long conversation. He asked me all about you, like a test. I didn't know everything. What's your favorite color?"

"Purple."

"Huh, I need to remember that."

"Yes, you do. Yours is *blue*."

"He asked why I thought you wanted to be with me. I said 'cause I make you feel safe. I said you trust me and don't trust people easy."

"That's true, but there's more—"

He shushes me. "He asked if you ever laughed when we was together. Said he never saw you have a real laugh, a happy one. I said fuck yes, you laughed all the fuckin' time—*at me*. 'Cept I didn't say fuck."

"Ooh, I hope not." My laugh is high-pitched, a wobbly squeal, like you'd expect from a girl my age. I'll never be that young again, but I like hearing my old laugh.

"He asked what I thought would make you happy. I said *hope*. Said no one can be happy if they ain't got no hope."

I swallow and nod.

"Told him I knew it for a fact. Said I lost hope a long time ago. Only found it again when I met the Amazin' Emily Calby."

I wipe my eyes.

"That seemed to make up his mind. Not surprisin', he wanted to know more about me than I was willing to share, but at the end he give me the address of your foster home. That's how I found you."

"He's a good man," I sniffle.

"I agree. Never thought I'd be sayin' that about the FBI."

"Maybe we're both changing."

The half-laugh, half-snort with the shoulder roll I missed so much. "Don't fuckin' bet on it."

"One more question," I say. "Last one." His doubt is obvious. "No, really. You said something about love. Do you ... love me?"

"Course I love you. You my daughter, ain't you?" He reaches out and musses my hair. "And you still one tough little motherfucker."

What did you think of *The Hiding Girl?*

THANK YOU for reading *The Hiding Girl*. We know you have lots of reading and other entertainment choices, so we really appreciate it. If you liked the book, please consider posting a review on Amazon and Goodreads to help spread the word. And thanks again!

Emily's Story Doesn't End Here

STAY TUNED for Book 2 of the Emily Calby Series, *The Girl in Cell 49B*:

Three years after her terrifying odyssey in *The Hiding Girl*, Emily is safe, living anonymously in relative normality with her mentor Lucas Jackson—before life blows up again on her sweet sixteen birthday. Arrested for carrying a stolen handgun (Lucas's birthday gift), a fingerprint scan reveals her to be the *missing Calby girl*, and worse. She's wanted for murder in another state.

Extradited to a corrupt juvenile prison in the middle of nowhere, Emily struggles to adjust to a new code of survival while battling a vindictive prosecutor willing to resort to any means to convict her. As *The Law* thwarts her every move, she begins to appreciate its awesome power. She discovers an unused prison law library and buries herself in books.

With her trial looming, the dark secrets behind the prison walls close in. Emily's fragile cellmate, so reminiscent of her dead sister, is in grave danger. So is her first love, a gentle boy sentenced to life without parole. She's desperate to protect them, but how can she when every day in court brings a new disaster? A courtroom thriller like no other.

Also by Dorian Box

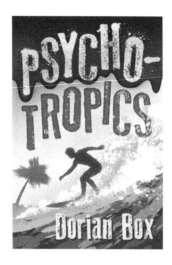

Psycho-Tropics

Writer's Digest Award Winner in Genre Fiction

A high school reunion in a South Florida beach town unburies the past (literally) in this dark mystery of revenge and redemption. Lottery-winning surfer Danny Teakwell seems to be living the life, but he's been hiding a terrible secret, punishing himself for two decades.

Now he's hit rock bottom. So he thinks. The ghosts from his past show up at the reunion, launching him on a mayhem-filled race through the Sunshine State to save a missing woman, and his soul.

The odds aren't good. He only has three days and his main allies are a pill-popping lawyer, crusty barkeep and seven-year-old embalming expert. Heart and dark humor combine with page-turning action and a twisty plot that will keep you guessing until the end.

Editorial Reviews of *Psycho-Tropics*

"An engaging thriller with plenty of humor, good characterization, and a memorable villain ...." — *Kirkus Reviews*

"Marrying humor with suspense is not easy, but it comes across masterfully .... A truly enjoyable read." — *Judge, 23rd Annual Writer's Digest Self-Published Book Awards* (Award Winner in Genre Fiction)

"Clues are tossed out like bait, twisting and turning the storyline along .... The characters are brilliantly constructed .... The dark humor serves to lessen the tension in all the right ways before it heightens again .... Effortlessly captures the wonderful eccentricities of life in South Florida ...." — *IndieReader* (Official Seal of Approval)

"A genuinely creepy sadist is the high point of Box's dark thriller set in Florida in 1995." — *Publishers Weekly*

"*Psycho-Tropics* is like riding Pipeline with a hangover. It's jaw dropping, heart thumping and addictively exhilarating, but with a hint of disorientation, dizziness and an unsettled stomach. But by the end you'll be smiling ear to ear and bursting to tell your mates how good it was." — *Surfer Dad UK*

Order it on Amazon

Locations in *The Hiding Girl*

Memphis

ICONIC MEMPHIS is a bucket-list city to visit for too many reasons to list. The Bluff City regularly appears on lists of top worldwide travel destinations. But Memphis is also a city that struggles with high rates of poverty and crime that take a disproportionate toll on predominantly minority neighborhoods.

Much of the first half of the book takes place in the 38126 zip code known as South Memphis. Bordering downtown and the vibrant Beale Street entertainment district, South Memphis was ranked as the most dangerous neighborhood in the United States in one crime-data analysis. Below is one of the "death bear" memorials Emily asks Lucas about—teddy bear memorials where people were killed—this one at the corner of Vance Avenue and Orleans Street.

Louisiana

SHREVEPORT is a brief, but eventful (like most) stop on Emily's journey. The bus station and federal courthouse near the Red River are real locations, although the bus station moved to a new facility during the writing of the book. In Lafayette, there is a downtown library and an Acadiana Park, but everything about them, including all characters inhabiting them, is fictional.

No disrespect is intended by the fact that one of the villains is portrayed as a Cajun. It happened more or less by accident, when I was seeking to distinguish the unnamed "two men" at the beginning of the book. They could have been anyone. Cajuns are spiritual, loving, authentic folks, known for their outlook on life called *joie de vivre* (joy of life). Recommended reading for those interested in learning about Cajuns and Cajun culture is Trent Angers' book, *The Truth About the Cajuns* (3d ed. 1998).

Other Locations

PENSACOLA is a city on the Gulf Coast of the Florida panhandle known for its beautiful beaches. There is no such place as Dilfer County, Georgia, where Emily's nightmare began.

Discussion Questions

1. Was Emily seeking revenge or justice? Is there a difference? Always, or is it a variable concept that depends on the circumstances? Chapter 32 explores the preacher's arguments against capital punishment and Emily's internal responses. The preacher disapproves of revenge, but concedes even some theologians believe in the concept of *just revenge*.

2. Moral equivalency—arguing that one bad choice is justified because it's better than another one—is regarded as a logical fallacy. But is weighing and balancing always required when faced with only undesirable choices? Or are some things absolute? Is killing one of them? Were Emily's choices rational or irrational responses to her circumstances?

3. Central to Emily's self-image is being a *good person*. The creeping belief she isn't torments her. Is Emily a good person? Can she ever be again?

4. Emily is a religious white girl from the rural South, Lucas a black former gang member from the inner-city. On the surface, they couldn't be more different. Looking back, do they have more in common than meets the eye?

5. Race floats in the background throughout the book. How does race inform the relationship between Emily and Lucas? Their behavior and world views?

6. Did Emily's transformation from a self-confessed *goody two-shoes* to a ... um, not-so goody two-shoes occur principally because of Lucas or was she already fundamentally altered by events and Lucas just provided an opportunity? Given Emily's circumstances when she arrived in Memphis, what would you have predicted her future to be if she had not met Lucas?

7. The funeral director called Lucas *righteous*. Is that possible? Synonyms for righteous include *pure* and *law-abiding*, but also *honorable* and *principled*.

8. If you believe in heaven and hell, where is Lucas going? How about Emily?

9. At its heart, *The Hiding Girl* is an unusual love story between two lost souls. How would you describe Emily's relationship with Lucas? List the adjectives that come most quickly to mind.

10. Why did Emily insist on wearing her hoodie, double t-shirts and long pants even in the stifling summer heat and humidity?

11. What roles and needs did Darla and Peggy fulfill in Emily's life?

12. The contents of Emily's backpack were important to her for obvious, tangible reasons, but did her backpack represent more than its individual parts? What would you equate it with losing in your own life?

13. Who is the real Emily: *Hiding Girl*, *Calm Girl* or *Scary Girl*? Is she parts of all three? While hopefully not dissociating like poor Emily, do you feel you have different aspects of self that take control in different types of situations?

14. What were your primary reactions to Emily's determined search for "justice"? Pity? Compassion? Disgust? Horror? Admiration?

15. Who do you think Emily will be in the future? Find out in book two of the *Emily Calby Series*, coming soon.

Acknowledgments

THANKS to the folks who helped with *The Hiding Girl*. My daughter, Caitlin, is a great resource when it comes to brainstorming plot next-steps and can be relied on for brutally honest feedback, which every writer needs. Sample text exchange:

> *Me: Caitlin, do you like this title idea? [Title]*
> *Reply: No!*

My niece, Lauren Dostal, a talented writer, read a draft and offered valuable suggestions that improved it. I look forward to watching her literary star rise. Mary Pat Treuthart's suggestions were delivered with her inimitable mix of practical insight and sharp wit. Author Andrew Diamond and I hooked up electronically as a result of reading and reviewing each other's first novels. I'm indebted to him for his generous advice and encouragement.

Thanks to Gary Wayne Golden, a gifted digital artist and designer, for the cover, layout and editorial input. Only Gary would catch issues involving the tides at Pensacola Beach or the difference between a .38 caliber pistol and a .380 pistol.

I bounced Emily's devolving psyche off of Dr. Randy Schnell on several occasions over beers. Nancy Buratto, a Louisiana gal blown from New Orleans by Hurricane Katrina, helped with the Cajun dialect she heard around her growing up. All errors are mine.

Props to Rory Miller for his book, *Violence: A Writer's Guide* (2d ed. 2012), which not only explained how to write effectively about sharp object violence, but stimulated a couple of plot points.

About the Author

"DORIAN BOX" is a graduate school professor and the author of eight nonfiction books, one of which was an Amazon Editors' Favorite Book of the Year.

The Hiding Girl is his second novel, the first in the *Emily Calby Series*, which follows twelve-year-old Emily's perilous life forward from the day two men invade her rural Georgia home and kill her family. Box's first novel, *Psycho-Tropics*, won a Writer's Digest Award in Genre Fiction.

In his academic life, Box is the recipient of numerous awards for both teaching and research. He's written thousands, possibly millions, of scholarly footnotes, and been interviewed by sources such as National Public Radio, the *PBS Newshour*, *New York Times*, *Washington Post*, and *Wall Street Journal*.

Dorian lives out his childhood rock star fantasies singing and playing guitar in cover bands, earning tens of dollars sweating it out in smoky dive bars until two a.m.

Follow Dorian at **dorianbox.com**
and on **goodreads.com.**

More Praise for *Psycho-Tropics*

Amazon Reviews

"A twisted, hilarious mystery with heart. ... When a seven-year-old embalming expert and James Garfield, the twentieth president, play roles in solving the case, you know something different is up."

"It's got it all: action, humor, pulse-raising suspense, pathos and warmth."

"Lots of writers have stories to tell—but can't. Box has stories to tell—and can."

"I thought this was going to be a typical Florida crazy book ... what a huge surprise. ... Great story and great characters, well told and believable."

"Carl Hiaasen on steroids."

"This book drew me in from the first sentence. ... Every time I thought I figured out what was going on, I was wrong. Every time I wanted to finish a chapter and put it down, the dramatic ending would propel me to the next chapter."

"Finished the damn thing in two days. I could not put it down. This is one of the best books I have read in a long time. ... The pacing was balanced, the characters were rounded and complex. Just when I thought I knew what was going to happen, the author threw a curve ball. The ending was truly a surprise."

"I am drawn to books with heavy character development. If there also happens to be a compelling story, all the better, but I've come not to expect it. It seems like most authors can't do both. This book has marvelous, complex characters, but also moves along at a fast pace and is completely unpredictable."

"As zany as this book is, it is intelligent and witty all the way through. The author has a knack for nailing the details of this well-crafted mystery about murder and mayhem in Florida firmly into place so that it remains believable."

"My daughter heard me laughing from across the house as I read this one. Don't let the humor fool you, though. This book has serious messages about forgiveness, redemption and self-examination."

"Wonderfully off-beat characters .... Suspense and comedy are hard to make work in novels, but Dorian Box has pulled it off beautifully."

"There's an amazing assortment of well-developed, eccentric and oddball characters ... all portrayed in a variety of vivid, and sometimes graphically gruesome, environments. ... I felt like a voyeur watching and feeling everything while I was reading."

"A brilliant mystery thriller, masterfully written."

"You will finish this book with a tear in your eye, a smile on your face, and very glad you took the time to read this incredible mystery thriller."

Printed in Great Britain
by Amazon

48957209R00199